Scarlet Wilson wrote her first story aged eight and has never stopped. She's worked in the health service for twenty years, having trained as a nurse and a health visitor. Scarlet now works in public health and lives on the West Coast of Scotland with her fiancé and their two sons. Writing medical romances and contemporary romances is a dream come true for her.

Susan Carlisle's love affair with books began in the sixth grade, when she made a bad grade in mathematics. Not allowed to watch TV until she'd brought the grade up, Susan filled her time with books. She turned her love of reading into a passion for writing, and now has over ten Medical Romances published through Mills & Boon. She writes about hot, sexy docs and the strong women who captivate them. Visit SusanCarlisle.com.

WITHDRAWN AND SOLD
BY
STAFFORDSHIRE
COUNTY LIBRARY

D0486717

3 8014 11127 0470

Also by Scarlet Wilson

Christmas in the Boss's Castle
A Royal Baby for Christmas
The Doctor and the Princess
The Mysterious Italian Houseguest
A Family Made at Christmas
The Italian Billionaire's New Year Bride
Resisting the Single Dad

Also by Susan Carlisle

Married for the Boss's Baby
White Wedding for a Southern Belle
The Doctor's Sleigh Bell Proposal
The Surgeon's Cinderella
Stolen Kisses with Her Boss
Christmas with the Best Man
Redeeming the Rebel Doc

Discover more at millsandboon.co.uk.

STAFFORDSHIRE
COUNTY LIBRARY

MILLS & BOON

LOCKED DOWN WITH THE ARMY DOC

SCARLET WILSON

THE BROODING SURGEON'S BABY BOMBSHELL

SUSAN CARLISLE

MILLS & BOON

All rights reserved including the right of reproduction
in whole or in part in any form. This edition is published
by arrangement with Harlequin Books S.A.

This is a work of fiction. Names, characters, places, locations
and incidents are purely fictional and bear no relationship to
any real life individuals, living or dead, or to any actual places,
business establishments, locations, events or incidents.
Any resemblance is entirely coincidental.

This book is sold subject to the condition that it shall not,
by way of trade or otherwise, be lent, resold, hired out
or otherwise circulated without the prior consent of the publisher
in any form of binding or cover other than that in which it is published
and without a similar condition including this condition
being imposed on the subsequent purchaser.

® and TM are trademarks owned and used by the trademark owner
and/or its licensee. Trademarks marked with ® are registered with the
United Kingdom Patent Office and/or the Office for Harmonisation
in the Internal Market and in other countries.

First Published in Great Britain 2018
by Mills & Boon, an imprint of HarperCollins*Publishers*
1 London Bridge Street, London, SE1 9GF

Locked Down with the Army Doc © 2018 by Scarlet Wilson

The Brooding Surgeon's Baby Bombshell © 2018 by Susan Carlisle

ISBN: 978-0-263-93359-8

MIX
Paper from
responsible sources
FSC® C007454

This book is produced from independently certified FSC™ paper
to ensure responsible forest management.
For more information visit www.harpercollins.co.uk/green.

Printed and bound in Spain
by CPI, Barcelona

LOCKED DOWN WITH THE ARMY DOC

SCARLET WILSON

MILLS & BOON

This book is dedicated to all the loyal readers
of Medical Romance all over the world.

Thank you for letting me write for you
and for enjoying Medical Romance.

CHAPTER ONE

AMBER BERKELEY LEANED against the wall of the elevator as it descended to the ground floor. The doors reflected a kind of odd image. She'd forgotten to check in the mirror before she left. Her half-up-half-down hair looked like some kind of bewildered lost animal on her head. She let out a laugh. She didn't even want to know what her bright pink lipstick looked like. Truth was, she didn't really care.

Tonight's ball was bound to be full of specialists and consultants who were all too important to breathe. She loved her job, but some doctors just seemed like a different breed entirely. Self-important. Self-interested. Amber didn't waste much time on people like those.

Tomorrow she was lecturing at one of the most prestigious conferences in the world. And she couldn't pretend she wasn't nervous. Hawaii was a magnificent setting. One hundred per cent more gorgeous than most of the places she visited. The Disease Prevention Agency tended to send their staff to investigate outbreaks and try and prevent the spread of infectious diseases.

Most of her time was either spent in the main base at Chicago, or on one of many expeditions as part of a team, generally to places with few or poor facilities.

This five-star hotel in Hawaii was like something out of

a dream. She'd even been greeted by the traditional colorful leis on check-in. And, corny or not, she'd liked them. The beach outside had perfect golden sand with sumptuous private loungers and straw parasols complete with serving staff. This part of the main island near Kailua Kona was a perfect piece of paradise.

Her first-floor room had a gorgeous view of the Pacific Ocean, which seemed to change color depending on the time of day. So far today it had gone from clear turquoise blue to light green. Shimmering like a tranquil soft blanket stretching to infinity.

As the doors pinged and slid open, the noise and the aromas of the food surrounded her. The room was full of people talking, a sea of dark tuxedos with a smattering of colored dresses in the mix. She threaded her way through, keeping her chin raised as she glanced from side to side. She had to know someone here. But the sea of faces didn't reveal anyone familiar. Amber's nose twitched. She wanted easy company. A chance to share a few drinks, grab a few snacks and get rid of the butterflies in her stomach for tomorrow.

She stared at a sign on the wall. Ah…there were two conferences on in the hotel—not just the one she was attending. It seemed that a world of business and economic experts were here too.

Just before she'd left, the director of the Disease Prevention Agency had called her into his office. She'd only seen the inside of his office walls on two previous occasions. Once, on the day she'd started. And second, on the day she'd received her promotion.

"Dr. Berkeley," he said solemnly. "I wanted to wish you well for tomorrow. There's been a lot of interest in our contribution to the conference. Thank you for presenting the meningitis research for us."

Amber gave a nod and a smile. "I've loved being part of the meningitis work. I'm honored to present on it."

The director nodded. "And you're confident you can answer any questions?"

Amber held up the list in her hand. "I've spent the last few months eating, breathing and sleeping meningitis. I think I've got it covered."

The director didn't even blink. "Oh, I'm not worried for you." His eyebrows rose as she stood from her chair. "I'm worried for them. Let's hope they're ready for you, Dr. Berkeley."

She'd smiled as she'd left. It seemed that her take-no-crap attitude was getting a reputation of its own. She wasn't embarrassed by it. Not at all. She'd never seen the point in beating around the bush. She'd always talked straight, to patients and to colleagues. Medics could be notoriously sexist. And Amber could be notoriously blunt.

Had it cost her a few jobs? Maybe. Had it earned her a few others? Definitely.

A guy with a paunch belly and gaping shirt approached her, beer sloshing from his glass. "Hello, gorgeous. Where are you going to?"

She didn't miss a beat. "Away from you." She didn't even glance at the lanyard round his neck. She had no intention of finding out his name.

She'd always vowed never to go out with a fellow medic. Life experience had taught her it wasn't a good idea.

She glanced around the room again. This was probably her worst-case scenario, wall-to-wall fellow medics, with copious amounts of alcohol flowing.

A few seconds later she met another charmer who refused to let her step around her. "We must stop meeting like this." He grinned as his hand closed around her forearm and his eyes ran up and down her body.

She didn't hesitate. She flipped his arm up and twisted it around his back, catching him completely by surprise and thrusting him in the other direction as the woman next to her laughed out loud. "Yes, we must," she said sharply.

The main bar in the center of the room was currently three people deep. Her chances of getting a drink were slipping further and further away.

Her eyes homed in on another bar on the far side of the room and through a set of doors. It looked much more sedate. She could have a glass of wine, check out the list of bar snacks then head back to her room and enjoy the view.

She threaded her way through the rest of the crowd. There were a few people who obviously knew one another sitting around tables. Even from here she could recognize the medic talk.

Right now she couldn't stomach that. So she headed directly over to the stools at the bar. There was a broad-shouldered guy already sitting there. He looked as if his whiskey was currently sending him into a trance.

Perfect. Too drunk to be a pest.

Or if he wasn't? She could deal with that.

She smiled as she sat down, crossed her legs and leaned her head on one hand. He might be tired but he was handsome. Actually, he was more than handsome. He was good-looking with an edge of ruggedness. His dark hair was a little rumpled and his suit jacket had been flung carelessly onto the bar stool next to him. She couldn't get a look at his eyes as his head was leaning forward toward the glass. But she could see the lean muscle definition beneath his pale blue shirt, the slight tan on his skin and the hint of bristle around his jawline. She smiled and just couldn't help herself. "Well, aren't you just the original party pooper?"

Jack Campbell blinked and blinked again. Nope. It had definitely happened. Or maybe he was just hallucinating. He stared into the bottom of his whiskey glass again and clinked the ice.

The warm spicy aroma emanating from the woman sitting next to him started to surround him, just as she crossed her long legs on the high stool, revealing the daring split in her floor-length black dress.

Even from here, he'd noticed her the second she'd appeared at the entrance to the ballroom. She was taller than most women, but wasn't afraid to use her height, combining her black sheath dress with a pair of heels and piling her dark hair with pink tips on top of her head. He'd watched her survey the room, ignore a few admiring glances, give short retorts to two men who dared to try and approach her and, now, she'd just crossed those exceptionally long legs and given him a clear view of them. Her black heels had ornate straps and crisscrossed up her calves.

At least he thought he'd watched her. Maybe he was dreaming. Truth was, he was so tired the only reason he was still awake was that his body was craving food. Food he seemed to have been waiting an eternity for.

He gave himself a shake. Maybe he needed another whiskey. The first one was putting him in that strange state between fact and fiction. His stomach rumbled loudly, so he lifted his hand to grab some nuts from a bowl on the bar. Quick as lightning, someone gave his hand a light slap.

For a second he was momentarily stunned. Then he shook his head and gave a smile of disbelief as he turned in his chair.

She was staring straight at him with a pair of bright blue eyes. He couldn't help himself. It was as if the fatigue coupled with a dash of whiskey had reduced all his usual politeness and social norms to a scattering of leaves beneath his feet. "Did you really just hit me? For trying to eat a peanut?"

She gave a shrug. "Yeah, sorry about that. Force of habit."

He raised his eyebrows. "You don't look too sorry."

She pulled a face and waved her hand. "Actually, I've just *saved* you."

Now he was amused. "Saved me from what?"

She shook her head and pushed the bowl away. "Probably some kind of horrible death. Best way to catch some kind of disease." She shuddered. She actually *shuddered*. "If I sent those to a lab I could horrify you."

He deliberately leaned over her, ignoring her orange-scented perfume, and plucked a nut from the bowl, holding it between his fingers. "One tiny little nut is going to fell me?"

She arched her eyebrows and blinked. There was black eyeliner flicked on her eyelid, enhanced by her thick extra-long lashes. With those blue eyes she really was a bit of a stunner.

"If I could put that in an evidence bag right now and send it to the lab I would." She shrugged. "But, hey, it's your poison. Your stomach."

"This is how you meet people? You attack them at the bar and steal their food?"

For a second she looked momentarily offended, but then she threw back her head and laughed. She put her elbow on the bar and rested her head on it. "Actually, my ambition this evening is not to meet anyone—I just wanted to grab a drink, some food and get out of here."

He gave a slow nod. "Ah, great minds think alike, then."

She looked a little more conciliatory. "Maybe. Sorry about the slap. Bar snacks make me testy. It really is an automatic reaction."

He laughed. "How many states have you been arrested in?"

She sighed. "More than you could ever know."

He could see the way her careful eyes were watching him, obviously trying to size him up. He liked her quick answers and smart remarks. He mirrored her position, leaning his head on his hand for a second as a wave of tiredness swept over him.

And then she spoke. "I'm trying to work out if you're drunk or just in a coma. I'm warning you—I'm off duty tonight."

The corners of his lips headed upward. Maybe he was imagining all this? Maybe he was already dreaming? Or maybe the jet lag was making him see things. If this was a hallucination, those words were *so* not what he was expecting. He let out a laugh. "I could actually be a bit of both. Jet lag and drinking—" he held up the whiskey glass "—are probably not the best idea in the world. But do I care right now?" He shook his head as he downed the remains at the bottom of the glass. "Not really."

Now she laughed as the bartender came over and set a coaster in front of her. "Well, the jet lag explains the accent. But not the complete disregard for your fellow man."

The bartender caught her eye. "What can I get you?"

She looked at his glass. "I'll have what Mr. Happy's having."

Jack raised his eyebrows at the bartender. "Better just put both on my tab."

She drummed her fingernails on the bar next to him. "Who said I wanted you to buy my drink?" Her overall presentation was quite glamorous but her nails were short and clean. Curious. Most women these days tended to have glittery painted talons.

"Don't drink it," he said smartly. "I can easily drink both."

She smiled. A genuine, wide smile. The pink tips of her hair matched the bright pink on her lips.

"You are easily the most crabbit man in the room." She gave a wink. "Is that Scottish enough for you? I learned that from a Scottish colleague."

He tried not to smile as he nodded his head and furrowed his brow. "It's a well-used word. My granny might have called a few people crabbit in her time."

She gave a smile. "Yeah, crabbit. I like that. It means you won't be a pest."

"But you will be."

"Ouch," she said as the bartender brought over the drinks.

She lifted the glass to her nose and sniffed. "What is this, anyhow?"

"Guess."

She tilted her head to the side. "Oh…guessing games. I know it's whiskey. I've just no idea what kind. And here was me thinking tonight was going to be totally boring."

He liked her. He was actually beginning to wake up a little. But that still didn't stop him putting his head on the bar for a few seconds. He closed his eyes and murmured, "I'm dreaming of snacks. I've only eaten airline food for the last twenty-eight hours. And you've stolen the peanuts."

She was still sniffing the whiskey but laughed anyway and grabbed a bar menu. "Haven't you ordered?"

He sighed as he lifted his head again. "I think I ordered around ten hours ago. Apparently the kitchen is busy, but—" his fingers made the quote signal in the air "—it'll get here soon."

She set down the whiskey glass and gestured to the bartender. "Actually, can you give me a glass of rosé wine instead, please?" She gave Jack a sideways glance as she pushed the glass toward him. "This is too rich for my tastes."

He was still leaning on his hand. After a few hours in a fugue, his brain was kick-starting again, along with his dormant libido.

"I've never really met anyone like you before," he murmured.

Her eyes narrowed. "Is that a pickup line?"

He laughed. "I'm too tired and too lazy to try and pick you up, right now. But, hey, look me up tomorrow. I'll probably have a whole new lease of life."

"With those circles under your eyes, I doubt you're even going to see tomorrow. I bet you sleep right through."

He shook his head. "Oh, no. I have to see tomorrow. I'm speaking—at the conference." He gestured behind her. "I should probably be in there right now, trying to charm my way around the room and into a new job."

"You're looking for a new job?" She gave a half smile. "What? Been fired from everywhere in Scotland?"

The bartender set down her wine in front of her, along with the biggest burger and plate of fries Jack had seen in forever. He couldn't help it. "Praise be. Food of the gods."

She sipped her wine and he could feel her watching him with interest as he snagged a fry. "I'm warning you. Try and put any of this in an evidence bag and I'll have to wrestle you to the floor."

She pushed up from her bar stool, leaning over to steal one of his fries. "You Scots guys. You think you're tough. You ain't got nothing on a girl from Milwaukee."

She bit into the fry and nodded. "Better than it looks. And, because it came fresh from the kitchen, I won't tell you any horror stories about it. I save them for the bar snacks."

Her stomach growled loudly and he couldn't help but laugh again.

He picked up his knife. "Okay, then, mystery woman. Since you're obviously the least boring person in the room, I'll make a deal and share with you." He waved the knife at her. "But let's be clear. This isn't normal behavior for me. I'm just too tired to fight."

He cut the burger in half and pushed her half toward her. "But no more insults. And—" he looked down at her long legs "—I still think I could take you."

She picked up her half. He liked that. A woman who didn't pussyfoot around her food. "Okay, then. Because I'm starved and can't be bothered to wait for room service, I'll take your offer." She gave him a sideways look. "You haven't even told me your name."

He nodded as he poised the burger at his lips. "Kinda like it that way."

Her eyes sparkled. "Me too."

She waited a second then added, "Are you really here looking for a job?"

He waited until he'd finished chewing. "I'm still officially in employment for the next two weeks. After that?" He held out one hand. "The world is my oyster. I've had a couple of offers. Haven't decided whether to take them up or not."

"Don't you need a paycheck?"

He paused for a second. "Of course I do. But right now, it's more important I take the right job, rather than just the first one that comes along."

She studied him for a few seconds. He could see a whole host of questions spinning around in her brain, but she was far too smart to ask. Instead she grinned as she stole another fry. "Makes you sound old."

"You think?"

"Definitely."

He shook his head. "I'm not old. I'm just…well-worn."

She laughed again as she took another sip of wine. "At what? Thirty? Thirty-five?"

He choked. "Thirty-five?" He patted one of his cheeks. "Wow. I was really conned by that moisturizer. I wonder if it's got a money-back guarantee."

He leaned a little closer. "I'll have you know I have a whole ten days before I reach the grand old age of thirty-five."

He narrowed his gaze as he looked at her again. "But two can play at that game." He gave a slow nod and took his time letting his gaze go up and down her length. "I'm guessing, forty? Forty-six?"

She let out a little shriek. "Forty-six! Oh, no way, buster. You've had it now." She leaned over him again, her soft skin brushing against his as she lifted the whole bowl of fries out of his reach.

"Not the fries!"

She perched the bowl in her lap and nodded solemnly.

"Surely you know a woman of my maturity needs to keep her strength up."

He liked her. He liked her a lot. The room opposite was full of anxious glances and too much "my qualifications are better than yours." Too many people wanting to talk about how wonderful they were as loudly as they could.

Jack was here for one reason. To present his research. To let people know he'd found something that had made a huge difference in a wartime setting. The difference between life and death.

That was the privilege of being an army doctor. He got to try things—sometimes out of desperation—that private clinics and hospitals around the world would throw their hands up at in shock.

But, so far, some of the best medical inventions ever had come from the battlefield. Freeze-dried plasma, handheld inhalers for pain relief, a specially designed applicator for ketamine to treat trauma casualties, and his own particular find—a type of wound dressing part clay, part algae that stopped severe bleeding in under twenty seconds. It had already saved over a hundred casualties who would have surely died. If they started using it in trauma bays around the globe, it could potentially save millions.

Ms. Mystery next to him leaned over and put her hand on his arm. "Hey? Everything okay?"

The feel of her warm hand sent pulses up his arm. He blinked. "Yeah, of course."

She gave a gentle smile. "Thought I'd lost you for a second there. Maybe the jet lag is getting to you after all." Her tone had changed a little. It was almost as if she'd just had a look inside his brain for a second and seen what he'd been lost in.

He gave a small sigh and tried to imagine meeting her in any other set of circumstances than these. "If I was any kind of gentleman, I should be trying to charm you and be swirling you around the ballroom floor in there."

She leaned her head on her hand. "But that's what I like. You're not trying to charm me. In fact, I should be insulted, because it seems as if you couldn't care less." She wrinkled her nose. "I did hear that Scots guys could be grumpy."

He straightened up. "Hey, that's the guys from Edinburgh. Not the guys from Glasgow." He tugged at his shirt, trying to make himself look more presentable. "And anyway, I have charmed you. I bought you chips."

She stared down at the bowl. "Chips?"

He shook his head. "You call them fries. We call them chips."

She pointed to a box behind the bar. "Oh, no. Those are the chips."

He smiled and leaned a little closer. "No, no. They're crisps. And I was just being polite earlier, calling them fries. Didn't want to confuse you."

She threw back her head and laughed, revealing the pale skin on her long neck, then shook her head and leaned a little closer. "The more tired you get, the stronger your accent gets. Any more Scottish and I'll need a translator."

His brow furrowed. "Nothing wrong with my accent. You just need to pay attention—concentrate a little more."

"Says the man who is sleepwalking at the bar."

He waved a fry with his fingers. "I'm not sleep-walking—I'm sleep-*eating*. There's a difference."

She leaned over and snagged another fry. They were dwindling faster than should be possible. This woman was smart, confident and full of sass. He liked that. "So, what brings you here?"

She waved her hand nonchalantly. "Yeah, yeah, I should be in there too. Schmoozing. But the truth is, I'm not much of a schmoozer."

He raised his eyebrows in mock horror. "You don't say?"

"Hey." She smiled. "It's my one and only true failing as an adult."

"You'll admit to one?"

She nodded solemnly. "One, and only one." Then she laughed and shook her head. "But you? I bet I could write a whole list."

Her stomach gave a little grumble and she started, putting one hand on it as a little pink flushed her cheeks. "Oops, I guess I'm hungrier than I thought."

He looked down at the plates. All remnants of the burger were gone and there were only a few fries left in the bowl.

"I could eat the whole thing again." He sighed.

She looked a little sheepish. "Sorry, I just stole half of your dinner." She waved over the bartender. "Can we order the same again, please?"

The bartender leaned closer. "I have to be honest. The kitchen is a little slow this evening and bar food is even slower. Between you and me, the quickest way to get served is to order room service. You'll get it in half the time because they prioritize those orders."

Jack paused for only a few seconds, and then he stood up. He nodded to the bartender. "You know my room number—can you put it through as a room-service order?"

The bartender glanced between them briefly then nodded. "Of course, sir. Any drinks to go with the food?"

Jack leaned on the bar. "Any drinks for you?"

Ms. Mystery looked stunned for the briefest of seconds. Then he saw that sparkle in her eyes again. He wasn't propositioning her—not tonight at least. He was still hungry and she was good company. He had no qualms about inviting her to his room.

"Diet cola," she said quickly as she stood up from her bar stool. There was a hint of a smile on her lips. He hadn't even had to make the invite; he'd just worked on the assumption she would join him. And it seemed she was taking up the challenge.

He turned back to the bartender. "Make that two, thanks."

The bartender disappeared and he crooked his elbow toward her. "Looks like I'm about to buy you dinner for the second time this evening." He glanced toward the packed ballroom, then paused. "You okay with this?"

Her eyes scanned the ballroom too and she gave the briefest shake of her head. "I have the strangest feeling I might be in safe hands with you, Mr. Grumpy Scot. I think I can take the chance." She laughed. "And to think, I took this position at the bar because you looked like the least trouble in the room."

As they headed toward the elevators, he couldn't resist. "Honey, I'm more trouble than you could ever imagine."

CHAPTER TWO

AMBER GLANCED AROUND the foyer and tugged nervously at her black suit jacket. She rubbed her cheek self-consciously, wondering if the imprint of her Scotsman's shirt button had finally left her skin.

It was embarrassing. One minute they were laughing and joking, legs stretched out on the bed after they'd shared the second burger; next she was blinking groggily, aware of the rise and fall of a muscular chest beneath her head. She'd peeled herself back oh-so-carefully, removing the arm and leg she had draped around his sleeping form.

For a few seconds she lay rigid on the bed next to him, her mouth dry, trying to work out what had happened. But it only took a few seconds to orientate herself. Nothing had happened. Nothing at all. She was still fully dressed—the only items missing were her shoes, which were strewn across the floor alongside her bag. He was minus his jacket and shoes too, but his trousers and shirt were still firmly in place.

She took a few steadying breaths. His room was almost identical to hers, so she slid almost in slow motion from the bed, gathered her things and tiptoed to the door. It was ridiculous. All that had happened was they'd fallen asleep. Now she thought about it, he'd fallen asleep first and she'd been so relaxed and so tired; she'd meant to get up a few minutes later. Instead it seemed she'd snuggled up for the night.

As she closed the door behind her while holding her breath, she wondered if she should be offended. They hadn't even kissed. And he was more than a little hot. Maybe he hadn't been attracted to her?

By the time she'd reached her room she'd started to get mad. Irrational and pointless, but, hey, that was just her. Half an hour later she was showered, hair tied back and looking as pristine as she could. She grabbed some coffee and fruit at the breakfast buffet and sat down at a table for a few moments.

This presentation was important. She was representing her agency to more than five hundred delegates. She could make connections today that could help her career. Not that she had ambitions right now. She loved her job. But the work the Disease Prevention Agency did was international. Having contacts across the world was always helpful. Last night had thrown her off balance a little. And she couldn't afford to be distracted right now. Nerves weren't usually a problem for her but she couldn't pretend her stomach wasn't currently in knots. She stared at the huge breakfast buffet then back to her untouched fruit. Apple. She picked a few pieces of apple out of the bowl with her fork then followed up with a large glug of coffee.

There was a rumble around the room immediately followed by heads turning. It was almost like being in a room of bobbing meerkats. Her eyes flickered out to the horizon. The ocean looked a little darker and there were some black clouds in the far-off distance. There were a few nervous laughs around her. "Maybe it was one of the volcanoes telling us all to behave," said some-one close to her.

"I don't know," said one of the women close by in a tone Amber didn't quite like. "I wonder if it could be something else."

Just then the doors to the main auditorium opened and people started to file inside. Amber glanced at her program. It was over an hour until she had to speak. The conference organizers had already told her the presentation was prepared. All she had to do was stand at the podium and talk. She'd initially planned to wait outside and practice, but her churning stomach told her that probably wouldn't do anything to quell her nerves. Maybe listening to someone else would be enough distraction to keep her calm.

She picked up her things and let herself be carried in with the crowd, taking a seat near the aisle in a row close to the back of the auditorium. Within a few minutes the lights dimmed and a professor from one of the national organizations delivered the introductory speech. "Our first speaker is Jack Campbell, Senior Medical Officer in the Royal Army Medical Corps. Dr. Campbell has just finished his second tour of duty. As many of you will know, some of our most widely used medical products were first introduced on the battlefield—and it looks like we're about to hear about a new revolutionary product that could help save lives across the globe. I give you Dr. Jack Campbell."

There was a round of applause in the room as a man in uniform walked across the stage to the podium. Amber blinked. Then blinked again.

A medic. He was a medic.

As he started to speak, her skin tingled almost as if his familiar accent were dancing across it. Jack. His name was Jack. The man she'd spent the night wrapped around was delivering one of the keynote speeches of the conference.

Every hair on her body stood on end. Nothing had happened last night. Nothing. But…it could have, if they both hadn't fallen asleep.

Her stomach did a flip-flop. She'd spent the last ten years avoiding any close relationships with fellow medics. And now she'd just accidentally spent the night wrapped around one. Hardly her most defining moment.

Why hadn't she asked more questions? The truth was, as soon as she'd realized he was Scottish she'd assumed he must be part of the business and economic conference. The UK had the NHS—a government-run health service. Her brain had automatically told her that it was unlikely the NHS would send a doctor to the other side of the world for a conference. But a private business—they probably sent employees to international conferences on a weekly basis. And she'd just automatically put him into that slot.

She gave a tiny shudder. That was what happened when you made assumptions. She lifted her head and looked at him again, angry with herself.

She'd found him attractive. She'd liked flirting with him. The truth was, more than she'd expected to. And now he was here. Standing right in front of a room full of professionals and addressing the room.

And boy, could he speak. She sat mesmerized along with the rest of the audience as he described his time in Afghanistan and the sometimes limited resources. He showed a new wound dressing he'd developed—a mixture of clay and algae that could stop severe bleeding and form a clot within twenty seconds.

Amber could almost see the ears pricking up in the room and people sitting a little straighter in their seats.

Those twenty seconds could be the difference between life and death.

His accent drew the audience in—as did his demeanor. He was a commanding figure, especially in uniform. He spoke with passion about his work, but was also realistic and even a little self-deprecating. All things that had drawn her to him last night. He acknowledged everyone who'd worked alongside him, fellow doctors, surgeons and army medics. He showed pictures of some of the soldiers who had been treated and had their lives saved by this dressing that had been used in the field. Finally he showed cost pricing for the wound dressings along with approximations of lives that could be saved across the world. She could sense the buzz in the air; it was almost infectious.

Then he just stopped.

After a few seconds people started glancing nervously at each other. The presentation had finished and his image was now being shown on the large screen behind him in intimate detail. As she watched she could almost swear she saw a little twitch at his right eye—those brown eyes that had almost seemed to bewitch her last night. She gave herself a shake. Where had that come from?

His eyes seemed to focus and he started talking again. "This product was conceived in a place of war. It was needed. It was essential to save lives—and it will be essential to saving lives in the future. War is never a situation you want to be in. People die. Families are devastated and lives change…forever."

He took a deep breath. "What makes me sad is that we need something like this. I'm sad that, even though we're no longer in a time of war, because of gun and knife crime, this product will continue to be needed."

His words echoed across the room. It was the way he said them, the change in timbre of his voice. She could hear the emotion; she could almost reach out and touch it. Even though the temperature in the room was steady, she could swear that a cool breeze swept over her, prickling the hairs on her arms.

People around her were openmouthed. Then slowly, but surely, applause started throughout the room. Within a few seconds it gathered pace and Amber couldn't help but smile as she glanced at the nods of approval and the conversations starting around her.

"Do you think we should get it?"

"It would be perfect for paramedics."

"What an investment opportunity…"

The professor crossed the stage again, shaking Jack's hand enthusiastically. He then launched into the next introduction. "Our next speaker is a doctor from the Disease Prevention Agency."

Amber felt a wave of panic.

"Amber Berkeley has been working there for the last five years. She specializes in meningitis and will be presenting some of the latest research into emerging strains. Please welcome Dr. Amber Berkeley."

Darn it. She stood up quickly. She'd come in looking for distraction and Jack Campbell had certainly met the criteria. Usually she would spend the five minutes before a presentation going over things in her head and taking some time to do controlled breathing. But she hadn't even thought about the presentation the whole time she'd been in here. Somehow her attention had all been focused on her mystery almost-suitor from last night.

She walked smartly down the auditorium, climbing the steps and shaking the professor's hand. Her heart was thudding so loudly she almost expected everyone else to hear it.

She glanced at Jack, who was giving her an amused look. Rat fink. Could he sense her panic? "Dr. Berkeley," he said with a nod of his head as the corners of his lips turned upward.

"Dr. Campbell," she answered as coolly as she could, trying not to take in how he filled out his army fatigues. She was sure he could have worn his more formal uniform for an event like this, but somehow the fatigues suited him—made him look more like Jack.

Her hands were shaking slightly as she set them on the podium, waiting for the professor and Jack to leave the stage. She tried to still her thoughts and let her professional face slide into place. She'd always been bothered with nerves. It was weird. Put her in a clinical situation—even an epidemic—and she could deal with the pandemonium of that no problem. Put her in a classroom setting, or even an interview setting, and her heart would race at a million miles an hour, making her thoughts incoherent and her words even worse. She'd had to work at this. She'd had to work hard.

She took a few deep and steadying breaths. Truth was, she could do this presentation in her sleep. She knew the information inside out. But could she present with the commitment and compassion that Jack just had? He was a hard act to follow.

A horrible queasiness came over her. That familiar feeling of not being good enough. The way she'd constantly tried to prove herself to her father by getting perfect grades, being the first in her class, qualifying for med school—all just to gain a second of his attention. Those memories ran deep—even though her father was gone.

She hated feeling this way. And as she looked out over the sea of expectant faces, she felt her anger spike.

She looked up as Jack descended the stairs to her right. At the last possible second he turned his head, gave her a cheeky grin and winked at her. *Winked at her*.

A little spurt of adrenaline raced through her body. The cheek. Right now, she could cheerfully punch him. Anything for an outlet to the bubbling frustration she was feeling inside.

She lifted her head and looked out at the still-waiting audience. She could do this. She could. She could be good enough. She could deliver her presentation with the same passion and commitment as he had. She would deal with Jack Campbell later. She tilted her chin upward and plastered her most professional smile on her face. "Thank you so much for inviting me here today…"

So her name was Amber Berkeley. It suited her. A tiny bit quirky, with a hint of grace.

He'd had no idea she was a speaker at the conference. That was the thing about not sharing names and trying to be a little mysterious—it made you miss out on other things.

He'd left the stage and stood at the back of the auditorium listening to her. Her nerves were clearly evident. Her hands had been shaking and she'd been white as a ghost as she'd stepped up to the podium. Last night she'd been brimming with casual confidence. He'd liked that better.

But as he'd stood and watched, the woman he'd met last night had slowly emerged. It was clear she knew and understood her subject matter. She spoke eloquently about meningitis and its spread, the way that the different viruses adapted and changed and the problems that could cause. He was impressed with the way she handled random questions that were thrown at her about the new emerging types of meningitis and the difficulties in diagnosing quickly enough for appropriate treatment.

He'd learned something new. And as she stepped down from the podium and walked back up the aisle toward him, he waited for her at the door, pushing it open as she approached.

The light in the foyer was bright compared to the auditorium. She stepped outside, blinked for a few seconds then unfastened her jacket and breathed a huge sigh of relief.

"You winked at me, you cheeky..." She left the last word missing.

"Did I?" He raised his eyebrows.

She shook her head and sagged against the wall for a second. "Thank goodness that's over."

He looked surprised. "You were good. What on earth were you worried about?"

She arched an eyebrow at him. "Who said I was worried?"

"Do your hands normally shake?"

Her tongue was stuck firmly inside her cheek. She waited a second before replying, then pulled her shoulders back and started to walk past him. "For that, you owe me breakfast. I couldn't eat anything earlier but right now I could probably eat the entire contents of the kitchen."

He held his arm out, gesturing toward the nearby hotel restaurant, trying not to fixate on the swing of her hips in that skirt. "Your wish is my command." Then he gave a little smile. "I seem to buy you a lot of food."

She tutted and shook her head as she walked past him, letting one of the waiters show them to a table looking out over the Pacific Ocean. The wind had whipped up outside, bringing the earlier dark clouds closer and making all the parasols on the beach shake.

Amber glanced outside. "What's that all about? I came here for sunshine and good weather."

Jack shrugged. "Almost looks like a day in Scotland instead of Hawaii. Must just be in for a bit of bad weather."

Amber sat down quickly as the waiter showed them to a table. She didn't hesitate to order. "Can I have coffee, please? Not just a cup—a whole pot. And some eggs, sunny-side up, and some rye toast, please."

Jack gave a nod and tried not to smile again. "I'll have what she's having—and some orange juice, please." He waited until the waiter had left. "So, you didn't want to hear the next speaker?"

She laid her hand on her stomach. "Are you kidding? If I'd stayed in there I'm sure all five hundred delegates would have heard my stomach rumbling. I had to eat."

Her hair was tamer today, tied back in a slick ponytail instead of piled haphazardly on top of her head. The pink tips were just visible when she turned her head. The simple black suit and white shirt were elegant, but as they sat at the table, she pulled off her jacket and rolled up her shirtsleeves midway, revealing a host of gold bangles.

"You ducked out on me."

She looked up quickly. For the briefest of seconds she looked a bit startled, but he could almost see her natural demeanor settling back into place. "How do you know I ducked out? You were too busy snoring."

He shook his head. "I don't snore. You, however…"

"You never told me you were a doctor." The words were almost accusing.

"Neither did you."

For a second she didn't speak. It was almost like a Mexican standoff.

He could see her swallow, and then she gave him a haughty stare. "I don't mix with fellow doctors."

Jack leaned forward. "What does that mean?" He held out his hands. "And what do you call this?"

"This," she said firmly, "is breakfast. Breakfast is fine."

He kept his elbows on the table, wondering if he could lean even closer. "Oh, so I can buy you food. But you can't spend the night with me?" He wanted to laugh out loud. She sounded so uptight, and that seemed a total turnaround from the woman he'd met last night.

But now he was curious. "So, what exactly is wrong with doctors? After all, you're one."

She gave an exasperated sigh. "I know. It's just…" He could see her try to find the words. "It's just that I don't like to mix work with…" She winced.

"Pleasure?" He couldn't resist.

She closed her eyes for a second.

He sat back in his chair and folded his arms. "So, if I'd told you last night in the bar I was a doctor, you wouldn't have come back to my room with me?"

She bit her bottom lip. He could tell she knew she was about to be challenged.

"Well, yes."

He held open his arms. "It's a conference full of medical professionals. The hotel is full of them. Who did you think you might meet in the bar?"

She shrugged. "There's more than one conference on in this hotel. I thought you were maybe one of those—" she waggled her hand "—business, economic-type guys."

He let out a laugh. He couldn't help it. From the second he'd started studying medicine it had felt as if he practically had *doctor* stamped on his forehead. He put his hand on his chest. "Me? You honestly thought I was some kind of accountant, computer, business-type geek?" He shook his head. "Oh, my army colleagues would just love that."

She looked distinctly uncomfortable and he tried to rein in his amusement.

"Why are you getting yourself so worked up? Nothing happened. You know it didn't." He gave her a kind of sideways glance. "Maybe…if things had been different and jet lag hadn't been involved then we could be having an entirely different conversation today."

He was probably pushing things. But it was true. There had been a spark between them last night. He wouldn't let her try and deny it.

Her face was pinched; there were faint wrinkles along her brow. He couldn't actually believe it. She really, really did have an issue with the fact he was a doctor.

He'd worked with colleagues in the past who didn't like to mix work with relationships. It wasn't so unheard of. Maybe if he'd adopted that rule he wouldn't have ended up losing someone. He wouldn't have felt the need to shut himself off entirely from the rest of the world.

But even as he had that thought he knew it was ridiculous. Relationship or not, they would still both have been posted to Afghanistan. He'd been tortured with what-ifs for a long time before he realized nothing would have changed.

He saw a glimmer of something in Amber's blue eyes. A spark at his words. Baiting her was easy.

She flung her paper napkin at him. "No way."

He raised his eyebrows. "Purely because I'm a doctor?"

She neglected to answer that part of the question and gave him a long stare. "Let's just say had you been some mysterious businessman…" She leaned back in her chair and crossed her long legs. "It's a bit insulting, really."

Was she changing tack? He mirrored her actions and leaned back in his chair. "What is?"

"A man inviting you back to his room, then promptly falling asleep and ignoring you."

He squirmed. When he'd woken up this morning he'd cringed. He remembered sitting up in the bed together to eat their second burger and fries. He also remembered watching some old movie with her and laughing along at the lines. And he could just about remember a warm body wrapped around his in the middle of the night. He'd tried not to remember the fact it had felt good because that flooded him with things he didn't want to acknowledge.

He lifted his hands. "Guilty as charged. Sorry. It was the jet lag." He put his elbow on the table and leaned a little closer. "But now? Jet lag is gone. Let's start again."

Even though she'd just tried to joke with him, she still looked the tiniest bit uncomfortable. She obviously took her "no fraternization with other medics" rule seriously. He couldn't help but be curious.

He waved his hand. "Relax, Amber. This is just breakfast. Nothing more. Nothing less. What do you have against fellow doctors, anyway?"

She didn't meet his gaze; she just sucked in a breath as her fingers toyed with the cutlery on the table. "Let's just say I lived in an environment with an absentee medic who was obsessed with his work. As a child I had no choice. As an adult, it's not a situation I ever want to repeat."

He wanted to ask questions. He did. But somehow he got the impression it wasn't really the time. He was curious about this woman. And after two years, that was a first for him—one that he couldn't quite understand.

The waiter appeared with the coffee and filled up their cups. Jack decided to take things back to neutral territory. "You might have told me you were a speaker."

She raised her eyebrows. "You might have told me you were starting off the conference." She gave a thoughtful nod. "You were good. I was impressed." Her eyes ran up and down his uniform. "I can't believe I thought you were at the business conference. I should have guessed. Your suit didn't quite fit perfectly—and, let's face it, those guys probably spend on their suits what I would on a car. I should have guessed you were an army guy. I'm still surprised you didn't mention it."

"I'll try not to be insulted by the suit comment— because you're right. I much prefer to drive a reliable car than buy a fancy suit. If you want to split hairs, you didn't mention you worked for the Disease Prevention Agency. Aren't you guys supposed to walk about in giant space suits?" He grinned and nodded his head. "Now I understand the comments at the bar about the peanuts."

She shuddered. "You have *no* idea what we've found on bar snacks."

He laughed as he kept shaking his head. "And I don't want you to tell me." This was better. This was more what he wanted. He could gradually see the tension around her neck and shoulders start to ease.

The waiter appeared with their eggs and toast, and Amber leaned over the plate and inhaled. "Oh, delicious. And just what I need."

She ate for a few minutes then looked back up at him. "Your wound dressing. It looks good. How on earth did you discover the science behind it?"

Jack was spreading butter on his toast. "There's been quite a bit of work on clot-forming dressings. My problem was they just didn't work quickly enough for the situations we were in. But—" he gave her a smile; she was watching him with those big blue eyes "—the Internet is a wonderful thing. I contacted a few people who'd led other studies and asked if we could try a combination. I knew the specifics of what I really needed. I needed something so simple that it could be slapped on by anyone—and so quick acting it could stop bleeding within twenty seconds."

The glance she gave him was filled with admiration. "I heard people talking after you finished. They think you're sitting on a gold mine."

Jack shifted uncomfortably in his chair. "It's not about money," he said quickly.

Amber didn't even blink, just kept staring at him with that careful gaze. "I know. I got that."

He picked at his eggs with his fork. "I know that for a lot of people medicine is a business. Britain isn't like that. The army isn't like that. Our health care is free—always has been and hopefully always will be. I'm not sure I can exist in a climate where every dressing gets counted and every profit margin looked at."

She took a sip of her coffee. "You've already been approached, haven't you?"

He bit the inside of his cheek, unsure of how much to tell her. Jack liked being straightforward. And from what little he'd seen of Amber, she seemed to operate that way too. That thing on the stage had just been a wobble—he was sure.

"Right from the beginning we had a contract arranged and a product license developed. It was developed during army time, so they have a part ownership, as do the original creators of the components." He sighed. "I knew this could happen. As soon as I realized how good it was, I wanted to make sure that it wouldn't end up being all about the money. That's not why I did this—it's not why *we* did this. And I know it's good. I know it could save lives around the world, and that's what I want it to do."

She tipped her head to the side and studied him for a few seconds. "I like that." The color had finally returned to her cheeks and she seemed more relaxed.

He gave her a smile. "Your presentation was good too. I know the basics about meningitis but not the rest. I had no idea just how quickly the strains were mutating."

She pushed her plate away. "Thank you. The presentation was important. I'm the only person here from the DPA this time, and I wanted to be sure that I gave a good impression." Her fingers were still wrapped around her fork, which she was drumming lightly on the table. "Monitoring infectious diseases is all about good international working." She let out a little laugh. "Let's just say that some of our counterparts have been a bit reluctant to share information in the past. In a world of international travel it makes contact tracing interesting."

"Ouch." Jack wrinkled his brow. He couldn't imagine trying to contact trace across continents. It was bad enough on the few occasions he had to make an urgent call to a far-off relative, and that was with all the army resources at his disposal.

He topped up his coffee. "Want anything else to eat?"

She shook her head. "I think I'm done. Thank you for this."

She kept staring at him, with a hint of a smile around her lips. He waited a few seconds then couldn't help himself.

"What?"

This was odd. It was the most relaxed he'd been around a woman for a while.

But he liked this woman's sense of humor. He liked her sassiness. And he was curious about the hint of vulnerability he'd seen on the stage. Not that it had stopped her—she'd gone on to deliver an impressive talk.

And he couldn't help but be curious about the No Doctor rule she'd obviously decided to follow.

There was a rumble outside and they both glanced out at the darkening and choppy ocean. "I thought Hawaii was supposed to be sunshine, sunshine and more sunshine." He frowned.

"Not forgetting the killer surf waves," she added as she kept her eyes on the ocean. "I think you were right. It looks like you brought Scotland's weather with you."

He shook his head. "Believe me, you wouldn't go into the sea in Scotland when it looks like that. Even on a roasting hot day, the sea still feels like ten below zero. On a day like today? You'd be a frozen fish finger."

She burst out laughing. "A what?"

He wrinkled his brow and drew a tiny rectangle on the table with his finger. "You know, cod or haddock, covered in bread crumbs. For kids. They're kind of rectangular."

"Oh…" She nodded. "You mean a fish stick."

The wrinkles grew even deeper. "A fish stick? What's a stick about it? It's a rectangle."

She folded her arms across her chest. "Well, what's a finger about it?"

He waved his hand in mock exasperation. "You Americans."

"You Scots," she countered just as quickly.

"Is this what we're going to do?" He couldn't help himself. He lowered his voice. The look she gave him through her thick lashes sent tingles across his skin.

"What do you mean?"

He gestured to the table. "Eat food and argue about words. We're starting to be a habit."

She glanced at her watch. "A habit? After less than twenty-four hours? Has to be a new world record."

He leaned his head on his hand. He really should go back in to the auditorium and listen to some of the other talks. He should be thinking about his career, and be circulating and making contacts the way he'd failed to last night. But somehow, like last night, the only contact he was interested in making was right in front of him.

Three days in Hawaii. That was how long he planned to be here. He could easily lose himself in three days with a woman like Amber Berkeley. She was smart. She was fun. And he could sense the spark between them.

In a way he was glad nothing had happened last night. It meant their flirtation could happily continue and he could find out a little bit more about her. All within the confines of the conference. Whether they attended any more talks or not was entirely a different story.

As for her No Docs rule? Rules were made to be broken. And they didn't work together—never would. Maybe she could be persuaded to spend some more time together. His stomach gave the weirdest little lurch. He couldn't believe he'd actually just thought like that.

He'd imagined landing in Hawaii to scorching sun, colorful flowers and interesting birds and wildlife. That was the picture he'd always had in his head.

He'd lived so long in his own little bubble that finding someone to exchange anything other than clinical findings with was odd. But odd in a good way.

He looked her straight in the eye. "You've never just met someone and clicked?"

She blinked for a second as if she wasn't quite sure how to answer. "Is this a trick question?"

He shook his head. "What? No."

Then she tapped her fingers on the table slowly. "Okay,

since you found out my name, did you look me up on-line?" She looked a little anxious.

He shook his head again. He was getting more con-fused by the second. "No. Why, should I?"

She hesitated for a few seconds then rolled her eyes and waved her hand. "There's no point hiding it. If you search up my name you'll find the whole news head-lines. A very long time ago, when social media was a mere babe, and I was working as an intern, I met a fel-low medic." She lifted her fingers. "And I clicked."

He folded his arms across his chest. "You clicked? Oh, no. You're not getting away with that. What hap-pened to the No Doctors rule?"

She sighed. "Let's just say this was a huge contribu-tion to the No Doctors rule."

"Tell me more."

She gave a slow rueful nod and held up her hands. He couldn't quite work out the expression on her face; it was a mixture of sad, exasperated and just…tired. "I was duped, I admit it. Or I was *charmed*."

"How charmed?" He was definitely curious. Amber didn't seem like the kind of girl to be either duped or charmed. Maybe there was a reason for the slightly brash exterior?

"Charmed enough to plan a wedding." She stopped for a second. "My father was a very accomplished sur-geon, notorious for only picking the best of the best for his residents. He was also notoriously sexist. There were no women on his team. Charles used me, to get to him." The words were matter-of-fact, but the way that she said them wasn't.

"He did?" Jack couldn't help the wave of disgust that swept over him and the way his heart twisted a little for her. "So what happened?"

She shrugged. "I found out on the morning of the wedding via an overheard conversation in the local hairdresser that he'd been boasting about getting on my father's team, and worming his way in through me."

"I thought women were supposed to drink champagne on the morning of their wedding."

"Oh, I was drinking champagne as they pinned my hair up. I thought about it all the way home. I thought about it all the time I stepped into my dress and little things came into my head, like a giant jigsaw puzzle slotting into place. By the time I reached the church and saw him standing at the top of the aisle, the smug expression on his face told me everything I needed to know. I turned on my heels, picked up my dress and ran."

"You ran?" He couldn't actually believe it.

She gave a small nod. "Do an Internet search of Milwaukee Runaway Bride. That's me." A long slow breath hissed out from her lips. "Not really something I want to put on my résumé." Her eyes looked up and met his. She gave a half shrug. "I hate the thought of people reading that about me online. It's like a permanent stain on my character."

She put her hands up to her forehead as if it ached, closing her eyes for a second. It was obvious she found this hard.

But she was being honest. He appreciated that. What would he have thought if he'd read this online? Probably, that she was a bit of an idiot, or that she was an attention seeker. Hearing it in person from her was an entirely different experience. He could tell that the whole experience had changed her.

"Regrets?" The words were out before he really thought about them, but Amber quickly shook her head as she lifted it from her hands.

"No. My father never spoke to me again. Nor did Charles. But then again, Charles lost his job the next day."

"You never spoke to your father again?"

She shook her head again but didn't look sad. Her words were more assured. "No. I was the ultimate disappointment. But then again, no matter how well I did, I'd always known that."

He could almost see her physically bristle.

"What kind of surgeon was he?"

"Renal. Top of his game—until the day he died."

"He wasn't proud that his daughter was a doctor too?"

"Don't think he even noticed." Her answer was short and snappy. "Truth was, I wasn't a boy. By the time I realized how little respect my father had for me, and my mother, I was done with him anyhow. He died a few years later and it actually set my mother free."

Jack was a little surprised at her words but at least now he had half an understanding about her No Doctor rule. Of course, it didn't make sense. But in her head, it did.

Then she took a deep breath and shook her head. "Let's change the subject." It was clear there was a lot more to this, but he could tell that she'd shared enough, and he respected her for that.

Her blue eyes met his and she sat up a little straighter in her chair, tilting her head at him. It was like a shock wave. When the anger and resentment left her face, Amber Berkeley was stunning. "You said last night you should probably be schmoozing. You're almost not in the army now. What's your plans, soldier?"

He raised his eyebrows. "Why, are you offering me a job?"

She straightened her back and narrowed her gaze, imitating some kind of stern interviewer. "Well, let's see. I know your qualifications. I know you're from Scotland. I know you appear to be quite bright, and maybe even a little bit of a humanitarian." She put her elbows on the table and leaned toward him. "Think you could cut it at the DPA?"

He gave a lazy kind of smile. "Not if you call chips fries."

She sighed and waved her hand. "Oh, well, that's it. Interview fail. I'm sorry, Dr. Campbell—looks like you have to work on your interpersonal skills."

He nodded in agreement. In the corner of the room one of the conference staff had a phone in her hand and was talking quietly to one of the waiters and pointing toward their table. After a few seconds she approached. "Dr. Berkeley?"

Amber turned around in surprise. "Yes?"

"Would you mind taking a call from one of your colleagues from the DPA?"

Amber stared down at her bag for a few seconds, and then her face crumpled. "Darn it. I switched off my phone before I came down because I knew I'd be in the auditorium. I hope nothing is wrong."

She held out her hand for the phone. "This is Dr. Berkeley." He heard it instantly. The change in her tone, her professional persona slipping back into place. He wondered if he should move to let her take the call in privacy, but she didn't seem to mind the fact they were still sitting together.

"Hi, Warren. Yes. No. Really?"

He watched as he could see her concentrating. After a few seconds she fumbled around in her bag. Jack reached into his fatigues and pulled out his pocketbook and pen, pushing them across the table toward her. She nodded gratefully as she flicked open the book and started to scribble. "Yip, what's the name? Oh…how awful. Which strain? Yes. Do you have a contact at the local agency? At the admitting hospital? Okay. Can Drew give me a lab contact I can work with? I might have more experience at identifying the strain. Sure, no problem." She glanced outside at the darkening sky. "No." She gave a little smile, then met his gaze. "Things have been a little different than expected. Let me get on this." She clicked the phone and sighed as she set it down on the table.

"Something wrong?"

She nodded. "A new unidentified strain of meningitis. One affected teenager. A request for assistance has been made to the DPA and since I'm here…"

She let her voice tail off. Jack spoke carefully. "It's your specialty area—of course they should call you."

She nodded. "I know. I'm lucky it's meningitis. In the DPA you have to do a bit of everything. I've been in Africa looking at polio and sleeping sickness, Chicago, when we thought we might have a smallpox outbreak, and Washington and Texas for flu." She gave a resigned kind of smile. "We get all over." She stared over toward one of the windows. "Let's just hope it's only one case. I'm here by myself. If there's any more and it turns into an outbreak, contact tracing could be a nightmare."

It was all he needed to hear and he made his mind up instantly. Jack was never going to schmooze his way around this conference trying to find a suitable job. No matter how much his head told him he should, it just wasn't in him to do it. He couldn't do it. He was far more interested in finding out more about the woman sitting opposite him. It had been so long since he'd felt like this. She was sparking his interest in so many ways—so many ways that he hadn't acknowledged in such a long time. He stood up. "Okay, then, let's go."

Amber's eyes widened. "What?"

He shrugged. "No point in you going alone. And I guess you could always do with another pair of hands even though it's not my specialty. If it turns into more than one case, you'll need help. I can be that help. Why don't you change, I'll grab a few things from my room and I'll meet you back down here in ten minutes?"

Amber looked a bit lost for words. She waved her hand toward the doors to the foyer. "But don't you have to work the room, find a job?"

"I just flunked my last interview." He gave her a wink. "I've been told I need to work on my people skills. No time like the present to start."

She stood up and picked up her bag. "Are you sure about this?"

He gave the briefest of nods. "Let's face it. You're the most interesting person I've met here. Better stick around."

He could swear that was relief on her face. "Okay, then, Dr. Campbell. I'll meet you in ten."

She'd never changed so quickly—just kicked off her heels and let her expensive suit crumple across a chair. She pulled on a pair of stretchy dark trousers, a short-sleeved shirt and a pair of flats. Because her wardrobe was mainly formal clothes for the conference—none of which she wanted to wear to the local hospital—she grabbed her least formal jacket, a khaki military-style one. She shook her head as she pulled it on. At this rate, she and Jack would look like a matching pair.

She dumped her purse and stuffed her wallet, phone

and notebook into a small backpack. She'd learned over the years to travel lightly.

She still couldn't believe he'd volunteered to come with her but she was secretly pleased. It didn't matter that she was confident in her practice. It didn't matter that she'd handled contact tracing for meningitis on numerous occasions. This was the first time she'd actually represented the DPA on her own. And it made her a tiny bit nervous. But from what little she knew of Jack Campbell, she hoped he would have her back.

He was already waiting as she walked back out to the main foyer. It was busier than she'd expected. Filled with anxious faces. Jack was standing among some other people.

"What's happening?" she asked.

"Look at that rain."

"What did they say about a weather warning?"

"I've never seen black clouds like that before. What happened to the sun?"

Jack was still wearing his fatigues; for the second time she tried not to notice how well they suited him. He smiled as he noticed her similar garb. "Are we ready to get started? I think we should move. Something seems to be happening."

She nodded. "We need to go to the Hawaii Outbreak Center and Lahuna State Hospital."

They walked across the foyer and out to the hotel main entrance. Both of the suited doormen were standing inside. They looked at her in surprise. "What's your destination?"

Almost immediately the sharp wind whipped her ponytail around her face and she had to brace her feet to the ground. She glanced around as her jacket and shirt buffeted against her. Rain thudded all around her, bouncing off the ground. The streets were almost empty and she could feel the stinging sand on her cheeks picked up from the beach across the road. All of the straw beach umbrellas had tipped over and were rolling precariously around. No one seemed keen on rescuing them.

Hawaii had never looked like this in any of the photographs she'd seen.

The doorman looked down at the deserted street. When she'd arrived the day before it had been packed with cars and taxis.

He gave a wave. "Come back inside and I'll call for a car. It may take a while. We've just had a six-hour emergency hurricane warning. The hotel is just about to make an announcement. All residents are going to be asked to stay inside. Could your journey wait? It's unlikely flights will be taking off anytime soon."

"What?"

"What?"

Jack's voice echoed her own. A wave of panic came over her. Did this mean she couldn't get to her patient?

She shook her head. The doorman was obviously assuming the only place people would try to get to right now was the airport. "I'm a doctor. I have to go to the Hawaii Outbreak Center then Lahuna State Hospital. I have to consult on a meningitis case."

The doorman gave her a solemn nod and didn't try to put her off any further. "Give me five minutes. I can get my brother-in-law to pick you up." He drew in a deep breath as he picked up a phone at his desk and dialed the number. "You might have to be prepared to lock down wherever you reach. Once we're on hurricane alert everyone is instructed to stay safe."

Jack stepped forward. "I knew that the weather was

looking bad, but when did they issue the hurricane warning?"

"Just in the last ten minutes. It seems to have picked up force somewhere in the mid Pacific. Apparently the hurricane has taken an unexpected sharp turn. We usually have more time to prepare. All hotels have been contacted and the news stations are broadcasting instructions."

"Is it normal to be so late letting people know?"

The doorman shook his head. "We usually have between thirty-six hours and twenty-four hours to prepare. We have statewide plans for hurricanes, but the truth is, Hawaii has only been affected by four hurricanes in the last sixty years. Tropical storms? Oh, they're much more common."

Jack met her worried gaze. She'd been in crisis situations before, but usually for some kind of an infectious disease—not for a natural disaster. It was almost as if he could sense her fleeting second of panic. He put his hand at the back of her waist and nodded toward the doorman. "Thank you so much for doing this. We're only going out because we have to and we'll be happy to lock down wherever appropriate."

Ten minutes later a taxicab appeared. They watched as a few large gusts buffeted it from side to side on the road. The doorman handed them a card with numbers. "We'll be keeping an inventory of guests in the hotel as we do the lockdown. I've noted where you're going and here's some contact numbers if you need them. Good luck."

They climbed quickly into the back of the cab and Amber leaned forward to give the driver instructions. The roof of the hotel pickup point rattled above them. The driver listened to her then rapidly shook his head, gesturing toward the empty streets. "No. Pick one or the other. Which is the most important? We don't have enough time to take you to both."

Amber blew out a breath and turned to face Jack. "If the phones are still functioning I could call the Outbreak Center. It's more important to be where the patient and lab are, particularly if I want to try and identify the strain."

She didn't mind batting off him. It was always useful to throw ideas back and forward with another doctor and he had a completely different kind of experience from her—one that was more likely to be suited to this.

He nodded seriously as his eyes took in the weather around him. "Sounds like a plan."

She leaned forward to the driver. "Can you get us to Lahuna State Hospital?"

The driver nodded. "It's near the city center. We should get there soon."

The cab wove through the streets and high-rise buildings. There were a few people practically being carried along by the wind as they rushed to get places. Some stores were already closed, shutters down and all street wares brought back inside.

A large white building with dark windows emerged through the rain. The main doors and ambulance bay had their doors closed, with security staff visible through the glass. They unlocked the door as Jack and Amber jumped from the cab.

"We've had to close the automatic doors," one told her. "The wind is just too strong and a member of the public has already been injured."

Amber gave him a grateful smile as he locked the door behind them. "Can you direct me to Infectious Diseases? I've been called about a patient."

"Third floor. Elevators at the end of the corridor. Take a right when you get out."

The hospital was eerily quiet, the main foyer deserted as they made their way through. But as they reached the corridor in the heart of the hospital they could see uniformed staff swiftly moving patients and talking in hushed, urgent voices. "I wonder if the windows will be okay?" said Jack thoughtfully as they reached the elevators.

"What?" She pressed the button to call the elevator.

"The windows." Jack looked around him even though there were no windows nearby. "A place like this? It must have around, what—three hundred windows? How on earth do you police that in the middle of a hurricane?"

Amber blinked. She hadn't even thought about anything like that at all. "The hotel too. Do you think they'll tell people to leave their rooms?"

The doors slid open. "They must all have disaster plans. Won't they just take everyone to a central point in a building, somewhere they can hunker down?"

He could almost read her mind. Both of them had rooms at the hotel that they'd literally just abandoned with no thought to the impending hurricane. If they'd had a bit more warning she might have closed her curtains and stashed her computer and valuables somewhere safer. Who knew what they would return to later?

They stepped inside and she pressed the button for the third floor. It only took a few moments to reach there and the doors to the infectious disease unit. Amber reached for the scrub on the wall outside before she entered, rubbing it over her hands.

She could already see through the glass that the unit looked in chaos.

She turned to face Jack before she pressed the entrance buzzer. "Ready?"

She felt a tiny glimmer of trepidation. She was it. She was the sole representative for the DPA. Was she asking him, or herself?

But Jack didn't hesitate for a second. "Absolutely. Lead the way."

CHAPTER THREE

FROM THE SECOND she walked into the unit she was in complete control. He couldn't help but be completely impressed. Whatever the little waver was he'd glimpsed outside, it seemed to have disappeared. There were actually two infected patients. It seemed that they'd been brought in only a few hours apart. Was that the start of an epidemic?

Amber took it in her stride and reviewed them—Zane and Aaron, both eighteen, who were clearly very sick. Then she phoned the Hawaii Outbreak Center and liaised with their staff, and then asked for some instructions to find the lab.

Her face was a little paler as they headed to the stairs. "I need to find out what strain of meningitis this is. These kids have got sick really quickly."

The lab was down in the bowels of the hospital and they had to change into white lab coats and disposable gloves before entering. It was a modern lab, with traditionally white walls, an array of machinery and computers and wide work benches. But somehow it wasn't quite as busy as he might have expected.

"Where is everyone?" he murmured.

Amber shook her head as they walked through. "Maybe

they've sent some staff home because of the hurricane warning."

The head of the lab was an older man, tall but thick and heavyset; he already knew they were on their way and walked over with his hand outstretched. "Mamo Akano. I take it you're my meningitis doctor?"

Amber nodded her head. "Amber Berkeley from the Disease Prevention Agency. Any further forward in identifying the strain?"

Mamo had deep furrows in his brow. "Maybe. The DPA just sent me some files over for you to consider. Come over here. I've opened them on the computer next to the microscope."

Amber hurried over and pulled up a stool next to the microscope. She glanced over her shoulder toward Jack. "Ready for this?"

It was the first time since he'd got here that Jack had felt out of his depth. This wasn't his forte. But he was always willing to learn. He gave a nod and pulled up a stool. "Tell me what you need me to do."

Three hours later her neck ached and her brain was fried. She'd spoken to her contacts at the Hawaii Outbreak Center, and her colleagues in Chicago. Their strain of meningitis seemed to be unique. It was definitely bacterial meningitis. The cerebral spinal fluid collected from both boys had been cloudy. But the gram stains hadn't given them the information that they needed. There was nothing like it on file—which was not entirely unusual, but just made things more difficult. It was closest to a previously identified strain of meningitis W135, but seemed to have mutated slightly. "What do we do now?" asked Jack.

Mamo sighed. He'd been by their side the whole time. "In theory, now we wait. But we can't really do that."

Jack frowned. "What do you mean?"

Amber gave a slow nod. "Mamo will need to see what the most effective antibiotic for treating this strain is. But sometimes we don't know that for up to forty-eight hours—even seventy-two hours. We can't wait that long. Both of these patients are too sick. I need to try and treat them now."

Pieces clicked into place in Jack's brain. "So, you guess?"

"Yip," said Mamo, "Amber has to guess." His voice didn't sound happy.

Amber straightened up. Her voice was confident and her manner methodical. "Zane was already started on a broad-spectrum antibiotic—Penicillin G—when he was admitted. But it already looks like it hasn't started working. Neither of these boys was immunized. So, we immunize against Men W, and we treat them with something more specific—more than likely chloramphenicol—and hope the strain's not mutated too much." She pointed to the phone. "Let me make one more phone call. Then I'll go back up to Infectious Diseases to speak to the consultant. Then…" She turned to face Jack. "Then we're on a race against time. We need to contact trace. If there are children involved they may already have been immunized against meningitis W. But because this strain is slightly mutated, I still want to give them antibiotics. I can't take any chances with this."

"Meningitis W is one of the most dangerous strains, isn't it?"

She nodded. "That's why it was included in the immunization schedule in lots of countries only a few years ago. These kids really should have had this vaccine.

But not everyone agrees with vaccination. Not everyone takes their kids for them, even though they can get them for free." She shook her head and turned to Mamo. "I need supplies. Where can I get oral supplies of antibiotics?"

Jack couldn't help but be impressed. She was on fire. This was her specialty and it was clear she knew the subject matter well.

Mamo walked over to another phone. "I'll talk to the hospital pharmacy. It's emergency circumstances—in more ways than one. Being part of the DPA will give you visiting physician credentials. You'll be able to get what you need."

She nodded again in grateful thanks. Jack got that. He was a medic too and part of the army. And, although he was confident in his abilities and credentials, it didn't matter where you were in the world—most countries had their own conditions and registrations for being a doctor. The US had different regulations for each state, so sometimes it made things difficult.

She nodded and laid her hand on Mamo's arm as he waited for someone to answer the phone. "Thank you," she acknowledged. He nodded as they made their way back out of the lab and to the elevators.

She leaned against the wall as the elevator ascended. A few strands of her dark pink-tipped hair had fallen around her face and shoulders, and he could practically see the tension across her shoulders and neck.

He leaned forward and touched the end of one of her strands of hair. "I never asked last night. Why pink?"

She blinked for a second as if her mind was racing with a million different thoughts, then glanced sideways as she realized he was touching her hair. "Why not?" she replied simply.

There was something about the expression on her face that made him suck in his breath. She appeared calm and methodical. He was seeing Amber Berkeley at her best.

He was so used to being in charge. But here? Here, he was just Jack Campbell. This wasn't a trauma situation. Here, he had to let the person with the most experience lead the case. And that was hard for him. "What can I do?"

He had to ask. He wanted to help. He'd help any colleague who needed it—whether it was his specialty area or not. The army had made him adaptable in more ways than one.

She fixed him with her steady blue eyes and gave him clear instructions. "I need to get histories. I need to find out where these boys have been in the last few days in detail. I need to know every contact. I need names, addresses, dates of birth—contact details if they have them."

Jack licked his lips and asked the first question that had danced into his brain. "And if they are too sick to tell us?"

She grimaced. "Then we ask their family. Their friends. Whoever admitted them. This is a potentially deadly strain. We can't wait. There isn't time." She shook her head. "I don't even want to think about what doing this in the middle of a hurricane means."

He gave a swift nod and reached over to give her arm a squeeze. "I can do detailed histories. I haven't done any for a while, but I still remember how. Let's split it. You take one, I'll take the other and then we can check if there's any crossover."

She looked down at his hand on her arm and gave a weary kind of smile. "Thank you for this, Jack. You didn't have to offer, but I'm glad you did. Usually I'm part of a team. So outside help is appreciated."

"You okay?"

She nodded. "The meningitis stuff? I can do it in my sleep. The hurricane stuff?" She shook her head. "I don't have a single clue. I feel completely thrown in at the deep end."

She gave a smile as the elevator doors slid open again. "Remember your first shift as a resident when it seemed like everyone on the ward was going to die simultaneously?"

He let out a wry laugh. Everyone felt like that their first day on the ward. "Oh, yeah."

"It feels a bit like that all over again."

He gave her a smile. "Well, think of me as your backup plan. You lead, I follow. Brief me. What do I need to know?"

She glanced over the notes she had. "Okay, these two kids were both part of a surf club. Zane became sick first, exhibiting some of the normal meningitis signs—high temperature, fever, signs of an early chest infection and, a few hours later, some confusion."

"So, there are at least a few hours between the disease progression in these kids?"

She gave a slow nod. "They were worried they might have to sedate Zane, but the lumbar-puncture procedure went smoothly and they started him on IV antibiotics straightaway."

"And the second kid?"

"Aaron came in a few hours after Zane with symptoms of shock. One of the other young guys had gone to see why he hadn't joined them and called 911 when he found him still in bed. The ER physician connected the cases pretty quickly. Neither of them had been vaccinated against Men W, and both had been bunking down at one of the local student residences."

Jack let out a slow breath. "Darn it. Close contacts?"

She nodded. "Close contacts. We need names and to find the rest of the kids who were in that residence."

"What else should I be looking for with close contacts?" He realized he was firing questions at her but he couldn't help it. He wanted to make sure he covered everything.

"The rules are generally people who've slept under the same roof, nursery or childcare contacts, and anyone they've shared saliva or food with. Dependent on age, they all need a two-day course of rifampicin."

Jack pulled a face. "Shared saliva with? You mean anyone they've kissed? For two teenage boys at a surf school we might have our work cut out. How far back do we need to go?"

"Seven days from first symptoms."

"Let's hope the surf school kept good records, then, and let's hope the boys know who they kissed."

The lights around them flickered and they both froze. "Please don't let us lose power," said Amber quietly. "This could be a disaster."

Jack sucked in a breath. He could tell the thought of the hurricane was making her nervous. Truth was, it made him slightly nervous too. But he had to believe that the authorities would have plans in place to take care of things. They couldn't control the weather. They also couldn't control time, and it was rapidly slipping away from them. "We have two cases. We can contact trace for these two cases and try and get antibiotics to anyone we think could be affected. Hopefully any younger kids will already be immunized."

Amber pulled a face. "Usually we would spend a few

hours discussing this with the local outbreak center and the DPA. The impending hurricane doesn't help. What if we can't get to the people that need antibiotics? We can't ask people to leave their homes as a hurricane is about to hit. And who knows how long it will last?" She shook her head.

"It's a disaster," he said simply.

"Just pray it isn't an epidemic," she said swiftly. "Then it really would be a disaster."

By the time they reached the infectious disease unit again it was in chaos. Bed mattresses had been piled against the windows. The curtains around the beds had been taken down and also stretched across the windows with large Xs taped on the glass. A few of the patients who'd been there earlier had been moved out, but Zane and Aaron were still attached to all their monitors.

There was only one adult walking between both beds. Amber and Jack walked over to meet him. "I'm Amber Berkeley with the Disease Prevention Agency. Are you Zane or Aaron's parent?"

He shook his head. "Ty Manners from the surf school. They've both been with me for the last ten days. I can't believe they're both sick."

He glanced toward the covered windows and put his hands on his hips. It was clear he was stressed. "Everything has just happened at once. I should be down at the surf school making it ready—and sorting out the other kids."

Jack saw Amber word her question carefully. "Ty, I'm sure you're worried about all the kids in your care, and the surf school. Do you have any records? Do all the kids that go to the surf school stay in the same place? We really need to trace all the contacts that Zane and

Aaron have had for the last seven days. It's really important we find out if other people have been immunized, and that we get some antibiotics to them if appropriate."

"It's definitely meningitis?"

Amber nodded. "It is. Both of their lumbar punctures were positive. And it's important that we treat things as quickly as possible. We don't want anyone else to get sick."

One of the nurses came and stood at Amber's shoulder with a clipboard in hand. "I've contacted both sets of parents. Zane's mother stays on Oahu. There's no way she can get here with the imminent hurricane weather but we're keeping her as up to date as we can. Aaron's mother and father live just outside Hilo. That's a two-hour drive to Kailua Kona. State police have told them not to leave their home but I have a horrible feeling they won't listen."

Amber walked over to the window and peeled back a tiny corner of the curtain. "Oh, my," she breathed as she looked outside.

The wind had picked up even more. Enormously tall palm trees were bending in the wind like drinking straws. Public trash cans were rolling down the street like empty soda cans. She watched as an awning at the café opposite was torn away before her eyes by the force of the wind and the red and white material disappeared like a kite being ripped from its string.

It made her heart beat a little faster. She turned to face the nurse. "How soon is the hurricane due to hit?"

The nurse glanced at her watch, then over to a TV screen they had in the corner of the unit. "In about an hour or two. It won't just be the winds. It will be the rain too. It's already started but this is nothing. Once it really hits we usually have floods. No one should be out there."

This was nothing? The rain she'd witnessed as they'd left the hotel had been bad enough. Even with the wipers at maximum their driver had barely been able to see out of the windscreen.

Amber spoke slowly. "But tell that to a parent that thinks their child is at risk." She closed her eyes for a second. "I wish I'd got a chance to speak to them. Maybe I could have played things down. Given them enough reassurance to wait."

Jack's voice was low. "But is that actually true? You suspect that this is an unknown strain of meningitis. The first antibiotics tried don't seem to hit the mark. Now it's up to the second. Are these boys really safe?"

Amber blinked back the tears threatening to appear in her eyes. "No," she said quietly. "Particularly when we don't know if our treatment is the right one. There's still a chance they could die—or have lifelong aftereffects."

She could see Jack's brain was trying to make sense of this all. His natural instinct as an army doc would be to prioritize. For a second there was a flash of something in his face. Something that made her step back. He looked as if he was trying to suppress his urge to take over. It was only the briefest of glances. But it brought back a surge of old emotions that she constantly felt around her father—as if she wasn't good enough for this. As if she couldn't possibly be good enough and someone like Jack, or her father, would have to step in and take over.

Her skin prickled. She hated that. Hated associating someone she'd just met with her father.

It wouldn't be the first time. She'd often met other doctors—particularly surgeons—who had the same old-fashioned attitudes and opinions. People who wanted to be in charge of everything—including her. These were the people she avoided wherever possible. Was Jack one of them?

Even that tiny flash of recognition in her brain would usually be enough to make her turn in the other direction. But in the circumstances, that was hardly possible.

The nurse interrupted her thoughts. "We're actually going to try and move these guys. They've done that in some of the other wards. Most of the corridors and central areas are full—and we have a lot of equipment we need to take. Someone is preparing a space for us down in the basement."

Jack's frown deepened. "Okay. We could help here. We should prioritize. Should we really be taking patient histories for close contacts right now when we might have no hope of reaching any of these people in the next few hours?"

Anger flared in her and Amber swallowed. She knew he was right. But she also knew how sick people could become with meningitis. She spoke in a low voice. "Jack, you offered to help. Not to take over. This is my specialty area, not yours. Of course I know this might be futile. But up until a few hours ago the hurricane wasn't heading in this direction. It might still turn. The prediction could be wrong."

Jack held his hands out. "Does it feel wrong to you right now?"

She held her nerve. She wouldn't let him tell her how to do her job. "Maybe not. But what if something happens to one of these guys? This might not be an epidemic yet—but it could be. It has the potential. And we have two young guys who've become really sick in only a few hours. What if something happens to one, or both, of them, and we've lost the opportunity to find their close contacts? What if we leave those people at risk? We also know this strain is slightly different. This could be the start of something." She pressed her hand on her heart. "I can't let the threat of a hurricane stop me from doing my job to the best of my ability. I have to take the histories. I have to collect the antibiotics and I have to try and talk to as many people as I can." She took a deep breath and her voice gave a little shake. "If the phone lines go down after this we could be in trouble. People might live near to medical centers. We can adapt. We could arrange for them to collect what they need from there."

His hands were on his hips. For a second she wondered if he was going to argue with her. Maybe bringing him here hadn't been a good idea after all. What did she really know about Jack Campbell? The army were used to being in the thick of things; maybe he was struggling with a back-seat role?

"I don't have time to fight with you about this, Jack. What are you going to be, a hindrance or a help?"

She could tell he was annoyed but she didn't have time to care. He had to do it her way, or no way.

There was a pause, and then he let out a sigh and gave the briefest shake of his head. "Let's be quick."

He grabbed a pile of paperwork and walked over to Aaron's bed. There was no chance of Aaron talking. He was ventilated with the briefest hint of a purpuric rash on his tanned skin. The new antibiotics were feeding into an IV line. If they were going to make a difference they would have to start working quickly.

Jack looked up at Ty. "We're going to have to ask you questions because you've spent the last few days with these guys."

Ty gave a nervous nod. "Can't go anywhere anyhow. What do you need to know?"

Amber started firing questions at him. "Where did they sleep? How many other people are there? Do you have names, ages and contact details? Have any left in the last few days? How many are still there? How many people work at the hostel and at the surf school? What have they been doing at nights?"

Once she started she didn't stop. Every now and then Jack quickly interrupted with the words "And what about Aaron?" ensuring that Ty was answering for both teenagers.

It seemed that there were around twenty people at the surf school. Things were pretty informal. Most had traveled to get there—some from the other Hawaiian islands. The people who worked there were all local. Timescales were important. Two teenagers had traveled back to other states in the USA yesterday, and a third had left for New Zealand in the early hours of this morning.

While all this was going on, hospital staff worked around them, attaching the two boys to portable ventilators that could be pushed out into the corridor with them; oxygen cylinders were attached to the sides of the bed and a portable emergency trolley was positioned near to the door.

One of the hospital administrators appeared and spoke in a low voice. "The patients in Surgical have been moved. The hospital front entrance has been completely cleared." Of course, it was covered in glass. "Medical CCU is the safest. It's right in the middle of the building with no windows, but we've already moved the sickest of our elderly patients in there. Pediatrics have been moved down to the theaters."

"Is the basement ready? Do you have the equipment that will be needed?" asked Jack. Transporting these patients would take more than the few nurses that were left in the department.

The administrator looked a little worried. "The staff room down at the laboratory has been cleared in the basement. The corridor down there is one of the most shielded in the building." The lights flickered around them again.

"As long as we don't have a power cut," said Jack warily.

"Let's go," said the head nurse smartly as the windows started to rattle around them. "I don't think it's safe to wait. We've packed up the equipment that we need."

She gestured to the nurses who were left. "You two with Zane." She looked at Amber. "You go with him too."

"Myself, Ty and Dr. Campbell will take Aaron down in the other elevator."

There was only one hospital orderly to assist—the rest obviously deployed to other parts of the building. How on earth did you lock down a hospital and keep all patients safe from a hurricane outside? She didn't even want to think about it.

They wheeled the bed out to the elevator, along with the portable ventilator, tanks and emergency trolley. The progress was slow; it was almost like a juggling act getting all the equipment they needed inside the elevator.

A few minutes later they arrived in the basement. This time she was familiar with the surroundings and backed out of the elevator first, pulling the bed with her. The lab staff must have been warned because a room to the right had been cleared. It looked as if it had been the large staff room, as a pile of chairs and large table were at the bottom of the corridor. The nurse guided the bed into the space and they quickly connected monitors to plug points and checked the ventilator was working properly.

It was weird. Amber actually liked being back in a hospital environment—even though this was a makeshift one. It always reminded her of why she did this job. Sometimes being stuck in an office at the DPA was tough. Only communicating with patients and fellow doctors by phone and email wasn't really how she preferred to work. She liked this. She liked being in the thick of things. She liked to see the patients, talk to them, be on hand when treatments were being tried and tested. A bit more like the role Jack had just done…

There was a weird sound from the corridor. The nurse looked up and frowned as she fiddled with some cables. "Go and check that, will you?"

The lights flickered again as Amber walked swiftly down the corridor. She automatically looked over her shoulder. It was like being in an old-style horror movie—never her favorite kind of entertainment.

The metal doors of both elevators were still closed. Shouldn't Jack be here by now with Aaron?

The lights flickered once more then went out completely.

Black. Everywhere.

She automatically sucked in a breath and held it.

"Darn it," came the shout from further down the corridor, followed by the flickering of some kind of light. Must be from a phone.

"You okay, Amber?" shouted the nurse. "We have a backup generator. It should kick in any second."

Something flooded into her brain. Keeping her hand on the wall, she walked quickly back to the room she'd just come from. The nurse had her phone in her hand and was using the light from it.

"Are the ventilators still working? Do we need to bag him?"

Even though it was dark, Amber moved to the bed, watching for the rise and fall of Zane's chest. The nurse was at the other side. She shook her head. "We should have three hours' worth of battery power. Honestly, the backup generator should kick in. Give it a few minutes."

There was a large thump from the corridor and some muffled voices shouting.

"Oh, no," said the nurse.

"What?" asked Amber.

"The elevator. I think your colleague's stuck in the elevator with Aaron."

Amber's heart started to thud in her chest. She lifted her hands from the bed. "Okay, you're okay here? I can go?"

The nurse nodded. Amber pulled her own mobile from her pocket and flicked the switch on as she walked back down the corridor.

The shouts were getting louder. "Jack? Are you okay?"

"Amber? Is that you? The elevator's jammed and the emergency phone isn't working!"

Amber ran over to the doors. It was ridiculous. She tried to pull them apart with her hands but it was obviously no use.

Mamo appeared from the lab. "Problems?" He shook his head. "Can't do much without power down here."

She pointed to the doors. "We've got one of the kids with meningitis attached to a portable ventilator in there."

Jack shouted from inside. "Is there anything outside you could use to try and pry the doors apart? I can try from in here, but I think I need you helping on the outside."

There was a strange sound from inside. Almost a whimpering. Oh, no. The nurse inside must be freaking out. Being trapped inside a black box wouldn't be most people's idea of a normal working day.

"Hold on." Amber held her phone up and tried to scan the corridor around them.

Something seemed to flick in Mamo's head. "Over here. I think there's an emergency fire ax next to one of the exits. Maybe we could use that."

Sure enough, on one of the walls there was an ax mounted in a red box behind a breakable panel. Mamo pulled his lab coat over his fist and broke the glass, grabbing hold of the ax.

"Give us a minute, Jack," Amber shouted. "Mamo is trying to pry the doors from this side." Something flashed through her brain. "Where's Ty?"

The reply was slightly muffled. "He stayed upstairs to make a few calls to the surf school. He wanted to check all the kids had been taken to an evacuation center."

Prying the doors apart was more difficult than it looked. Mamo put the edge of the ax into the gap at the doors and tried to turn it sideways to widen the gap. After a few minutes he turned to Amber. "You keep holding it," he said gruffly as he slid his hands and foot into the space that was only a few inches apart.

Amber kept trying to turn the head of the ax wider, while keeping it in the space. Her shoulder muscles ached. Her jaw was tight. From the other side she could see a flash of light. The nurse inside must be using her phone. White knuckles appeared on the inside of the door. She could hear the grunts and groans from Jack. "Grrr…"

After a couple of minutes the doors started to release a little further; both Mamo and Jack stuck their shoulders and body weight in the doors, using their feet to push the opposite door apart.

The elevator wasn't completely aligned with the floor—probably the reason they'd had so much difficulty prizing the doors apart.

The nurse looked numb. Amber ducked inside and grabbed the end of the bed. "You get the ventilator," she said to the nurse. "There will be a bit of a bump as we push out."

Mamo and Jack stayed at their doors, holding them back with their body weight as they guided the bed through between them. The nurse jerked as the bed thudded the few inches to the floor, then steered the portable ventilator alongside. The lights flickered in the corridor again.

"Got everything?" checked Mamo. Jack nodded as he pulled out the emergency trolley and let it roll across the floor. The two of them glanced at each other, then gave a nod and both jumped. The doors slid back into place swiftly just as the lights flickered back on in the basement.

"Thank goodness," breathed Amber.

Mamo gave a nod of acknowledgment as he glanced at Aaron in the bed. "Everyone okay? I need to go back to the lab and check the machines."

Amber, Jack and the nurse pushed Aaron into the room in the basement. It only took ten minutes to make sure he was safely set up alongside Zane and that the power supply was working as it should be. The IV infusions with fluids and antibiotics stopped pinging, as did the cardiac monitor and ventilator.

"We're good." The nurse nodded. "I've phoned one

of the ICU doctors and they're going to base themselves downstairs with us." She gave a rueful smile. "Don't worry. I've told them to take the stairs."

Amber walked back over to where she'd abandoned her paperwork. She had to get back on task. Time was ticking.

This was her responsibility and she was in charge. "Jack, how do you feel about making some calls? Let's do the international ones first. I can give you numbers for the public health agencies in the countries our patients are heading to. Following the patients up will be their responsibility."

Jack gave a nod. That tiny little feeling she'd had that he might want to take over seemed to flutter away. "Yeah, I'm not sure how long our phone lines will work. Let's try and do these as quickly as possible. Then we could look at the people who've returned to any of the surrounding islands. See if we can get someone local to prescribe and supply the antibiotics."

She was pleased. He was methodical and logical. Definitely what she needed right now. It was odd to think that last night she'd fallen asleep next to a man she barely knew and now she was working with him in a virtual blackout.

One of the nurses gestured to them. "There's an office over there. Why don't you go and try the phones?" She pulled her watch from her pocket. "According to this, we have about ten minutes before the hurricane hits."

It was like a chill rushing over her body. Should she be scared? Should she actually be terrified? She'd faced plenty of disease disasters, but never a natural one like this. "What happens next? What happens to everyone out there?" she asked the nurse.

"They've moved most of the tourists from the beachfront hotels into emergency shelters. Hawaii has a hurricane preparedness guide. Unfortunately we've not had the warning time that would normally be in place. Things have changed quickly."

There was a tiny wave of panic. "Is there anything else I should know about a hurricane?" She hated the fact her voice sounded high-pitched.

"There's a standard set of instructions." One of the nurses pulled a leaflet from her bag.

Stay indoors away from windows, skylights and glass doors.
Secure and brace exterior doors. Store as much water as you can.
Close interior doors and take refuge in a small interior room, like a closet or hallway, on the lowest level of your home.

Jack pulled a face. "How do these apply to a hospital?"

The nurse gave a nod. "We've moved all the patients away from windows, mostly to the central corridors, and we've evacuated the top floor and ground floor. We're filling the baths and sinks with water to keep the toilets flushing, but the kitchen says it has ample supplies of drinking water." She closed her eyes for a second. "After that—we pray. This hospital has been standing for thirty years. We've had a few hurricanes in that time. We just hope that it will hold together again."

Amber gulped. "What about the staff? Do you all have to stay?"

She wasn't thinking about herself. She was thinking about all the local staff that might have families of their own close by to worry about. With the emergency warning coming so late, most of them might not have had time to make plans.

The nurse held out her hands. "We'll manage. The hospital has an emergency plan. Extra staff get called in as relief. They help transfer the patients and stock the ER. Some of the rest of the staff had to go home to sort out family issues. I came in early to let my friend go home to her disabled mother." She pointed at the nurse dealing with Aaron. "Nessa only started here a few weeks ago. Her family are on Oahu. She wouldn't have time to get there, so decided just to lock down here where she could be useful."

She gave an anxious glance between Amber and Jack. "No matter what your experience, after the hurricane hits, we'll need doctors. Probably more than you know."

Jack gave the briefest of nods. His face was serious, but he didn't seem intimidated at all. "I'd rather be working than holed up in the hotel. Let us sort out what we can about these meningitis cases. After that, put me where you need me."

The nurse gave a nod. "I'll phone up to the ER and let them know we might have some additional help." Her eyebrows rose a little in question. "What will I tell them?"

His voice was firm. "Tell them I'm an army doc and can deal with whatever they need." His eyes met Amber. "Dr. Berkeley works for the DPA. She'll help out where she can."

"Great." The nurse picked up the phone and turned her back on them.

Amber gulped. For infectious diseases she was fine. But she wasn't quite as confident as Jack at being thrown in at the deep end. It wasn't that she didn't feel capable. She would always help out in an emergency. She wasn't sure how qualified or equipped she'd be to deal with things. She'd never really worked in an ER setting. She'd been part of team expeditions for the DPA. But she'd never been in charge. Never had the full responsibility herself. But those expeditions had been more co-ordinated. She'd always ended up working in pre-ready emergency clinics or vaccination hubs.

Her director had already mentioned he thought she was ready to try her hand as a team leader on a field mission to further her experience. But this was entirely different—totally out with her normal expertise. It was almost as if Jack sensed something from her. He leaned over and whispered in her ear. "Don't worry. I've got your back."

Then he did something completely unexpected. He turned her toward him and lowered his forehead onto hers. It was a gesture of security. Of solidarity. Of re-assurance.

Warmth spread through her. She looked up and met his gaze. His dark brown eyes were fixed on hers. They were genuine and steady.

She pressed her lips together and took a deep breath, so many thoughts flooding into her mind. Her brain was such a mess. All she could concentrate on was the feel of his hands on the tops of her arms and the gentle way his forehead pressed against hers. His warm breath danced across her skin. Her gaze was naturally lowered and she could see the rise and fall of his chest.

He was a doctor. The type of guy she'd spent most of her life trying to avoid any romantic entanglements with. And this was crazy. She'd already seen a flash of something in him that reminded her of the focused way her father used to be.

So, if she already had alarm bells flashing in her

head, why wasn't she running for the hills? She could pretend it was the hurricane. That the only reason she wasn't moving was because she was stuck here.

But that wasn't what was anchoring her feet firmly to the ground.

That wasn't what was letting the heat from the palms of his hands slowly permeate through her jacket and trickle its way through her body. Her last few boyfriends had been as far removed from medicine as possible—a landscape gardener, then a chef. But somehow she hadn't felt this. This connection.

And she couldn't understand it. She'd only met Jack last night. And yes, they'd clicked. There was no doubt the man was attractive. There was no doubt her mind was imagining so many other places they could go.

But the timing wasn't right. It wasn't right at all. Her mother's face flashed into her head. The tired, weary look that had always been visible. The sadness when she'd glanced at a clock and realized Amber's father wouldn't be home that night. The endless amount of wasted dinners scraped into a trash can. The times when Amber had sat at the dinner table, desperate to tell her father about her day, and he could barely pay attention— talking over her as he launched into yet another story about work, or surgery, or research. Or when he left the table again as soon as the phone had begun to ring with another call from the hospital.

She'd spent her whole life feeling like an unimportant spare part. Constantly trying to earn the approval of a man who barely knew she existed. When Jack had spoken on the stage earlier on today, he'd had the same conviction, the same passion and dedication as her father.

She sucked in a breath as she realized the similarities between them both.

Having any kind of relationship with Jack Campbell was a complete nonstarter. She'd already lived part of her life being second best in someone's life. She was determined never to allow herself to be in that position again.

She wanted to step away. She should step away.

But for the briefest of seconds her eyes just fixated on the rise and fall of Jack Campbell's chest under his fatigues. She tried to focus. She had a purpose. She was a physician. She was here as the representative of her agency. She had a job to do. She could continue to monitor Zane and Aaron to try and keep them stable. To chart the progress of the infection and its reaction to treatments. Information like this was vital right now—nearly as vital as stopping the potential of any spread.

Aaron's parents might be on the road here and in the path of the hurricane. Her skin prickled. The logical part of her brain told her that these people were Hawaiians. They would know all the emergency plans for hurricanes. They would know how to keep safe. But would they follow their heads or their hearts?

Two years ago she'd had to make a heartbreaking call to another parent. She'd been called to an ER overwhelmed with flu patients. A small child had been admitted straight from school with a history of asthma, difficulty breathing and a high temperature. She'd called the parents and told them they should attend as quickly as possible. They never got there. In their sense of panic they'd been involved in a car accident and it had etched a permanent memory in Amber's brain and a scar in her heart. If she'd said something different, maybe if she hadn't let them know the urgency that she was feeling, they might have taken more care.

But the truth was, in the midst of a chaotic ER, she'd held that little girl's hand—angry that the parents hadn't got there in time—and tried to assist as they'd attempted to resuscitate her. They'd failed. And then she'd got the news about the parents.

No one had blamed her. No one had needed to. She'd blamed herself.

There were always going to be tough times being a doctor. She knew that. She expected that. But this one had hit her harder than others.

And it had affected her more than she'd realized. Her confidence at work and around others was mainly just bravado. It also helped her erect a shield around herself.

Her heart wasn't safe. She didn't feel in a position to form relationships. Not while she felt like this. Not when she couldn't open herself up to others. It was safer to be single. Safer to surround herself with colleagues who didn't seem to recognize her detachment, but, instead, thought of it as self-assuredness and confidence.

She told them she didn't date colleagues and let them think that her life was full of a hundred other potential suitors at any time of the day.

She didn't tell them that she'd run out of series to watch on her paid Internet TV.

For the briefest of seconds earlier today she'd thought she'd recognized something on Jack's face.

That expression. That look. A flashback—a haunting. It was momentary. Only lasting a few seconds.

But it made her feel *something*. A connection.

And even though there was a hurricane outside, that scared her more than anything. So she turned on her heel and walked away.

CHAPTER FOUR

HE WASN'T ENTIRELY sure what was going on. Maybe he'd been too forward with the woman who'd shared his bed last night. He'd wanted to envelop Amber in a hug, but her demeanor had told him not to, and he'd ended up just pulling her toward him and gently touching heads.

He still couldn't work out what had possessed him. He hadn't held a woman that close in…how long?

Two years. Two long, hard years.

One minute she was there. Next minute she was gone.

Jill Foster had been a bright-eyed medic he'd met in Afghanistan. She was one of the best he'd worked with. As a teenager she wanted to be a doctor but couldn't afford to go to university, so she joined the army instead. Her skills and natural talent were picked up and she excelled in her role.

They worked side by side for six months. And as soon as he got home he missed her. By the time they redeployed again they were dating. Right up until the day he was felled by abdominal pain. The bothersome ache that had been distracting him had turned into an acute pain and he'd collapsed after finishing a long emergency surgery. Twelve hours later he'd woken up and life had changed.

Life had changed completely.

He'd had an appendectomy. It seemed that the army doc hadn't recognized his own appendicitis. But in that twelve hours there had been an emergency—a group of soldiers had been caught in some cross fire and had needed to be retrieved. He was usually part of the emergency call-out team. But, when he'd been under anesthetic, Jill had taken his place. And it had cost her her life. While going to pick up their injured comrades the vehicle had driven over an IED, the effect instant.

Gone. Just like that.

He'd never forget the face of the base commander who'd been there to tell him as soon as he came around from anesthetic. The guy looked ill, his face pale underneath his tanned skin. The other soldiers had been retrieved, but Jill and three other members of the team Jack normally worked with had been wiped out.

The numbness spread through his body immediately. He pushed up from the gurney, ignoring any wound pain, and staggered across the compound toward the mortuary. Two squaddies saw him and ran over to help, throwing their arms around his waist to keep him steady.

But no one would let him see Jill.

And he knew why. He did. Surgeons knew better than anyone what the effects of an IED could be.

So, he sat on the floor of the mortuary for the next six hours and vowed to make his time in Afghanistan meaningful.

Everything after that became about the wound dressing.

Wartimes were tough. Surgeons dealt with explosive injuries that no normal surgeon would ever see. And because of his postings he'd grown familiar with the faces around the camp. The cheeky squaddie in the armory. The quiet Yorkshire lad who liked to read books. The gung-ho female sergeant who could give any guy a run for his money. All of them had ended up on his table.

Not all of them had lived. But Jack had done his best. He agonized over any person that he lost. Replayed everything in his mind, wondering what he could have done differently—could have done better.

Once he was in the desert setting, work was everything. He became almost obsessed. The research too was entirely in his focus. He quickly realized how good their dressing worked and what the life-saving implications were. It was everything to him.

It gave him something to focus on. It allowed him to build a shell around himself and close out the rest of the world. He still went above and beyond for his colleagues— he always would. But he'd lost the connection, he'd lost the emotion and empathy that he'd always had within the job.

He'd lost a little part of his heart.

And now? He had no idea what he was doing—in more ways than one. He wasn't worried about helping after the hurricane. The infectious disease stuff was beyond his professional expertise. But if he had to hunt down people to deliver emergency antibiotics, he could live with that.

What he wasn't so sure about was the fact that the first woman he'd held in two years had just blanked him and walked away. Was his heart so numb that he couldn't pick up on female cues anymore?

Amber looked as if she was sucking in some deep breaths as she scrubbed her hands at one of the sinks. The noise seemed to echo around them in the basement. He couldn't stand it. Should he apologize for holding her?

He shook his head and stalked across the corridor to the other room. The IV antibiotics were feeding slowly through to both Zane and Aaron. Both of them were still sedated and ventilated. He glanced at the monitors and then at their charts. The nurse came over and stood with him at the end of Zane's bed. She gave her head a slight shake. "I still don't know if he's reacting to the medicines. He still seems so flat." She gestured toward the rise and fall of his chest.

Jack nodded. He understood what she meant. All of Zane's accessory muscles were working around his chest area. With ventilation and sedation he should be in a much more stable position. It was almost as if his body was fighting against everything.

Aaron seemed much more settled. His heart rate, temperature and blood pressure were good. It seemed that he was reacting better to the treatments and medications.

The lights flickered again and the television monitor in the room across the hall shorted out. The nurse's face paled. "This is it," she said warily. "The TV signal is gone. The hurricane is about to hit."

Amber appeared back in the doorway. She looked awful. "What do you do next?"

The nurse gave the briefest shake of her head. "Hunker down."

For the next four hours they held their breaths as they waited to see if they would come out the other side of the hurricane. It didn't matter they were in the basement with no windows or possibility of flying glass. At times the whole foundation of the building seemed to shudder and Jack wondered if the whole hospital could end up on top of them. Doors and windows throughout the hospital must have been affected as the doorway to the stairwell at the end of the corridor continued to rattle incessantly. It was impossible to stay still for four hours. They had patients to look after, and Jack couldn't help but worry about the patients above them and the people outside. They tiptoed around each other in a kind of unspoken frustration. The phone lines had died. Between them they'd managed to reach fourteen of the local people who had stayed overnight in the same accommodation as Zane and Aaron.

"I thought the eye of the hurricane was supposed to be silent. Quiet even," he said to one of the older nurses.

She shook her head. "Maybe in a movie. Or in a fairy tale. I've only seen two hurricanes. And there was no silence. Except when they were over. We're being hit by the fiercest part of the storm right now. Anything or anybody out there right now probably doesn't stand a chance. Anything not anchored or cemented to the ground will likely never be seen again. Or end up on one of the other islands." She sighed, and he realized she must be thinking about her family on Oahu. He put his hand on her arm.

"I'm sure they're safe. Just like we are."

She gave the briefest of nods and then marched over to the monitors and started pressing buttons again. Jack was exasperated. He needed to be doing something. Anything. But he'd done everything he could down here.

Ty had been started on the antibiotics too. And he, in turn, had been concerned about his employees with young families.

Amber took the time to explain how meningitis passed from person to person and how, at the moment, unless an employee showed signs themselves, their families weren't at risk.

She seemed to circumvent Jack wherever he went. And that was fine. If he'd overstepped he was glad of the message.

They monitored Zane carefully, watching his limbs

closely for any visible signs of septicemia. Eventually, Jack finally made his way up the stairwell to see if he could be of assistance in any other part of the hospital. He'd only made it to the first floor before he could hear the rattle throughout the building. The door at the stairwell had been juddering loudly, obviously being buffeted by wind that had found a way inside the hospital.

Jack stuck his head through tentatively. No patients should be on the first floor or the top floor. Flash flooding and roof damage were two of the major probable issues. The evacuation plan dictated that most patients were moved to central areas on the second and third floors.

"Hello?" he shouted. He concentrated and listened hard. All he could hear was the wind whistling through the building and the sound of thudding rain.

He pulled his head back in and started up to the second floor. There definitely would be patients and staff up there. There was a crowd of people in green scrubs standing at the entrance to the stairwell on the second floor. A few glanced in his direction as he pushed through. He held out his hand to the nearest member of staff with a stethoscope around his neck. "Jack Campbell, Senior Medical Officer, British Army. Can I do anything?"

He could see a myriad people in the corridors with swabs held to arms and heads. The man gave a brief nod. "Oh, yeah, the army guy. I heard about you. I'm Ron Kekoe. Head of the ER. We've had to move upstairs in case of flash flooding." He glanced at his watch. "We're going to give it a few hours then move back down, and send out teams as required." He pointed toward a makeshift desk just along the corridor. "Phones are down but we've got radios to contact other emergency services and the evacuation shelters." His face was serious. "We've already had a few reports of winds up to one hundred and eighty miles an hour and roofs being torn off buildings. There will be casualties." He frowned for a second and Jack realized someone had appeared beside him.

Amber, breathing heavily. She must have run up the stairs after him. His first thought was for the teenagers. "Zane? Aaron?"

She shook her head. "No. They're just the same. But I realized I probably wasn't much use down there. One of the residents is staying with them. I thought I should probably come and help."

He could hear it. That little edge of nerves in her voice. It was clear, however, that Ron didn't hear it. He just gave a nod. "The infectious disease doctor?"

Amber didn't seem to mind the label and held out her hand. "Amber Berkeley, DPA."

Ron gave her a half-suspicious look. "Someone mentioned you wanted to take antibiotics out." He shook his head fiercely. "No way. Not anytime soon. First vehicles that go out will be heading up portable trauma bays. If it's near to where you need to be, you're welcome to tag along—provided you do some doctoring."

He didn't even wait for Amber's reply. Jack got that. Everything about this was familiar territory to him. This was all about triage, all about prioritizing. Ron gave them both a nod. "Can you deal with some minor injuries? There's nothing too threatening. Just flying glass and debris. A few staff were caught. If you could clean and stitch that would be great."

Amber gave a quick nod of her head and walked around Jack, heading toward the first person with a bloody wound pad pressed to their forearm.

He watched for a few seconds as he could see her

swallow nervously. This was different for her. And he got that.

He moved on over and started treating the next member of staff who had a cut on their forehead.

He was methodical. And he was quick. All the injuries were relatively minor.

But as he worked steadily he noticed the continued chaos around him. Although the external phone lines weren't working, the internal phones rang constantly. Staff seemed to be disorganized, and Ron, as Head of the ER, seemed out of his depth.

Jack couldn't help himself. He walked over. "How about you let me do some of this?"

Ron looked up from a prescription he was writing. Three other members of staff were waiting to talk to him and the radio was crackling constantly on the table.

"What can you do?"

Jack pointed to the desk. "I have experience of crisis triage. How about I field all the radio calls? I can take the details and liaise with the other agencies. We need to know what's needed and where. As soon as the winds die down we could have teams packed up and ready to go. What do you say?"

He was trying so hard not to overstep. He could see Ron was struggling with the volume. He might not know Jack, but surely he would let him help?

Ron only paused for a few seconds as the radio continued to crackle.

"Perfect. Let me know if there's anything major."

"You got it." Jack settled at the desk and picked up the radio. There were a few notes already about building damage—but no reports about casualties. There was a footnote querying whether a home with disabled residents had been evacuated, with a note to check with the nearest evacuation center. There were a few other notes from a care agency who had several housebound residents that they hadn't been able to get to. Chances were they were safe. Most Hawaiians knew about the potential threats and what to do. But the infirm or frail would probably not have been able to put all preparations in place without assistance.

There seemed to be no standard way of keeping track of all the information, so Jack added all the names and addresses to a list for checks and pulled out a citywide map to start charting where everyone was.

Some staff were reporting that the sky was almost black now. No one with any thought to safety could possibly go outside.

The chatter on the radios was constant, along with the background noise of the hammering winds. Even though they'd been told not to, some of the staff squinted past mattresses at the windows and let out squeals and gasps. "Did you see that?"

"That car just flipped!"

"Oh, my, look over there. The roof's coming off that building like a tin can!"

"Those trees are bending like drinking straws."

"That one's going to snap for sure!"

The rain thudded off the windows, battering down in among the wind's fury. Debris flew through the air, randomly hitting windows and shattering glass.

Jack tried to tune it all out, focusing on the task he'd been given and trying to keep a clear head. But even though he tried, his eyes were distracted by the woman who'd pulled her hair back into a ponytail and seemed to be cleaning and stitching wounds precisely. She had a quieter nature when working with staff who were patients, and, even though he'd seen a smattering of nerves earlier today, he would never question her clinical skills.

Reports continued to come in and his list grew longer and longer. By the time Amber came over and sat down next to him, he'd started to separate out all the calls by seriousness and area.

She looked down at the lists and charts he had spread across the table. "Wow. You're really keeping on top of this. How many teams do we have?"

"Probably less than we actually need." He didn't mean his answer to seem quite so brusque.

Amber shot him a strange sideways glance. "Do you know how many staff we have, and how many transportation vehicles?"

He glanced over at Ron, trying to hide his frustration. "Ron hasn't told me yet. Search and Rescue say no one leaves unless they deem it necessary. There can be risks of flash flooding."

Ron appeared next to Jack and blanched when he saw the list and map covered in colored dots. Jack stood up. "The eye of the hurricane has passed. How about we send staff back down to the first floor to reopen the ER? It's important that people have a central point to come to."

Ron nodded in agreement.

"Makes sense." Amber pulled a crumpled piece of paper from her pocket and smoothed it out in front of her. "So, do any of the areas where teams will be sent have patients we'll be looking for?"

He could tell she was trying to sound reasonable. He knew perfectly well that as soon as the winds died down she wanted to find a car and get around all the contacts immediately.

He pulled out his own list. He hadn't forgotten that he'd offered to help her. "Trouble is, it's so dark out there now. With all the debris, the roads will be hard enough to maneuver along. What with no street lighting, things will be much worse." He pointed to colored dots he'd stuck on the map. "The blue dots are addresses where we need to give people antibiotics. What complicates things is that some of these people might not have stayed in their own homes. The statewide evacuation shelters are all based in high schools or elementary schools. Chances are, some of them might have gone there."

"We have no way of telling?"

Jack shook his head. "Not right now. There could be thousands of people in each of the evacuation shelters. With limited communications, there's no way for us to find out."

"Any news about Aaron's parents?"

Jack shook his head again. "I've not heard a thing about them. If I do, I'll let you know."

He could see her swallowing nervously as she pointed to another part of her notes. "These people, there's fourteen of them. That includes the three close contacts who had traveled internationally. We've contacted Florida, Texas and New Zealand. It's up to their own public health departments to make contact and issue the antibiotics. We also had four kids go back to Oahu. Honolulu staff are coordinating for them. Another two kids are on Maui and one more on Kauai. Local doctors will deal with them."

"So that leaves us the kids and staff from the Big Island. How many do we need to still track down?"

"Four. That's not too many. Hopefully we can coordinate with any team that's going out." She was toying with a strand of her hair. It must be a nerves thing. But it made him feel instantly protective.

"We still have the other six teenagers that were still staying at the surf school. Ty hasn't been able to get hold of anyone else, but he's pretty sure they'll have been evacuated to the Deltarix High School. Six close contacts in one trip. That should make things a bit easier."

Amber bit her bottom lip. She looked over at the map. "So the red dots are the reports of damage or destruction, and the blue dots are the places we still need to go for contact tracing?"

"Yellow are the people that need to be checked on. That doesn't necessarily need to be medical personnel, but since that information is being passed between agencies, I thought it wise to keep it up there." He sighed. "We still have no idea if there's a threat of flooding, or what the roads will be like."

Ron pointed to a part to the north of the city. "During the last tropical storms, these roads were impassable between mudslides and flood damage."

There was a blue dot very close to that area. Jack leaned forward. "Where's the nearest evacuation center to there? Maybe because of what's happened in the past, the residents will have evacuated anyway?"

The radio next to Jack crackled and he picked it up. "Reports of major incident at Deltarix High School."

Amber glanced at the list on the wall and her face paled. "That's one of the evacuation centers. The one we were just talking about."

Jack's pen was poised. "Can you give us some more information?"

"Roof's been torn from the high-school gymnasium where hundreds of the evacuees were waiting out the storm. Reports of serious injuries and multiple minor injuries."

Jack glanced over toward Ron. He waved his hand to attract his attention. "Do you have any idea of numbers?"

The voice crackled at the end of the radio message. "Around six serious. Two head injuries, three with chest injuries or breathing difficulties and another with multiple fractures. Also a number of children with fractures, and another child reported to be seizing."

Jack ran his fingers through his hair and looked at Ron. "It's time. We've got to load up and get out there." He didn't want to be at the end of a radio, manning a desk. He'd never been that type of guy. He'd been asked to triage. Well, the time for triage was over. It was time to get out on the ground and use the skills that he'd been trained in.

Right now he wasn't afraid of the hurricane. Right now he was afraid that people would die if they couldn't get the medical attention they needed—people like Jill.

And no matter what, he couldn't let that happen.

He was trying so hard to give Ron his place. He handed the lists he'd made to him. Jack had been watching the staff in the department for the last two hours and could guess exactly who'd be sent on the teams. "How about you call everyone together and let them know?"

It was the first time since she'd got here that Amber's head had really cleared. She'd stopped thinking about Aaron's parents. Her brain had already worked overtime on that one, imagining a million different ways they could have been injured trying to get to their son. She hated the way her stomach churned over and over. The logical part of her brain just couldn't override the emotional part.

She had patients to seek out—people who were at risk of developing meningitis. And she had other patients to help. Cleaning and stitching had almost felt therapeutic. Getting back to basics. She'd even reviewed a few elderly patients on the medical ward who had taken a downward turn in the last few hours. She was almost sure one had a chest infection and the other a urinary tract infection. Because of the hurricane, X-rays and lab tests would likely be delayed, so she'd ordered antibiotics and IV fluids for them both.

She'd felt useful. She'd felt part of something. And it had sparked something inside her. Which was why she'd finally found the courage to sit down next to the guy who had sparked something else inside her earlier.

Now was not the time to get freaked out. Now was not the time to worry about someone breaching her inner shell.

There was too much else to worry about. There was too much else happening. She wanted to move back into the tough and sassy woman he'd met at the bar last night. Was that really only twenty-four hours ago?

Jack grabbed some tape and put up the map on the closest wall. He started moving sticky notes around at lightning speed. Ron was at his shoulder.

"We definitely need a team at the high school. There are twenty known casualties, with probably more." Jack looked over his shoulder at the melee of staff. "Another team here." He pointed at a care home. "We know that seven elderly residents were unable to be evacuated along with three members of staff. Red Cross have reports of injuries of a group of tourists on a bus tour."

There was a flash of frustration across Ron's face. "Why on earth didn't they take shelter as instructed?"

"The radio on the bus wasn't working, they didn't

hear the alerts, and once the driver realized there was a storm, he pulled over to the side of the road. That bus has overturned just outside Kona."

Ron threw his hands up. "Well, too late now. Any more information on the numbers?"

Jack shook his head. "No. The mobile masts must have gone down just after it was called in. Apparently the caller was given standard advice about sheltering, but there wasn't time for anything else."

Ron had his hands on his hips as he shook his head. "The tour buses are pretty standard—usually single-deckers with around fifty passengers." He ran his fingers across the map, paying attention to the notes Jack had given him and then looking back among his staff and nodding. Jack pressed his lips together. It was hard not to try and take charge. His army ranking meant he was usually the one in charge of any emergency planning.

It was almost as if Ron sensed his thoughts as he gave Jack a sideways glance. "Okay, army doc. Which team do you want to lead?" Jack felt Amber flinch next to him. He knew that her eyes were currently fixed on the blue dots on the map, while her brain did the countdown in hours. The residential home was closest to a few addresses they had to visit, but the nearest evacuation center could also house some of their close contacts. No matter the temptation, he kept his mouth closed.

He wasn't the boss. This time he was only here to assist. He didn't know the area and he didn't know the skills of the staff. This was Ron's team. Not his. He turned to face Ron. "I'll go wherever you need me. Just let me know how I can help."

There was a glimmer of amusement on Ron's face—almost as if he knew Jack was trying to resist interfering.

Ron glanced around, whistled and then put his hands

about his head, clapping loudly. "Right, everyone—pay attention. We have work to do, so listen up, people. Okay, Marie Frank, Akito, Sarah, Leia and Tom, I want you all back in the ER with the doors open to receive casualties as soon as we have the all clear. Abram, Jess, Sito and Amal, you'll be team one." He pointed to a position on the map. "I want you out here. Collect your emergency kits. There's an overturned bus with an unknown amount of casualties. Coordinate with the Red Cross. They gave us the initial information. They may also have some staff that can assist."

He turned to face Jack and held his hand above his head. "People, some of you might have already met this guy. This is Jack Campbell, an army doc from Scotland who has offered to assist at this time. In an emergency, we take all the international help we can get. Follow his instructions as you would mine."

He turned toward Amber. "And this is Dr. Amber Berkeley from the Disease Prevention Agency. We have two teenagers in the basement with a strain of meningitis W. Before the hurricane, Dr. Berkeley identified a number of key contacts who require antibiotics. At the moment we only have a rough idea of where those people might be. Dr. Berkeley will give you a list of names and addresses, and some spare antibiotics. If you come across any of these people at evacuation centers, or you are near to the addresses and it's safe, feel free to try and make contact. In the meantime—" his pale gray eyes turned to Amber "—Dr. Berkeley will also be assisting in the field."

Ron pointed to two other members of staff. "Dr. Campbell will be leading team two along with Dr. Berkeley and Lana and Jamal. Guys, show our new doctors where they can pick up supplies and radios. You guys will be covering the high school where the roof has been damaged. Team three."

He pointed to some other staff and shouted names. "You'll be covering the elderly care center, and also check on the additional needs facility nearby. After that, head to the high school with team two." Ron stopped and took a deep breath. "As soon as we get radio confirmation it's safe to go outside, the police will be here to assist us. Chances are, none of us are going to get any sleep anytime soon. Stay safe, people. Now, let's do what we're trained to."

Amber hadn't even realized she was holding her breath as Ron spoke. It was almost as if he flicked a switch. The buzz began immediately. But instead of more bedlam, it was like a weird kind of organized chaos.

She'd recognized something in Jack during Ron's talk. She could see how hard he found it to defer to someone else. How had that really worked for a guy in the army? An army was all about rank and discipline.

But she'd seen him swallow and tell Ron that he'd go wherever he was needed. Ron must have recognized the struggle too, because he'd almost laughed out loud, then decided they should go to one of the most challenging areas.

It was clear he had faith in the skills of an army surgeon.

But would he have the same kind of faith in her? Her stomach twisted. That awful feeling of having to prove herself all over again.

"Let's go," said Jack. He was already following the two staff they'd been assigned to work with. Amber gave herself a shake and pushed everything else from her head. They followed Lana and Jamal tentatively down the stairs, and after a quick check through the doors, they braced themselves against the continuing wind sweeping through the building and headed toward the ER.

All the staff who arrived in the ER moved seamlessly, locating emergency packs and handing out tabards for all staff. Amber found herself wearing a bright orange vest over her jacket with the word "DOCTOR" emblazoned across it in fluorescent white letters.

It was odd. She'd thought she might feel more awkward than she did. But she seemed to find her place and slot into it. Maybe it was the complete air of calm around Jack. Or the sideways glances he kept shooting at her when he thought she wasn't watching. She tried to keep her professional face in place. There was so much going around about her, it was easy to follow every instruction given and pay attention to the briefings about equipment they could carry, potential patients and what they might face outside.

Lana and Jamal seemed confident in their roles. Lana showed Amber where everything was in her pack and handed her an emergency supply of drugs. They'd moved down to the ER and other staff ensured the department was ready to open. The wind was still fierce outside but the intensity had started to diminish. Eventually, they heard a set of sirens outside. Jack appeared at her shoulder, stuffing something in the bag on her back. She tried to turn around. "Wh…what?" she asked.

"Extra pads," he said casually. Somehow the sense of him beside her was reassuring. It didn't stop her head going to the place it wanted to be—finding a way to the patients she was supposed to see. Finding out where Aaron's parents were. Keeping to her mission.

Amber was nervous. She couldn't help it. What she really wanted to do was find a working phone and contact the DPA to see if someone else could coordinate information on her patients. Jack seemed a little distant. He did things automatically, almost without any thought. He'd seemed so passionate about his work, it was weird to see him behaving in this oddly detached way. What was it like to do things on automatic pilot?

And her stomach was still twisting in knots about Aaron's parents. Information seemed a bit chaotic right now. She so wished she'd had a chance to talk to them. Maybe she could have persuaded them to stay at home until after the storm. Her gut told her that most parents would have got behind the wheel of a car if their child was at risk, but somehow it just made her feel worse. She hadn't even had the opportunity to try and stop them. That was the thing that frustrated her the most.

The bright orange pack on her back wasn't light. It was jam-packed with just about everything she could need. Her hand still held a copy of the list of patients they hoped to find. As she heard the sound of sirens outside, her heart gave a little lurch. She stepped back over to a desk and picked up an internal phone. "May I?"

The nurse at the desk gave a nod and she quickly dialed the room downstairs. "It's Amber. We're just about to leave. How are Zane and Aaron?"

The nurse gave her a quick rundown. "Holding steady" seemed to be the most appropriate phrase. One minute later the doors were pulled open and some of the Fire and EMS personnel came in. All were wearing heavy gear, helmets and visors. They started handing out similar headwear to the emergency teams. One of the guys shook hands with Ron and had a quick conversation. He turned to face the waiting teams.

"Okay, people. Remember, hazards will be encountered after a hurricane. Live wires, gas leaks, building fires, unsafe structures, flooding, hazardous materials, victims of the trauma and displaced animals. No one travels alone. Everyone keeps in radio contact. If the wind speeds increase again above fifty miles an hour, you'll all be told to stand down until it's safe. All of my staff have flood maps. Listen to what they tell you. Areas may look safe but the ground under the water may be unstable. All our mobile masts are down. Several of our utilities are down. The rainfall is still heavy. Be safe out there, people."

As soon as the fire chief had finished, several of the EMS staff came forward. "Team one, over there. Team two, you're with me. Team three, let's go."

The first things that struck Amber were the wind, the noise and the driving rain. Even though the eye of the hurricane had passed, the weather was still a force to be reckoned with. It wasn't an ordinary ambulance that sat outside. This vehicle looked more like an army vehicle. It still had emergency markings, but also had bigger, thicker tires and an overall heavier build.

They climbed inside and Jack checked over the map with the driver. "Dave," he said as he glanced around at the team. "Consider me your scout. We aren't sure of all the roads as we've only come from the emergency center. It's a few miles to the school, so be prepared."

The radio was fixed to the dashboard with the channel open so they could hear any updates.

Amber stared out of the windows as the vehicle started to slowly move. Some of the trees looked permanently bent in the wind. Some shop fronts with shutters appeared undamaged. Others weren't quite so lucky with gaping holes in the front of their stores. Most of the high-rise buildings they passed were eerily quiet. The city center had plenty of offices that should have been safely evacuated. Some of those windows had obviously been hit by flying debris too, and a few curtains were buffeting in the winds from high floors.

The streets were littered with random and sometimes odd items. Signage, chairs, a table, kitchen utensils and lots of city trash cans rolled around. A few cars were turned on their sides. The wind continued to sideswipe them, but Dave held the vehicle steady. "It's like a disaster movie," breathed Amber.

"Except it's real life," answered Jack, his voice gravelly.

She could hear it. The edge of wariness in his body. He was perched on the edge of the seat, looking constantly from side to side, as if he were waiting for something to jump out at them. It unnerved her. Inside the hospital they'd been relatively safe. Out here? Anything could happen. And even though there were parts of Jack that reminded her of her father, right now she was glad he was at her side.

They turned the next corner. "Darn it!" yelled Dave, and the vehicle came to a screeching halt. They hadn't even been going fast, but Amber found herself flung forward, despite being strapped in.

Part of a building lay in front of them. It was as if the edge of the latest block of apartments had disintegrated onto the road. She looked up and couldn't help but gasp. She could see inside the second-floor sitting room. Pictures were on the wall. There was a door leading…somewhere. Half of a settee was still sitting in the room. But then? Then a whole corner of the room had just disintegrated over the road. "How on earth did that happen?"

Dave very slowly edged the vehicle around the rubble, mounting the pavement on the other side of the street, continuing to stare upward. "Has to be the roof," he murmured. "Part of it looks torn off, part of it has collapsed downward, taking the edge of the building with it."

Jack shook his head as he adjusted the backpack at his feet. "This hasn't been called in. There could be people in that building."

Amber blinked and looked at the debris on the road. It all just seemed like a pile of bricks, along with an up-turned armchair, lampshade and parts of a window. Thankfully, she couldn't see anyone among the rubble. But Jack already had his hand on the door handle.

"I'm going to check the building," he muttered to Dave. "Radio in. The entranceway and stairwell look safe. I'll run up and have a shout, check there's no one stuck inside."

Amber's first thought was to say no. But Dave nodded and Jack was out of the car before she could object. He stuck his head back in the door. "Wait here, you lot. I'll only be five minutes."

"Wait. That can't be a good idea. Should he be going in there?"

Dave shook his head with a half smile. "Nope. But we shouldn't go in any building without a health and safety check after a hurricane. Do you honestly think that's going to happen anytime soon? They're sending us to a high school with half the roof ripped off."

The irony struck her hard. Of course they were. This was always going to be dangerous. Dave radioed in about the damaged building and partially blocked road, while the rest of them stared out of the vehicle windows, waiting for any sign.

A few minutes later Jack appeared with a bundle in his arms. Amber couldn't help it. She was out of the vehicle immediately, Lana and Jamal not far behind her.

"It's okay," said Jack as he strode toward them in the

strong winds. The elderly woman was huddled in toward his chest. "This is Mary," he said as he placed her
inside. "She was sheltering in the stairwell. No serious
injuries, just some cuts and bruises. And a whole lot of
shock since she was in her sitting room as it collapsed."
He gently sat her down and put his hand at the side of
her face. "It's okay, Mary. You're safe now."

There was something so caring and tender about the
way he spoke to her. It tugged at Amber's heart. What
was it about this guy? One second he reminded her of
her father and she wanted to sprint into the distance;
next second he did something like that and it just melted
her heart.

He looked up for the briefest of seconds and his dark
brown eyes met hers. He didn't say anything. He didn't
have to. Whatever the weird connection between them,
it was obvious he felt it too.

After a second he broke their gaze and nodded to
Dave. "Nothing serious. We can go on to the high school
and tend to her there with the others."

Amber settled in the back with Mary as they set off
again. Jamal patched the few small wounds Mary had
on her legs and arms, then bundled her under his arm
and held her tight, talking to her the whole time.

It was clear she was shocked. Her voice was shaking
and tired. She'd missed the transport to the evacuation
center and decided to lock down in her house until the
hurricane passed. Amber's stomach turned over. Where
would Mary go after the storm? Where would anyone
go whose house had been damaged?

Fifteen minutes later they reached the high-school
evacuation center. Half the roof was missing from the
auditorium and gymnasium. Debris was strewn across
the football field. There was another emergency vehicle

outside, so the team piled out and headed to the main entrance of the school.

Someone with an orange tabard was waiting for them. "Are you the team from Lahuna State Hospital?"

Jack nodded and held out his hand. "Jack Campbell." He nodded over his shoulder toward the rest of them. "Amber, Lana, Jamal and Dave. We've also picked up a woman with a few minor injuries." There was no need for more formal introductions as they all had tabards too with their designation.

The woman put her hand on her chest. She looked as if she might cry. "I'm Chrissie. We have a number of injured people and a whole lot more to assess." She pointed toward one of the classrooms. "Your lady can go in here. We have a few volunteers."

"Take us to the people that are injured," said Jack.

"Wait," said Amber quickly. She handed a note to Chrissie. "Do you have a register of the people here?"

Chrissie looked confused. "We tried to do that, but things got a bit chaotic."

She squeezed Chrissie's hand with the list in it. "Please, can you check these names? It's really, really important we get in touch with these people."

Chrissie stared down at the list in her hand. "I'll do my best."

Amber followed Jack further into the building.

There were a few firefighters already in the building. They were moving debris and assessing damage. One of them shook his head as they approached. "We have a few power issues. Electrical faults. We've put tape over some of the doorways so no one goes inside."

Jack nodded and headed into the main gymnasium. Rain was thudding down onto the floor on the half where the ceiling was missing. Everyone still inside had been moved to the other side. There were a number of people lying on the floor.

Jack shrugged his pack from his shoulder and walked over, setting it down on the floor next to one of the injured. "You over there." He pointed to Amber, then turned to Jamal and Lana. "One over there, and one over there. Let me know what you've got."

Amber took a deep breath as she approached the young woman lying on the floor ahead of her. The woman looked around the same age as herself but her arm was lying at an awkward angle and she had a gash on her head.

Amber knelt down next to her, reaching in her pack for some supplies. "I'm Amber. I'm one of the doctors. What's your name?"

"Kel," she breathed.

Amber tried to do a quick assessment of the patient, pulling a small flashlight from her pack and checking her neuro obs. The woman gave a little groan and her eyelids fluttered open for a second. She attempted to move then let out a yelp. Her arm was obviously broken. Amber grabbed a dressing and covered the wound on the woman's forehead after she'd checked it. The arm was going to take a bit more than a wound dressing.

"When was the last time I dealt with broken bones?" whispered Amber to herself. She touched the woman's other shoulder. "I'm going to give you an injection for the pain," she said lowly, "before I try and move your arm." It only took a matter of seconds to draw up the injection. Amber kept talking to the woman the whole time. She gave her the injection and waited a few minutes for it to take effect. She found a sling in among her supplies. Once the woman's pain was under control, she very gently put the injured arm in a sling.

Where was Jack? She couldn't see him and there were a number of other patients to deal with. Jamal and Lana were dealing with patients of their own, checking wounds and patching dressings. Amber moved on to the next patient. Then the next, then the next. It seemed that lots of people in the evacuation center had been injured, some before the storm, some on the way to the center and some as a result of the roof being ripped off.

Eventually one of the firefighters came to her side. "Dr. Jack said to come and find you. He needs a hand, and wants a rundown on your patients."

A hand she could do. But should she be offended he wanted a rundown on her patients? She asked one of the volunteers to keep an eye on a few people and followed the firefighter outside, then followed him down a corridor into a back entrance of the damaged gymnasium.

There were a few people who looked as if they were standing guard outside one of the doors. "What is it?" she asked.

"The school janitor. He was already injured trying to help someone. Now we think he's been electrocuted."

Amber gulped. Water had seeped into every part of this building due to the roof damage and storm. One of the firefighters handed her a pair of rubber boots. "Put these on before you go any further."

She threw her shoes to the side and pulled on the rubber boots, nodding to the firefighter once she was ready.

But when he opened up the door, she realized she was anything but ready.

Jack was almost hanging from the ceiling, above a floor covered in a few inches of water, and holding on to a man who was trapped in twisted bleachers. He had a plastic portable gurney in two bits next to him.

"Great," he said once he saw her. "Amber, can you

bring an airway? I need you to maintain this guy's airway for me." His hands appeared to be on the patient. "But don't touch the floor. You'll need to climb around, across those bleachers. Get a pair of gloves from somewhere."

She tried to make sense of the room. The bleachers were twisted into an almost unrecognizable state. One of the large ceiling lights had landed in the pool of water on the floor. The firefighter next to her spoke into her ear. "The janitor pulled a kid out of here just before that light landed on the floor. He was flung up onto the bleachers with the shock. He's been groaning ever since." The firefighter nudged her. "Your Dr. Jack is quite the gymnast. He managed to make it over there better than some of our boys."

Amber was trying to plot her course along the edge of the water-lined floor then up toward the tangled bleachers. After a few seconds, she gave a nod. "Okay, I think I can do it." The firefighter handed her some gloves.

"Wait," she asked. "What's Jack going to do while I hold the airway?"

The firefighter pressed his lips together. "Oh, he's also trying to stop the bleeding."

"What bleeding?"

She looked back at the floor again and directly under the bleachers to where Jack and the patient were. The water was stained with red. This guy was bleeding heavily. However he'd landed on those bleachers, it hadn't been pretty.

She shook her head. "Don't worry. I get it."

It was obvious that Jack couldn't take his other hand from wherever the wound site was. She bent down and pulled one of his wound pads from her pack and stuffed it inside her jacket. It took a few moments to maneuver her way around the edge, taking care to avoid any hint of water, to where one of the firefighters was waiting to give her a punt up onto the bleachers.

"Ready?" he asked.

"As I'll ever be," she replied. Her hands caught on to a plastic chair and she moved from one to another, ducking between them and squeezing her body from side to side.

"Any word from the power company?" shouted Jack. "If we could be sure the power was off, things would be a whole lot easier."

"Can't even get through," replied one of the firefighters. "Ironic, really. The one place we actually want a power cut is the place we can't get it."

Another guy came up alongside him and shouted over to Jack. "We've looked for the breakers but we think the box has been covered by the debris from the roof."

Jack pulled a face as Amber continued to thread her way through the twisted bleachers. The last part was the toughest; she had to shrug off her jacket and push it through first before she could squeeze through the small space, finally ending up breathless next to Jack.

"How on earth did you get the plastic gurney up here?"

Jack raised his eyebrows. "It's plastic. We just threw it across the floor then had to work out a way to pick it up on this side without getting shocked." He gestured to the large plastic pole next to him and a thick pair of rubber gloves. As she looked down at them she caught sight of the blood on Jack's clothes.

"Are you okay?" she asked, instantly worried.

"It's not mine," he replied quickly. His jaw was tense with a little tic at the side, as if his muscles were straining. One hand was positioned at the patient's head and neck, keeping his airway propped open, the other pressed hard against the patient's side.

Something flickered in her brain. "Wait," she said quickly as she unfolded her jacket. "I brought one of your wound pads."

His eyes lit up. "Great. Thanks." He rolled his eyes. "I left my pack behind when I came in here. We thought he'd just been shocked. I didn't realize there were other injuries." She opened the wound pad and held it toward him. He grabbed it and replaced it with the one he'd been using. As he pulled it upward Amber could see that the traditional dressing had virtually disintegrated.

"Let me help," she said as she moved her position to near the head of the trolley. She pulled an airway from her pocket and worked around Jack, inserting it into the janitor's mouth. Once she was sure it was safely in position, she placed her hands carefully on either side of the janitor's head, her fingers covering Jack's. He looked up and met her gaze.

"You got it?" he asked.

There was something about his words and the expression in his gaze. All the way along she'd felt as if his natural position was to take over everything. To take charge. But now Jack was the one asking for help.

She'd thought she'd have to ask him a million questions out here—out of her comfort zone. But he hadn't been around and she'd coped fine. Maybe the director at the DPA was right—maybe she was ready for more field missions.

"I've got you," she whispered in reply.

In that second she felt a wave. A connection. An understanding of the overwhelming pain in his eyes. A deep, fathomless hurt that he never revealed or let bubble to the surface. Jack Campbell never asked for help. He never counted on anyone else. He was solitary in his life. For reasons that she couldn't even begin to imagine. It was the first depth, the first exposure she'd seen from him, and it was the truest thing she had ever felt.

Even though she'd only just got to know him, she got the overwhelming impression that he'd have her back. A warm feeling flowed through her, filling her with the confidence that she sometimes lacked. This strong, fearless army surgeon needed her help and she was happy to give it. Always. And something about it felt good. Special.

He released his hand, pulling it gently out from under her firm grip. For a second the tension left his shoulders, but a few seconds later he put his second hand down with his first on the wound.

"What's he done?" asked Amber. The sky was dark above and there were no artificial lights. From this position she couldn't really make out what was wrong.

"He's been pierced by a bit of the bleachers. From the amount of blood, I think he might have damaged his spleen."

She licked her lips. "How's your wound pad doing?"

Jack gave a brief nod of his head. He lifted one hand from the wound site. The glove he was wearing wasn't smeared in blood this time. It was more or less wiped clean. He put it back down. "I think things are clotting. The blood loss has certainly slowed. Before it just seemed like a steady flow. Nothing I was using was stemming the blood flow."

She gave an appreciative nod. "That's another life, Jack. Another life saved."

She shifted a little. Her position was awkward, her legs spread across an unstable base above the still-wet floor, her back starting to ache already. The space across the floor was vast, with easy access to the door if only there weren't a chance of water filled with electricity in their way.

"Jack, how are we going to get out of here? We might be able to clamp this gurney around him but there's no way we can fit it through the spaces we climbed through." She wrinkled her nose and stared down at the floor. "The gurney is plastic. Could we lower it to the floor and push him across again?"

Jack raised his eyebrows. "You want to take that chance?"

She pulled a face. "Not really."

"Me either."

She stared at the rope around his waist, looped around something hanging from part of the ceiling and allowing him to slightly change position as needed. "How on earth did you do that?"

He grinned. "One of the firefighters is some kind of mountaineer. At first they were worried I shouldn't actually touch the bleachers. They rigged the rope and tied it to me before I set off. Theory was it would keep me off the floor if everything else around me collapsed."

She stared down at her waist and raised her eyebrows. "Great. Where's mine?"

He nodded toward her feet. "You got the rubber boots. That's your insurance policy." He wiggled one foot at her. "I'm still on the regular army boots. Not quite the same."

She noticed he was still keeping his hands firmly down at the janitor's wound. She watched carefully the rise and fall of the janitor's chest. At least he was maintaining his airway, without any oxygen. That was good. Even if he had suffered some kind of electric shock, he was still breathing. If only she had a spare hand right now to reach for his pulse.

"Any idea about his cardiac situation right now?"

"I'd love to know about his cardiac situation. But I've run out of hands. You have too. Let's just say, due to the amount of blood loss, we know his heart has kept beating. I just wish he'd regain consciousness so I could try and assess him."

Amber shook her head. "With that wound, I'm not sure you do. How much pain will he be in? I don't know how still he would stay and we're not in the most stable of positions."

Jack gave a reassuring nod. "I know that." For a second his dark eyes twinkled. "Did you ever imagine when you met the jet-lagged Scotsman in the bar we'd end up working together in the middle of a hurricane?"

She let out a quiet laugh and shook her head. "If you'd asked me to place bets that night, I'm pretty sure this would never even have been on my radar."

"Still annoyed I didn't tell you I was a doctor?"

"Till my dying day." She laughed.

Jack's face changed. There was the briefest flash of something and Amber's insides flip-flopped, cringing. She'd said the wrong thing—but she had no idea why.

"Dr. Jack!" came the shout behind her.

She wanted to swivel around but her position made it awkward. Jack replied for them both. "We're almost ready."

"What are they doing?" asked Amber as she tried to see out of the corner of her eye.

"It's the backup plan," said Jack. "Just think really big planks of wood."

There were loud noises behind her. Scraping, thudding and the odd splash of water. She could also hear quite a lot of groans and moans behind her as the firefighters positioned the planks of wood.

After what seemed like forever, there was a voice not too far behind her. "Okay, Docs, we think we're just about ready. The wood is in place. We're on it. We're going to come toward you and help you clamp that gurney into place. Then we'll try and bring you all down together. Whatever you do, as you come down from the bleachers, make sure you step directly onto the wood. We're still not sure about the state of the electrics and the main floor is still wet. Nobody touches the floor. Are we clear?"

Jack glanced at her. "We're clear," he shouted back.

But the firefighter didn't seem to be happy with that response. "Dr. Berkeley, did you get that? I need to know you understand before anyone moves."

Amber shouted back. "Okay, I've got it. Just let me know when."

From that point, Jack was her eyes. He told her where everyone was, and how soon it was until they were at her back. And they were a good partnership. She held her hands steady, supporting the janitor's airway, even though they felt as though they could cramp. It was the longest time until she felt a pair of large hands at her waist. It made her start a little. "Right behind you, Doc," came the deep voice at her back. "I'm going to come around your side and grab one side of the gurney."

She felt his large body brush against hers as the firefighter came around her side, squeezing his body next to one side of the gurney. Another guy appeared at the other side and they coordinated with Jack and Amber.

"We'll take the weight of the gurney. Your job is to keep doing whatever it is you need to do. We're going to move slow and steady. Let us know if there's an issue. Dr. Berkeley, we know you're going to be walking backward. We're going to have someone else behind you to guide you, and make sure you don't step off the planks."

It was the first time she actually felt a bit nervous. Of course. Stepping off the planks could result in a nasty shock. Jack met her gaze again. "Okay?"

"Okay," she replied, her voice a little shakier than she'd like. She really wanted to move her hands, just for a second, just to stretch them to stop the cramp setting in. Last thing she wanted was her hands to spasm when she was holding this airway.

She took a few breaths and concentrated on the rise and fall of the janitor's chest. That was what she needed to focus on. She could do this.

The firefighter to her right started talking slowly and steadily. "We're going to take the weight on three. Ready? One, two, three."

The gurney lifted just a little under her hands. She felt another pair of hands at her waist and heard the voice of a female firefighter. "Dr. Berkeley, I'm Kate. I'm here to guide you. I want you to take one slow step backward."

It was harder than it should be. She wasn't on a flat surface. She was still halfway up the twisted bleachers. Her hands were already fixed in position. Now she was stepping downward with no weight to steady herself. But the hands at her waist were strong and firmly reassuring. Not only did they feel as though they could take part of her weight, they also felt as if they could keep her straight and steady. She felt her way with one foot, finding another part of the bleachers to stand on. Then she shifted her weight, ready to move the next foot.

The firefighters watched her constantly, as did Jack, the gurney sliding steadily closer toward her. Jack was finding it easier to move; he could put a little weight on the gurney as he found his footing to move. Amber concentrated on the firm hands at her waist and the steadying voice of Kate. When she finally felt her foot reach a thick plank of wood on the floor, she let out a huge sigh.

Kate gave a laugh. "Don't be too relieved," she said. "We've still got a bit to go. And, believe me, these guys couldn't put planks of wood in a straight line if they tried."

Slowly and steadily they moved. Jack's eyes were on hers. He didn't talk. He just kept watching her. In any other set of circumstances she would have been slightly unnerved. But it wasn't like that. It was reassuring.

Once they reached the entranceway and stepped off the wood and onto the normal flooring in the corridor outside, Jamal was waiting with a bag and mask to take her place. He gave her a gentle nudge. "Let me take over for a bit," he said as she stumbled back wearily and stretched out her aching hands.

The gurney was lowered to the ground. Jack moved instantly to the side of the gurney and lifted the edge of his wound pad. Amber couldn't help herself. She had to see too. She knelt on the floor next to him. Lana had appeared too and fixed a BP cuff around the janitor's arm, checking his blood pressure and taking his pulse with her fingers. "Can't beat old-fashioned methods." She winked at Amber.

Amber could see a bead of sweat on Jack's brow. Just how long had he been in position while she'd been dealing with other patients? "Has it worked?" she asked.

Jack gave a relieved breath. "I hope so. It looks as if a clot has formed." He looked at the readings that Lana had taken. "His blood pressure is low. His pulse fast and thready. He's not regained consciousness. He really needs to be back at the hospital."

Amber nodded. "I agree. I've got another patient next

door with a broken arm, and a possible head injury. I also patched up a woman with a shoulder injury and another with a whole array of cuts to her face and arms."

Jack sighed. "Before I got called here, I dealt with an older man with a crush injury to his lower leg. Part of the ceiling caught him when it was ripped off. And a woman who sheltered some kids and ended up with a spinal injury." Amber's eyes widened but he shook his head. "She's not paralyzed but she's got a loss of sensation in one of her legs. She needs proper assessment. We've got two kids who had asthma attacks because they forgot their inhalers. We managed to find some and they're stable now. Another kid had a minor seizure but that's stopped and he's come around."

Jamal pulled a list from his pocket. "Here. I collated some details while you two were trying to get electrocuted," he said wickedly. "We radioed in, and they're sending a few extra ambulances in our direction." He looked at Jack. "You just need to decide who goes first."

A list. She'd forgotten. She'd forgotten about her own list.

Jack must have caught the expression on her face, because he raised own eyebrow in silent question. She shook her head and stood up. "You've got this. Let me see if there's anyone else needing to be patched up before the ambulances arrive. I'll let you know if there's anything serious."

She stretched out her back for a few seconds, trying to relieve the ache she was feeling, and made her way back to the main gymnasium. There were a few more staff, helping patch patients up. She found her pack again and emptied its contents on the floor next to her, then made a quick check of Kel and her broken arm, giving her some more pain relief and checking her neuro obs again.

The evacuation center had over two thousand people in it—they were lucky there weren't more seriously injured. Lots of the people in the center volunteered to help and some had first-aid certificates or previous experience in the health service.

Jack appeared at her side. "Have you finished sorting out who goes first?" she asked him.

"We've got fourteen people who need transport to the hospital sometime soon. I found out our janitor is called Hugo. He's going, along with the lady with the spinal injury, a woman with a head injury and the older gentleman with the broken tib and fib. We only have two ambulances initially, so I've had to prioritize."

Amber leaned in a little and looked at the list in his hand. She could see Kel, the woman with the broken arm and head injury, on the second list. On any other day of the week, she would have wanted to get her assessed sooner. But things were different here. She wasn't unconscious. The other patients would actually take priority.

Jack must have noticed her expression. "You don't agree?" He seemed surprised, but held up the list for her to look at. "If you think differently, let me know."

She swallowed. She hadn't expected that. He actually wanted to know if she had other ideas—even though this wasn't her specialist area. Her fingers crumpled around the list in her pocket as she shook her head. "I don't disagree. I understand why you've prioritized them. How much longer until we get ambulances again? I'd like to get Kel checked over in the next round of patients."

He pulled out the radio from his pocket. "The first should arrive in around ten minutes. It could be an hour before they're back."

"Do we stay here?"

Jack gave her a curious stare. "You can't let it go, can you?"

"What?"

He smiled and shook his head. "Don't pretend with me. You're itching to find out about the close contacts of the meningitis, aren't you?"

He handed her the radio. "Here. Call in. Check on Aaron and Zane and see if anyone has recorded seeing any more of the close contacts."

Amber took the radio gratefully. She wanted to find out how many people were still out there without any medicines. She talked into the radio as she walked back toward the entrance point where Chrissie was based. It only took a few minutes to find out that Chrissie had managed to find the group of boys who had come from the surf school. They'd thought there were six, but it turned out to be seven. One of the boys who was supposed to go someplace else had been delayed by the weather and ended up here. Amber signaled to Lana, and she came and helped her talk to the teenagers and distribute the antibiotics.

Jack appeared at her side. "Ambulance is here. We're loading the first patients. How are Zane and Aaron?"

She gave her head the briefest shake. "Good, and not so good. Aaron has picked up. He's started to respond and come round. Zane is still the same. No change. His BP and temp are in normal limits but he's just not woken up yet."

"Has there been disease progression? Septicemia?"

"Thankfully no. But this whole strain worries me. I'd be much happier if I could find the rest of the close contacts."

Jack seemed to stare ahead for a few seconds. Then the edges of his lips seemed to hint upward. "I was going to ask if you wanted to head back to the hospital with the patients, or if you wanted to stay here and treat any more casualties that come in."

She could hear the slight edge in his voice. He was teasing her. Just a little. "Or...?"

He drew himself up and pushed his shoulders back. It was that second—that second that she saw the man who had served in the army and done two tours of duty. The man who had saved lives and had to juggle priorities in a way she probably never would.

He met her gaze with his dark brown eyes. "Or we could volunteer to stay out here. To help at the bus, or elsewhere, and see if we can drop any more of the antibiotics off."

Her heart gave a little leap. He got her. He understood her. She smiled and folded her arms across her chest. "I think I'll take option three."

CHAPTER FIVE

It was dark. More than dark—with the power cuts throughout the city it was virtually a blackout. It seemed that only sporadic places had power, so parts of the city glowed like little bulbs on a Christmas tree. Total wrong time of year.

It made Jack catch his breath. Dave, their driver, had helped take people back to the hospital and they'd coordinated with Ron in ER and managed to visit a few of the addresses in the surrounding area where close contacts resided, along with a few other addresses where they'd been asked to check on vulnerable adults.

They decided to go back to the evacuation center and help as best they could. The school kitchens had been opened and manned by a whole host of volunteers. Chrissie pressed some food into their hands and pointed them down a corridor. "We're short of space. But you'll find somewhere down there to sit down for the night."

Amber looked down as her stomach growled loudly. Her hair was pulled back from her face in a haphazard way and there were tired lines around her eyes, but somehow they still had a little sparkle. "Oops. I'd forgotten how hungry I was. It's been a crazy day." She leaned her head against his shoulder.

Jack paused in the corridor; he couldn't help it. "I feel

like we should go back to the hospital in case there are other patients to see."

She lifted her head back up. "Jack. Take a breath. We've been working all day, and if we have to pull a night shift, then we will. But let's just sit down for five minutes."

He took a deep breath. That angsty feeling that had been in his stomach all day was still there. It was constantly there. He'd just learned to live with it. Learned to live with the fact he was always looking over his shoulder, waiting for the unexpected.

Every part of his body wanted to keep living on the adrenaline. To keep going, to find the next person to help. But the truth was, his muscles ached. The aroma coming from the food in his hand was tempting. And the thought of sitting down for five minutes didn't seem quite so alien as it might have. Particularly when he was with Amber.

He nodded. "Okay, then—you win. But five minutes. There's probably still a whole host of people that need help. The damage from the hurricane seems huge."

He followed Amber down the corridor. Every room they reached seemed packed with people, some sitting, some lying on the floor. Amber frowned as they struggled to find somewhere to sit.

Suddenly Jack had a brain wave as they kept walking. He bent toward her ear. "I have an idea. Back this way, I think."

Two minutes later he found what he was looking for. The janitor's storeroom. He nudged the handle with his elbow to open the door. Sure enough, it was empty, even though it was tiny. There was a metal cage packed with supplies. A large chair in one corner and a mop and bucket in the other. Amber turned toward him. "Good call. Now let's sit down."

He thought about being polite for a second, then realized they were past that point, so he let her sit down first, then crushed in next to her.

She laughed as he joined her, giving him a last glimpse of those bright blue eyes as the door slowly closed behind them.

"Oops," giggled Amber as they sat in the pitch darkness. "I guess there's no light in the store cupboard."

"I guess not," agreed Jack. "Looks like we might need to eat in the dark."

"I can do that. I can eat anywhere. I'm so hungry," said Amber.

Within a few minutes their eyes started to adjust to the darkness, the only light being the thin strip at the bottom of the door from the corridor outside.

Amber finished eating and set her paper plate on the floor, sagging back into the chair. Jack finished too and clashed shoulders as he rested back beside her.

"Do you think this is really a chair for one?"

"I don't care." Amber waved her hand. "After the day we've had, I'm happy to share. Hey, do you think we should have gone back to the hotel?"

Jack shook his head. "I was wondering though—we weren't the only doctors at the conference. There were lots of others. I wonder if anyone has thought to draft them in to help."

Amber sighed. "Please tell me that in an emergency situation, some of them will have volunteered like we have. It can't possibly just be us."

She stretched out her arms in front of her, then clasped her hands to stretch out her fingers too.

"Are you stiff? Sore?" It suddenly struck him that

he'd asked Amber to do things today that were totally out of her comfort zone. When was the last time she'd had to support an airway? And she'd done it expertly—just like checking broken bones and assessing a potential head injury.

"I'm just trying to stretch out the sore bits," she confessed. "I thought my hands were going to cramp at one point when I was supporting the airway." She shook her head. "And we definitely didn't need that to happen."

Jack smiled at her. "You did well today, Amber. Better than others that I've worked with in the past."

It took her a few seconds to answer. "Thanks… I think. Truth was, I *was* worried. I thought I might forget everything and have to ask you to remind me. But once I started, everything just kind of fell into place." She let out a sigh. "Maybe the director was right. Maybe I should do more field missions."

"The director?"

"Of the DPA. He's been at me for a while, telling me it's time to do some more field missions."

"I thought you'd already done some."

She nodded slowly. "Oh, I have. But I've always been part of a team. I've always had other medics and nurses around me. I've never actually been the one in charge. I guess I've just been a little afraid."

Now he was curious. He shifted onto one hip so he faced her a little better. "Afraid of what? You're a capable and competent doctor."

Her head dropped and her hands kneaded together in her lap. "Amber?" he pressed.

She let out a long slow breath. "I know I am. I know that I'm capable at what I do. Infectious disease is my comfort zone. I like it—more than that, I enjoy the work. The variety. The locations." Her head lifted and even in the dark he could see her meet his gaze. "But…" Her voice tailed off.

"But what?" He couldn't understand why she would doubt herself.

She leaned her head back against the chair, her eyes staring out in the darkness. "I guess I've spent my life feeling as if I wasn't good enough."

Jack shook his head. "Why on earth would you think that?"

She blinked and he thought he could catch a glimmer of moisture in her eyes. "It was just the life I was brought up with," she said slowly. "My father was obsessed with his work as a surgeon. My mother and I barely saw him. Even when we did, he would spend his time at home, studying journals or taking hospital calls. My mother was basically a widow on the day that she had me. It was never a marriage, and he was never a father."

Jack held his breath at the intensity of her words. He could hear the pain in her voice. The rawness of it all. This obviously ran deep.

He remembered small parts of their original conversation at breakfast. He still couldn't really get his head around it. "Surely, he was proud of the results you got to get into medical school, then the fact you qualified?" He put his hand on his chest. "I don't have kids, and would never want to push them in any direction, but if any of my kids went after their dream and achieved it, I would be over the moon for them. Isn't a parent's job to be proud of their kid?"

Her voice cracked. "Maybe. In an ideal world. Instead, I had a father who never seemed to notice or acknowledge me, or my mother, and now, after he's gone, I feel as if my mom wasted forty years of her life on someone who never loved or appreciated her."

He reached out and took her hand in his. He could tell how upset she was by this. "But she got you. And I bet she's prouder than you can ever imagine. I can't second-guess your parents' relationship, but she probably has a whole host of reasons for why she never left. But now? Now she can pursue whatever she wants, and know that her daughter has her back." He squeezed her hand. "And I'm sorry about your dad. When did he die?"

Amber cleared her throat. "A couple of years ago. It was ironic, really. The surgeon had an aortic aneurysm. He could have been screened at any point, but hadn't found the time."

Jack nodded. He didn't need to ask any questions. As a fellow surgeon, he completely understood how fatal a ruptured aortic aneurysm was.

He couldn't help but try and lighten the mood. "So, runaway bride, are you still dead set against dating doctors?"

It was almost as if something in the air changed between them instantly.

Her voice rose in pitch. "Oh, we're going down that road again, are we?"

"Yeah, well. It seems I've got five minutes on my hands."

"Okay, then. So, I've had a lifetime's experience of an almost vacant father, then a follow-up with the jerk of the century."

Jack gave a little laugh. "Yeah, the guy you left in full tuxedo standing at the end of an aisle."

She gave a smothered laugh too. "Yip. But I did it because he was a butt-licking, using social climber." She turned to face Jack, their faces just a few inches apart. "It seems I have terrible taste in men."

His lips automatically turned upward. He could

smell a hint of her floral scent. It had been there earlier, but after the day they'd had, he would have expected it to vanish. But, as they sat together with their bodies pressed close, he could smell it again. If he reached up right now he could touch her cheek—the way he should have done after he'd met her in the bar. But in a way, it was probably better that he hadn't. At least now he knew why this intriguing, smart, sassy woman wanted to brush him off. And although her exterior was sassy, her interior was entirely different. How many people actually knew that about Amber?

"Hey," she said quietly. "I've spilled a whole lot more than I ever usually do. What're your dark secrets? You've just told me that you've got no kids. Well—none that you know of. But what else don't I know? After all, I have spent the night with you. Will I get messages at some point from a wife, an ex-wife, a girlfriend, and have to reassure them that actually nothing happened between us?"

He sucked in a breath. Even though his eyes had adjusted, they were still in the dark. He could see her profile, her eyes and her eyelashes, all highlighted by the tiny strip of light at the bottom of the door. There was something so private about this—even though they were in an evacuation center with around two thousand other people. They'd found a tiny little spot where they could be alone. And he was grateful for it.

Even though they were in the dark, he closed his eyes. It seemed easier somehow. "I'm single. I've never been married. I don't have an ex-wife."

Even as he said the words out loud, he knew how they sounded. As if he were telling part of a story but not it all.

"But…"

He sucked in another breath. "But then there was Jill."

Amber's voice was a little more high-pitched than normal. "Jill? Who is Jill?"

"Jill was my girlfriend. For just over a year." He let out a wry laugh. "Though she didn't like to be called that. She preferred The Boss."

Amber's voice was wary. It seemed she'd picked up on the fact he was using past tense. "Sounds like someone I would like."

The words struck a chord with him. Jill would have liked Amber. He could imagine them as friends. Jill would certainly have put Amber straight about her choice in men—him included.

"She was good. She was…great." This time it was more difficult to suck in a deep breath. He never really discussed Jill. Not with those who'd served with her, nor with her family after the funeral. It just made everything too real. Too human.

"I was sick. I was operating on a soldier who'd lost his lower limb. It was a tricky op—long—and I started to have abdominal pain. I just ignored it and kept going. By the time I finished I collapsed. My appendix had ruptured."

"What? For crying out loud, Jack, how much pain must you have been in? Wasn't there anyone who could take over from you?"

He winced. "Probably. But the guy on the table was a friend. And he'd already lost so much. I knew how he would feel when he woke up. I also knew that he'd want to get back on his feet. I had to do the best surgery I could to give him a chance of a prosthetic limb. I didn't want him to have to spend the next eighteen months needing revision after revision, when I could take the time to try and get things as good as they could be."

Amber nodded slowly as if she understood. "So what happened next?"

Jack squeezed his eyes closed again. "When I was in surgery…there was a retrieval—when something's gone wrong in the field they sometimes send out a medical team to bring back the injured. It can be the difference between life and death." They were still holding hands, but this time her other hand closed over his, holding it tight, supporting him to continue. "I was always the person that went. Except this time—this time I was in the operating theater on the table. So Jill went. She was an army-trained medic and she was good. As good as any doctor. But they never made it. Their vehicle hit an IED."

Amber didn't hesitate for a second. She pulled her hands away from his and wrapped her arms around his neck, enveloping him in a bear hug and pressing her face next to his. Her breath warmed the skin at the bottom of his neck. "Oh, Jack. I am so, so sorry. That's cruel. I can't even begin to imagine how that feels."

He stayed there. He let her hug him. He let her hug him in a way he'd never really let anyone hug him since it happened. He'd had a few awkward hugs at the funeral from Jill's mom, dad and sister. But he'd only met them on a few occasions briefly. He didn't really know them the way that he'd known Jill.

So it just hadn't felt right. Not when he was so busy building a shell around himself. One that wouldn't let him feel. One that would let him channel all his emotions and energies someplace else.

The sensation gripped him so much it was almost a physical pain. Amber just kept holding him. She didn't let go. And after what seemed like forever, the tension in all his muscles that he permanently held tight finally started to dissipate. He was so conscious of her cheek against his. She didn't seem to mind the fact his bristles must be scraping her skin.

He could feel the heat emanate from her body, and after the fierce winds of the hurricane it was like a warm comfort blanket. Only trouble was, the reaction his body was having was nothing like a warm blanket. It was more like a spontaneous firework.

And his head was trying to work out what was going on around him.

It had happened again. He'd actually *felt* something.

It had happened on the bleachers, when Amber had lifted her head and just stared at him. The connection had been like a punch to the stomach. The way she'd held his gaze, even though they'd been in the middle of something major, and just looked at him. Unflinchingly. As if she'd seen more than was actually there, and buried deep down to find the rest.

He hadn't really wanted to believe it then. He'd been holding his hands against a man's side, trying to stop him bleeding to death. For the last two years his mind had never been anywhere but on the job.

But for the briefest few seconds those big blue eyes had connected with something, tugged at something inside him, in a way he hadn't expected.

Or had he? The last few days had been crazy. He'd been attracted to her as soon as he'd seen her sashaying across the room and slaying potential suitors with a mere look. From her casual, unhindered and sparkly chat in the bar, to her professional, passionate, presenting face she'd shown at the conference. To her dismissal of him at breakfast when she'd found out he was a doctor, to the moment that he'd stepped forward and pressed his head against hers because it had just felt as if she'd needed it.

In every subtle way, he'd found himself drawn to this improbable woman. Someone who, it turned out, had just as many layers as he had.

He didn't even know where to start anymore.

But his body seemed to.

He lifted his hand to her face and touched the side of it gently, pulling back from their hug just enough to give him room to maneuver.

He should ask permission. Because his brain was so muddled he clearly wasn't thinking straight. So he just kept his hand on her soft cheek, tilted her head up toward his and put his lips on hers.

He was hesitant. But Amber wasn't. As soon as he brushed against her lips she ran her fingers through his hair at the back of his head, urging him closer, and her mouth opened to his. What started as tentative and questioning progressed quickly. Amber Berkeley knew how she wanted to be kissed. His hands tangled through her hair, tugging it from the ponytail band. His kisses moved from her lips to her ear and neck, but she was too impatient for that, pulling him to her mouth. She changed position, straddling him on the chair so she was on his lap, letting his hands run up and down the curves of her waist. Her hands moved from his neck to his chest, resting there while they continued to kiss.

There was a noise outside. A shout that permeated the dark world of the storeroom they'd claimed as their own. They both froze and pulled apart, listening to see if the shout would return.

This time it was Amber who pressed her forehead against his. She let out a light laugh. Her breath warmed his skin as she whispered, "Just so you know, I don't date doctors."

He laughed. "Just so you know, I don't kiss on the first date."

She tapped his chest. "This isn't the first date. This is about the third. And anyway, it doesn't matter because—"

"I don't date doctors." He said it simultaneously with her. "Well, that's a relief."

Amber climbed off him as another shout came from outside. "Think we should see what's happening?"

He nodded as he picked their food containers from the floor. "Let's face it. Someone's going to need something from the store cupboard eventually."

He thought for a second she was going to say something else as her hand paused on the door handle, but her head gave the tiniest shake and she pulled it open toward them.

There were more people in the corridor outside, but if anyone wondered what they were doing in the store cupboard, no one mentioned it. Jack walked over to the main entranceway. A number of firefighters and police were gathered there, comparing maps and discussing next steps.

"Give me two minutes," said Amber. "Lana's just given me a wave to check someone over." He nodded as she disappeared.

"Anything I can help with?" Jack asked as he approached the main desk.

"Oh, there you are." Jamal walked up behind them and handed over the radio. "Ron was wanting to talk to you."

Jack turned the dial on the radio and put it to his ear, checking in with Ron. "Where do you need us?"

One of the firefighters turned around as he heard the

instructions Jack was given. He waited until Ron was finished then gestured Jack over toward the main table.

"We're getting short of drivers. We can give you a vehicle. But at this point you'll be on your own." He pointed to part of the map. "There's been some flooding around the coastal areas. We're more inland here, but we think there has been around twelve inches of rainfall during the hurricane—and the rain hasn't stopped yet. There's still a chance of flooding from swollen rivers and rain coming off the hills."

The firefighter looked at Jack a little warily. "It might be better to wait until daylight."

"Wait until daylight for what?" asked Amber as she walked back up.

Jack turned to face her. He knew exactly how the words he was about to say would affect her.

"To be part of the search party for Aaron's parents. They've never arrived and are now presumed missing. It's time to go look for them."

CHAPTER SIX

ONE MINUTE SHE was kissing a man she shouldn't; next minute her heart was plummeting into her shoes.

"They haven't appeared?"

Jack shook his head. "Someone has reported a car off the road. It was an ambulance who were resuscitating another patient, so they couldn't stop. But they glimpsed a black car in the trees just outside the city. It's the road they would be expected to be on if they were traveling between Hilo and Kailua Kona."

She gulped. "Then we have to go. We have to go and see if it's them. Even if it isn't them, someone could be hurt." She looked around, trying to remember where she'd left her pack.

"Give me a minute." His voice was authoritative. It was the kind of thing she'd expected earlier from Jack. He walked back over to the table and started talking to one of the firefighters while she scrabbled around locating her jacket and pack. "Lana? Are you coming?"

Lana shook her head. "Can't. Sorry. I've got a sick kid that I'll need to transfer with to the hospital. She's asthmatic and is having problems."

"Anything I can help with?"

Lana shook her head. "I can cope. I should be gone in the next five minutes. But, hey," she said, "I've got another one from your list." She pointed to a name. "This family are here. The younger kids are nephews of Zane and had contact in the last few days. I've given them the antibiotics that they should need."

"Thank you." Amber gave her a relieved hug but Lana wasn't finished.

"Here." She bent down and pulled something from Amber's pack. "I think you should keep this handy. On a night like this, you'll need it."

Amber stared down at the heavy flashlight in her hand. Of course. Exactly what she'd need on a dark roadside. Her heart was starting to beat a bit erratically and she was starting to regret eating that food as her stomach churned.

Jack appeared at her elbow with a different dark jacket in his hand. He was already wearing one with his luminous "DOCTOR" tabards over the top. "Here, one of the firefighters gave me this for you. Apparently the rain is still really heavy and they think we might need it."

She automatically pulled her tabard over her head, shrugged off her own thin jacket and pulled on the thicker, sturdier one with a large hood. "Should I be worried that they've given us this?"

"Let's hope not," replied Jack quickly.

She'd seen him. She'd seen him at his most exposed. She'd held him. She'd kissed him after he'd told her things that could break her heart.

But right now it was almost as if that had never happened. It was almost as if he'd pulled a mask—an invisible shield—into place. Something she'd never been able to do. Everything now seemed so precise. So clinical.

"Where's Dave?" she asked as she slung her backpack over her shoulder.

"We have to drive ourselves. There are too many reports right now to deal with. One of the firefighters has given me directions. The roads were apparently passable a few hours ago. Let's hope they're still the same."

"They've been out there for a few hours?"

Jack held up his hands. "Truth is, I don't know when it was called in. All I know is we've been asked if we can go." He held up the radio. "If we need assistance we let them know. They don't have any spare people to come with us."

Amber shivered. She hated this. Everything about it made her fear the worst. But she tilted her chin and looked Jack in the eye. "Then let's go."

The road leading away from the high school started out relatively debris free. But as they started to wind further out, tree branches and bushes were scattered all around them. Jack drove slowly, taking care around corners. The wind was still strong, buffeting them from side to side, but they only passed one other emergency vehicle on the road. It seemed that everyone else had listened to the instructions to stay inside until they got word it was safe to go back out.

The rain was relentless and Amber was glad of the change of jacket. "I'm going to slow down a bit," Jack said to her. "You watch one side of the road and I'll watch the other. Hopefully we'll come across the car soon."

It was still black outside. They left the city behind and moved out more toward the mountains and green landscape. The few glimmers of light were left far behind them. It was hard trying to scan the dark landscape as they traveled forward. Trees and bushes lined the road. And on a few occasions they stopped at a felled tree, mistaking its dark outline for something else. But eventually their headlights swept over the familiar outline of the back of a car, protruding slightly at the side of the road.

"There!" shouted Amber, her heart rate quickening instantly.

Jack slammed on the brakes and they both jumped out, leaving the engine running and lights facing the foliage.

Amber's heart raced madly as she waded through the foliage on one side, as Jack strode through on the other side.

There were definitely two people in the car. There was condensation on the inside of the windows. The front end of the car had impacted on a large tree trunk and had completely crumpled. She could see where the airbags inside had deployed then gradually deflated again.

Jack yanked the door open on his side. Amber pulled at the door on her side. It had a large dent in it and wouldn't open. The ground was muddy beneath her feet and she struggled to stay upright as she put one foot on the back passenger door and pulled again at the handle of the driver's door. It finally gave and she landed in a heap in a bunch of wet leaves.

A groan came from the car and it made her heart leap. Noise was good. Noise meant that people were alive. She scrambled to her feet and leaned inside the car. Jack was checking the pulse of the woman in the passenger seat. Amber did the same with the man on her side, wrinkling her nose a little. The smell inside the car was a little unpleasant. How long had they been trapped?

Something clicked into place in her head. Top-to-toe survey. The way any doctor was supposed to assess an unknown patient. She started speaking. "Hi there.

I'm Amber. I'm a doctor. I'm just going to take a look at you."

The man under her hands gave another groan and his eyelids flickered open. She smiled at him. "Are you Aaron's parents?"

She could see the instant panic on his face. "How is he?" The words were weak and hoarse.

"He's holding steady," she replied. "I'm just glad we've found the right people." Her hands checked his arms, shoulders and chest. There was no apparent head injury, but his lower legs were pinned in place by the crumpled dashboard.

Jack had his head down low, speaking to the woman. He gently touched her arm and gave her a little shake. "Hi there. Can you hear me? I'm Jack, a doctor. How are you doing?"

His eyes met Amber's and he mouthed the words. "Color is poor."

He bent to the crumpled foot well and pulled out a purse, rifling through it until he found what he was looking for. "Bess. Bess, it's Jack. Can you open your eyes for me?" He'd pulled out a stethoscope and blood-pressure monitor from his bag and Amber did the same. She didn't want to move Aaron's dad's position in the seat, so she just had to wrap the cuff around his covered arm to try and get some kind of reading. She followed Jack's example and put her hand inside his jacket pocket, pulling out his wallet and checking for his forename. "Maleko… Maleko, can you open your eyes for me again?"

The man grunted and opened his eyes. "Can you tell me where you're hurting? Any pain around your neck or shoulders?"

He shook his head slightly, then groaned loudly and pointed to his legs. She glanced up at Jack. "It's difficult to see because of the collapsed foot well." She pulled on a pair of gloves and gently felt with her hands. When she brought her hand back out it was covered in blood.

"I think we might need some help getting him out of here. Looks like a fractured tib and fib. I'll give him something for the pain. What about you?"

Jack's brow was creased. "I could really do with some oxygen. I'm thinking she's got some kind of chest injury, either from the seat belt or from the airbag. Probably a punctured lung." His gaze met hers. "Can you give me a minute until I radio in and try and get some support from Fire and Rescue? We're going to need help getting them out of the car."

Amber nodded and edged further into the car so she could keep an eye on both of the patients. Maybe opening the doors hadn't been such a good idea. The heavy rain was driving hard against her back. She reached over and touched Bess's face. "Hold on, Bess. Aaron's waiting for you. I know he'll be so happy to hear both of your voices."

Her stomach twisted and coiled. She couldn't go through this again. She couldn't be the person who had to tell a family that their relatives had been lost in a desperate attempt to reach their child on time—particularly when she still didn't know what the outcome for Aaron would be. It was all just too much.

The hurricane. The fear. The worry about whether she was good enough. The injuries well outside her area of expertise. And Jack. The first man she'd kissed in forever. A doctor. He should have a red flashing warning light above his head to tell her to stay away. But she'd kissed him anyway. What was she thinking?

She reached into her bag to find some pain relief for Maleko, and to try and squeeze some wound pads in next to him to stem the slow flow of blood. If she knew he didn't have a spinal injury, she could help remove his jacket and get a true blood-pressure reading. But she didn't have that guarantee right now. She didn't have a cervical collar or a spinal board, let alone any cutting equipment to release his legs from the cramped space they were trapped in.

Jack was still busy on the radio. He hadn't climbed back into the vehicle and she could see the rain drenching him as he stood in front of the headlights. She sucked in a breath. From his gestures, she could tell he was annoyed. He didn't like not being in charge. He didn't like not having complete control. She could sense all these things even from here. The resolute single-mindedness and obsession with the job were written all over his face.

It was so reminiscent of her father that it almost felt like a punch to the stomach.

She closed her eyes for the briefest of seconds. She was soaked now too. The rain was running down her face and cheeks, hiding the tears that were sneaking out alongside. She'd kissed this man. For a brief second she'd felt connected to this man—even though every part of her being told her to run in the other direction.

He'd told her about his girlfriend. He'd had his heart broken. Chewed up and destroyed by a set of circumstances that he'd had no control over. That on any other day might never have happened.

How did a guy who at heart was a control freak get over that?

How many nights had he spent awake asking the what-if questions?

She ducked her head back inside the car and rechecked Maleko's obs. "We're trying to get some more help. Hopefully you'll be a bit more comfortable until we can get you out of here."

She frowned as she looked at Bess's complexion once more. Were her lips slightly more blue? She pulled out her flashlight. The headlights from the other car just weren't strong enough and she needed to see a little better.

Darn it. Bess looked terrible. She clambered through the muddy ground around the car, her rubber boots almost being pulled from her feet. Jack was still arguing with someone on the radio.

She pulled out her stethoscope and slid it under Bess's jumper. Definite decreased breath sounds on the right-hand side. It was likely that she'd broken one or more ribs. There was a good chance one had pierced her lung and caused it to collapse. Trouble was, she had no idea of Bess's medical history. She knelt down and watched for a few seconds. All of Bess's accessory muscles were trying to pull air into her body. While a collapsed lung would always cause problems, most people would still be able to get enough air through their other lung. Could Bess be asthmatic? Where had Jack put that purse?

She rummaged around the floor again and emptied the contents of the bag out onto the ground next to her, shining down with her flashlight to get a better view.

"What on earth are you doing?" came the angry voice.

"Quiet, Jack." A wallet, lipstick, credit cards, pens, a phone with a cracked screen and about ten missed calls, a strip of paracetamol, another blister pack of blood-pressure meds and, yes, an inhaler.

She picked it up and checked it, then gave it a shake. Jack sounded annoyed now. "Can you let me back in?"

It was clear he wasn't really paying attention to what she was doing—partly because the car door was blocking his view. She flipped the cap off the inhaler. "Bess, I'm going to give you a few puffs of your inhaler. I know you can't really breathe in properly, so just try and get as much as you can."

Bess was aware enough to form her lips around the inhaler as Amber administered the medication.

Jack obviously lost patience and nudged her with his shoulder as he tried to see what she was doing. But Amber wasn't having any of it.

She rooted her feet to the sticky ground and held firm. "That's right, Bess. You're doing great. Let's see if your breathing eases a little while we wait for some help."

She shot Jack a dirty look as she straightened up and pulled her head out of the car. "Back off, Jack. I'm just as capable a doctor as you. You can't be in charge of everything."

Even as she said the words, she felt an instant pang of regret. The flash of pain across his face—her recognition of what he'd revealed earlier. She understood the theory of why he had an inbuilt feeling of wanting to be in control. She just couldn't live with it.

They were incompatible in every which way.

Even though she wanted to reach up and brush some of the rain from his face right now. Even though as she looked at his lips all she could remember was that kiss.

She'd gathered confidence in the last few hours that she wouldn't let anyone take away from her—not even Jack Campbell.

An hour later Ron looked at them both as they climbed out of the back of the fire truck. The ER was swarming with people. Some clearly patients, others with a whole variety of colored tabards on. It almost made her head ache as much as her body currently did.

"Oh, my missing docs." Ron looked over as the patients were unloaded. He seemed much more comfortable now he could focus only on his ER. "What have we got?"

Amber spoke first. "This is Bess and Maleko. They were on their way from Hilo and were involved in a car accident." Ron opened his mouth to interject but Amber kept talking. "Their son Aaron is one of the teenagers with meningitis."

"Ah…" Ron's eyebrows rose.

"Maleko has fractured his left tib and fib and had to be cut out of the car. He's had ten of morphine at the scene around an hour ago. Bess is asthmatic and looks like she has a right-sided pneumothorax. Her color has only improved since she had some Ventolin, but she's been struggling with her breathing since we found them."

She was conscious of Jack standing behind her. She could almost feel him itching to talk but she was determined to do the handover properly.

Ron didn't seem to notice any issue. He just turned and issued instructions. "Him, Cubicle Three, and her, Resus Room Four. Get me a portable chest X-ray and a chest tube tray. Find me a surgeon for Cubicle Three."

He turned to face them again. "Quick question. They're expecting to have some emergency flights available tomorrow for any tourists that want to leave. I can't tell you what to do. But the next week or so will be mad. We'll move into disaster relief and emergency services mode. I still need doctors. Any kind of doctors. All kinds of doctors. And don't expect to be paid. So, do have someplace you need to be in the next few days, or can you stay?"

"I'll stay."

"I'll stay."

There was no hesitation. Their voices sounded in perfect unison. And Amber turned on her heel and locked gazes with Jack.

Both of them looked in surprise at the other.

Her heart gave a couple of flips. What had possessed her? But as she looked around the crowded ER, she knew exactly why she'd agreed.

This wasn't about her. This wasn't about Jack.

But that still didn't explain the fact she was secretly glad he'd also said yes.

CHAPTER SEVEN

BY THE TIME they reached the apartment that had been designated to emergency rescue workers, both of them were ready to collapse with exhaustion. Another emergency worker glanced at them as he was about to leave. He threw them a set of keys. "Your room is the one at the back. I hope you brought some extra scrubs. We've no spare clothes."

He disappeared out of the door and they were left staring at each other. Jack shrugged. "Your room" made it sound like one room. Amber walked down the dark corridor and pushed open the door. Sure enough, there was one—not particularly big—double bed.

"I'll sleep on the floor," said Jack quickly. He didn't want to make her uncomfortable—even though they'd kissed. It was clear Amber still had issues with him.

Amber shook her head. The moon was the only light in the room at present. "Don't be silly, Jack. I'm tired. You're tired."

She gave a half shrug. "After all, we've managed to share a bed before." She held out her hands. "We could be here for the next few days. Let's not make things difficult."

He glanced around. "It's a pretty small space." He knew exactly what she was saying. They hadn't had an official fight, but things just seemed uneasy between them.

She nodded. "It is. So let's make the best of it."

He gave a resigned nod as he stripped off his jacket. "Fine by me."

He tried to keep his face neutral. Last time he'd shared a bed with Amber, he'd barely known her, but had been acting on the flirting and glimmer of attraction between them. She hadn't known his hang-ups and he hadn't known hers. This was different. This was another step. They'd already kissed. In among this disaster there was something in the air between them. Something he hadn't quite managed to get his head around yet. He knew he acted like a control freak sometimes. He knew that Amber had her No Doctor rule in her head. But where did that really leave them?

"Fine by me." Amber's words echoed his as she sat down at the edge of the bed and took off her boots.

Jack smiled at the back of her head. They'd reached an uneasy truce, and somehow he knew he wouldn't sleep a wink.

She was sharing a room with Jack Campbell. In the midst of chaos someone had obviously decided they were together and given them a temporary room in an apartment—the hotel was literally under siege as it now had to accommodate people who had lost their homes. So it had seemed churlish to object.

Lack of power was still the main issue. The power companies were working hard to safely restore power to the island. But they were stretched beyond capacity. And safety was more important than being able to turn on your lights at night.

But it meant that nights could be long.

They'd reached an easy compromise. They worked wherever the disaster relief coordinator sent them. Her little outburst and subsequent bristliness couldn't be helped. The work was constant and exhausting. She'd managed to track down all of the close contacts for meningitis and ensure they had antibiotics. Aaron now seemed to be on the slow road to recovery. Zane's progress was picking up. For a short while there had been a question over septicemia and how it was affecting his hands and feet. But the blood flow had improved and the toxins seemed to be leaving his system.

Amber was still concerned that in among the chaos there could be more cases that might be overlooked. There were so many voluntary agencies now that coordination of information seemed nigh on impossible.

Her director at the DPA had supported her decision to stay for the next week and told her that he trusted her. That meant a lot.

"Amber, do you know if we have any food in this place?"

It had been four days since the hurricane. By the time they got back to the apartment at night they were too tired to even talk. Most of the local businesses were waiting for insurance assessments before opening again, and there was only one tiny corner shop that had managed to open its doors.

Jack was staring at a box of cornflakes they'd eaten for the last two days straight. It was empty.

"I think we had soup." She walked across the kitchen and opened a cupboard. Empty. There were four other emergency service workers sharing the apartment—any one of them could have eaten it. "Maybe not." She shrugged as she closed the door. Her stomach grumbled loudly.

She put her hands on the counter and stretched out her sore back. "I guess the only place we can go is back to the hospital, or to one of the evacuation centers. At least we know the school kitchens are open."

Jack pulled a face. "Is it wrong if I say I can't stand the noise?" He rubbed his eyes. "I've spent most of the day surrounded by bedlam. I'd kind of like five minutes of quiet."

She paused for a second as Jack's stomach grumbled loudly then burst out laughing. "Well, there's no food at the inn. So, we have to go somewhere. Hospital or school?"

He sighed. "Okay, then." He grabbed the keys for the emergency vehicle they were still using. "Let's go to the school."

Ten minutes later they reached the high school that was still doubling as an evacuation center. Although all people who were evacuated when there was a hurricane had been told to bring enough food with them for seven days, the logistics of trying to store and manage that amount of food was more difficult than anyone had previously predicted.

After two days, the high-school kitchens had been opened with volunteers and aid agencies cooking in shifts. Further emergency supplies of food and bottled water had been shipped in so that no one was left hungry or thirsty.

Jack was right. It was beyond noisy. A constant clamor of people all trying to be heard above one another. Amber noticed a little family holed up in a corner, a dark-eyed woman trying to get two small children to sleep on a mat and blankets on the floor. "What must it be like in here at night? Do you think all these people have damaged houses?"

Jack seemed to follow her gaze. "Maybe. One area had some flash flooding too. I was down helping earlier today. Some of the houses were virtually washed away."

She frowned. She'd spent part of the day in ER, part with Aaron and Zane, and part in a temporary clinic. It was hard to keep track of everything. "What were you doing there?"

"It's a bit further away and some of the people were desperately trying to salvage what they could from their homes. Lots of dirty water, some of it waist-high."

Amber nodded. "Dirty water, dirty wounds. High chance of infections."

"Exactly."

They joined the line for food at the kitchen. Jack picked up a couple of bottles of water for them both. "How much longer will you stay?"

She shook her head. "I don't know. The director was happy for me to stay for a week in the first instance. But I don't know how much leeway I'll get after that. What about you?"

"I'm officially on leave. Holidays. Then I need to look for another job. So I can stay as long as I'm needed."

She pressed her lips together and nodded. "I heard Ron asking you earlier about surgeries. Are you going to help out?"

He nodded. "Probably starting tomorrow. There are lots of bone injuries and I got loads of orthopedic experience in Afghanistan. One of the hospital surgeons was injured himself, and another's had an MI. So, they're kind of desperate."

They reached the front of the line and took the plates offered to them. Amber lifted the plate to her nose and inhaled. "It's some kind of curry. It smells great."

All the seats were taken, so they walked back through

the foyer and outside. For the first time in days the rain had finally stopped. The sky was dark again but now they could see a smattering of stars glistening above.

Amber looked from side to side. Disaster still echoed around them. Remnants of the roof were still lying on the football field. A few broken windows in the school were boarded up. But the wind that had whipped around them for days had eventually died down and the night seemed almost peaceful, even if the place around them wasn't.

They walked over and sat on one of the stone walls near the front of the school. The car park behind them was littered with emergency vehicles and cars.

They ate in silence for a few minutes. "When do you think this will ever get back to normal? I can't believe that the beautiful place we landed in a few days ago has changed so much."

Jack stopped eating and put down his plastic fork. "I didn't even really get a chance to appreciate the beauty due to the jet lag. My eyes were closed the whole way from the airport. Seems like such a waste now."

Amber sighed. "I heard in the hospital today that a hotel on one of the other islands collapsed. We're lucky that didn't happen here." She held up one hand. "But look now. The rain and wind have gone. If we were lying on the grass right now looking up at the sky, we might think that nothing had ever happened."

There was a loud clatter and some raised voices behind them. Jack smiled and glanced over his shoulder. "Yeah, and then you hear the noise."

Amber nodded in agreement. "Yeah, the noise. Or how different it is."

"What do you mean?"

She smiled. "I mean, no mobile phones. Limited electricity. No TV. No Internet. No music."

Jack groaned. "And no real water."

Four days on there were still no mobile masts and it didn't look as if they could be replaced anytime soon. None of the regular utilities were working properly and the apartment they were staying in only had water switched on for two hours a day. It meant limited showering and limited toilet facilities.

"I can't wait to get back to a hotel at some point and just stand in the shower for an hour."

Jack laughed. "I don't see that happening in the next few days. I'm not sure we'll even get back to the hotel. Did you leave anything important there?"

Amber couldn't help but pull a face. "Just business suits, other clothes and my laptop. Nothing that can't be replaced. There's only one thing I'm keen to get back and it's a locket my mom gave me for my twenty-first birthday. I'd left it in the safe." She turned to face him on the wall. "What about you?"

He blinked for a second and breathed out slowly. "Like you, clothes, a laptop."

"And?" She knew. She just knew there was something else.

He stared up into the sky for a few moments. "It's nothing that I couldn't replace. It's just…"

"Just what?"

He looked back down and stared at the plate still in his hands. "A photo. A photo of Jill from years ago. She's sitting in the camp in her army fatigues, laughing at something someone said. We had quite a lot of photos together. You know, it's a modern world. Everyone has a phone constantly. But after…the photo that made me catch my breath was this one. We're not in it together. I have no idea what we were doing at the time. Probably just taking a five-minute break between scrubbing for

Theater. But it's her. It captured her essence, the person who she was."

Amber bit her lip. Her heart ached for him. The grief seemed raw. Was that wrong two years on?

But before she had a chance to say anything, Jack continued. "I know it's stupid. It's just a photo. I don't carry it in my wallet. It's in my suitcase." He let out a wry laugh. "Jill would call me an idiot. But, sometimes, when I get carried away with things, it helps to remind me why I do this."

"You do this for her?"

He leaned forward and put his plate on the ground, then rested his head in his hands. "I do this for them all." He turned his head toward her and looked sideways through wounded eyes. "The wound dressing—the science behind it. It was all so much easier than realizing I'd lost Jill." His voice broke and he sat up and held out his hands. "I don't even know what would have happened. We might have stayed together. We may have grown apart. The one thing I am sure of is that we would always have been friends."

Her heart twisted inside her chest. She'd never felt a pull to someone like that she felt toward Jack Campbell. It didn't matter that it was all wrong. It didn't matter what her brain told her. What made her heart twist was the fact she was sitting with him and he was talking about another woman. One who'd obviously meant a lot to him.

"Friends is good," she said, trying to keep any emotion from her voice.

Jack kept his brown gaze fixed on her. "Is it?"

Her skin prickled. "What do you mean?"

"Are we friends?"

She shifted on the wall. "Well, I'm not sure…" Her

brain couldn't think straight. Was that the word she would use for the guy she'd met barely a few days before, shared a bed with, kissed and quarreled with? "Are we?"

Jack was leaning forward, his elbows resting on his knees, his gaze unwavering from hers. When he spoke his voice was hoarse. "What if, for the first time in a long time, I've looked at someone and wanted to be more than friends?"

The words swept over her skin. Half warming, half making every tiny hair on her body stand on end. Was that even possible?

Her hands automatically crossed her body and started running up and down her arms. "But I don't date doctors." It was like her default answer. She'd been saying it for so long that her brain found it easiest to resort to the familiar.

"I know. But you kiss them."

Her mouth opened. She hadn't quite expected him to be so direct. "You kissed me."

"You kissed me back." He straightened. There was a glint in his eye that seemed to be highlighted by the stars above them.

The world around them was a wreck. They were both wrecks.

But underneath them and underneath the land around them was a beauty that was hinting to get back out—to get back to the surface and let itself be revealed.

He drew in a deep breath. She tried so hard not to let her eyes fall to his broad shoulders and chest. To drink in the stubble on his jaw, and the way the expression in his eyes was so deep it just seemed to pull her in, like some kind of leash.

"I don't know what this is." The edges of his lips curled upward. "I know that our timing sucks. I know

you think you shouldn't date a work-obsessed doctor."
He put his hand on his chest. "I know that I've spent the
last two years virtually avoiding all contact with anyone
of the opposite sex. Some might call me work-obsessed."
He ran one hand through his hair. "But it's so much easier
to focus on work. To let it take over. To let it consume
all your thoughts."

She frowned. "I'm not sure you're doing a good job
of convincing me that we should be friends."

He nodded and stood up, stepping in front of her and
gently taking her by the elbows so she was facing him.
They were only a few inches apart.

"How about if I tell you that I'm confused? How about
if I tell you that my judgment may be skewed by hurricanes, lack of sleep, lack of food, forced proximity and
a hypnotic smell of rose and orange that seems to follow me around?"

Her scent. He was talking about her perfume. She
couldn't help but smile. "I'm still not sure about the
friends thing. I have standards, you know."

"What kind of standards?"

"You know, they have to like the same books, the
same movies and, most importantly, the same chocolate."

"Ah." He raised his eyebrows. "These could be im-
possibly high standards. I could be suspicious that you're
trying to stack the odds against me because I'm a doctor."

She smiled and shook her head. "Quit stalling for
time."

He lifted his hands and rested them gently on the
tops of her arms. "The answers would have to be crime,
sci-fi and…a kind of chocolate that is only available in
Scotland. I'm very loyal."

She wrinkled her brow and gave her head a shake. "Oh, no, we're not a good match for friends at all. It has to be romance, action movies and old-fashioned American chocolate bars every single time."

He smiled and leaned a little closer. "I have another way we can check our compatibility level."

"You do?" Now she could smell him. A mixture of earthy tones and soap.

His eyes were serious but he was still smiling. And she couldn't help but smile too. She slid her hands up his chest as he leaned in toward her, and she tilted her chin up toward him. This time there was no dark store closet.

This time there was a background of noise, and a smattering of stars in the sky. Last time around things had been more tentative. This time, Jack didn't hesitate. His lips were on hers straightaway. His fingers tangling through her loose hair, tugging her even closer to him.

She breathed in, pushing all the confusing thoughts from her head. She knew exactly where she was. She knew exactly what she was doing.

It didn't make a bit of sense to her. But she'd spent the last few days with this man at her side. And even though they weren't together, even though they weren't a couple and even though he carried a photo of someone else in his suitcase, she still didn't want to step from his arms.

His kisses were sure, pulling her in and making her want more. His body was pressed against hers; all she could feel were the strong muscular planes next to her curves. It wasn't often that she met a man who wasn't intimidated by her height. In general she could look most men square in the eyes. On a few occasions, heels had been a complete no-no on a date. But with Jack she had to tip her head upward to meet his lips. Her eyes barely came to his shoulders.

As he kissed her, his hands slid from her hair to her waist. If she were anywhere else she might be tempted to wrap her legs around him, but somehow, in the middle of a disaster, and in front of a school, it just didn't seem appropriate.

She actually laughed and took a step back.

"What? What is it?" Jack glanced around as if he'd missed something.

She shook her head and held out her hands. "We're in front of a school that's currently an evacuation center for around two thousand people. And…I'm still trying to decide if we are friends or not." She was smiling as she said the words. Parts of her brain were screaming, but other parts of her were warm.

Jack sounded ready to move on. It seemed as though he'd looked inside and realized he'd spent too long blocking out the world and just focusing on work. Maybe now he would take a breather and decide what he wanted to do next.

That could be anywhere, with anyone. But that flicker of something she'd felt that first night in the bar was igniting wildly.

So when he held out his hand toward her she didn't hesitate to take it.

CHAPTER EIGHT

HE'D KISSED HER. He'd kissed her again and again even though his brain couldn't seem to formulate any clear thoughts.

Then they'd gone back to the apartment and kissed some more.

They'd fallen asleep with their arms wrapped around each other just as they had the first night. Except Jack hadn't slept much.

He'd been too busy caught between staring at the woman in the bed next to him and looking out of the window at the bright stars above.

He felt...different. He'd spent so long focused on work and shielding his heart from any hurt that he'd never even thought about connecting with someone again.

And this had just crept up on him. Out of nowhere, really. One minute he was jet-lagged at a bar; next he was focused on the woman with the pink-tipped hair striding across the ballroom. And everything after that he just couldn't really work out.

This was a woman who had told him straight-out she wasn't interested. She didn't date doctors, ever. But the sparks that had flown at the first meeting had never died. No matter what she said.

She was a good doctor. Conscientious. Caring. Even when completely out of her depth. No wonder she was doing so well at the DPA. They were lucky to have her.

His stomach gave a few flip-flops as he thought about what came next. He hadn't been able to access emails for days. He'd been having a few tentative exchanges about job possibilities. He'd need to make a decision soon.

Amber groaned and shifted position, her arm draping across his chest. He wanted to nudge and kiss her awake. Every cell in his body was currently screaming at him. But he couldn't do that. Not like this.

They'd been pushed into a forced proximity. It didn't matter how much of a pull he felt toward Amber. After waiting two years to connect with someone, he wanted to be sure. And he wanted *her* to be sure. Because Amber Berkeley gave off a whole host of conflicting signals. Oh, sure, she kissed really well. But just because she kissed him didn't mean she wanted anything to progress between them. And how did you have that conversation with someone you'd really only just met?

Amber moved again, her lips brushing against the skin at his shoulder. Jack almost groaned out loud.

One thing was clear. Carrying on like this would drive him plain crazy.

Amber checked the obs chart in front of her. Aaron was on his way to a good recovery. Zane was finally making progress too, allowing her to breathe a big sigh of relief.

Jack came up behind her. "How you doing?"

He'd been a little awkward this morning. Not unpleasant. Just a little brisker than before. When she'd woken up and found herself wrapped around him again, all she'd been able to think of was how right things felt.

By the time she'd got her five-minute shower she'd

tried to be more sensible. In a few days she'd have to leave and get back to Chicago and the DPA. Jack still had no idea what to do next. And she'd no right to have an opinion on anything about that.

He nudged her again. "Hey? Are you with me?" His voice was soft, like velvet touching her skin, and she jerked back to attention.

"What? Yes. I've just finished checking on Aaron's mom. Her lung has reinflated and she's feeling a lot better."

Jack nodded. "I checked his dad. The pins in his tib and fib look good. He's got a walking cast on and they've had him on his feet already. Once he's mastered the hospital stairs on his crutches, he'll be good to go."

"Aaron should be ready to go in a few days. I've taken some more bloods this morning and he seems to be responding to the antibiotics well."

Jack gave a nod. "How about if I told you that I managed to find a shop that's opened?"

"Really?" That had her instant attention. She wanted to buy some toiletries and some food. Probably in that order.

He nodded again. "Apparently they had a delivery today from the mainland. They have some fresh food. I might have bought some."

"You might have bought some?" She arched an eyebrow at him. "What exactly *might* you have bought?"

"Chicken. Potatoes. Veg. Bread. Butter."

She rolled her eyes upward. "Sounds like heaven. Do we get to eat this food in a place that doesn't hold two thousand other people?" She wrinkled her nose. "And smell like two thousand other people."

"Oh, yeah," breathed Jack. "I also heard a rumor that

the utilities might be turned on for a bit longer tonight. We might get more than an hour of water."

"Now, that would really be bliss." She leaned back against the nearest wall. Then something came into her head. "Hey, tonight, who's cooking? Shall we flip for it?"

He gave a sneaky kind of smile. "Well, since I managed to find the food…"

She shook her head. "Oh, no. Oh, no, you don't. We flip for it."

"Or?"

"Or I steal the food and eat it myself."

He pulled a quarter from his pocket. "Okay, then. Heads or tails?"

"Tails."

He flipped the coin. It spun in the air and landed on his palm.

She grinned. "Tails." She lifted one finger and prodded his shoulder. "Just remember. I prefer barbecue chicken. Or maybe chicken cordon bleu."

She gave her stomach a little rub to tease him.

He shook his head. "Don't let it be said that anyone calls you Bossy Britches."

She batted her eyelashes. "Dr. Campbell, I have absolutely no idea what you mean."

He was strangely nervous. And he had no idea why. He was a perfectly capable cook. He could throw together a dinner without too many problems—even with his eyes on the clock to make sure he coordinated it with the bursts of power. The apartment they were temporarily residing in was only a few streets away from the beach. Since there were still a number of other emergency helpers using the apartment, Jack decided it might be easier to pack up the food and take it outside.

Their belongings had been dropped off from the hotel around an hour ago. In the chaos after the hurricane, the hotel was being used as a temporary shelter for some families. It seemed that his belongings had been more or less thrown into the case. But everything seemed to be there.

He undid the zipper on the inside lid of the case and slipped his hand inside. The wave of relief passed over his body instantly as he felt the battered edge of the photograph, but he froze as he went to pull it out. He knew it was there. He knew he hadn't lost it. But he'd lost her.

Did he need to keep looking at her photograph?

His fingers released the edge of the photograph as he knelt by the case. He breathed for a minute. In. Out. In. Out.

He pulled back his hand and fixed his eyes on the door. He'd used to have the picture on permanent display. That had stopped a few months ago. Would he ever get rid of it? No. Never.

He would always be respectful of Jill's memories. Her life. Her love. Her laughter.

But in the last few days it was as if the shadows had lifted from his eyes. And from his heart.

His head had stopped focusing only on the research. He'd never been interested in the business side of things. He'd only ever been interested in developing the best product that might actually save lives. Now he'd done it and he had the evidence base to prove it. But his obsession had started to diminish.

Today, he'd finally managed to access a working computer for a few minutes. Seven hundred emails. Mostly about the wound dressing.

But the only ones that he'd opened had been the

emails about job opportunities. Doctors Without Borders. Seven private clinics throughout the world. Six NHS posts highlighted to him by friends and colleagues who thought he would be suitable. Three possible aid agencies postings in far-off places that would be similar to what he was actually doing right now in Hawaii.

He'd always thought he'd know the right job opportunity as soon as it came along. But somehow, in among all of this, for the first time he was uncertain.

He'd always had a career path in his head. Up until this point it had served him well. But now? Here, in Hawaii, with his senses awakening for the first time in years, he just didn't know what path to take.

The door banged and Amber walked in. She was wearing a pair of thin blue scrubs with her hair tied up on top of her head. Her eyes widened as she saw him crouched on the floor. "Our luggage? We have our luggage?"

He nodded, and before he got a chance to point her bright green suitcase out, she'd spotted it and ran across the floor, throwing herself on top of it. "Come to Mama, clean clothes, shampoo and moisturizer." She laughed as he shook his head at her while she stayed in position.

"What? Are you trying to tell me that you haven't craved your own clean shirt and underwear in the last few days?"

She jumped up and dragged her case toward the bathroom. "Leave me alone. I might be some time." Her eyes were gleaming.

He smiled and stood up, waiting for a few seconds until he heard the inevitable signs of the shower running. He lifted his hand and knocked on the door.

"What?" came the impatient shout.

He leaned on the wall and folded his arms across his

chest as he kept grinning. "Amber? Just to let you know, you have—" he glanced at his watch "—nine minutes."

"What?" Her horror-struck face appeared at a tiny gap in the door. "Tell me you're joking?"

He tapped his watch as he walked away. "Tick, tick, Amber."

It was the quickest shower in the history of the world. She'd been vaguely aware of the smell of cooking food as she'd entered the apartment, but the sight of her suitcase had been too good. When she'd flung it open inside the bathroom there had been a note on the top asking her to collect her valuables from the hotel and to bring her passport with her. That had to mean that they'd emptied the safe in her room and taken her locket someplace else.

She ran across the hallway with only a towel wrapped around her so she could blast her hair with the hair dryer. Sure enough, in around two minutes, the lights and power flickered off. She let out a groan. Jack appeared at the door smiling, dressed in a T-shirt and jeans. "What? You didn't quite make it in time?"

She threw back her still-damp hair. "Darn it. At least I've got rid of some of the wetness." She frowned as she remembered the state of the clothes in the bathroom. "But I think I'm going to look like some kind of dishrag tonight. I wasn't able to iron any of my clothes."

Jack gave her a steady glance. "I think you'll look fine, no matter what you're wearing."

A little tingle ran over her skin. There were a few flickering candles in the main room but very little other light. She licked her lips and wondered if she could put on some makeup in the virtual darkness. It was almost as if he read her mind. He strode through the main room and walked back with a candle. "Here. You'll need it to get dressed. I'll pack up the food in the kitchen."

She was surprised. "Aren't we eating here?"

He gave her a wicked glance. "We're sharing with four other people—what's the chances of them coming in and stealing our food? The beach nearby looks safe enough. I thought we could eat down there and pretend we were still in the Hawaii we came to."

She reached out and took the flickering candle as her stomach gave a little squeeze. "Give me five minutes. That's all I'll take."

And she did. Grabbing a red beach dress from her case that she'd planned to wear for a more casual day, and a pair of flat sandals. Her hair was still damp but she left it around her shoulders in the hope it might dry in the warm evening air. Finally she slicked on some red lipstick as she squinted in the mirror in the candlelight then grabbed a light black cardigan.

When she walked back out in the corridor, Jack was standing with a package wrapped in aluminum foil in one hand and a bottle in the other. She laughed and shook her head as she walked up. "What? No wicker basket? No picnic rug or crystal glasses?"

"I'm all out." He shrugged. "This is going to be more like some high-school midnight feast than some big seduction scene."

She stepped forward, closer than she would normally dare. They were currently alone. The only light was the flickering candles. "Is that what this is?" she asked teasingly. "A big seduction scene?"

Jack's pupils seemed to dilate a little. She liked that. She liked that a lot.

He gave the slightest raise of his eyebrows and dared

to lean a little closer, letting her inhale the dark woody aftershave he'd put on.

He adjusted his package and held one hand palm up. "Let's see. We've already shared a bed—how many times? We've kissed." He gave a little smile. "Maybe twice. Do we need a seduction scene?"

She was fixed on his eyes. Had he always had such thick eyelashes? Why was she just noticing them now? She licked her lips subconsciously. "You can't seduce me," she said, her voice more hoarse than she'd expected. "I don't date doctors, remember?"

He slid his arm around her waist and pulled her closer. "Who said anything about dating?"

Maybe it was the dim lighting. Maybe it was the slow buildup of momentum in their mutual attraction. Maybe it was the combination of reasons that they shouldn't really be together.

But whatever their pasts, whatever the world had against them, it seemed that somewhere above those stars had aligned for tonight.

They walked down to the beach with her hand tucked inside his elbow. The tidy-up around them had started. There were lots of areas still needing attention. Buildings still requiring massive repairs. The path to the beach had a number of heavily bent palm trees, one appeared to have been completely torn from its roots, but other than that there were no major issues. The beach was deserted, just a pale expanse of sand and a virtually black sea.

Jack had grabbed a towel from the apartment so they had something to sit on. They settled down and he eased the aluminum foil open. The crinkling sound seemed to echo around them.

Amber bent down and inhaled, her hair falling around her and shielding her face. He resisted the temptation to reach out and pull it back. She sat back up, smiling. "You made it. Barbecue chicken." Her eyes were gleaming in the pale moonlight. "You actually made it."

"Of course I did. You requested it." He gave a simple shrug as he handed her one of the plates that he'd brought from the kitchen. It only took a few moments to share out the chicken and potato salad that he'd made. Ingredients had been few but it was still better than eating at the evacuation center. He also opened the wine he'd acquired at the nearby shop.

"Darn it." He shook his head. "We have no glasses."

Amber gave him a fake look of horror. "You mean we'll have to drink from the bottle? How classy." She shook her head as she took the bottle from his hands and expertly removed the cork with the bottle opener. "Do you honestly think I'm that kind of girl?" She winked and put the bottle to her lips, extending her neck and tipping her head back, giving him a perfect view of her profile in the moonlight.

He caught his breath. It had been a long time since that had happened—in fact, had it ever happened before? In the space of a few days Amber Berkeley had started to burrow her way under his skin. He'd found himself looking for her constantly. Picking up on the sound of her voice, even when they weren't in the same room. Wondering what she thought of him. And that last kiss—it had haunted him. In more ways than one…

Amber handed the bottle back to him, still smiling, then leaned back on her hands and sighed. "Wow."

"Wow?"

She nodded. "Yeah. Look around. From here we can hardly see any sign of the damage. Just a beautiful beach with a mile of sand, an endless dark ocean with stars in the sky above." She nodded in appreciation. "This is the Hawaii I imagined coming to. The one I had in my head. The daytime being yellow sand, bright blue ocean and a multitude of colored flowers, and the nighttime being beautiful, quiet and romantic."

Jack smiled as he shifted to face her. "Romantic?"

From here she was bathed in the pale moonlight. It caressed her skin, showing the glow and the vitality. She closed her eyes for a second and breathed again. Then turned her head to face him. "Yes. Romantic."

He paused. "What happens next, Amber?"

She licked her lips. He knew exactly what he wanted her to say.

She shifted on her hips so they were face on. She hadn't stopped smiling. "I guess I'm not entirely sure. The last few days have been…strange."

"Strange?"

She held up her hands. "Challenging. In a whole host of ways. Challenging for work. Challenging for life and…challenging for me."

He could tell she needed to talk out loud. He nodded. "It's been…different. I didn't come here expecting to find anything."

"And have you?" Her eyes were wide with expectation.

He put his hand up to his chest. "I feel like I have. I came here wondering what came next. I came here just to present at the conference—to tell the rest of the world about our product. And that was it. That was all that I was here to do."

"So what happened?" There was a teasing edge in her tone.

He met her twinkling gaze. "I met an unstoppable

force. And it made me feel as if I found a little bit of myself again."

"You did?" Her voice broke.

He nodded slowly as he licked his lips. "*She* made me feel as if I found a little bit of myself again."

Amber moved. She hitched up her dress and put one leg over him, so she was sitting facing him.

"This is getting to be a habit," said Jack hoarsely.

She slid her arms around his neck and tipped her head to the side. "I think it might be."

His hands went to her waist. "Maybe we need to re-think your rule. Don't most people say that rules were made to be broken?"

She lowered her head and whispered in his ear. "How about you convince me?"

"I think I can do that…"

And he did.

CHAPTER NINE

THE DOOR TO the room burst open. Amber sat bolt upright in the bed then remembered she didn't have quite as many clothes on as she usually did. Kino, one of the emergency workers who was sharing their apartment, only momentarily blinked. "Amber, Jack. You're needed. We've all been called in."

Jack moved seamlessly. He stood up, grabbed a set of scrubs that were lying on the floor and stepped into them. He pulled on his shoes and immediately started asking questions. "What is it? What's happened?"

Amber was still in the process of waking up and Jack was already dressed. Of course. An army doc. He was used to emergency calls. She'd never been good at the intern hours of putting your head on the pillow only for a page to sound yet again.

Kino kept talking. "A landslide. It's caught one of the villages on the outskirts of Kailua Kona. Multiple casualties."

Kino moved away. "I'll wait for you outside."

As soon as he left, Amber retrieved her underwear and grabbed a clean T-shirt, jeans and sneakers. She didn't have time to worry about appearances, so she clipped her hair up on her head and met Jack at the door.

"Ready?" His face had become almost a mask. The

warmth and emotion she'd glimpsed last night seemed to have been put back in their box. He seemed totally focused.

She grabbed her jacket and followed him out to the car. They were lucky they still had it on loan—and that their emergency packs were in the trunk. Jack handed her the radio as Kino climbed in their car. "Might as well come with you," he said as Jack nodded.

Jack started the engine. "Call in, Amber. See if we've to go to the hospital first, or straight onto the site."

Their instructions were clear. They were to be part of the first responders on site.

They traveled the rest of the way in virtual silence with only the occasional crackle from the radio. Kino was able to point out directions as he was from one of the other Hawaiian islands and was familiar with this area. Most of the major roads had been cleared of any fallen trees and debris by now.

But as they ventured nearer the village, the extent of the damage was evident. Four emergency vehicles were ahead of them, bright flashing lights causing Jack to slow down on the road. It was just as well, because the rest of the road had vanished in the landslide.

Amber had never seen anything like this before and she stepped out trying to survey the scene. "Where's the village?" seemed the obvious question.

Kino's voice was shaky. "It was there," he said, pointing to the mass of rubble and mud ahead of them.

Amber shook her head. "I don't get it. What's happened?"

One of the other emergency responders walked over. "It's because of the hurricane and the amount of rainfall. The earth around the volcanoes and mountains hasn't been able to stand the strain and extra pressure. It's always a risk a few days after any major event. It's just never happened before."

Her eyes were starting to pick out things in the debris. It was mainly mud and earth, along with a million uprooted trees. But in among the rest of it she could see a few things sticking out. Part of a roof of a house? A brick wall that seemed to have been carried away by the flow of the landslide.

"How many people?" she breathed.

"About five hundred," replied the first responder. He dug into his pack and pulled out tags. "Triage. That's your first duty. Red, amber and green. We'll set up the tarp emergency tents for first responders here. Find them, pull them out, assess them."

Jack had been silent this whole time—almost as if he was creating a plan in his head. A fire truck had just pulled up and the firefighters were out instantly.

Amber opened her mouth to shout over to them as the first responder put his hand up to her face. "Don't."

"What?" She was confused. She was only going to ask if they wanted to split into groups with the doctors.

"First rule of a landslide. The first big danger is the possibility of a further landslide. Keep noise to a minimum. No shouting. Only use the radios we'll give you." He pointed up to the mountainside. "There's always a chance that not everything has found its way down yet. There could be boulders, more trees, a million rocks, all waiting to slide back down here."

She felt her skin chill. She was walking into a situation she knew nothing about. Could she really do this? She took a few deep breaths. Jack had already started reorganizing things in his pack as some of the firefighters came over to join them, carrying radios. Another car pulled up and she recognized some of the staff from ER. They divided quickly into teams.

Her first few steps were tentative. The ground was unstable in places, and they were on an incline. But Amber followed the instructions she was given and moved as quickly as she could. Within minutes they found their first patient. A woman, who was half covered in mud and looked completely stunned. Half of her clothes were missing. Amber did a quick check and nodded to the firefighters that she was safe to move. "I was in the bathroom," the woman whispered. "I was getting dressed."

"Anyone else in your home?" asked Jack quickly.

She shook her head and Jack moved rapidly on as two of the firefighters assisted the woman back up to the almost constructed triage station.

For the next hour they worked in almost silence. Finding people trapped in the mud and earth. Some were badly injured. Others were lucky—they only had cuts and bruises. A few weren't so lucky. Amber found one man who seemed to have died of a severe head injury and another who had suffocated under the mud.

Jack was methodical and fast. He didn't waste a single second. Her stomach was in a permanent knot as she watched him. He barely acknowledged her existence. He seemed too focused on the task at hand. And she knew that was entirely how he should be. But somehow it still hurt. It still reminded her of her father. And she just couldn't shake the association.

She pulled out a child covered from head to toe in mud. But as she bent to do a quick assessment, Jack more or less elbowed her out of the way—just as he had at the car the other night. She bristled. She couldn't help it. She was perfectly capable of assessing this child. But was now really the time to fight about it?

She left him and moved on to the next spot where a firefighter was waving over to her. He pointed downward. "We've got a house buried under here." He had his ear pressed to the ground. "We think this is part of the chimney stack. Or it used to be. Is it maybe wrong way up? Who knows. We can hear them beneath us."

"Can you get them out?" She was currently up to her knees in sticky mud. The thought of being trapped underneath that made her feel queasy.

The firefighter nodded. "The space looks wide enough. I'm going to send someone down."

"Is that safe?"

His eyes scanned the surroundings. "Is anything here?"

She swallowed and stood to the side, allowing the firefighters to sort out their gear and lower their colleague. After a few minutes the guy radioed back up. "I've got four. All badly injured. Two adults and two kids. Can you lower me a cage? I'll need to strap them in one at a time."

It was a painstaking operation. The cage was carried over from one of the specialist fire and rescue trucks. First to come up was a woman whose color was verging on gray. She took the briefest seconds to assess. "Flail chest." Amber put a red tag on her. "Straight to hospital whatever way you can get her there."

The next up was a little girl with an ugly fracture of her arm, sticking through her skin. She was wailing at the top of her voice, making everyone nearby look around anxiously. Amber calculated in her head the little girl's size and weight. She hated approximating but it was the only way to try and ensure a safe dose of analgesia. Twenty seconds later she gave the little girl an injection to try and relieve her pain and handed her over to another firefighter to take her away. The next child was unconscious but breathing steadily. There was a slight graze to his head. She tagged him as amber and sent him on.

"There's a problem down here," came the crackle of the radio.

"What is it?"

"I can't move him. He's pinned down and I can't get him free. I need some assistance and he looks in a bad way."

Amber didn't hesitate. "Send me down. Let me look after him."

The firefighter frowned. "I'm not sure. Things are too unstable."

"You let your own man go down there—and you'll probably have to send another." She was determined. She was a doctor. This was her role and she wanted to play her part.

"I don't know." The firefighter hesitated.

"Well, I do. Where's a harness? Get me a harness and lower me down."

Of course she was nervous. Of course she was scared. But this was an emergency situation and she could deal with it. A tiny part of her brain objected. She could almost hear her father's condescending tone. But she brushed it away as she stepped into the harness.

"Amber? What do you think you're doing?"

Mud was streaked across Jack's face and clothes.

"My job," she replied as the firefighter clipped on her line.

"Ready?" he asked.

"Ready." She nodded.

Jack's voice cut across everyone's. "No. No way. No way is she going down there. It's too dangerous. Not a chance." His voice was louder than it should be and sent a wave of irritation over her.

She turned toward him. "Stop it, Jack. There are more than enough patients to deal with. Go and look after your own."

His hand came down on her arm in a viselike grip. "I said no." His voice was steely but it was the expression in his eyes that made her swallow. In a flash she saw a million things she didn't want to. This wasn't the man she'd laughed and loved with last night. This was a man who thought he should be in charge. This was a man who didn't believe in her as a doctor. He didn't respect her as a person and he didn't respect her as a doctor.

She turned to face the firefighter. "Tell him to get his hand off me." Her voice was shaking with rage. A few of the firefighters around them instantly stood up.

"Cool it, buddy."

"You heard the lady. Step back."

Jack's eyes flashed furiously but Amber just jerked her arm away then tugged at her harness to ensure it was secure. She grabbed a few things from her pack and stepped to the opening. "I'm ready." Her heart was thudding frantically in her chest. She felt anything but ready. But delaying now could make things more dangerous for everyone.

"This isn't finished," said Jack hoarsely.

"Oh, yes, it is," she replied as she was lowered down into the darkness.

He could barely contain his rage but he understood exactly how he'd come across. There were four pairs of eyes currently watching him with suspicion. "She's a great doctor. But she's not an emergency doctor. She's never worked in a situation like this."

One of the firefighters met his gaze. "Neither have I. Doesn't mean I won't do the job."

The words almost stung. The guy had a point. But had that guy lost a woman before that he'd loved? Jack should be down there. Jack should be the one in the position of risk. It shouldn't be Amber. She hadn't asked to be here. She'd just volunteered her services. He didn't doubt she could deal with whatever she might find down there—he didn't doubt her medical abilities at all. What he did doubt was his ability to survive if something were to happen to her.

From the second she'd stepped into that harness, his brain had had to remind himself constantly he wasn't allowed to shout. Because shouting was exactly what he wanted to do right now. Amber didn't need to be at risk. She didn't need to be in a situation that could rapidly go out of control.

He felt himself start to shake. And he couldn't stop it. It was like being dunked in a giant bowl of ice. He wanted to grab that line and haul her back up here. Back up here into his arms where she might actually be safe. Back up here where he could tell her he loved her—despite it only being a week, and despite the fact she still wasn't sure about dating a doctor.

He didn't want to date her. He wanted to marry her. He wanted to tell her that he could find a job anywhere so long as he was with her. He wanted to tell her that life was too short to wait. That when you knew, you just knew—no matter how hard you tried to fight it.

He lifted his shaking hands to the guys around him. "What can I say? I love her. I don't want anything to happen to her."

There was momentarily a flicker between them all. Then one guy put his hands on Jack's shaking arms. "Then I guess when she gets back up you should tell her."

Jack nodded and took a deep breath. "I guess I should."

* * *

She could barely breathe. What should be the inside of a home was a strange hotchpotch like one of those upside-down houses they had at an adventure park. She thought she'd come down the chimney but now she wasn't quite sure. What she was sure of was that the man on the floor beside her was barely alive. She needed oxygen. She needed a chest tube, and any longer and she'd need a defibrillator too. She had to concentrate right now, so why was her head so full of Jack?

She'd been a fool. She'd spent the night with a guy that every warning flag in her brain had told her to stay away from. But she'd done it. She'd let him in. She'd started to believe that all her previous fixed beliefs had been irrational. She shouldn't judge anyone else because of her father. Now the first time she'd opened her heart a little, he'd stamped all over it.

She was more than a fool. She was a stupid fool. And she hated herself more than anything right now. That look he'd given her. As if she were incapable. As if he had a right to tell her what to do.

She couldn't live like that. She *wouldn't* live like that.

There was a loud creak around her and the sound of shifting. A cloud of dust surrounded them and mud was seeping through a gap in the wall near to them—indicating what was waiting. The firefighter on the floor next to her looked up with his eyes wide. "Darn it. We need to move."

The second firefighter who'd come down just behind her was trying to find a way to prop up the huge boulder that had pinned their man to the floor. She finished fastening a collar around her patient's neck. His blood pressure indicated massive internal bleeding. His pulse rate was over one hundred and thirty. She slid her arms under her patient's shoulders. "Okay. Guys, is there any way you can take a bit of the weight even for a few seconds? If you can, I'm going to just yank him out of there."

The two guys nodded and attempted to slide some kind of wedge under the boulder. "You'll have a few seconds. This has an emergency inflatable action. But it won't hold—not with this weight. We'll fire it on three and try and take some of the weight too. Are you ready?"

Amber looked at the strange wedge-shaped contraption that after much manipulation was barely shoved under the huge boulder. Of course it wouldn't hold but it might give her a few seconds. She pressed down low to the floor behind her patient. All she had to do was pull. "Okay."

"One, two, three, *go*!"

She pulled with all her might. There was a tiny explosion followed by a colossal boom. She landed backward on the floor with the patient's head and shoulders planted between her legs. The two firefighters were covered in gray dust and choking madly. The boulder was back squarely on the floor where her patient had just lain.

The creaking sounded again and both guys exchanged a glance. "Let's get him into the cage." Amber didn't have time to recheck his obs as they bundled him into the cage and yanked the cord sharply to get him pulled up. She could hear frantic voices above her as the patient blocked their little light as he was pulled up. Seconds later three lines were dropped down. She didn't even have time to think as one of the firefighters clipped her harness instantly, then yanked her line.

She jerked roughly upward through the thin gap above, banging her shoulder. Arms grabbed her and threw her to one side. The noise was massive. Like a roaring in her ear. She didn't even have time to make sense of any of it. She saw the flash of orange and yellow as the firefighters were pulled up alongside her. "Take cover!" came the shout.

She still hadn't caught her breath when Jack landed on her, covering her body with his. He had his jacket pulled over his head, which in turn covered hers. Seconds later the ground moved beneath them, then over them, tumbling and tumbling around. Rocks pounded her body. Trees scratched her face and legs. Dirt crowded around her, and when she tried to inhale, mud slid over her mouth, choking her completely. Over and over they went like tumbleweed on a desert landscape. Jack's arms were around her, holding her in place. Nausea washed over her. Her head was spinning.

Finally, the tumbling seemed to slow. She was able to snatch a breath along with a mouthful of leaves. Every part of her ached. She tried to pull her hands up to protect her head, clawing at the jacket that had partially protected her. Jack's.

They finally stopped moving. She wheezed, then choked, spluttering up mouthfuls of dirt and mud. As she turned onto her hands and knees, there was a wave of pain from her ankle. But breathing came first. There was a heavy weight on her back. She pushed up, struggling to move. She tried again, ignoring all her pain and putting all her energy into curling her back around. Dirt and earth moved around her. She coughed, as she burst up through the mounds of debris. Her breathing was stuttered, her head still swimming.

Another landslide. They'd been caught in another landslide. She looked around, trying to work out where she was. Trying to work out where *anyone* was.

At the top right of her vision she could see the flicker of dark green tarpaulin. The triage tent. It seemed a million miles away now.

She shook her head, pulling twigs and leaves from her hair. She blinked. Something warm was beneath her palm.

She looked down, her eyes taking a few seconds to focus.

Jack. It was Jack.

She shifted her hand. "Jack? Are you okay?"

He'd dived on her. He must have realized the landslide had started. He must have known she was about to be caught in it.

Why hadn't he moved away? Why hadn't he got to safety?

She blinked again. He hadn't moved. More important, his chest wasn't moving. His lips were distinctly blue.

She felt a wave of panic. He'd tried to save her. He'd tried to shield her from the landslide. He'd put himself in harm's way deliberately for her. But at what cost?

"Jack! Jack!" She started thudding down on his chest. Trying desperately for any kind of reaction.

Nothing. Nothing at all. She thrust her fingers in at his neck, trying to locate a pulse. Nothing. She moved them again. Still nothing.

Panic gripped her. No. Not Jack. Not now.

"Help!" she shouted, waving one hand frantically in the air. "I need help!"

She started doing chest compressions, letting her doctor mode send her into automatic pilot while every other part of her being screamed out loud.

She loved him. She hated him. She couldn't possibly be with him. But did she really want to live without him when he'd connected with her in ways she'd never felt before?

The pain in her chest was immense. Stress, fear and terror all at once.

She could feel the movement of his chest beneath her palms. His color hadn't improved. He wasn't breathing. She couldn't feel the beat of a heart beneath her hands.

A tear dripped down her cheek and landed onto his chest.

This couldn't be how this ended. It just couldn't be.

She wouldn't let it.

She *couldn't* let it.

CHAPTER TEN

ONE SECOND HE was trying to contain himself; next second he was watching the mass of boulders and tree slide toward them as he dived on top of Amber.

He couldn't remember anything after that.

Except that his chest hurt. *A lot.*

And so did his shoulder. And so did his head.

He blinked, then squinted at the bright white that met his eyes.

A face appeared above him. "Oh, you're back to the land of the living. About time. I know someone that will be pleased."

His brain was still trying to focus. She was vaguely familiar. "Please don't make me do neuro obs on you, Jack. You haven't exactly been the easiest patient these past few hours."

She winked at him and something flooded into his brain. "Lana?" The ER nurse who had been sent out with him and Amber.

Amber. This wasn't a flood; this was a tidal wave. "Amber? Where's Amber?" He tried to sit up in the bed, yelping as his shoulder let him know who was in charge.

Lana smiled. "Oh, good. No neuro obs. You do know who we are." She pointed to his shoulder. "You dislocated that. It will probably be sore for a few days. And you've got a few cracked ribs where someone got a little overenthusiastic when you needed CPR."

"What?" He sagged back on the bed and put his hand on his chest. That was why it was so sore.

"As for Amber." Lana nodded over her shoulder. "Don't let it be said we're not accommodating. She's just back from Theater. Her ankle needed to be pinned. She's just about ready to wake up."

Jack turned his head to the side. There, in the bed next to him, lay a very pale-faced Amber, her dark hair fanned around her, doing her best impersonation of Snow White.

He shook his head, but, no, even that hurt. Lana walked over and lifted a cup with a drinking straw. "Try some water. Then we can chat. Do you need some more analgesia?"

He shook his head. "What...what happened? Last thing I remember was the landslide."

Lana nodded. "I think I'll leave Amber to discuss that with you. She used a few choice words." Lana laughed; her eyes were twinkling. "Give me five minutes to wake her up."

Lana pressed a button and the top of Jack's bed rose behind him, giving him a better view of the room. From the noise outside, the hospital was still crazy. He should be helping. He shouldn't be in here as a patient.

But he couldn't deny the pain in his chest. His heart gave a leap as he heard a few quiet words from the bed next door. He could hear Lana speaking to Amber. "Yeah, I'm the girl with all the gifts. I've been in the ER, Maternity and Surgical in the last day. I just go wherever I'm needed." Lana glanced over her shoulder and gave Jack a wink. "Here, have a little drink and I'll sit you up. Your partner in crime has woken up too."

"He has?" Jack's breath caught at the tone of her voice. She sounded almost...happy?

Lana stepped back and glanced from one to the other as she placed a buzzer next to Amber's hand. "Okay, people, things to do. Ring if you need me." She was laughing to herself as she walked out of the door.

For a few seconds there was silence. And Jack was glad of it. He was just so glad to see her there. Seeing that giant amount of earth moving toward them had terrified him. There had been no chance to move Amber out of its path. He might have had a chance to run for it. The firefighters next to him had run like lightning, carrying the patient in the rescue litter. He only hoped they'd managed to get out of the way of the landslide.

"You made it," he finally said, his voice breaking a little.

"Of course I made it," she snapped. "I haven't finished being mad at you yet."

He rested his head back against the pillow, closed his eyes and smiled. Just the way he liked her.

"What are you smiling at?"

He put his hand to his chest. "I'm just thanking someone up above that we're both still here." He opened his eyes again. She was too far away to reach out to. But that didn't stop him wanting to.

She cleared her throat. "I'm still mad at you."

He met her gaze. Somehow he'd never seen anyone look quite so beautiful. "I get that. Do you think being mad could last a lifetime?"

Confusion swept her face. "What are you talking about?"

He breathed slowly, then winced. He should have remembered about the ribs.

"Are you okay?"

He shook his head. "Just feels like someone has been tap-dancing on my chest. I broke a few ribs, and dislocated a shoulder. I still have no idea how we got out of that."

She blinked. Her eyes looked wet. "Sorry. My technique might be off."

Something clicked in his brain. "You did CPR on me?"

She let out an exasperated laugh. "Well, you'd shielded me from a landslide. It would have seemed kind of bad to leave you there when you—" her voice broke "—you weren't breathing." He saw her try to take a deep breath. "Blue really isn't your color."

His brain was trying to compute. He'd just figured that one of the search and rescue guys or gals had pulled him from the landslide.

She kept talking. "How could I walk away? You tackled me to the ground like you were some kind of superhero. Then you just threw a coat over us and didn't let go all the way down the mountainside."

He wasn't imagining it. A tear was sliding down her cheek.

"Some people are worth holding on to," he said softly.

Amber shook her head. "But we're wrong for each other. You don't believe in me. You second-guess me. You make me feel as if I have to prove myself around you." Her head-shaking got fiercer. "That's not what love is about. That isn't how someone who loves you should make you feel."

He could see it. The pain on her face that had been etched there since he first met her—always just hiding beneath the surface as she slipped on her bravado and her game face.

"Is that how I make you feel, or is that how you already feel, Amber?" he probed gently. "Because I think you're a wonderful doctor. I've seen you in situations that should be completely out of your comfort zone and taking it in your stride. Am I a control freak? Yes. I've lived the past eight years in a place where discipline and control is everything. But where acting first is sometimes the only chance you get. I know that. I recognize that.

"I've had a situation where everything was out of my control and I woke up the next day having lost someone that I loved. How do you think I felt when I saw you put yourself in danger? Did I overreact? Probably, yes. Will I do it in future? Maybe. It doesn't make me a bad person. It makes me know that I feel again. That I love again. Do you think I could bear waiting to see if something might happen to you? I saw that ground start to move, felt the rumble beneath my feet, and there was no way I was letting go of you." He could feel his hands start to shake again. It was almost as if all his emotions were finally coming to the surface.

"Love isn't perfect, Amber. I don't even know if I'm any good at it. I just know I want to try. And I want to try with you. I know we're right at the beginning. I know anything can happen from here. I just want you to give me a chance. I just want to try."

"You love me?" She said the words in disbelief.

"Of course I love you. What's not to love? You fight with me. You tell me I snore. You tease me. You make me work harder. You challenge me at every turn." He gave her a smile. "I don't think I've ever met anyone so perfect for me in my life."

Tears were tumbling down her cheeks. "But…but…"

"But what?"

He fumbled around the edge of the bed until he found

the button that lowered the side. He swung his legs to the edge of the bed and waited a few seconds while his head spun, then yanked the blood-pressure cuff from his arm.

The first step was shaky. The second was determined. Nothing would keep him from being by her side. He reached the edge of her bed.

"Tell me how you feel, Amber. Tell me how you feel about me. I might be completely crazy here." He lifted his hand to the bandage on his head. "Maybe I've got a head injury." Then he took his hand back down to his chest. "Or maybe I'm finally listening to my heart." He reached over and brushed one of the tears away from her cheek. "I've spent the last two years focused on work. Locking myself away from everything and everybody." He held up his hands and smiled. "Here. This place." He laughed and shook his head, ignoring the pain. "We came here expecting a busman's holiday. Expecting the beauty and wonder of Hawaii. Instead we got this. A hurricane. Chaos. A landslide." He moved closer and took one of her hands in his. "I'm glad, Amber. I'm glad. Because something brought us together. And whatever you want to do in the future, wherever you want to be—" he smiled at her "—I'm just praying you'll let me tag along."

He moved his other hand over hers too. "I'm not your father, Amber. I'm not your ex. I'll never be those people. I'm Jack Campbell from a tiny mining village in Scotland. Auchinleck. I'll teach you how to say it. I'll take you there. I can promise I'll introduce you to things you've never seen before." As his mind filled with the thoughts of his village back home and the characters it was filled with, he couldn't help but laugh out loud. "They'll love you. Just like I do."

Amber's tears were flowing; she started to laugh. "I

wanted to shout at you. I've wanted you to wake up so I could tell you how mad I was at you."

He leaned one arm on the side of her bed. "And what exactly were you mad about, Dr. Berkeley?"

It seemed as though all her emotions welled up at once. "I...I was mad because you put yourself at risk to try and save me." She was struggling to get the words out. "I was mad because you were trying to stop me doing something dangerous... I was mad because I was scared to do it...but I didn't want to be. I was mad because I constantly felt as if I had to prove myself to my father. To earn his respect. To earn his approval. To show him I could do it. To show him I was capable. And...I... I..." She stopped talking and sucked in a deep breath. Her tear-filled eyes met his. It was almost as if something had just clicked into place. He could see the glimmer of recognition in her gaze. She squeezed his hand. "And...I don't need to do that with you."

He could see her whole change in stance. Her shoulders went down as if the tension had left her body. "I don't need to do that with you," she repeated in a whisper.

"No." He smiled. "You don't, Amber. I've got your back. I'll always have your back. You specialize in infectious diseases. How much of that have you got to do in the last seven days? Have you complained? Have you said no? Not once. You've put your head down and got on with it. And have you stopped when you were scared? When you put yourself in a situation where you could be electrocuted? When you put yourself in the path of the landslide?" He cupped her cheek. "Who would do that, Amber?" Then he laughed again. "What normal, sane-minded person would do a thing like that?"

She started laughing too. "Jack Campbell, I do believe you may be a bad influence on me."

He fumbled around, looking for her button to lower the bedside. "Where is this dang thing? Ah…finally." He put the side down and moved closer, wincing as his ribs let him know he wasn't quite as healed as he might want to be. He put one hand on his side. "Dr. Berkeley, I believe we may need to talk about your technique."

"Hang the technique." She smiled as she put her hand around his head and pulled him closer. "You're alive, aren't you?"

He moved closer, inches away from her lips. "I believe that might put me in your debt."

She licked her lips. "You bet it does. You don't think I saved the man I love for anyone else, do you?"

Before he could ask her to repeat that, she kissed him. And he had absolutely no intention of stopping that…

EPILOGUE

One year later

EVERYTHING WAS PERFECT. The beach was perfect. The brightly colored flowers in her wedding bouquet were perfect, and the overwater bungalows in the perfect green sea in front of them were perfect—especially when she knew one of them had their names on it.

"Ready?"

Her mother stood in front of her dressed in a bright orange dress, complete with an over-the-top hat on her head. So right for the mother of the bride.

Amber stared down and wiggled her pink-painted toenails in the yellow sand. They were always going to come back to the place they'd met to cement their union. Hawaii had recovered well and returned to the beautiful lush state it had been on the morning she'd first arrived. She ran her hand across her pale cream wedding dress. She'd opted for a three-quarter-length dress, lightweight, with lace across her décolletage and shoulders with cap sleeves. Covered enough for a bride but quirky enough that she could get away with being barefoot. Her only jewelry was her gold locket.

She nodded and breathed slowly. "Oh, yes. I'm ready."

Her mother stepped in front of her and put a hand on

each shoulder. "I always wondered if I'd have to tell my daughter not to make the same mistakes I did. You have no idea how happy I am that I don't need to do it. I love Jack. He's perfect for you. Grumpy sometimes. Doesn't let you get away with anything. But most importantly he adores you, Amber. I see it in his eyes every time he looks at you. Work hard at this marriage, honey. You found a keeper."

Tears threatened to spill down her cheeks. She leaned forward and hugged her mom, almost sending the bright orange hat tumbling down the beach in the light winds. "Thank you, Mom, for everything. You've always been my biggest supporter and I love you."

"Come on, Amber! Are you stalling, girl?"

The broad Scots voice of Jack's dad drifted down the beach. His family were waiting in the shaded area, tugging at the collars of their shirts in the searing heat. They'd been ecstatic to come to Hawaii for the wedding, even though it was a long flight. It was a small wedding with only a few other members of Amber's family, and a few of the residents they'd met in Hawaii. Lana, Jamal and Ron were all waiting patiently for things to start, as were Aaron and Zane—who'd both made a good recovery from meningitis—both with their respective parents.

Amber laughed and turned around, catching her breath at the sight of Jack waiting for her in his kilt. "Oh, wow."

Her mother gave her hand a squeeze. "Yip. Wow. Let's not keep your handsome man waiting. These Scots guys can't seem to manage the heat," she joked.

Amber met Jack's gaze. She'd never been so sure of anything in her life.

He gave her his trademark cheeky grin. His heavy dark kilt was swaying in the breeze from the ocean and his cream open-necked ghillie shirt outlined his muscled chest. As she walked toward him, he held out his hand to her.

She handed her flowers to her mother and he took both her hands in his so they were facing each other.

"You've still got a few seconds," he whispered. "If you want to do the runaway bride, you should do it now."

She smiled at the celebrant who was waiting to start the ceremony as she let go of Jack's hands, slid her hands around his neck and stepped closer.

"Where would I run to? I'm exactly where I want to be, with exactly who I want to be with. Now and always."

The celebrant gave a short laugh. "Hey, folks. Aren't you supposed to wait for me?"

Jack winked. "Just give us a minute. We'll be right with you," he said as he bent to kiss his bride.

And the guests all applauded, even though they weren't quite husband and wife.

And everything was just as it was destined to be.

* * * * *

THE BROODING
SURGEON'S
BABY BOMBSHELL

SUSAN CARLISLE

MILLS & BOON

To Jeanie.

The best sister-in-law I could have ever wished for.

PROLOGUE

THEIR NIGHT OF passion had started so innocently.

Dr. Gabriel Marks had taken the only open seat at the dining table. The petite young woman with the light brown hair and quick wit he remembered from the committee meeting six months earlier sat to one side of him. She smiled and said hello, as did the rest of the committee members.

Their chairperson had organized the dinner for those members flying in that evening. The next day they would all be attending the meeting at the High Hotel at Chicago's O'Hare Airport.

As a transplant surgeon, Gabe was honored to serve on the liver committee of the National Organ Allocation Network. The group met twice yearly to discuss issues involving liver donation and policy. The professionals who made up the committee, as well as family members of patients, came from all over the country and represented different areas of liver transplantation. What they did was important and saved lives.

If he remembered correctly, the woman dining beside him was Zoe somebody, a former registered nurse who now worked for the Liver Alliance, a group that educated people with liver disease and assisted patients needing a liver transplant. The Liver Alliance did good work. He'd had some dealings with the group in the past regarding patients with special considerations, but he'd never met Zoe before joining the committee.

The discussion around the table was lively during their meal and he appreciated Zoe's quick wit and infectious laugh.

The next morning, they had acknowledged each with a warm hello but had sat on opposite sides of the table during the six-hour meeting. When Zoe had spoken up, her remarks had been intelligent, enlightened and spot-on. He'd been impressed.

After the meeting had adjourned he'd headed to the airport to catch his plane home. But his quick check of the flight board revealed his plane had been grounded because of thunderstorms. Gabe was watching the word *Canceled* cascade down the panel when a groan of dismay had him turning around. It was Zoe.

She looked at him, her face screwed up. "Sorry. I hadn't meant to be so loud. This wasn't in my plans."

"It never is," Gabe responded.

"You're right about that." She looked up and down the concourse. "I guess I'm going to spend the night in the airport."

"I bet if we hurry we can get a room in the hotel before everyone figures out what's going on." Gabe turned back the way they had come.

"A room?" Her voice squeaked.

He gave her a pointed look. "I meant a room apiece. Are you always so literal?"

She grinned, walking past him at a fast clip. "I knew what you meant. I just wanted a head start if there was only one left."

He chuckled and hurried to catch up with her. A short time later they had rooms for the night. As they walked toward the elevator Gabe said, "I'm sorry, but I've racked my brain and still can't come up with your last name."

"Avery. Zoe Avery." She chuckled. "That came out sounding a little James Bondish, didn't it?"

He laughed. "Maybe a little bit. Would you like to meet for supper? Unless you have other plans." He rarely had a night free of paperwork and he wasn't going to spend this one by himself. Not when he liked this woman and was fairly confident she'd accept his invitation.

They entered the elevator. "What other plans would I have but to channel surf?" she answered with a grin.

Her mischievous talk appealed to him. As a transplant surgeon at a San Francisco hospital, he didn't have many people in his life who dared to speak to him so freely. He found it refreshing.

The elevator doors opened. As she prepared to exit, he held the doors open. "Meet you at seven in the hotel restaurant?"

"There's not a wife who's going to be mad at me, is there?" Her playful grin belied the serious concern in her eyes. Had a date ever lied to her about being married?

"No wife. How about your husband?"

"No. Not one of those either." There was a sad note in her reply, yet she cheerfully confirmed, "See you at seven, then." She waved as he stepped out.

Gabe took a moment to appreciate the gentle feminine sway of her hips, anticipating the evening to come.

He was waiting at the restaurant entrance when Zoe strolled up. There was a bright smile on her face. "Sorry, I didn't have anything else to wear." She brushed a hand across the front of the simple navy dress she'd been wearing earlier in the day.

"You look great to me." And she did. Something about her pulled at him. He wanted to know her better.

She grinned. "Thanks. You know the right thing to say to a stranded woman."

He chuckled. "If we have to be stuck somewhere, I'm glad it's a place with hot running water."

"I'm surprised you didn't say food."

"Now that you mention it, that's important too. Our table won't be ready for a few minutes. Would you like to wait in the bar?"

"Sure." Zoe walked ahead of him. She was a tiny thing with a powerful personality.

He ordered their drinks and carried them to a small table. They sat and talked about that day's meeting until the waiter came to get them.

Zoe stood, brushing against him as she moved to avoid someone sitting next to them. Gabe's blood heated. He had no doubt her movements had been unintentional, but his body reacted just the same. It had been some time since a woman had gotten to him on so many levels so quickly.

The waiter showed them to a corner table and handed them menus. They discussed what they would order and were ready when the waiter returned.

After he'd left Gabe remarked, "If I remember correctly, you're a patient advocate with the Liver Alliance and live in the Washington, DC, area."

"That's a good memory. I'm impressed. You were paying attention."

Feeling ashamed, he said, "Apparently not when you said your name."

"It's okay. It happens."

"So have you always been with the Liver Alliance?"

"I went to work in an ICU when I was fresh out of

school. I worked a lot with liver patients and really liked it. I decided to go back to school and become a liver transplant coordinator. About a year ago I needed something with regular hours. The Education Chair position came open and it was a perfect fit. Good, stable hours, a tiny office, and I'm still working with the people I love."

Gabe nodded. "And you like living in DC?" He didn't normally quiz his dinner dates, but his curiosity about Zoe was uncharacteristically strong.

"I do. There's always plenty to do. Museums to visit, music festivals and just the excitement of being in the center of our government."

Her enthusiasm for the area was contagious.

She leaned back and looked at him. "And you're from San Francisco. Pretty city."

Obviously, she'd been paying more attention than he had during introductions. "Yep."

"That's a pretty tough commute for these meetings." She ran her finger down the side of her water glass, leaving a trail of condensation.

What would it feel like to have her do that over his chest? He shifted in his chair. They were having dinner. That was all. They didn't really know each other. "I try not to schedule surgery for the day I get back. It makes it easier to deal with the time change." Gabe took a sip of his drink then said, "You seemed pretty upset about not flying out tonight."

"Yeah. My mother has the beginnings of Alzheimer's and I don't like to leave her alone overnight. I'm worried she might not handle being by herself."

"You worked it out?"

"I did. I got a friend to go over and stay with her." Worry flickered in her eyes as she glanced away.

"She's why you needed the job with regular hours.

I understand caring for someone with your mother's illness can be difficult." He was an only child whose mother turned to him often for help and emotional support, but she still possessed her mental faculties. If she didn't and he had to provide her with constant care even while he traveled…?

Zoe looked at him again, brow furrowed. "It is. I hate watching her wasting away. And good care is costly."

"My mother is all I've got. My father died before I was born. I can only imagine how I would feel if she got sick."

Her eyes took on a dark look before she said, "Growing up without a father can be tough. Do you have a stepfather?" Zoe seemed to have changed the subject on purpose.

"Nope. Mom never remarried." He'd often wondered why. She'd always said it was because his father had been the love of her life, but he'd thought there might be more to it. As a kid, he had overheard her tell a friend she felt like she might be doing Gabe a disservice by not marrying. That she worried her decision not to do so had left Gabe with no male role model or father figure.

"She must be a great mom," Zoe commented, bringing him back to the present. "You seemed to have turned out all right."

His mother had been and still was a good mother, but truth be known, his grandmother had been the primary adult during his formative years. His mother had worked full-time to provide for him. "Thanks for saying so. But lately she's been applying pressure to become a grandmother. It gets old."

Zoe's head turned to the side, her look quizzical. "You have no interest in making her one?"

"No. I'm not good family material. My job, my career, doesn't leave me any room for a family. I'm far too busy. More than one girlfriend has accused me of being a workaholic. A wife and children deserve a full-time husband and father. I decided long ago that that drama wasn't for me."

A peculiar expression came over her face, but before he could ask what was wrong, the waiter brought their meals. Zoe started talking about places she had visited and would like to go to and he dismissed her unexplainable expression in favor of her entertaining conversation. When they were done with their meal, Gabe said, "It's still early. Would you like to go to the jazz bar downstairs?"

She hesitated a moment. It really mattered to Gabe that she said yes. She finally quipped, "Why not? It sounds like fun."

Relief washed over him and he smiled. Why was it so important that she go? He placed his hand at her back and guided her out of the restaurant toward the circular stairs. His hand fit perfectly in the hollow of her back. At the club, he asked for a table close to the band.

They had been there a few minutes when Zoe touched his arm. She leaned in close and said into his ear, "I needed this. Thanks for asking me."

He smiled, glad she was having a good time. His body tightened with awareness. It was overreacting, big-time. Or was *he* overly conscious of his body's natural response to an attractive woman he genuinely liked? They were both single and old enough to know their own minds, so why shouldn't they enjoy each other's attention?

Several couples moved to the open area of the floor. On impulse Gabe asked, "Would you like to dance?"

"I'm not very good." She sounded more disappointed than rejecting.

He stood and offered his hand. "You don't have to be. Just follow my lead."

Zoe smiled. One he would remember. "Hey, I can do that."

Gabe held her hand as they stepped out onto the floor. Pulling her into his arms, his hand went to her waist. It was so small his arm almost wrapped all the way around her. The top of her head came to just below his chin. The sweet scent of her filled his head and his body stirred. He resisted the strong urge to pull her tight, but firmly squelched the idea. His arousal would be evident. This was the nicest evening he'd had in a long time and he had no intention of ruining it by scaring her off.

The sultry sound of the saxophone swirled around them.

She looked up, commanding his attention. "I'm impressed. You've a surgeon's touch even on the dance floor, gentle and skilled."

"Thank you, ma'am." He brought her a little closer in spite of his resolve. There were other things he was good at he'd like to show her. He needed to squelch those types of thoughts too. Gabe missed a step.

Her hand squeezed his shoulder when she stumbled. He looked at her, mumbling, "Sorry."

"I'm sure it's your partner," she said.

Searching the depths of her eyes, he muttered, "I assure you it isn't."

"I've not had much opportunity to dance since my prom, years ago."

Her eyes were so green. "You're doing great."

She stared back. They continued to move slowly around the space. It wasn't until there was a mumble going around the room that he forced his attention away from her seductive gaze. The music had stopped. They were the only ones still on the dance floor.

Zoe looked around. Her cheeks were spots of red. "Oops. I guess we got carried away." She focused on him. "It's been a long day and time I head upstairs. It's later in my time zone than it is in yours."

"Okay." Gabe hated to let her go. He held her hand as they returned to the table. She picked up her bag and he left a few bills on the table for their drinks. "I'll see you to your room."

Zoe grasped her bag with both hands. He would have liked to have one of them in his. Somehow it seemed to belong there. What would she do if he kissed her? Would she push him away? Did he dare take a chance? He'd regret it if he didn't.

They entered the elevator and rode up to her floor without a word. The need to touch her, hold her gnawed at him. Tension, thick as a wool blanket in the winter, lay between them. She glanced at him once, her soft, questioning eyes uncertain. He was painfully aware of what he wanted but did she feel the same? The decision must be hers.

At her door, she pulled her keycard from her purse and turned to face him. "Thank you. I really enjoyed this evening. Especially the dancing."

Was she flirting with him? Testing the water?

She gave him a long look as if reaching a decision. With a blink, her hands came to rest on his shoulders as she stood on her toes and kissed him.

That was all the encouragement Gabe needed. He reached out, pulling her against him, his mouth crushing hers, his tongue finding a warm welcome. Her arms wrapped his neck and she hung on during the most passionate kiss he'd ever received. He wanted her. Right now. Based on her actions, she wouldn't deny him.

He steadied her on her feet and growled, "Key."

Zoe put it in his hand, her lips finding his again. He had no problem with that. Backing her against the door and with a minimum amount of fumbling, he managed to get the door opened and them inside.

It closed with a click behind them. Zoe's legs wrapped around his waist. His hands cupped her butt as he stumbled toward the bed, his blood boiling and his body alive with desire for her.

He eased her down onto the mattress, moving over her. Had he ever been this hot for a woman? Supporting himself on his hands, he searched her face. She stared back. He saw the second doubt creep in. Gabe gently kissed her. "I want you. Badly."

Silent for a moment, she whispered, "Make me feel good tonight, Gabe. Forget everything."

"I can do that." His mouth took hers while his hands worked to remove her clothes.

She followed suit with equal frenzy. Her moans of desire combined with the kneading of her fingers on his bare back made him more aroused than he'd ever believed possible. Their mating was blistering, fast and very, very satisfying.

Hours later Gabe rolled over. His hand brushed warm, soft skin. *Zoe.* His body stirred once more. He wanted her again.

"Mmm…" she murmured before her kisses teased his chest.

His hand skimmed the rise of her hip. "Damn, I don't have another condom."

Her hand brushed his length as she murmured, "I'm on the pill."

Unable to go without her any longer, he saw to her pleasure then found his. Having no barrier between them felt so right.

When he woke again, Zoe was dressed and stuffing her belongings into her luggage. "Where're you going?"

"I have to catch my plane." Her back remained to him.

"You've already rescheduled?" He was still in a haze.

"They texted me." She did glance at him then. "I have to go. I need to get home to Mom."

Gabe could see the glass wall rising between them. Unbreakable. All the warmth they had shared last night was now frigid air. Zoe was embarrassed by her behavior. It shouldn't bother him. He wasn't looking for forever, but he didn't like the idea of being something she regretted.

"Zoe—"

"I have to go." She was out the door before he could untangle the sheets from his body.

CHAPTER ONE

ZOE CLUTCHED THE restroom door handle in the conference area of the High Hotel. It had been almost six months since she'd seen Gabe and she was hiding from him. She suspected he was impatiently waiting for her in the hall. Not facing him wasn't a choice she had. Her entire world had changed in that amount of time. Her mother was worse. And Zoe was pregnant.

Guilt hung on her like a heavy necklace of stones she wore all the time. She should have told Gabe. It wouldn't have been that hard to contact him. She'd used him to escape her life for a night and now there was a baby to consider. He'd deserved better on a number of levels. When she'd kissed him at her hotel-room door she hadn't planned on becoming the "drama" he had been adamant about not having in his life.

He knew now. He'd seen her protruding belly when she'd stood. She'd heard his gasp from halfway across the meeting room. There had been no mistaking his shocked expression when she'd glanced back. Would he care if it was his? Did he want to know? Regardless, he deserved to be told he was going to be a father. Even though he'd stated a family wasn't for him.

She paused before pulling the door open. Hopefully Gabe had already returned to the committee room. At first she had thought the stomach rolling had been a virus. After a few weeks she'd had to admit it might be something else. But couldn't believe it. She'd been taking the pill. She'd dragged her feet about buying a pregnancy test because she'd just been unable to wrap her mind around the idea she might be expecting. She'd thought of contacting Gabe the moment she'd seen the test was positive, but had immediately found an excuse not to. Each time she'd convinced herself she had to tell him, she'd come up with a reason not to call him. Too tired, working too late, her mother needed her right that minute, and the list went on. The truth was Gabe had said he wasn't interested in being a father and she felt guilty for her part in involving him.

How would he react when he found out? She'd vowed after each of their committee's monthly conference calls to call and tell him. As time had gone by, she'd decided he deserved to hear the news face-to-face. Their semi-annual in-person meeting was soon and she'd planned to tell him then. What she hadn't counted on was not seeing him the night before. She'd fully expected to have a chance to tell him in private before their committee meeting. Sadly that hadn't happened.

Her fingers flexed on the handle. What if Gabe had found someone special since they had been together? The idea disturbed her more than it should have. Any relationship he might have could be hurt when the woman learned of the baby. Just another reason Zoe shouldn't have put off telling him. She hadn't intended to hurt him. Ever.

Was he mad? Glad? Would he believe it was his? She'd been such a coward.

Her body had hummed with tension all morning as she'd anticipated telling Gabe. More than once she'd had to remind herself to breathe. Had even had to force herself to eat a bite or two of the croissant she'd gotten off the breakfast buffet. Despite being five months along, morning food still didn't always agree with her. Her temperamental tummy was made worse by nerves strung so taut they would hit a high note if plucked.

She had glanced at Gabe several times. His gaze had met hers on a number of those. When it had, ripples of pleasurable awareness had zinged through her. She wasn't sure if it was the flapping of wings in her belly or the baby kicking, but her body had a definite reaction to the sight of him. She was still attracted to him. There had been an uneasiness in his eyes, but a glint of pleasure as well. Had he been glad to see her before she'd stood up, revealing her condition?

Their night together had been memorable. Extremely delightful and erotic. She'd let go like she'd never allowed herself to do before. Her life had been becoming more complicated and she'd just wanted to live a little. Gabe was there, tall, dark and handsome with a Southern drawl, her fantasy come to life…almost.

Her dream man would want to marry and have a family.

Yet despite that one character flaw, she'd wanted Gabe to give her the attention she'd craved. Had been greedy about it. Being with him had made her feel alive, desirable and carefree. She'd taken shameless advantage of their night of passion. The fear it might not come her way again had had her agreeing to things she was normally cautious about.

Not only was Gabe easy on the eyes but intelligent, thoughtful, funny and a great conversationalist. He really listened. She liked him, too much. Now fate had them in its grasp. Like it or not, against all odds, they were having a child together.

Finding the right man had been difficult for her. She refused to settle or compromise. She wanted a man devoted to her, who would feel the same way about their family. More than once her mother had said Zoe was dreaming of someone who didn't exist. Zoe resisted that idea, knowing her mother was jaded from being an abandoned wife and mother. Still, Zoe believed there could be a happily ever after out there for her. She just had to find the right man.

The one time Zoe had thought she had, she'd ended up devastated. While confident their relationship had been progressing toward marriage, she'd caught Shawn having dinner with another woman. When she'd confronted him, he'd announced they didn't want the same things out of life. That no man could live up to her expectations. That Zoe had an unrealistic view of life and relationships. To believe a man could be devoted to just one woman was antiquated.

Other men had implied the same thing. She still vowed not to lower her standards, even when she realized her pledge might mean she'd never have the family she'd dreamed of. Gabe's assertion about not being interested in a wife or family only meant he wasn't any different than the other men she'd been interested in. They'd all been like her father and left when life had turned inconvenient.

She'd fully accepted Gabe was not Mr. Right when she'd let go of her inhibitions that night, confident in her birth control.

Zoe lightly banged her forehead against the bathroom door, her hand aching from the prolonged tight grip on the handle. She just wanted that one man who would love her forever. If that was being too picky, so be it. As her mother's condition gradually deteriorated, it was becoming more difficult to date, even if she had a chance. At least now, with a baby on the way, she had one of the two things she'd always wanted.

With a sudden surge of resolution, Zoe gripped the handle even tighter, her knuckles going white. She had to face Gabe. It was time. She ran her free hand over the rise at her middle, unable to keep the smile from forming despite her anxiety. When she had finally accepted she was pregnant, she'd been filled with joy. The only disappointment was that she didn't have a husband to share her happiness with.

She rolled her shoulders back, forcing them to relax, took a fortifying breath and stepped out into the hallway. As she suspected, Gabe was there. Waiting.

Gabe gasped when Zoe stood. He felt like he'd just been sucker punched in the gut. His throat constricted as his heart recovered and went into high gear, pounding like a drum against his ribs.

Zoe was *pregnant!*

It was obvious beneath her pink dress.

For the past two hours she'd been sitting across from him, so involved in their committee's discussion she hadn't left the table. At least he'd assumed that was why she hadn't stood until the midmorning break.

Gabe clamped his mouth shut and swallowed, trying to slow his thundering heart. Tearing his gaze from Zoe's rounded middle, he glanced wildly about the conference room. *Was it his?*

Numerous times over the last months he'd thought of her. Of their night together. More than once he'd picked up his phone with the intention of calling her, only to put it down, afraid his intrusion into her life wouldn't be welcomed, especially after the way she had left the morning after.

He'd hoped to get to the hotel earlier so he could talk to her but his flight hadn't cooperated. His surgery schedule hadn't either. Instead of coming in the night before, he'd had to take a morning plane.

After he'd gasped, Zoe had glanced back at him before she'd hurried toward the conference-room exit. *Was she running from him again?*

Standing, he'd pushed his chair away with so much force he'd had to catch it before he could make his way around the table. He'd been stopped by one of the other committee members but had ended that conversation in short order.

He'd stalked down the hall toward the restrooms, his best guess for where she'd gone.

It could be someone else's.

His heart did another tap dance. Zoe could have found someone just after they'd been together. He shook his head. His gut told him that wasn't the case. Maybe it was the way he'd caught her uncertain look before she'd headed from the room.

The unending fascination he still felt for her hadn't been part of his plan for a one-night stand, but it was there anyway. Now it appeared that night had had bigger repercussions than the memories that haunted him.

Gabe stationed himself across from the women's restroom. Zoe had to come out sometime.

When the door finally opened, Zoe stepped into the hall and Gabe met her in the middle of it. Despite the large area around them, the space seemed to zoom inward until it was just he and Zoe.

"Is it mine?" His words were low and harsh.

She nodded, before she looked away then back to him.

"You don't have to worry. I can take care of it. I won't make any demands on you."

Gabe's head jerked back in disbelief. "What? Of course I'll help. This is my child too."

"It was an accident. I can take care of us." Her hand brushed her middle. "You don't need to feel obligated in any way. I just wanted you to know about the baby." Her voice grew stronger and she tried to step around him.

He blocked her path. "Yes, I can tell how eager you were to tell me. Must have been damned near impossible for you to keep it a secret all these months." He almost winced at the sarcasm in his voice. "You should have told me. Not blindsided me."

Zoe put a protective hand on her middle. Her eyes turned sad. "I wanted to. Tried. Sorry."

At the sound of footsteps, they both glanced up the hall in the direction of the committee room. It was one of the other members coming their direction.

"Please, let's not make a scene," Zoe begged.

Gabe took her elbow. He was gentle yet firm. "Come. We need to talk." He led her to a small alcove some distance down the hall from the restrooms.

Bile rose in his throat as Zoe stepped as far away from him as the space would allow. Just months ago, she'd been so alive in his arms. He took a deep breath in an effort to regain control, perspective.

"This isn't the time or the place for this." The desperation in her eyes and tone was unmistakable.

He glared at her. "Would you have ever told me if you hadn't had to? Did you really think I wouldn't notice? Did you manage to forget I've seen all of you, knew your body down to the smallest detail?"

Heat filled her cheeks. It was plain she remembered as well as he did, perhaps more clearly.

Gabe watched her closely. "Why didn't you tell me?"

Her hand went over her middle again. "This wasn't supposed to happen. I take full responsibility. I just thought you deserved to be told to your face."

"It seems to me that you could have at least picked up the phone and called."

"I know I should have, but I just kept making excuses. Then I knew I was going to see you here, but you didn't come to the dinner last night…"

The tension in his shoulders eased. She must be under a lot of pressure. Could he believe her? "I got stuck in surgery. Look, you're right. Now isn't the time for us to talk. We're expected back in the meeting. When does your plane leave?"

"Just after the meeting." Zoe glanced at the opening as if anxious to leave.

His voice softened. "You can't change it?"

"No. I have to get home to see about my mother. Just being gone overnight has become a problem. I've got to go." She shifted toward the opening.

"Okay. We'll have to figure something out later. But we *will* talk." He nodded his head toward the opening. "Why don't you go back ahead of me? I'll be along in a minute. I'd rather there be as little talk as possible."

With a curt nod of apparent agreement, she slipped past him and hurried away.

He was going to be a father. Gabe's chest had a funny ache in it. Was it joy? Being a father had never been in his plans. He'd always been so careful. Zoe had changed that.

He'd grown up without a father. That had been the deciding factor in his decision to forgo the family route. Yet now that his plans for his life had just been rewritten permanently, he was determined no child of his would grow up not knowing his father. Zoe could protest that he wasn't obligated all she liked. If she'd thought that feeble opposition would make him walk off as if nothing had ever happened, she'd badly underestimated him.

More annoying still was his body's reaction to her nearness. She'd been standing so close. Her soft floral scent still lingered in his nostrils. That fragrance would forever be hers. Memories washed over him. Zoe soft and willing in his arms. The sweet, lilting moan she'd made as they'd joined. It was a night he'd replayed over and over in his mind. Yet this wasn't the outcome he'd planned. But one he would accept. Deal with.

In the last few minutes his world had altered irreversibly. In a few months he would be a father. Next month he would be in a new job. A very visible one. He needed to look professional, be in control of his life. Gabe took a deep breath, gathered his emotions. Life had just grabbed him by the tail.

Zoe made her way back to the conference room on weak knees. Gabe had been right. They didn't need to return at the same time, especially after one of the committee members had caught them arguing. Had the woman overheard what they'd been talking about? Yet Gabe's sensible suggestion that they enter separately troubled her. Was he ashamed of her?

Maybe it was best. They shouldn't draw attention to themselves, so that they'd have to explain what was going on between them. All she'd planned to do was tell Gabe and now he knew. She didn't expect anything more from him and had made that plain. They would part ways today and that would be it. He'd have his life, his career, on the West Coast and she and the baby theirs on the East.

Except Gabe had said he wanted to talk. Would he be making demands? She had been surprised by the ferocity in his tone when he'd stated he would be in his child's life. Where had that come from? Especially after he'd told her he wasn't interested in a family. It must have been the shock of learning he was going to be a father. That was all it was.

She had just settled her shaking body in the chair when the moderator called the meeting back to order. Gabe slipped into his chair a minute later with an apologetic nod in the chairperson's direction. Zoe refused to meet his look, the one she felt on her. The rest of the day would be long. Picking up her pen, she doodled on a page of her agenda to keep herself from glancing at him. The few times she dared to look, his thoughtful light blue gaze was fixed on her. She still found him attractive.

At their lunch break, Gabe started her way but was stopped by someone asking him a question. That gave her the chance to grab her meal and hurry back to her place, avoiding interacting with him again.

By midafternoon the meeting was ending. Zoe hadn't heard much of it. She had been busy berating herself for failing to think through the consequences of not telling Gabe sooner.

"Dr. Marks," the chairperson said, and the room erupted in clapping.

Zoe's head jerked up. What had just been said? She gave a half-hearted pat of her hands as she watched Gabe. He smiled, nodding, as he looked around the room.

His gaze met hers briefly before he said, "Thank you. I look forward to becoming the head of transplants at National Hospital."

The earlier fluttering in her stomach took off like a

covey of quail. Gabe would be moving to the East Coast. To the same area as her!

She stared at him in disbelief.

He shrugged.

The rest of the people in the room stood and gathered their belongings. Zoe didn't move. She'd believed Gabe would be three thousand miles away when he'd talked about being involved with their child. Now he would just be down the road. He might want to see the baby not only during the summer, while taking a few weeks of annual vacation, but regularly. He could even want part-time custody. This situation was spinning out of her control.

By the time she pulled her thoughts together, the room was practically empty. Gabe was still being congratulated by a couple of people when she was ready to go. In a stupor of shock, she snatched up her purse and grabbed the suitcase handle, hurrying out, unable to think clearly. Gabe had upended her envisioned future as a happy single parent.

"Zoe."

She looked over her shoulder to see him striding toward her, and walked faster.

"Wait up," he called.

"I need to catch my plane." She had too much to process. Needed time to think.

Gabe pulled level with her. "But we need to talk."

"If you wanted to talk so badly, why didn't you tell me you had accepted a job that had you moving for all intents and purposes into my backyard?"

His mouth gaped in shock as he grabbed her arm, forcing her to stop.

"Maybe because I was too busy trying to recover from the bomb you dropped on me."

He did have her there. She inhaled and said on the exhalation, "I think we both need some time to consider what we need to do." His touch made her tremble, triggering memories of his hands all over her that night. How was she supposed to think?

"I already know what I want," he snapped. "I intend to be as much a part of my child's life as possible."

"Does it matter what I want?" Zoe jerked free, took hold of her luggage handle again and started out of the hotel attached to the airport by a tunnel that led under the street.

Gabe matched her stride. "You didn't think I'd want to know my child, did you?"

"I thought you deserved to know he or she existed, but I never imagined you'd want to be involved as closely as you're talking about." She kept increasing her pace, lugging her bag behind her. "You made it perfectly clear you weren't family material before we went to bed together."

"Oho, so that's it. You didn't think I'd care about being a father. It so happens that now that I am one I intend to be one. You have a problem with that?"

"I don't know. I might if you keep applying this much pressure all the time," she hissed.

"If I keep... You've had months to adjust to having a child. I only just learned I'm going to be a father." His frustration was loud and clear.

Guilt assaulted her. "I'm sorry about that. It wasn't fair, but you can't expect me to make a life-changing decision for my child while I'm on the way to the airport."

They continued through the tunnel into the terminal. Gabe remained beside her, larger than life. Why couldn't he give her some space? She was already tied in emotional knots. She needed to get away, get home and regroup.

Zoe had other things to consider besides Gabe's newly found parental outrage. Her friend had just sent a text to say that her mom was anxious, constantly searching the apartment and asking for Zoe.

Her thoughts were too scattered. She needed to consider carefully everything she said or agreed to. What happened would affect her and her child forever. "Gabe, I'm not talking about this right now. You're moving across the country and you need time to get settled into your new job before you agree to shoulder the responsibilities of fatherhood. Responsibilities you need to carefully weigh first. Meanwhile, I need time to handle other issues in my life."

"Is there someone else involved here?" His question was a demand. "Are you involved with someone?"

"No, nothing like that." She glanced at Gabe in time to see him visibly relax. What did it matter to him if she had a boyfriend—or a lover, for that matter?

He touched her elbow to steady her when she rocked back as they headed up the escalators to the security area. Heat zipped through her. "You need to hold the handrail."

"I'm perfectly capable of taking care of myself. Pregnancy doesn't make me feeble-minded." She'd covered her reaction to him with feistiness she didn't completely feel as she pulled her arm from his hand.

"Neither does it mean you shouldn't be careful or unwilling to accept help."

Zoe's look met his. Gabe's didn't waver. He appeared sincerely concerned. She had to admit it was nice to have someone care about her welfare. So much of her life revolved around helping others, her patients and her mother. Being worried over was a pleasant change. They stepped off the escalator and continued down the concourse. "I promise I'll be careful."

She looked ahead. A young woman with a baby strapped to her chest was pushing a rented luggage cart piled high with bags. Standing on the front, holding on, was a boy of about four. Seconds before they passed Zoe, the cart wobbled and the boy fell backward onto the unforgiving floor with a sickening thud. The mother screamed as blood flowed.

Even as the accident registered in Zoe's mind, Gabe was down on one knee beside the child. The boy's screeching echoed off the high glass ceiling as the mother pushed Gabe's shoulder in her effort to reach the boy.

He half turned, catching hold of her as he said in a level, calm manner, "Ma'am, I'm a doctor. Don't move him. You could make it worse. What's his name?"

"Bobby. Bobby's his name," the woman said between crying huffs.

"Bobby, hush. I'm Dr. Gabe. I'm going to help you." Gabe continued to speak softly and reassuringly to the boy.

Zoe noticed a diaper bag sitting on top of the woman's luggage pile. Grabbing it, she opened it and searched until she found a diaper. Laying it as flat as possible on the floor, she carefully slipped it beneath the boy's head, then held his head steady to stop him from squirming.

Gabe nodded to her then said, "Bobby, I need to see if you're hurt anywhere else. Your mom's right here. She can hold your hand, but you must be still."

The boy's crying quieted, although tears continued to roll down his face.

A crowd circled them yet Gabe's full attention remained focused on the child.

The mother moved to the opposite side of the boy, going down on her knees beside Zoe. Taking his small hand, she said, "I'm here, honey." The baby on her chest started to cry and she patted her on the bottom. "Don't cry, Bobby. You're making me and Susie cry too."

The boy gave her a sad smile. His chest shuddered as he struggled to stop sobbing. The mother's eyes were wild with fear as she stared expectantly at Gabe.

"Bobby, do you have a dog?" he asked, reaching for and pulling his suitcase to him.

"Uh-huh." The boy grew quiet and watched Gabe.

Nimbly, Gabe unzipped a side pocket and removed a stethoscope. "What's his name?"

"Marty."

"Marty—that's a good name for a dog. Did you give it to him?"

Zoe shifted closer to the mother. Placing her fingers on the pulse of the boy's wrist, Zoe checked his heart rate.

"One-ten," she told Gabe. Thankfully it wasn't very high.

Zoe looked up to see a security guard hurrying in their direction. When he arrived she said, "I'm a nurse and he's a doctor." She nodded in the direction of Gabe. "Call 911. This boy needs to be seen at a hospital."

Thankfully the man didn't waste time arguing and spoke into his radio.

Meanwhile Bobby was saying, "No, my mom did. I wanted to name him Purple."

Gabe grinned. "Purple. That's an interesting name. Is he a purple dog?" While he spoke to the boy in a low tone, Gabe listened to his heart, checking his pulse and looking into his eyes.

"There's no such thing as a purple dog," the boy stated. "It's my favorite color."

Gabe chuckled and patted Bobby on the shoulder. "I'm sure you'll be playing with Marty soon." He spoke to the mother. "I think he'll be fine, but he may have a concussion and need to stay in the hospital overnight for observation."

Blinking, she swiped away the wetness on one cheek.

"I'll see that you're taken care of. Don't worry," Gabe assured her.

Seconds later the emergency medical techs arrived. They relieved Zoe and she stood. Her hands were a mess and one of the techs handed her a wet towel to clean them.

Gabe had been tender with Bobby, even able to distract him, which was a talent in itself. He showed promise at being a good father. Caring concern was every bit as evident in his interaction with the boy and mother as it had been during the night they had shared. Maybe it wouldn't be so hard to accept him as part of her and the baby's life. If he was truly serious about it. Her fear was that when reality set in he might change his mind. Right now, he was just being noble.

Gabe was busy giving the EMTs a report about what had happened when Zoe found her bag and headed to the nearest restroom to wash her hands. When she came out, Gabe stood nearby.

She checked her watch and shook her head. "I have to go. It's almost time for my plane. I have to get home."

He didn't look pleased with her putting him off once again. "I'll be in touch."

"Okay." She pulled a card from her purse and handed it to him. "My phone number is on it. 'Bye, Gabe."

CHAPTER TWO

TWO DAYS LATER Gabe was on his way out of surgery when his phone rang. "Hey, Mom."

"Hey yourself. I've not heard from you in weeks." His mother sounded eager to talk.

"I've been busy."

"Too busy to check in with your mother?" Her tone held a teasing note but there was also some scolding as well.

"I've been trying to wrap up things here. Planning a move at the same time has kept me tied up." Along with finding out he would soon be a father...

"I'm so proud of you and pleased you'll be moving closer. I don't see enough of you."

With his schedule, he couldn't promise it would be much different, but he did need to tell her about the baby. At least that would make her happy. "Mom, I'm glad you called. I've got some news."

"I hope it's good?"

"It is. I'm going to be a father." Even though he'd had a couple of days to adjust to the idea, the words still sounded strange.

"You are! I didn't even know you were seeing anyone!"

Gabe chuckled. His mother was as excited to hear the

news as he had expected she would be. "I'm not really." He didn't want to get into it.

"Okay… Well, when is she due?"

"Sometime after the first of the year."

His mother shot back, "You don't know the exact date? Is it a boy or a girl?"

He really didn't know much. He and Zoe were going to have to really talk. Today. "I'll have to ask Zoe."

"I'm guessing she's the mother?" Curiosity filled her voice.

"Yes, her name is Zoe Avery."

"Where did you meet her?"

"At a professional meeting." He wasn't surprised his mother was full of questions.

"Gabe, I'm guessing this wasn't planned?" It sounded more like a question than a statement.

"It wasn't, but we're working all that out." His pager went off. He was needed in ICU. "Mom, I've got to go. I'll call you soon. I promise."

"Okay. I love you, son."

His mother might not have been around much, but he *had* known he was loved. His child would at least know Gabe cared, even if he couldn't be there for him all the time. He'd learned early from his mother that sacrifices were necessary to survive and succeed in a profession. That focus was important to get what you wanted. For him, that was to build a renowned liver-transplant program.

He checked on his patient in ICU the nurse had paged him about and increased the dosage of pain medicine, before giving instructions to his physician's assistant to notify him if there were additional issues. Then he headed to his office for some privacy. It was time he and Zoe had that overdue conversation. He just hoped she wouldn't try to evade it. They needed to discuss things whether she liked it or not.

She answered on the second ring.

"Zoe. It's Gabe. Please don't hang up."

"I wasn't going to." The soft voice that he'd know anywhere as Zoe's sounded distracted.

"Uh… How're you doing?" He felt like a teen calling a girl for the first time. It mattered too much.

"I'm fine."

His chest tightened. She didn't sound like it. "Are you feeling okay?"

"I'm fine and so is the baby."

He was relieved to hear that. It amazed him how quickly she and his unborn child had become so important to him. "Uh, what's the baby's due date?" He'd been so shocked to learn she was pregnant he'd not thought to ask earlier.

"January twenty-second."

"My father was born in January." He shook his head. That was an odd statement. He'd not thought of that in a long time. "Do you know what it is yet?"

"No. I'll find out soon."

"You'll let me know as soon as you do?" Why should he want to hear so badly? How much time would he spend being a father anyway? More than Zoe apparently thought he should. Fatherhood wasn't what he'd planned for his life but now he had to adjust and adapt. He was determined to be the best father he could be.

"I will if you want me to."

He would like to tell his mother the sex. She would be so excited. Would start buying clothes. "Zoe, how did this happen?"

She tittered. "Why, Doctor, I thought you, of all people, understood the birds and the bees."

The Zoe with a sense of humor had returned. This was ground he was comfortable on. He huffed. "I don't mean the physical process. I thought you had things handled."

"I thought so too. I guess the pill failed." She sighed. "Or maybe the condom was bad. I don't know. I just know I'm pregnant. I'm sorry, Gabe. I realize this isn't what you wanted."

It wasn't, but he could tell by her tone that she hadn't planned it either. "Maybe not, but I'll deal with it. Meet my responsibilities."

"This baby needn't ruin your life. I have things handled. I can raise it. I want to. There's no reason for you to change your lifestyle because of us. I know this wasn't in your life plan."

"You're not going to handle this alone. I'm here to help. I should help."

In the background, a woman called Zoe's name. Was that her mother?

"I'll be right there, Mom," Zoe said in an exasperated tone.

"Is everything okay?"

"Yes. And no." Zoe sounded bone weary. "Mom's Alzheimer's has really progressed. She's more confused these days. More demanding."

The faint sounds of Zoe's name being shouted again reached Gabe's ear.

"Sorry but I've got to go," Zoe said. "'Bye."

The click of them being disconnected was the last he heard.

The next day between surgeries he couldn't stop himself from texting her.

Is there a good time for me to call?

A few minutes later he received her reply.

Tonight. No later than ten-thirty my time. I have an early meeting in the morning.

Gabe typed back.

Will call at ten.

He needed to discuss his trip to her part of the world the next weekend. He would be looking for a house and wanted her to set aside some time to see him and discuss the baby's future.

His phone buzzed. He was needed in the emergency department. There had been a car accident. It turned out that his patient was a teenage girl who required surgery right away.

Hours later, Gabe left the operating room and checked his phone. He groaned. It was already after ten-thirty. Remorse filled him. He'd promised Zoe he would call her earlier. This was just another example of why he shouldn't have a family. He was so focused on his job. A wife and children deserved better than leftovers and afterthoughts. He would soon be a father. Where was he going to find the time? He had to show Zoe how serious he was about being a parent.

His child. Somehow that sounded weird and right at the same time.

Regardless of the time, he needed to talk to Zoe, even if just to make plans for the weekend.

She answered on the first ring. "Hello." The word was said quietly as if he had woken her.

He remembered her voice sounding like that the night they had spent together. "It's Gabe."

"I know."

Was that because of caller ID or because she recognized his voice? He hoped the latter. Now that he was actually speaking to her, he was a little unsure. "I'm sorry I'm late calling. I didn't think you'd be asleep yet. There was an emergency and time got away from me. How're you doing?" he finally asked.

"Fair, all things considered."

"Has something happened to the baby?" Gabe's middle clinched at the thought. He was surprised at how quickly his mind had gone that direction.

"No. The baby is fine. The doctor said today it measures just right. Heartbeat is strong."

An odd feeling washed over him. He was relieved to hear it. "Was everything all right with your mom after last night?"

"Yeah, she was just confused. She gets more anxious and demanding these days. She's asleep now."

"That must be stressful." He couldn't imagine what he'd do with his job demands if his mother required his attention like Zoe's did.

"I don't wish this disease on anyone."

Gabe had heard Alzheimer's was difficult to deal with, but this was the first time he'd known someone facing it daily. "Do you have any help?"

"Not really. My sister lives about four hours away and travels for work, so she can't come often." There was a pause, and then she asked, "Do you happen to know how the boy from Chicago is doing? His mother was beside herself."

"She was, but she was much better after she knew Bobby was going to be all right and they had a place to stay for the night. I spoke to her the other day and Bobby is doing just great."

"You called her?"

Gabe grinned. "Don't sound so surprised. I did. I like to keep track of my patients. She said if it weren't for the stitches in his head she wouldn't even know anything had happened."

"Good. I'm glad to hear it. You were good with him. Both as a doctor and a person."

"Thanks. I like to see that my patients get complete care. You weren't half-bad yourself. Using the diaper to stop the blood flow was quick thinking."

"It's my turn to say thanks."

The self-assured Zoe had returned. Smiling to himself, he got down to business. "I wanted to let you know I'll be in town this weekend, looking for a place to live. I'd like to see you. Discuss things without being interrupted."

"Look, Gabe, I appreciate what you're trying to do, really I do. But you don't need to feel obligated. I'm fine. I can take care of the baby."

His blood ran hot. Why did she keep pushing him away when he was offering to help? Did she expect he'd be satisfied with a phone call here and there and a few school pictures? It was time to make himself clear. "Zoe, I have every intention of being an active parent in my child's life. You're not going to push me out of it. I'll gladly handle my share of the expenses. I not only want to be involved, I *will* be involved. Let's try to keep this between us and not drag others into the situation."

Silence lay heavy between them.

She must have gotten his less-than-subtle hint about hiring a lawyer. He didn't want to go there but he would if he had to. Growing up without a father hadn't been fun. At baseball games there hadn't been a man in the stands cheering him on or coaching on the sidelines.

When he'd liked his first girl and she had wanted nothing to do with him, there had been no man to listen and offer advice based on experience. His mother had tried but it just hadn't been the same. Those memories only made him all the more determined to be a present father to his child. It was his child, his responsibility.

After his and Zoe's night together, he'd like to believe they had parted friends, albeit uncomfortable ones, but civil nonetheless. He wanted to build on that. He had no interest in angering Zoe, so he volunteered in a conciliatory tone, "I'll be looking at houses most of the day on Saturday, so how about having dinner with me that evening?"

"I can't. I don't have anyone to watch Mother."

"Then I'll pick up something and bring it to your place. I'd really like for us to talk about this." He wasn't letting Zoe run from him forever. He saw another call was coming in. He'd have to get it. "The floor is paging me. I'll be in touch on Saturday."

By Wednesday, Zoe had red-rimmed eyes, a runny nose and was sneezing.

"Of all the times to get a head cold," she murmured as she headed down the hall of one of the local hospitals to see a patient. She already had her hands full with life and her job, and to feel awful was almost more than she could take. Since Gabe's call, she was still trying to sort out her thoughts and feelings.

The reality of him moving to the area, of seeing him on a regular basis was slowly seeping in. Against her better judgment she looked forward to seeing him again. That was a road she needed to close but how could she when their lives were becoming more intertwined, both personally and professionally? Her life was changing so fast she was racing to catch up. What more could happen?

She sanitized her hands using the liquid in the container by the patient's door and pulled out a mask from the box on the shelf nearby. Mr. Luther was her most difficult patient but one her heart went out to. Why, she didn't know. He didn't make it easy. It could be Mr. Luther was the father figure she was missing in her life or that he just didn't have anyone else. He reminded her of a bad-tempered grandfather who hid his huge soft spot well. For some reason she was the one person he would listen to. Maybe he sensed she liked him despite his rough outer shell. Regardless, she was determined to do whatever she could to help him.

Knocking on the hospital door, she waited until she heard the gruff "Yeah."

She took a deep breath to fortify herself for what was coming. Pushing the door open, Zoe entered the dark room where the TV was blaring. The sixty-four-year-old man who sat in a chair beside the bed didn't even look her way as she entered.

He'd been in and out of the hospital for months with advancing inflammation of the liver caused by hepatitis C. Because of it he had a yellow tint to his skin and eyes and ongoing nausea and fatigue. It didn't look like he would have any improvement without a transplant. She hoped that Gabe might help her there. When the time was right she'd ask him. With any luck, Mr. Luther would be transferred to Gabe's care at National Hospital and listed for a transplant.

"Hello, Mr. Luther. How're you doing this morning?"

"You know as well as I do how I'm doing."

She might but she wouldn't let him get away with ignoring her. "Do you mind if we turn the TV down?"

"I do but I guess you'll do it anyway."

Zoe grinned as she found the remote and lowered the volume. She'd learned long ago that his bark was worse than his bite. "I need to give you a listen and have you sign a couple of forms so I have permission to look at your chart."

"The others here have already listened to me today."

"You know how this works by now. I have to do my own listening and looking at lab results if I'm going to help you get better. I'm your advocate. I don't work for the hospital. I work for you. I'm here to help you."

"Aw, go ahead. You will anyway."

Zoe stepped to him. Pulling her stethoscope out of her pocket and placing the ends in her ears, she proceeded to listen to his heart. It sounded steady and strong, which pleased her. She then listened to his lungs and checked his pulse rate. Removing her small penlight from her lab coat pocket, she said, "I need to look in your eyes."

"I was afraid of that." Mr. Luther lifted his face to her.

She pointed the light in his eyes. What she found there she wasn't as happy with. The whites still weren't clear.

"Well? Will I be getting out of here soon?"

"That's not for me to say. Your doctor here makes those decisions. But I will be in touch. If I don't see you here next week, I'll be calling you at home to check on you." She didn't have to keep such close tabs on him, but as far as she knew, there was no one else to do it. Zoe placed her hand on his shoulder. "Please do what they say, Mr. Luther."

He grunted. "Always do."

She looked back at him as she went out the door. He was going to need a liver transplant much sooner than the doctors had originally estimated.

As she traveled to different hospitals to check on other patients and completed paperwork in her office over the next few days, she continued to search for reasons not to see Gabe while he was in town. The longer she could put him off, the better. Dealing with him was the last thing she needed at this point in her emotionally and physically overloaded life.

Preparing for her baby's birth, dealing with her mother's rapidly deteriorating condition and now the urgent need to get Mr. Luther on the fast track for a liver transplant... If only Gabe would stop pressuring her to make decisions about her baby's future, decisions that could wait until closer to the due date. If Gabe sincerely wanted to help her, maybe she could convince him to give her those precious three months before her baby was born to deal with her other problems by priority. Would he understand her genuine need for time and distance? Or would he be self-centered, accusing her of trying to push him out of the baby's life?

On Saturday afternoon, her mother had gone to her room for a nap and Zoe was trying to get some much-needed rest on the sofa. The cold was taking its toll on her. She'd just closed her eyes when the phone rang. Anticipation zinged through her. Would it be Gabe?

"Hey," he said when she answered, not giving his name. It wasn't necessary. Zoe would have known his voice anywhere. "Have you changed your mind about going out to dinner?"

"No." Even to her own ears she didn't sound welcoming, yet blood whipped through her veins at the mere fact she was speaking to Gabe.

"You sound awful. What's wrong?"

"I woke with a cold the other morning."

"Are you taking care of it? Getting enough rest?" His concern somehow made her feel better. She liked knowing Gabe cared about her, even if it was just because of the baby.

"Yes. I'm just tired."

"Then I'll pick up dinner. Bring it to you. What's your address?"

She gave it to him.

"I'll see you in about an hour and a half. 'Bye."

Knowing she was about to see Gabe again caused her stomach to flutter. Despite feeling bad, she still rushed around, putting her apartment in order in anticipation of his visit. Her life was already a tightrope and Gabe was tying complicated knots in it as well. With one more tiny twist she might snap.

Zoe finally settled on the sofa to wait for him. She hadn't missed his poorly veiled threat about getting a lawyer involved if she didn't talk to him. The nervous waves in her stomach crashed harder, despite him brushing off his threat with a dinner offer. He'd made it plain he didn't want a wife and children the night they had been together. His declaration of lifelong bachelorhood over five months ago contradicted his current insistence on being involved with their child. How long would his sense of obligation last? Until "his" child started making demands on his time? Would he still be sharing parental duties when they started to interfere with his career? Maybe he didn't mind being a father as much as he hated the thought of being a husband. If that was the case, she was left with the conclusion he would never marry her.

That hurt. It shouldn't, but it did.

She had no doubt Gabe wouldn't consider marriage as a practical solution to their situation. In the unlikely event he did, she would say no. Being wanted because she was the mother of his child wasn't good enough. When she married it would be for love. Her hand went to her middle. Right now, her focus would be on the baby. She wasn't going to let Gabe continue making immediate demands that would needlessly confuse her life further.

The door buzzer woke Zoe. Panic filled her. She'd had every intention of having time to apply some makeup and fix her hair before Gabe arrived. She stopped in front of a mirror on the way to the door and pushed at her hair, creating some order, before she checked the peephole, getting a distorted view of Gabe. Even then he looked amazing. Why couldn't he be everything she *didn't* want in a man?

Zoe unlocked and opened the door. Gabe had two large white bags in his hands and one small brown one. She'd never seen him casually dressed. The white-collared shirt he wore rolled up his forearms set off his dark hair and California tan. Jeans hugged his slim hips and loafers covered his feet. He could be a model for a men's cologne ad. He took her breath away.

For seconds, they just looked at each other. He broke the silence. "May I come in?"

"Yes." Zoe pushed the door wider.

Gabe entered, looked around, then headed toward the kitchen table, where he set the bags down. "You sit down and rest. I'll get things on the table. Just tell me where they are."

Zoe closed the door and followed more slowly. Her apartment went from small to tiny with Gabe in it. She needed to get a grip on her attraction to him or she would lose control of the situation.

Her mother joined them, looking from Gabe and back to her, perplexed.

Zoe put a reassuring hand on her mother's arm. "Mom, I want you to meet a friend of mine, Gabe Marks."

"Friend" might be stretching their actual relationship, but she didn't want to explain more.

Gabe came around the table with a smile on his face. "Mrs. Avery, it's a pleasure to meet you."

Her mother smiled. "Hello."

"I brought you some dinner. I hope you're hungry." He pulled a chair out from under the table and held it for her.

"Thank you. I am." Her smile broadened as she sat.

Zoe sank into a chair.

Gabe returned to the bags, continuing to remove cartons. "Zoe, I hate it, but I forgot drinks."

How like him to take control and look comfortable doing it. "I have iced tea made."

"Sounds great." He looked at her mother and smiled. "That work for you too, Mrs. Avery?"

Her mother grinned, an endearing expression Zoe hadn't seen in some time, and nodded to Gabe. The devil was charming her mother out of her fog.

Zoe stood.

"I said I'd get things." He waved her down and headed into the kitchen. "Just tell me where they are. Plates? Silverware?"

"I don't feel that bad." Zoe joined him. Gabe took her by the arm and gently led her back to her chair.

Her body trembled at his touch. She sat, forcing him to release her. If he had noticed her hypersensitive reaction to him, he didn't show it, much to her relief. She had to somehow smother her physical desire for him. She couldn't spend the rest of her life fighting it and hiding it from him.

"You may not feel very bad at the moment, but you

don't need to exert yourself any more than absolutely necessary. You don't want to get worse." His tone said he'd accept no argument.

Zoe huffed then gave him directions to which cabinet and drawer he needed. He soon had the table set and was heading into the kitchen again.

"Glasses?"

"Cabinet next to the refrigerator."

After the chinking of ice dropping into glasses, Gabe brought two drinks to the table and returned to get the other. He took the seat at the head of the table. For some reason that held significance. As if he was taking on more importance in her life than she wanted.

"Who are you?" her mother asked. In a different situation Zoe might have thought it was funny. Her mother might be as overwhelmed by Gabe as Zoe was, but in this instance she was afraid her mother just didn't remember.

Gabe answered before Zoe had a chance to. "I'm Gabe."

"Oh, yeah, that's right."

He didn't miss a beat and started opening containers. "Would you like a piece of fried chicken, Mrs. Avery?"

"Yes, that would be nice."

Gabe picked up her plate and placed a piece on it. "How about potatoes, green beans and a roll?"

"Please."

Gabe finished serving her plate and put it in front of her. "Mrs. Avery, did Zoe tell you that I'm moving to the area?"

She looked at Zoe. "No, she didn't. You'll like it here. Henry and I moved here when we were newlyweds."

"So you've lived around here for a long time," Gabe said as he scooped food onto another plate.

Zoe watched her mother become dreamy-eyed as memories surfaced. "We had the best time together."

That was until Zoe's father had left and never returned. In her mother's illness she only remembered the good times, but Zoe clearly recalled the hurt and devastation her father had left behind. She never wanted to live through that again.

"I'm sure you did." Gabe smiled at her then opened the brown bag. He looked at Zoe. "I forgot. I made a special stop for you." He pulled out a plastic container of liquid. "Chicken soup. Let me get you a bowl and spoon." Before she could say anything, he was on his way back to the kitchen. When he returned, he poured the soup in the bowl and placed it and the spoon in front of her.

He'd made a stop just for her? When had someone last made her feel so special? The soup smelled heavenly. She met Gabe's expectant expression. "Thanks. This hits the spot."

"Who're you?" her mother asked.

Zoe couldn't help but chuckle this time. She was asking herself the same thing. Was there another man like him? If there was, she'd never met him.

"I'm Gabe."

"That's right. Did you know that Zoe's having a baby?" She looked at Zoe.

Gabe looked at her as well. "Yes, ma'am, I see that."

"She'll be a good mother. She's a nurse, you know." Her mother's attention returned to her food.

"I do know." He continued to watch Zoe. "I also think she'll be a good mother."

"Are you Zoe's boyfriend?"

"Mom!"

Gabe's eyes questioned her as if asking permission to answer. Was he wondering how much her mother knew? It was time to come clean. "Mom, Gabe is the baby's father."

Her mother studied him closely. "You will get married." That wasn't a question but a statement.

Embarrassment flooded Zoe. She couldn't even look at Gabe. "Mom! You can't go around telling men to marry me."

Her mother ignored her and went back to eating. "This is good," she said, not missing a beat. As if she hadn't created a cloud of tension in the room.

It took a few minutes for Zoe to find the courage to even glance at Gabe. He seemed to have taken the exchange in his stride.

After their meal Zoe settled her mother in her room to watch TV and returned to find Gabe had cleaned up the table. "I'm sorry about that. I don't expect you to marry me. I've never thought you should."

"Don't worry about it," he said in an even tone. "I put some coffee on. I hope you don't mind. It's been a long day." He hung the washcloth up.

"I'm not surprised. You pretty much came in and made yourself at home." She hadn't meant to sound irritated, even though she was…a little.

A shocked look came over his face. "I'm sorry. That wasn't my intent. I hadn't eaten since early this morning, having looked at houses all day. Plus, I knew you didn't feel well and I guess I just got carried away."

Was she being too sensitive? He had her so out of sorts she'd not even thought about him, his needs. This situation couldn't be any easier on him than it was on her. If she met him halfway then maybe it would be better. She could at least try. "Why don't you go have a seat in the living room and I'll bring you a cup of coffee. How do you like it?"

"Black is fine."

With coffee in hand, she found Gabe sitting on the sofa, legs stretched out with his head back and his eyes closed. Was he asleep? Why did it seem so natural to have him in her home?

He quickly straightened when she set the mug on the table closest to him. He ran his hands through his wavy hair. "Thanks. I'd rather do two transplants back-to-back than look at houses all day."

She settled in the chair facing him.

Gabe took a sip of his coffee.

"Did you find a place?" Was it nearby? Could she handle him being so close?

"I did. It's out in Vernon Landing."

Zoe breathed a sigh of relief. It wasn't as local as she'd feared. The traffic alone would make him think twice before he just showed up. She wouldn't allow that anyway. He was right—they needed to talk. They needed to at least agree on visitation guidelines before the baby was born.

"I'm glad you found something." She couldn't help but ask, "When will you be moving in?"

"Two weeks."

Her heart did a thump-bump. "That soon."

"Yeah. I'm to start my new position on the first of the month."

Zoe had hoped for more time to adjust to the idea of him living nearby.

"I know this is going to be an adjustment," he remarked as though he could read her mind. "Neither one of us planned how things have turned out."

That was an understatement if Zoe had ever heard one. Her hand went to her belly.

"Zoe."

She looked at him.

"I have no intention of taking the baby away from you. All I want is to be in his life. See him or her occasionally. Do my share financially."

That declaration did make her feel better. He sounded sincere, not threatening. Having him help financially would be nice, especially since her mother was going to require ever more costly care as time went on. However, she wouldn't let Gabe think for a moment he could do as he pleased where the baby was concerned. "You know, you can't just show up here unannounced."

He put his mug down, placing his arms on his knees with hands clasped between them, and leaned toward her. "I would never do that."

"We're going to have to set rules and guidelines. I'll be raising him or her." How matter-of-fact she sounded pleased her. *She* was in control of this discussion.

"Agreed. But big decisions like schools, medical care, moving out of town should be discussed with me." Gabe's dark expression warned of his unwillingness to negotiate.

"Moving?" That he had given the future that much thought startled her. She was going to have to make a change of living space soon.

His expression didn't waver. "I won't allow you to take him or her to the other side of the country to where it makes it hard to be a part of their life."

She appreciated his rights as a father, but she wasn't going to build her world around his wants. She started to say as much but he cut her off. "When I get settled, why don't I get a lawyer to draw up an agreement? That way we'll both know where we stand. You can make a list and I will too. Then we can compare and come to a satisfactory compromise."

Zoe considered his suggestion with care. She had intended to tell him his role in their child's life wasn't to dictate how she would raise her child, but doing so would result in arguing about it. "All right. I can do that."

Gabe stood. "Then I'd better go. I have a bit of a drive to the hotel."

Zoe rose too and followed him to the door. "Uh, Gabe, before you go, could I ask you about something?"

He looked at her. "Sure."

"I hate to ask you this before you even started your new job, but I have a patient, Mr. Luther. He's medically fragile and his liver is failing. He could really use your expertise. He can be a difficult patient but he's getting sicker and sicker..." She'd had other patients sicker than Mr. Luther, so why was she so concerned about him? He would end up being like the other men in her life and just pass through—but she still wanted the best for him.

"Email me his file and I'll have a look."

"Thank you." Why did she believe Gabe would make it all right? It would be so easy to lean on him in her professional life as well as her personal one. But could she count on him always being there?

His gaze met hers, held. Heat built in her. That same effect he'd had on her during their night together was there, curling around her, tugging her closer to him. Gabe's hand gently brushed a thread of hair away from her cheek. "You're welcome. I should go. Take care of yourself. Please tell your mother I said 'bye. See you soon."

That sounded like a promise. Zoe couldn't help but wish for more even as she told herself that was the last thing she needed. She closed the door behind him. Something about Gabe made her want to ask him to stay longer. Yet she knew those feelings, if she acted on them, would only make matters worse.

CHAPTER THREE

GABE STEPPED INTO an empty conference room at the hospital and tapped Zoe's number on his phone for the second time that day. A couple of days had passed before he'd allowed himself to call her, convincing himself he should check on her, the baby. He could have texted, but for some inexplicable reason he was eager to hear Zoe's voice.

She'd sent the files as he had requested. He was still reviewing them, but he'd already decided to examine Mr. Luther as soon as possible. Why hadn't Zoe at least called or texted him about the patient she was so concerned about?

After a number of rings there was still no answer. What was going on with her? Had something happened to the baby? To Zoe? Her mother?

He was thousands of miles away with no way of knowing. Why didn't Zoe answer? He would try her one more time. If she didn't pick up he'd call the police and have them stop by her place. Gabe touched the green icon and listened to three rings.

On the fourth a breathless voice said, "Hello?"

Relief flooded him, the tension ebbing away from his shoulders. "Zoe, I've been calling you all day."

"Gabe, I don't need this today."

"What's wrong?"

There was an exasperated sound on the other end, and then Zoe said, "Mother decided to cook bacon. She left the pan on the burner. The kitchen caught fire. I'm at the hospital right now."

His gut felt like someone had it in their fist and was twisting it. "Is she all right? Are you?"

"They're treating her for smoke inhalation. She'll be in the hospital at least overnight. The fire alarm went off and one of the neighbors called the fire department. They got there quickly or it could have been much worse." She paused. "I'm fine and the baby is too."

He said gently, "It may be time to find your mother a place where she'll have full-time care."

"I know, but that's costly. I can't afford an apartment and pay for a place for her to stay. Her insurance doesn't kick in until she is fifty-nine and a half. That's another seven months. I'll just have to figure something out until then. The doctor has just come in. I have to go. 'Bye."

"'Bye." He spoke into silence.

Unable to stand not knowing what was going on any longer, Gabe took the first opportunity he had and called again around midmorning the next day. He tapped his pen against his desk in his apprehension about how she would react to his suggestion that she come and live with him. Zoe answered on the first ring.

"How're things today?" he asked.

"Better." She sounded tired.

He wished he was there to hold her. Whoa—that wasn't a thought he should be having, or the type of relationship they had. "That's good to hear. I'm concerned about you. Are you taking care of yourself?"

"I told you—the baby's fine," she informed him, as if he hadn't just asked about her welfare.

Did she think he was only concerned about the baby and not her? "I want to know about you as well. Have you been able to make some plans?" Would she consider his idea? For some reason it really mattered to him that she accept his plan.

"A few. The doctor said Mom could stay in the hospital a week. That'll give me time to look for an assisted-living home for her. I don't want her to make any unnecessary moves. She's already confused enough."

Strength and determination had returned to Zoe's voice. "Can you go back to your apartment?"

"No. It's so damaged it's uninhabitable. I'll have to find a new place."

This was his opening to offer his solution. "I have something I want you to consider and I want you to hear it out before you say anything. Right now, your most urgent problem is twofold: finding somewhere your mother will be safe and that has adequate full-time care, *and* somewhere for you to live. Let me help."

"Gabe, I'm not taking money." She sounded iron-rod strong. "I can handle things on my own."

"Please hear me out." Why wouldn't she let him help her? Zoe's independence would get her into trouble one day. "I'm sure you can, but if you'll listen, I think you might find my plan practical and helpful."

She huffed then said, "Okay. What do you think I should do?"

"I think you need to move in with me."

"What!"

He jerked the phone away from his ear.

She came close to yelling, "That's not going to happen. No way."

Gabe interrupted, using his giving-order-in-the-OR voice. "Just listen. You need to find a place for your mother. Money is an issue. If you stay at my house, where I have plenty of room, you'd be able to pay for a place for her while you wait for her insurance to start."

"Thank you, but I don't think so." Her words sounded as though they were coming through clenched teeth.

"Why not?" He'd offered a practical solution. Couldn't she see that?

"Because you don't need to be involved in my problems, my private life." She sounded as if he should have known that.

"If it'll make you feel any better, I'm interested in seeing that my child comes into the world with a mother who hasn't been sleeping on a couch in someone's living room. Who isn't stressed out over finances. It'll just be for a few months. We'd only be housemates. You can pay rent if you like."

"I appreciate your offer, but I don't think it would work." Her voice had calmed, but her resolve was loud and clear.

What was that supposed to mean? It was a practical solution. "Just think about it."

"I have to go. Mother's calling me. Her nurse has just come in."

Silence filled his ear. He wasn't surprised that she'd shot the idea down and ended the call. If nothing else, he'd learned Zoe was stubborn.

Zoe resisted the impulse to kick something. How dared Gabe think that she would move in with him? She didn't even know him. Just because she was having his child, it didn't mean he had any say over her life.

Up until a week ago they hadn't really talked, and even then all they'd done was agree to make lists of what they wanted. And have a lawyer make it legal. She mustn't forget that part of his idea. She should have rejected his idea outright and told him what he could and could not do when it came to his rights. Instead she'd meekly agreed to avoid an argument.

Now he was trying to move her around like a pawn on a chessboard. She wasn't having it. Taking care of her mother, her baby and herself was her job, her decisions to make. She didn't need or want him butting into her life anytime he pleased. Besides, if she started letting him make major decisions about her life, what would she do when he got tired of playing daddy or didn't have time for her when the next crisis cropped up? One thing she had learned was that she must be careful who she depended on.

Two days later Zoe wasn't feeling nearly as confident. Since she couldn't return to her apartment, her renter's insurance was paying for a hotel room until she found a place to live or for fourteen days, whichever came first. Her priority over the weekend had been to locate a place for her mother to live. That had turned out to be more difficult than anticipated.

She'd visited every assisted-care facility in the immediate area. Responsibility weighed heavily on her about having to put her mother in a home. She had found one that would be suitable, but it was way beyond her budget. Guilt squeezed her heart.

Between searching for facilities for her mother and her full-time job, there hadn't yet been time to look for a place for herself. Her apartment manager told her that there wasn't an empty apartment available in the complex. Since her lease was almost up, Zoe would have to look elsewhere. Fourteen days in which to see to her mother's needs and find a new home for herself, not to mention getting packed to move. There simply wasn't enough time. She was almost at her wits' end.

Her workload was heavy, but she'd managed to squeeze in checking on Mr. Luther. He'd been discharged from the hospital, where he'd been treated for stomach pain and fatigue. These were just symptoms of a larger issue that wouldn't get better without a transplant. It was time he be admitted to National Hospital for a transplant workup. Thankfully he wasn't so sick he couldn't go home until that time, but that wouldn't be the case for much longer. When she could think straight again she must talk to Gabe about him.

That night at the hotel while Zoe sat eating takeout food, her phone rang. It was Gabe. She hated to admit it, but his unwelcomed suggestion was starting to look like the only answer. "Hello."

"It's Gabe." He sounded unsure. Was he afraid of her reaction after his last call?

"Hi." She was so tired and disheartened she was glad to have someone to talk to, and Gabe was a good listener.

"How're things going?"

She loved the deep timbre of his voice. There was something reassuring about it. "They could be better." Zoe sounded as down as she felt. She refused to show weakness. Appearing needy wouldn't help her either. Gabe was already making plans regarding the baby she'd not counted on.

"Your mother?"

"She's actually recovering well." For that Zoe was grateful.

"What, then?"

"I've been out looking at homes for her." Her hand cradled her baby bump. The weight of her responsibilities was growing.

"And?"

"They were awful. I can't stand the idea of putting Mother in one. I hate myself for having to do it." Why was she spilling all of this to him? What was it about Gabe that made her want to lean on him? Their relationship was nothing like that, yet she was becoming more deeply involved with him each time they talked.

"What's happening with your mother isn't your fault. You know for her health and safety she needs to be in professional care where she'll be safe and well cared for. What occurred a few days ago proves it. You're not abandoning her. You're doing it because you love her."

His voice was gentle and reassuring, washing over her tight nerves like a warm balm. "Thanks for saying that. I just wish it wasn't necessary."

"You didn't find any place you liked?"

"I found the better of the evils." If only she had the money to put her mother there. Even if she emptied her savings she'd still be short. It was just as well there was no room available. She'd have to settle on one of the other places that weren't as nice as Shorecliffs House.

"So, will you move her in when she's able to leave the hospital?"

"Yes. I'm making arrangements tomorrow."

"I'm glad you found a place for her. Any luck on a new apartment for you?"

"I haven't had time to worry about that. I'll be good in the hotel for at least a few more days. I have to see what I can salvage out of the apartment. I know the living-room furniture will have to go. It smells too much like smoke. I can keep the tables and such, but everything has to be wiped down and packed up." It wasn't a job she was looking forward to, even if she would just be overseeing things.

"You'll have some help with that?" Concern filled his voice.

She pushed pillows behind her and leaned back against the headboard. "The insurance company has a crew coming in. I just have to find some place to put what's salvageable, like another apartment."

"I'm sorry this happened."

She could imagine him pulling her into a hug. "Me too, but at least it made me face the inevitable. Mom needs more help than I can give her."

"Tough way to figure that out." Sincere sympathy surrounded his words.

"You're not kidding." Why was it so easy to talk to Gabe? She should be putting distance between them, not making him a confidant.

There was quiet on the line before he said, "Have you thought about my offer?"

She'd suspected that question would come up before the call ended. "Gabe, I'm not living with you."

"The invitation remains open if you change your mind. I'll be moving your way on Friday. I hate it but I've gotta go. Surgery is paging me. 'Bye."

Suddenly Zoe felt utterly alone. He seemed to always be rushing off somewhere. If only Gabe could have talked to her longer. She needed his logical reasoning because she hated the idea of her mother going into a care home. There was no one else to lean on. Her sister was out of the country. Zoe hadn't even been able to get in touch with her to tell her about the fire. Zoe had friends, but they had become rather distant since she'd had to spend so much time with her mother. Now that she needed someone, Gabe was filling that spot. It was odd. They knew so little about each other, yet they seemed to click.

She ran her hands over her belly. They certainly had clicked that one night. He'd been easy to be around then and he was now. Too easy.

Zoe stuffed her leftover meal into the paper bag and threw it in the garbage. Going back to bed, she slid between the bedsheets. Curling into a ball as she hugged a pillow to her, she let the tears she'd held in check flow. What would it be like to have strong, sure arms around her? Comforting arms? Someone to share her pain with?

That was what she'd always dreamed of. Gabe's face popped into her mind. She couldn't depend on him. He didn't want a wife and family. Just like her ex-fiancé and her father. She couldn't let her heart be hurt again like he had so easily done. She had to wait for the right man to give her heart to. The one who wanted the same things out of life that she did.

She did have her baby. Zoe smiled. Another person to take care of but she was looking forward to it. Would her child have Gabe's big blue eyes and dark hair? Or look more like her? In a few short months she would know. Hold him or her in her arms. Out of all this darkness there would be a shining star. With a slight smile on her lips, Zoe fell into an exhausted sleep.

The next afternoon she received a call from Shorecliffs House, the assisted-living home she couldn't afford. The administrator said they had a room opening after all. Before the woman had hardly finished, Zoe had said she would take it. When the conversation was over Zoe put her head against the wall and tapped it a few times. She knew what she had to do. The only way she could afford it was by moving in with Gabe until her mother's insurance would cover the cost.

Backing down and agreeing to Gabe's plan put her

in a vulnerable position. There must be ground rules. Above all else they would not be sharing a bed. Ever. That rule couldn't be broken regardless of how tempting it might be.

With a lump in her throat she worked to swallow, Zoe pushed Gabe's phone number. He didn't answer, so she left a message. "Please call me."

A few hours later, while working at her old apartment, her phone rang. With shaking hands and banging heart, she said, "Hello?"

"Hey, what's going on?" He sounded distracted.

"That proposition you made about me renting a room from you—did you really mean it?"

"Yeah, I really mean it. Wouldn't have offered if I didn't." He seemed totally focused on their conversation now.

"It looks like I'm going to need to take you up on a room. But there have to be some rules."

"Such as?"

"I pay rent. I have my own room. I'm strictly a roommate. I'll only stay until my mother's insurance starts. We lead our own lives without reporting in to each other."

"Okay." He drew the word out. "Do you mind if I ask what changed your mind?"

"The home I wanted to put Mom in had an opening. I had to jump at the chance when they called. Having a roommate is the only way I can afford it. I don't have time to look for one, so…"

"I see." By his tone he did.

"The arrangement will only be temporary. I'll be out in six months, tops. I'll have found my own place by then." Hers and the baby's.

"I don't have a problem with that. My house is plenty

big enough for us both. My bedroom is on one side of the house while the other two bedrooms are on the other. We might meet in the kitchen occasionally.

"With my new position, I'll be super-busy, so I probably won't be around much. I'll be moving in on Friday. Why don't you let me make the arrangements for the movers to pick up your furniture?"

"I don't really have much. Everything I own smells like smoke. The insurance had to give me money for clothes. I'm at the apartment, boxing up family pictures and such now. I'll put whatever I decide I don't need in storage. I think my bedroom suite and Mom's should be all right but the mattresses may have to go. Anyway, I don't need to bore you with all that. I'll figure it all out and get back to you."

"Zoe, I already have my movers coming. You have enough going on. Let them take care of moving your stuff as well."

"You've got your hands full with your own move. I'll take care of mine." She had to start setting boundaries now. This she would do for herself. At least she could feel in control of one area of her life.

He huffed. "If that's the way you want it. Let me know when you're ready to move in and I'll make sure you can get into the house."

Someone in the background called his name. To them he said, "Yeah, I'll be right there. I need to do it myself." He spoke to her again. "I've got a case that needs my attention, so I've got to go. Take care of yourself."

Gabe didn't like the thought of Zoe handling her own moving arrangements or of her lifting boxes, but with her attitude, he wouldn't be doing himself any favors by pushing her further. He decided to keep his distance, trying not to think about what she was doing and why. He made a point of not calling her, even though he was anxious to know how she was doing.

Had her mother's move gone well? This personal interest in Zoe perplexed him. It wasn't like him. He put it down to the fact that she was the mother of his child. And he genuinely liked her. If he didn't hear from her soon he'd be forced to call her. On Thursday evening, he flew to Richmond and resisted the urge to try to see Zoe. If he hadn't heard from her by Friday evening he would call.

Early the next day he was standing on the porch of his new home, waiting for the movers to show up. He didn't have many belongings, had never cared much about what his home looked like as long as it was comfortable. With his more-gone-than-home lifestyle, he had never felt the need to decorate his places.

Apartments had always been where he'd lived as an adult, but with a child coming, a house had seemed like the right thing to buy. A boy needed a backyard. Or a girl. The idea of having a place for his son or daughter to play like he'd had appealed. He may not have had a father but he'd had a good childhood. He looked around him at the tree-lined street with the sidewalk running along it and the other houses with their green lawns and shook his head. A subdivision wasn't where he'd ever dreamed he'd be living.

Next thing he knew he'd be driving a minivan. The very idea made him huff. Yet he'd made a step in that direction today. He had sold his sports car and picked up his new four-door sedan. His argument to himself was that he was being practical, because it would be easier to get a car seat in and out of.

A moving van pulled into his drive. The large truck

held his meager belongings—bedroom suite, kitchen table, sofa, boxed kitchen items and household goods. There would be a large amount of space in the house sitting empty. Maybe what he needed to do was hire an interior decorator to come in and suggest what he needed to buy. A few hours later the movers had left, and he was searching through a box for the coffee maker when his phone rang. His heart beat faster. It was Zoe. "Hey."

"I just wanted to let you know that I'm not going to move in until Sunday."

He was both disappointed and surprised. "Oh, okay. Why not earlier?"

"I've had to deal with Mother. And the guys can't help me until Sunday afternoon. I've spent most of the morning organizing what needs to go into storage and packing up the rest."

"Guys?" What guys was she talking about? She wouldn't let him help her; instead, she'd chosen to ask some other men. There was a pang in his chest he didn't want to examine closely.

"Some friends from work," came her offhanded answer.

"It sounds like you have everything in hand." Could she hear the testiness he felt?

"Why I'm calling is to see if it's all right for me to come over and see what my room looks like. I need to decide what to bring and what to store."

His ego took another hit. She was only interested in seeing the house, not him. It occurred to him he was taking this all too personally because he was operating on the assumption they were more than merely accidental parents. Which they weren't, so why was he feeling this way? He had to get control of his imagination, be ruthlessly realistic about the foundation of their relationship. Starting now. "Sure. That'll be fine."

"How much longer do you think your movers will be? I don't want to get in their way."

She was all business. He could be that as well. "They left hours ago, so you're welcome anytime."

"Great. Please text me your address. I'll see you later." She hung up.

Gabe lost track of the number of times he'd checked his watch since Zoe had called. It amazed him how excited he was at the thought of seeing her again. The doorbell finally rang as he finished unpacking the last box in his bedroom.

He wiped his hands on his jeans and hurried to the front of the house. Through the pane glass of the door he could see Zoe. His heart beat faster. She was as amazing as he remembered. Her head was moving one way then another as if she was taking everything in. Pulling the door open wide, he stepped back and said in a welcoming manner, "Come in."

Zoe gave him a slight smile. "Hi. I like your house. It's…big."

He wasn't sure how to take that statement. Was she being complimentary or expressing relief they wouldn't be living in close proximity? Or both?

With a tentative step, Zoe entered Gabe's new home. Stepping into his living space symbolized how drastically her life was changing. It wasn't an unpleasant feeling, just one of uncertainty. As if she'd been forced to open a door without knowing what lay behind it.

It was a new redbrick home in an exclusive neighborhood that she'd only driven through a couple of times. She was a little surprised he'd chosen the area and such a large house. This was a subdivision of family homes, not where single men tended to live. Gabe didn't impress her as a spacious-home kind of person. So why had he decided on this one?

It did have one appealing advantage, though. It was large enough they would most likely have little or no contact while she resided here. That was what she wanted. To get through the next few months then move on. Or at least that was what she was going to keep telling herself.

She ran her fingertips over the smooth wooden door with its beautiful glass panels and large oval in the middle. A hardwood floor gleamed in the shaft of afternoon sun flowing in through the open doorway. Beyond the foyer was a sunken living area with a fireplace filling one wall. She took a timid step forward. Along the back were tall windows, revealing a circular brick patio and manicured yard. Her breath caught. It was perfect. If she'd been picking out a house this would have been the one she chose.

The corner of her mouth lifted a little. The living area's massive space held only a leather sofa, matching chair and large TV. How like a man to have only the essentials. What would it be like to snuggle up on that sofa next to Gabe in front of the fire? Something she wouldn't be doing. "You have a beautiful home."

She watched his lips curve up. Was he pleased with her compliment? Did it matter to him what she thought?

"Come on in and I'll show you around."

He led her through the living area, giving her time to admire the backyard anew through the windows as she followed him into the kitchen by way of a bay-window alcove that served as an eating area. A small table and two well-worn chairs were stationed there. The kitchen was spacious, furnished with all the latest appliances. She could only imagine what a pleasure it would be to cook for a family here. Hardly the galley-sized kitchen she'd been using.

It was a shame that no woman would share this house with him. If it was her… No, those thoughts were better left alone. That was one place she didn't need to go. He'd already made it clear what he wanted out of life and that didn't include her.

From there he pointed down a small hallway. "That's my suite and the way out to the carport. This is the way to your side of the house."

It might be, but she was afraid it wouldn't be far enough. Just being near him had her dreaming of what could be.

They crossed the living area and went through an arched doorway into a hallway that ran from the front of the house to the back.

"You have a choice between two bedrooms. You can have them both if you want them." Gabe turned to the right, bumping her as he did so. He grabbed her before she rocked backward. "Whoa there. We wouldn't want you to fall."

Gabe's hands were brand hot on her waist. He watched her intently for a moment. His eyes focused on her lips before he released a breath he'd apparently been holding and let her go.

Zoe tingled all over with the desire to have him touch her again. Living in such a virile man's home wouldn't be easy.

He led her into a sunny room at the front of the house. It was larger than she'd had in her apartment. The street was out the front window and a neighbor's house could be seen in the distance through the other. "There's a full bath right there." Gabe pointed to a doorway. "The other room's down this way."

He didn't give her time to look before he walked out into the hallway. He acted as if he was making a point to keep as much distance as he could from her. Zoe caught up with him by the time he reached the doorway of the other room. This one was as large as the first but the view was nicer. From the window facing the back she could see the yard and trees.

"There's another bath in here." Gabe stood in the entrance and flipped on a light switch. "This bath isn't quite as large as the other one but it's a nice size."

He sounded almost apologetic. Did it really matter to him what she thought of it?

As she pondered those unsettling questions, he added, "You're welcome to store anything you like in the room you don't use."

"I appreciate that, but I've already put stuff in storage. I'll just be bringing my bedroom suite, a chair and TV. That should be enough. The less I bring, the less I have to worry about moving the second time." It was important she be practical about the arrangements because she *was not* living here long.

She caught sight of Gabe's odd expression a second before he glanced away. "Whichever one you don't take I'll make the baby's room."

Her look met his again. "The baby will be living with me."

"I know that, but he or she will be regularly visiting me. I'll need a bedroom for my child."

His assertion solidified her resolve that when she was settled they were going to sit down and decide on Gabe's visitation schedule. His insistence on being involved wasn't going to overrule what she thought best for her baby. This was *her* baby. She would be making the final decisions about raising her child, regardless of what Gabe wanted. However, she knew this wasn't the time to broach that issue. She was juggling far too many things as it was. "We'll talk about your visitation rights later."

"Just because you keep putting it off, it doesn't mean the issue will go away. Or me, for that matter." He arched an eyebrow in challenge.

Before her temper got the better of her, Zoe headed for the front door. "I've got to get going. It's been a long day."

"Have you eaten? I could call for Chinese takeout or pizza."

She didn't slow down. "I have to go. I'll just do drive-through and go to bed early."

"Do you need any help moving? I can meet you Sunday morning."

Why did he keep being so nice to her? "Uh… No, I have it all taken care of. You've got your own stuff here to worry about." She walked out the front door but stopped on the porch. "By the way, did you have a chance to look at Mr. Luther's file?"

"I did. I plan to talk to his primary doctor just as soon as I can."

She stepped to him and touched his arm briefly. That was a mistake. Even that had her blood humming. "Thanks, Gabe. I really appreciate it."

He glanced down before his earnest look met hers. "No problem, but still no promises."

"I understand." She smiled and removed her hand. "I'm grateful for any help you can offer him. See you on Sunday." She closed the door behind her and headed for her car.

As she slid into the driver's seat, Gabe stepped out onto the porch, his face unreadable. As she drove away, Zoe looked in her rearview mirror. Gabe was still standing there, hands in his pockets.

Why was she already missing him? He truly was a decent guy. She couldn't think of another person who would have been as understanding or helpful as he had been under the circumstances. Still, she must not forget he was only being so generous because of the baby. What would it be like to have someone like Gabe to come home to at the end of a weary day?

At least for a short while she and the baby had a nice place to live and, better yet, her mother was in a safe place that provided quality care. That was what really mattered.

Not the feelings Gabe brought out in her.

CHAPTER FOUR

LATE SUNDAY AFTERNOON, Zoe led the way in her compact car to Gabe's house. A couple of guys from work, John and Rick, were helping her move. They had managed to stay right behind her despite their trucks being heavy with her furniture and boxes of possessions.

She was grateful that Shorecliffs House encouraged residents to bring their own furniture when they moved in. Having familiar belongings around had definitely made her mother less anxious. To Zoe's surprise, her mother seemed content with her new residence.

In a few months Zoe would be living in her own place as well. If she could find the right small house she would buy. A child needed space, other families around them. A neighborhood similar to Gabe's.

She had managed to salvage the end tables in her living room. With those and one comfortable chair she'd bought with some of the insurance money, she planned to set up a small living area in her bedroom. That way she wouldn't disturb Gabe when he was home. If she didn't take steps to keep her distance, she could easily become too involved in his life. That wasn't what he wanted and she would respect that.

As Zoe pulled into the drive, Gabe stepped out onto the front porch. Had he been watching for her? She pulled as far up the driveway as she could so the two trucks would be as close as possible to the front door. Moments later she climbed out of the car and started toward him.

He wore a T-shirt and worn jeans with tennis shoes. His casual dress somehow made him even more attractive. It would be nice to have him greeting her when she came home every day. What was wrong with her? That fantasy she shouldn't entertain.

She joined John and Rick, who were already in the process of untying ropes securing her furniture. Gabe came down the two steps toward them.

"Gabe, this is John and Rick." She pointed to one then the other. "They work with me."

He shook hands with the men. "I'll get this end," he said to John as he pulled her headboard off the truck. Gabe maneuvered the bulky item, and then he led the way into the house with John carrying the other end.

Zoe pulled a box off and carried it inside. Gabe was on his way out of her room when she entered.

"You don't need to be carrying that. Give it here." His hands covered hers as he tried to take the box.

Awareness zipped through her. It was always there between them. Even the simplest touch from Gabe had her thinking of that night they had spent together. "I'm fine. It's not that heavy." She gave it a tug, removing his hands. "These guys can't spend all evening here. I need to help."

"Then why don't you just tell us where to put things and let us handle the moving?" Gabe followed her back to the room.

John glanced at them then slipped out the door.

She set the box down. "You need to understand

right now that you do not tell me what I should or shouldn't do."

"And you need to think less about proving your independence and more about what's good for the baby. Now let us handle it."

Anger washed through Zoe as he left before she could respond. A minute later Rick and John entered with the footboard. Gabe was right behind them with the rails. Gabe and John put the bed together while Rick returned to the truck. She pointed to the wall she wanted the bed against. Rick returned with a couple of boxes stacked on top of each other. All the men left once again. Zoe started removing bedsheets, pillows and a blanket from a box. She'd stay put and start unpacking if it would keep Gabe from making a scene.

All three men made a couple more trips to the truck.

After one trip she and Rick were left alone. He asked, nodding toward the doorway, "Who is this guy you're renting from?"

Before she could respond, Gabe entered the room with an end table and said in a tight tone, "I'm the father of her baby."

John came in right behind him. He and Rick looked at her with wonder then back at Gabe.

Holding up a hand, John said, "No offense, man. We just wanted to make sure Zoe was safe."

"None taken." Gabe's voice still held a hard note. "I'm sure she appreciates having friends who care about her." Gabe set the table down and stepped beside her.

"Come on, Rick." John tapped him on the shoulder. "We only have a couple more boxes."

"Why didn't you tell them who I am? Are you ashamed?" Gabe asked.

Zoe couldn't have been more shocked. Why would he

believe that? He was an excellent doctor, well respected in his field, smart, had good taste in homes and, most of all, was a wonderful lover. Where had he gotten the idea she might be embarrassed by him? She couldn't imagine any woman not being proud of being associated with him. "I can assure you that's not the case. I just don't broadcast my private life. John and Rick are my friends but not that close."

"They sure sounded protective of you. I thought there might be more going on." His tone implied he might be jealous.

No man she knew even came close to measuring up to Gabe. She turned her head and gave him a questioning look. He had to care on some level to have those feelings, didn't he? Warmth flowed through her at the possibility. The self-assured man for once needed her reassurance. She stepped toward him. "Gabe, there's nothing to—"

"Well, that's it," Rick announced as he and John came in with a box apiece.

Zoe stepped away from Gabe but she felt his attention on her as he said, "Thanks, guys."

John and Rick headed for the front door, and she and Gabe followed.

There Gabe shook their hands, saying, "Thanks for your help. I appreciate it. I know Zoe does too."

There he was again, speaking for her. It made them sound like a couple. They weren't. "I do. I don't know what I'd have done without you guys." She hugged John then Rick. "I owe you big-time."

"Maybe you can make it up to us by bringing us some of your peanut-butter cookies. They're the best in the whole DC area."

Zoe was both flattered and embarrassed by such high

praise of her cookies. She promised them a batch as soon as she settled in. They said their goodbyes.

"Thanks again," Zoe called and waved. She turned to see Gabe standing in the front doorway, leaning against the frame. Her nerves buzzed. Not only was she alone with him, she was now living in his house. She walked toward him. "Well, I guess I'll go finish straightening my room."

"Wouldn't you like to sit down for a few minutes? Have something to eat. Not that I have anything here. I was going to order a pizza."

"I should get some unpacking done. I have to be at work early in the morning. I've been gone for a week." For some reason she needed to get to her room, take a moment for herself without Gabe nearby.

Gabe followed her more slowly into the house. Had he made the right decision by inviting Zoe to live at his house? Could he have offered a different solution to her living arrangements? He'd never counted on this attraction roaring through him. He had to keep his emotions in check. Focus on the baby and not the mother. It would be tough, but he would manage it.

Zoe was hiding from him. He was as certain of that fact as he was his name. She wasn't the type to run from problems. She had more than shown her ability to handle difficult circumstances. Yet he didn't doubt his judgment. He'd give her space. He still had boxes of his own to empty.

While he worked in the kitchen, he listened for sounds from the other side of the house. There were none. It was as if Zoe wasn't even there. Unable to stand it any longer, he walked softly to her room. As he was about to knock on the open door, he saw her. She lay sound asleep curled up in a ball on the half-made bed. After the last few days she'd had, or the week, she must be exhausted. He spied a blanket on the cushioned chair near the rear window. Picking it up, he placed it over her.

Zoe moaned and pulled the edge of the blanket up under her chin.

She looked so peaceful. Beautiful, with her eyelashes resting against her creamy skin. This was the woman who was the mother of his child. Would she look like Zoe? *She.* Did he want a daughter? Could he be a good father to a daughter? Girls needed special care. He wasn't even sure he could give what was needed to a son.

Zoe would make an excellent mom. He had no doubt of that. The care and concern she'd given the boy at the airport when he was hurt and the love she'd shown her mother all indicated he was right. As open and expressive as she had been with her friends when she'd thanked them for helping her was just another sign of her capacity to love. He could take lessons from her.

He'd been jealous of John and Rick when they had arrived. Had been resentful of the carefree way she'd treated them, especially when she seemed so guarded around him. He would like him and Zoe to at least be close friends. They had been friends at least during that one fateful night. Surely they could build on that beginning? Their baby at least deserved that kind of parental unity.

Unfortunately, standing here and staring down at Zoe wouldn't win him any friendship points if she woke. Unable to stop himself, he ran the back of a finger along her cheek. Zoe sighed. She truly was lovely. Before he got into trouble, he slowly lowered his hand and backed out of the room.

A couple of hours later he was waiting for his pizza to arrive when a loud "Dang it," followed by a crash, came from the direction of Zoe's room. Gabe ran across the house and down the hall as fast as the twists and turns would allow. When he reached the doorway, his heart almost stopped. Zoe teetered as she stood on the cushioned chair with a hammer in her hand. Around her on the carpet was a broken frame and pieces of glass. She rocked back. Gabe rushed forward, catching her against his chest.

The feel of her in his arms brought back erotic memories: hot kisses, tender caresses and willing woman opening in welcome… Desire like he'd never felt before washed over him. He must master his libido or he'd scare her.

As he lowered her to the floor, his protective instinct propelled his hands to her waist to steady her. The curve there was no longer tiny, but knowing the reason for the change excited him all over again. Without thought, his hands moved to her middle. The gentle bulge fascinated him. *His child.* He'd never planned to have one, but now he was and everything about the miracle filled him with awe.

Zoe leaned back against him for a second then straightened.

The part of him better left dormant reacted once more to her nearness. His lips brushed her temple.

She stiffened and stepped away. "I'd better clean this mess up."

"I have a pizza coming. You're welcome to some." He moved to the door. "Don't stand on anything again. Call me if you need to do something above your head."

Zoe went down on her knees and started picking up broken pieces. She still hadn't looked at him. "Okay."

Her tone implied she wasn't promising anything.

"Zoe." He waited until she looked up and into his eyes. "I mean it."

Her expression went hard. "I heard you. But I thought I made it clear to you earlier you have no right to tell me what to do while I'm here."

He wasn't going to allow her to push away the importance of what had almost happened just now. "Then I suggest you think through what you're about to do before you act on it. You or the baby or both could have been seriously hurt if I hadn't been here to catch you."

"Ow!" She stared at her hand.

He took an involuntary step toward her. "What happened?"

"I cut my hand." A stream of blood ran over her palm.

"Give me that." Gabe took the pieces of glass from her and dumped them into a trash can nearby. Cupping her elbow, he helped her stand. Reaching over his shoulder, he grabbed a handful of his shirt and pulled.

"What're you doing?" Zoe asked, the pitch of her voice rising in alarm.

"Taking off my shirt to use as a bandage," Gabe explained impatiently, his words muffled by the material covering his head.

"Isn't that a little dramatic?"

Pulling the shirt off, he retorted, "Not if you don't want blood on the new carpet or one of your towels." He glanced around. "Even if we could find one." He wrapped the shirt around her hand and applied pressure. "I have a first-aid kit in the kitchen. Go into the bathroom and clean up. I'll be right back."

Gabe returned to find Zoe had obeyed his instruction, which surprised him. He had fully expected her to argue or defy him. Putting the kit on the counter, he opened it. After a quick search he found a bandage and removed the covering. "Let me have a look. I want to make sure you don't have any glass in the wound."

"I cleaned it well. There's nothing there. Hand me the bandage and I'll put it on."

Gabe ignored her, seizing her hand and turning it palm up. The bleeding had stopped but there was a fine line of red across the pad, gaping slightly at the center. He looked closely for any slivers. "Does it hurt anywhere?"

"No." Her breath brushed his bare shoulder, setting his pulse humming.

They were so close. Her sweet scent filled his head. He reached for the bandage and applied one end of it. "Hold this end."

She placed her finger where he indicated, and he pulled off the paper cover of the other adhesive strip, smoothing the bandage into place. Her hand felt so fragile, soft. He ran his fingertip along the line in the center of her palm. Zoe shivered.

Her gaze met his. Time hung suspended. Their faces were so close. His attention fell on her full lips. He'd wanted to taste them earlier but had stopped himself. Here was his chance again. All he had to do was lean forward the least bit to experience them. Did he dare? Would she let him?

Want like a live sizzling wire buzzed through him. His gaze met Zoe's again. She was watching him, eyes wide with questions. Did she need his kisses as much as he wanted to give them? His mouth moved toward hers as if it had a mind of its own.

The tip of Zoe's tongue darted out to dampen her bottom lip before her eyes fluttered closed. His blood heated and his body jerked to attention. Her actions were the confirmation he'd been waiting for. There was no stopping him now. A second later his mouth found hers.

The touch of Zoe's lips was all he remembered and more. So much more. Her mouth, plump and inviting, pulled him in. This wasn't the flurry and fiery urgency of that one torrid night. Instead it was slow, easy, experimental, answering questions and creating so many more.

Zoe sighed softly and leaned into him, her hands running up his chest. His arms circled her waist, bringing her against him. Gabe deepened the kiss. Zoe opened for him, eagerly greeted him. Her fingers played with the hair at the nape of his neck as his hands roamed her back, before pulling her tighter. She tasted so good.

The doorbell rang.

Zoe jerked away. Her eyes were wild like a startled animal looking to escape. "We shouldn't have done that."

Gabe leaned to kiss her again. He hadn't had enough. "We've done far more."

Her hands fanned across his chest, pushing, stopping him. "Gabe, we don't want the same things. You don't want a spouse or the full-time responsibility of a family. I do. We aren't living together. I'm your roommate. I only moved in here because I couldn't think of what else to do. If you cannot respect my boundaries, I'll have to find another place to go."

Anger flared in him. It was obvious she felt the attraction he did. The spontaneous spark of their kiss was undeniable proof. Yet she was steeling herself, refusing to act on it. His eyes met Zoe's, held. "Don't go. I'll keep my hands to myself. I'll stay in my half of the house."

The bell rang again.

"I'd better get that before the delivery guy leaves." At the door he stopped and turned back to her. "Just know this. You'll have to do the asking next time."

* * *

Zoe stood in the bathroom, shaking. Her heated blood zipped through her trembling body. She looked into the mirror. A woman who had been thoroughly kissed stared back at her. Bright eyes, rose-tinted cheeks and swollen lips all told the story. Zoe ran her fingers over her still tingling mouth.

Every fiber of her body wanted to rush to Gabe and tell him she wanted him to touch her again. Kiss her. Love her. Yet her coldly rational mind said no. There would be nothing but pain if she once more allowed her body to overrule her heart. She couldn't let her desire for him control what she really wanted.

Gabe hadn't even suggested marriage as a convenient means of helping her with the responsibilities and mounting expenses of being pregnant by him. Oh, he was being noble, very nice, and even willing to "pay his share" of the expenses of her pregnancy, but nothing more. From what she'd learned about Gabe, he would have done the same for any other woman he'd accidentally impregnated. Even if he had asked, she wouldn't have accepted. What if he left her when he felt his obligation was over? She wouldn't survive. Nothing but a commitment born of love was enough for her.

Her breath had caught when he'd pulled off his shirt. She'd seen him shirtless before but the light had been dim. This time she could make out every nuance of his wide, muscular shoulders. She'd not missed the flex of his arm muscles as he'd applied the bandage or the light dusting of hair in the center of his chest narrowing into a line leading beneath the waist of his jeans. Large enough to carry heavy loads, both physically and metaphorically, it would be so easy to let him share her burdens without that all-important commitment of love.

Gabe smelled of male heat and his own special musk. His scent surrounded her. She was tempted to inhale deeply, memorize it, only to realize she already had. His tender touch had undone her as his finger had traveled over her palm. She wanted more of his kisses. Longed for his lips to cover hers again. All her vows to herself had evaporated like water on a hot day the second his mouth had found hers. There had been no thinking, only feeling. Only Gabe for that one eternal moment.

Thankfully the pizza guy had arrived, snapping her back to reality.

"Food's in the kitchen if you want any," Gabe called.

She was hungry and had to face him sometime. Also, she'd made her reasons for rejecting him crystal clear. There was no purpose in avoiding him with the ground rules of their relationship established. The aroma of cheese and tomato sauce drew her to the kitchen.

Gabe had pulled on another shirt and now sat at the table with the pizza box open and a slice in his hand. A canned drink sat in front of him.

"I haven't had time to go to the grocery. Help yourself to a soda. If you'd rather have water, the glasses are to the right of the sink."

Apparently, Gabe had recovered from their moment in the bathroom. He was treating her like the roommate she'd asked him to. So why wasn't she more pleased about it? "Thanks."

Gabe didn't even look her direction while she filled her glass with water and took her chair. He pushed the box toward her. She selected a slice. "We haven't talked about any house rules."

He gave her an incredulous look. "There are no house rules. You're free to do as you please. Treat it as yours. There don't have to be rules for everything."

His aggravation rang clear in his tone. Had she pushed him too far? Her common sense kicked in. All she'd done was hold to her vow, hold her ground about what their relationship would be while she lived here. His ego was no doubt bruised, but what was he really after? The best she could tell was sex while he waited for his child to be born.

"Thanks. It would be nice to use the kitchen. I like to cook healthily, especially for the baby."

"Then cook to your heart's content." He took another bite of his pizza. After swallowing, he asked, "Do you mind if I ask you a question?"

What was he after now? Was he going to put her on the spot about what had happened a few minutes ago? Her feelings about him? "No. Ask away."

"Why did you pick the room you did?"

That particular question was totally unexpected. Why would he care? "Because of the view. I like the trees and the yard."

He nodded thoughtfully.

Gabe had her curiosity up now. "Why do you want to know?"

"I just wondered if you saw the front room as a nursery and chose the other for that reason." He watched her.

"Truthfully, I didn't, but it would make a lovely one with all the natural light."

"Then that's what I'll make it. I need to do something with this place. I was thinking of hiring an interior decorator to help. Unless you would like to do the room. After all, you'll be here for a little while after the baby is born."

"I'll think about it." Could she stand to see her dream nursery become reality and then leave it? Yet the thought of bringing the baby home to a pretty little world excited her.

Gabe didn't offer any more conversation. And she couldn't find a comfortable way to initiate one. She didn't like this stilted silence between them. He must be angrier about her rejection than she'd first thought.

"Do you want another slice?" he finally asked.

She shook her head.

Closing the box, he stood. "Well, I'm going to call it a night. I need to be at the hospital early on my first day." He walked to the refrigerator, opened it and put the box inside. "I'll see what I can do about Mr. Luther as soon as I can. It may not be tomorrow. Night." With that he went down the hall toward his room.

Zoe sat looking out at the dark patio, feeling deflated. Something was missing. Something she hadn't known was special until it had gone. Zoe glanced in the direction Gabe had gone. She wanted it back.

"Hey, I forgot to give you this."

Zoe jumped at Gabe's voice. She hadn't heard him returning. He was barefooted and bare-chested with only a pair of sports shorts riding his slim hips.

He slid a key across the table toward her. "You'll need that."

"Uh…thanks."

"I'll see about getting you a garage door opener as soon as possible so you can park in the carport."

"Okay."

"Night, Zoe."

"Good night." She watched him leave, wishing she was going with him.

After putting her glass in the dishwasher, she straightened the kitchen and put the chairs back into place before going to her room. Stepping into her bathroom brought back memories of Gabe's kiss. Would it be like that every time she went in? She feared it would.

Moving in with Gabe had been a calculated risk. One she'd believed she could handle, but it was proving more difficult than she had anticipated. Yet her mother now had the quality care she needed, deserved, so the risk Zoe was taking with her heart was worth it. At least living with Gabe was temporary. Knowing there was a time limit on the intense temptation did help.

Tonight was an example of why she needed to strengthen her resolve to keep their relationship on a business basis. There would be no more moments of weakness on her part if she could prevent it.

After a hot bath she crawled under the covers. She'd never felt more alone in her life. Gabe was only steps away, but she wouldn't go to him. What would it be like to sleep with her head on his shoulder? Heaven. Yet she couldn't allow herself even the pleasure of that fantasy because it would weaken her self-control.

CHAPTER FIVE

GABE HAD FORGOTTEN what it was like to start a new job. The stress, anxiety and the feeling of always being one step behind. He didn't like that. Knowing what was happening in his sphere of influence was important to him. Indirectly Zoe had accused him of being controlling. In her case and with his patients, he believed it was more about caring. Either way, he was determined he would be placed on the surgery schedule sooner rather than later. The more surgery he did, the faster his career would grow.

Even in the OR there was an adjustment period. It would take time to put a staff together that would interact smoothly with each other. For now it would be trial and error. Yet this was the position he'd been working toward his entire professional life. What he hadn't planned for was becoming a father while trying to create the finest liver-transplant program in the world.

Worse was his growing desire for his "roommate."

It had been three days since he'd seen Zoe and he didn't anticipate slowing down long enough to see her anytime soon. If she'd been worried they'd have too much time together, these past few days had proved her concern groundless. As far as he could tell, she was asleep when he came home and getting her morning shower when he left. He'd known his job would be demanding and had accepted it. That was just one of a number of reasons why he wouldn't make a long-term commitment to a woman.

Since he'd not seen Zoe after giving her a house key, he'd left his garage door opener on the kitchen counter because he had not had time to get another. He wrote her a note.

This is for you. Sorry I didn't think to give it to you the other night. Been busy. Call me if you need something.

When he pulled into the drive late that night, Zoe's car wasn't parked in her usual spot, just to the right past the front door. A light burned in the kitchen. She must have taken him up on his offer to park in the carport now she had a door opener.

He studied the glow in the window. At least Zoe had thought about him. He'd been living with his mother the last time he'd come home to a light left on for him. There was something about it that said, *I care about you.*

As he entered the front door, a wonderful smell filled the air. Making his way to the kitchen, he discovered a plate of cookies with a note beside them. He dropped his keys and picked up the piece of paper.

Made some for the guys. Thought you might like a few.

Gabe took a bite of a peanut-butter cookie. "Mmm." His grandmother used to bake them. His mother never had much time for that sort of thing. Most of her efforts revolved around her job. Her actions had taught him that success was only gained through hard work and personal sacrifice. Picking up the plate, he flipped off the light and headed for his bedroom with a smile. He would eat the rest before he went to bed.

The next morning he left another note.

Thanks for the cookies. They hit the spot.

Note-passing wasn't as satisfying as seeing Zoe, but at least they weren't ignoring each other.

How good her cookies were was on his mind as he started his rounds just after noon. The first patient he planned to see was Mr. Luther. Gabe had contacted Mr. Luther's physician, Dr. Patel, and they had agreed that he should be transferred to Gabe's care. Mr. Luther's health had deteriorated to the point where a transplant was the only option. The hepatitis C had taken its toll. Following Dr. Patel's instructions, Mr. Luther was admitted to National Hospital for an evaluation before being placed on the liver transplant list.

Gabe rapped his knuckles on the door.

A gruff voice called, "Come in."

Gabe pushed the door open. "Mr. Luther, I'm…" He stopped short. Zoe stood at the bedside of a grizzly man who obviously hadn't shaved in a number of days.

"Gab—uh… Dr. Marks, hello." Zoe's smile was cautious.

His heart gave a little extra beat. "I hadn't expected to see you."

"I wasn't sure if I'd see you either." She looked at him shyly.

"Thanks for the cookies. They were great."

She glanced toward their patient, who was looking from one of them to the other with curiosity, and said to Gabe, "It's part of my job to keep tabs on Mr. Luther."

The older man pointed first at Gabe then at her and back again. "I'm guessing you two know each other, him eating your cookies and all."

Gabe nodded, stepping forward and extending his hand. "I'm Dr. Marks. Dr. Patel has thoroughly reviewed your case with me."

"So you're why I'm in one of these dang uncomfortable beds again." He didn't sound happy but shook Gabe's hand.

Zoe placed her hand on the man's other arm. "Mr. Luther, Dr. Marks is going to help you. If you want to blame someone, it should be me. I asked him to see you."

Gabe couldn't believe how big a heart Zoe had. She was emotionally invested in her patient far more than was required by her job. Was Mr. Luther an exception to her rule or did she, as Gabe suspected, care deeply about all her patients, and Mr. Luther in particular? What would it be like to be under her umbrella of loving concern? *Focus on your patient*, Gabe sternly ordered himself. "She did ask me, and the first thing I need to do is examine you. Then we'll run some tests."

"More of them, you mean," the man grunted.

Gabe shrugged and removed his stethoscope from around his neck. "Now, would you lean forward for me?"

The man did as he asked and Gabe listened to his heart. He then had him breathe deeply as he checked out his lungs. "I'm going to turn this overhead light on. I need to look at your eyes."

The switch was on Zoe's side of the bed and she flipped it on.

"I've not spoken to his nurse yet, so I don't know his vitals, Zoe. Would you mind getting his BP for me? Check his pulse points?" Gabe placed his stethoscope around his neck and removed a penlight from his pocket.

She laid the folder in her hand on a chair and went to work.

Gabe looked at the man. "I understand you were diagnosed with hepatitis a number of years ago."

"Yeah." Mr. Luther nodded.

"When did you first seek help for it?" Gabe looked into his eyes.

"Maybe six months ago."

"He was referred to the Liver Alliance by Dr. Patel three months ago," Zoe said, as she placed the cuff on the patient's arm. She pumped the cuff then listened through her stethoscope for his pulse. Done, she looked at him. "One-thirty over ninety."

Gabe nodded. "Not perfect but not as bad as I expected. Mr. Luther, have you been a heavy drinker in the past?"

The man glared at him. "I've drunk."

Gabe gave him a pointed look in return. "You do understand that there can be no drinking again if you have a transplant."

"I'm not even sure I want a transplant," the man grumbled.

Zoe looked up from where she was checking Mr. Luther's pulses on his feet. "Mr. Luther, you need to think hard about that. Without it you'll die."

"Gonna die one day anyway."

Gabe slipped his penlight back into his pocket. "That's true, but without a new liver you have at best a couple of years and you'll get increasingly sicker. There won't be much quality to your life. We're going to do the workup on you to consider listing you for a transplant, but you need to know that your attitude will affect the decision-making. New livers are hard to come by. If you're not going to do your part to keep a new liver healthy, you'll not be listed."

"Yeah." The man picked up the TV remote. "I'll think about it." He nodded toward Zoe. "I'd better not hear that you've been giving Avery here a hard time or you'll answer to me."

"Noted." Gabe made eye contact with Zoe and nodded toward the door. She gave the man a concerned look and followed him out.

Zoe closed the door behind her and looked at him with such hope. "So what do you think?"

Gabe shook his head slightly. "I'm really concerned about his compliance. He's a gruff bear, I know, but to be listed, the committee must know he'll do what he's supposed to do."

"I'll talk to him. Make it clear."

"*He* has to want this," Gabe stated emphatically. "You have done all you can do for him by bringing him to my attention."

Zoe glared at him. "I know that."

"Even if he does agree to cooperate, I can't guarantee he'll be a candidate. I'm just one person on a committee of eight."

She touched his arm. "I appreciate you trying."

Gabe nodded. He hated that he couldn't give her more encouragement. "I have to go. I have other patients to visit."

That evening, Gabe found a note from Zoe waiting on the counter.

There's supper in the refrigerator if you're interested. Thanks for all you're doing for Mr. Luther.

He felt himself smiling, unable to contain his satisfaction. Why was this particular patient so important to her? Even though he'd not given Zoe much reassurance on Mr. Luther's prognosis, she was expressing her gratitude by cooking for him.

He'd not eaten since lunch, so he was tickled to have a home-cooked meal. His day had been so exhausting he'd not even bothered to get drive-through. Zoe's cooking, even though it would be rewarmed, was heaven sent. He could get used to this treatment.

Gabe had just sat down at the table when the patter of feet drew his attention. Looking over his shoulder, he saw Zoe. He smiled, glad to see her. Her appearance, on top of her meal, was totally unexpected.

She wore a short fleece robe tied above the rise of her belly. His gut clenched with pride. That bump was his child. Had he ever seen a more beautiful sight? Zoe's hair was mussed as if she had been running her fingers through it in angst. Was she nervous about approaching him? Why should she be? She'd recovered her self-control the moment the doorbell had interrupted their bathroom interlude.

"Hey," Gabe said. "Thanks for the meal."

"You're welcome."

"Sorry if I woke you." He picked up his fork, ready to take a bite.

Zoe said softly, "I've been waiting up for you."

She had? Hope, warm as a fire, welled in his chest. "Really?"

"I wanted to talk to you about my rent."

Disappointment smothered his anticipation. She wanted to talk about that now? Shaking his head in refusal, he turned back to the food. "I've had a long day. Make that a week. I'm in no mood to talk business now."

Zoe moved around the table, facing him. "I have to pay for my mother's housing, so I need to know what my budget will be."

That made perfect sense, but it didn't give him the energy to hash out her rent right this minute. "Then make it a dollar for this month. When I get time, I'll figure something out."

She leaned toward him slightly, giving him an amazing view of cleavage. Her breasts were larger than he remembered. Pregnancy had changed her there as well.

She announced with more volume than necessary, "I'm not just paying you a dollar!"

With effort, he turned his attention to cutting his pork chop. "Then you decide what you can afford to pay when you work out your budget. Right now, I'm hungry and don't want to talk about it. Instead, why don't you sit down and keep me company? Tell me how your mother's doing."

He glanced up in time to catch her perplexed look as she slowly sank into the other chair.

She didn't immediately start talking, so between bites he asked, "So? How is she?"

"Still confused but otherwise okay. The staff assures me she's adjusting quite well."

A moment of silence followed, and then Zoe remarked, "You know, you really should take better care of yourself. You're eating like you haven't had anything all day."

He shrugged. "That's pretty close to the truth."

"Gabe!"

"Yeah?" He met her look as he poked his fork at some green beans.

"You've got to do better than that. You can't keep that up."

This was the tables being turned. He was the one who normally scolded her. Now her anxiety was for him. He liked it. "Thanks for your concern. I do appreciate it. But I have my hands full at work. I've had to hit the ground running every day since I started. Hopefully it'll get better soon." He cut into the pork chop again. Lifting the piece on the end of his fork, he said, "This sure is good."

"I'm glad you like it. You know if you don't start taking care of yourself you won't be healthy enough to care for your patients."

He finished off the last of the roasted potatoes, wishing there were more. She was a good cook. Or maybe the food was made better by the fact that someone had cared enough to think of him. It would be so easy to get used to, even if she'd done it out of gratitude. "Zoe, I know you look after the welfare of others all the time, but I can take care of myself. I'm all right."

"What makes you think you can give me a place to live for virtually nothing because you're concerned enough to help me, but I can't respond in kind?"

She had him there. It made him feel good having someone waiting for him at home who would talk to him over a freshly cooked meal, instead of always eating carryout or fast food in front of the TV. Yet Zoe had made it very clear that she was only renting space from him, that they were not "living together." It was time to move the conversation off him. "Give me until this weekend to think about the rent and I'll have a figure. Will that do?"

"I can wait that long. There's one more thing I wanted to talk to you about."

Gabe almost groaned out loud. He was in no mood for this. If he had to have a discussion with her, he'd rather discuss whether or not she preferred being kissed on the neck or behind the ear. "And that is?"

"I noticed you haven't bought any food. I'm planning to stop by the grocery on my way home tomorrow. Would you like me to pick up some things for you?"

"Uh… I usually eat at the hospital or get takeout." She frowned at that, so he amended, "But you've made an excellent point about taking better care of myself. I do need to have something here. If you don't mind, could you get a few boxes of mac and cheese, some frozen dinners and protein bars? That should hold me until I can get to the store myself. Take the cost out of your rent when we settle on the amount."

She turned up her lip and looked down her nose at him. "That's your list? As a doctor, you should be ashamed of yourself."

He shrugged. "You asked."

"I did. Well, I'd better get to bed." She rose. "Night, Gabe."

He watched her walk away. The more distance she put between them, the cooler the room became. If only he was going with her. "Good night," he whispered when she was out of sight.

Gabe finished his dinner, put the dirty plate into the sink, flipped off the light and went to his lonely room. With any luck, he was so tired he would go to sleep quickly and not think about the desirable woman just steps away. Was this what his life would be like? Always wishing for more?

Two evenings later Gabe came home before it was dark for the first time in a week. He'd had a replacement garage door opener for the one he gave Zoe delivered to the hospital, so he was now able to park beside Zoe's car in the carport. There was something strangely intimate about their cars sharing the same close space. He shook off that thought. Zoe didn't want that. Had made it very clear. Still, that didn't mean he hadn't lain awake late into the night, thinking about her.

Entering the house, he inhaled the delicious aroma of lasagna. He must be doing something right in Zoe's eyes. As he took another deep sniff, his stomach growled. Following the scent, he fully anticipated finding Zoe standing in the kitchen. Disappointment washed over him. She wasn't there. He headed toward her side of the house but along the way his attention was diverted out the window to the patio. There she was, sitting in a cheap fold-up lounger. Her head was back, her face lifted to the late-afternoon sun. Was she asleep?

Her head turned. Had she sensed he was there? Their gazes met through the glass, held. Zoe reminded him of an old master's painting where the yellow light surrounded her feminine form as if she was a heavenly being. That was the thought of a lovesick man. Which he was not!

Zoe blinked and half lifted the hand lying over their baby and waved. Gabe smiled and headed in her direction. She was a temptation he should stay away from but was drawn to as if he were in her gravity field. Stepping out of the French doors of the living room, he strolled across the patio.

"I'm surprised to see you home so early." Zoe looked back over her shoulder at him.

"I decided it was time to come home at a decent hour." He continued moving until he was facing her then nodded his head toward the house. "Something smells delicious. Do you have enough for two?" Did he sound as pitiful as he felt?

She smiled. "Yes. I made enough so that I'd have some to leave in the refrigerator for you."

Even after their somewhat strained conversation a

couple of nights ago, she was still trying to take care of him. Doing it despite her insistence that they were nothing more than roommates. He suppressed a spark of hope she'd changed her mind and managed to answer in a neutral tone, "Thanks. That's really nice of you."

"It's the least I can do since you're helping me out."

That explanation left a sour taste in his mouth. He would've liked it better if her kindness was motivated by a more intimate reason. Why did he keep wishing for more? She'd made it so plain on numerous occasions there would be nothing between them but the baby. He needed to accept it and get on with his personal life. Maybe it was time to ask about the available female staff at the hospital.

Zoe was saying, "I'd better get up and take it out before it burns. If you hadn't come home it really might have. The sun feels so good." Zoe swung her feet off the lounger to the bricks. "The day is so beautiful I couldn't pass up the chance to be outside. I saw this lounger in the grocery and had to have it."

Gabe stepped closer. "I'm sorry there's no patio furniture. I've never had a need for it before."

"This is such a nice space I'd furnish it before anything else." A shocked look came over her face. "I'm sorry. That's none of my business."

"Why can't it be? As far as I'm concerned, you can have a say in how I furnish the house where our child will be spending a lot of time. I don't know anything about that stuff. How about going with me to pick something out? You'd have a better idea of what I need than I do." He wasn't sure what had made him extend the invitation, but any reason that might coax her into spending time with him was worth a try.

She looked at him as if weighing the pros and cons. "I guess I could, if you really want me to."

"Tomorrow work for you?" The question had just popped out. He'd had no intention of doing it that soon.

"I have to visit Mother first thing in the morning, but I could go after that."

"Great! We'll go visit your mom then head for the furniture store. I've not seen where she's living, and I'd like to."

"Why?" She watched him suspiciously.

"Why what?"

Her look didn't waver. "Why would you want to go with me to visit my mother?"

He couldn't really answer that, so he settled on, "Because I like your mother and she'll be the grandmother of my child. Also, you've practically gone into debt because of the quality of this place, so I'm curious."

Zoe shrugged then pushed off the lounger. When she teetered backward, he caught her elbow and helped her stand. Her chuckle was a nervous one. "Thanks. I'm getting more off balance by the day. If you want to go, you can. I need to get the lasagna out." She walked toward the door.

Gabe followed her. *And more beautiful.* In the kitchen, he watched while Zoe removed and cut the pasta. He could hardly wait to taste it. To resist digging in before it made it to a plate, he busied himself with the dishes.

"I'm impressed. A man who knows how to set the table correctly." Zoe picked up a plate and returned to the stove.

"My grandmother taught me. She'd be happy you noticed." He took glasses from the shelf and filled them with ice.

"Not your mother?"

"Mom wasn't around much. She was busy making a living. I spent a good deal of time with my grandmother in my early years." Why was he telling her all of this? He didn't make a habit of sharing his personal life.

"You must've missed your mom."

He had. She'd told him throughout his childhood that it must be that way since his father was gone. Gabe's child was never going to know that feeling if he could help it. But would that really be possible with his current job, the future demands of his career? "I did, but it was what it was."

Zoe looked at him for a moment as if she understood everything he wasn't saying. Moving to the table, she set down the plate of food. "Go ahead and start. It's better hot." Picking up the other plate, she returned to the stove.

Gabe finished pouring the tea and took his place. Zoe had included a small salad and a piece of toasted bread as well. The aroma was divine but still he waited for her.

Zoe joined him with her plate in her hand. "I told you to go ahead and start."

"And my grandmother taught me that the cook deserves to be waited for. Sorry, her teaching trumps what you want."

Zoe smiled. "Smart woman."

"She was. I miss her every day." Zoe reminded him of his grandmother, who had been the most giving and caring person he'd ever known until he'd met Zoe.

"Tell me about her." Zoe placed her napkin in her lap and picked up her fork.

"I guess she was like every other grandmother. Tough when she needed to be but loving all the time." Gabe took a bite of the hot lasagna and his taste buds screamed with joy. Zoe could get a permanent job cooking for him. He would miss her when she left. That looming event he didn't want to think about. "This is wonderful. I didn't think anything could be any better than the meal last night."

Her eyes twinkled and her cheeks turned rosy. She enjoyed a compliment. Had the other men in her life not done that enough? He'd like her to always look at him the way she was now. In spite of her curt refusal to allow a personal relationship between them, her happiness mattered very much to him. But why?

"I'm glad you like it," Zoe said with a hint of shyness. As if she hadn't been sure he would.

"Anyone would."

"Not anyone."

There it was. Just what he'd suspected. "Has someone said you weren't a good cook?"

Zoe made a sound low in her throat. "Oh, yeah, in no uncertain terms."

Annoyance hot as fire flashed through him on her behalf. "Like who?"

"My ex-fiancé. Nothing I prepared for him seemed to suit. He always complained. Too salty, too hot. I guess that's one of the reasons he's my ex. Along with a few other, larger character flaws."

She'd been engaged? Had cared about a man enough to want to marry him? It shocked Gabe how much that bothered him. If she'd married that guy, they wouldn't be sitting here now. Wouldn't have had that night or be expecting a baby. He would have missed knowing Zoe. He swallowed hard and put his fork down. "What happened?"

"I caught him out to dinner with another woman. Turned out he was a jerk. He made it embarrassingly clear in front of the entire restaurant that I wasn't who he wanted. That I was too old-fashioned. Wasting my time waiting for a knight in silver armor to ride up and pledge to love me until death did us part. That expecting the man who said he loved me to be faithful and plan to be with me forever was naive nonsense. He said I needed to grow up. What a fool I was! I know what I want, and I have no intention of settling or compromising."

Gabe had the sudden urge to hit something. If her ex had been there he would have punched him in the face. Although he was pretty sure he wouldn't like the answer to the question before he asked it, he couldn't stop himself. "What do you want?"

"To find someone who will love me for who I am. Who'll put me first in his life and grow old with me." She looked at him. "To have that happily ever after."

Her answer was worse than he'd expected. She wanted everything Gabe was confident he couldn't provide.

CHAPTER SIX

ZOE WOKE THE next morning to the sun shining through her bedroom window and the birds chirping. She stretched. Now that she was well into her second trimester, she was feeling more energetic. A flutter in her middle made her pause. She couldn't stop a smile of happiness curving her lips. The baby was kicking. Butterfly taps, but they were there nonetheless.

At dinner after she'd told Gabe she was holding out for a man who would love her unconditionally and commit the rest of his life to their marriage and family, the conversation had become stilted, punctuated by awkward silence. His reaction had not been a surprise. It had merely reinforced his original revelation that he had no interest in getting married and having a family. With his logic, his career wouldn't allow it. When she'd risen to clean the kitchen, he'd insisted he would do it. Sensing Gabe was still uncomfortable with her answer, she'd left him to it and gone to bed. She'd slept well and deeply.

Thinking about the way their evening had ended, she feared their visit to her mother's and the shopping trip might be tense as well. Debating whether or not to spend the day with Gabe, she was surprised by the smell of frying bacon wafting into her room.

Gabe was cooking?

She pulled her robe on and tugged the belt tight, making certain she was completely covered. More than once when she'd been talking to Gabe about rent, she'd caught his gaze slipping to the V of her robe. His hot glances had brought to mind passionate memories that would have weakened her resolve if she'd allowed herself to revisit them.

The scent led her to the kitchen, where Gabe stood at the stove with his bare back to her, the view of wide shoulders with thick muscles tapering to a trim waist and slim hips clad in well-worn jeans hung low. She swallowed. He had such a nice behind, was a magnificent specimen of a male. Her fingers twitched with the temptation to touch him. Would he mind if she did? The question set off mental alarm bells. She must stop tormenting herself with fantasies of forbidden pleasures.

She stuffed her hands into the pockets of her robe and cleared her throat. "Good morning."

Gabe half turned. "Morning. I don't have your culinary talents but I can cook eggs and bacon. Interested?"

Zoe battled to master her physical reaction to him as she shrugged in what she hoped was a nonchalant manner. "Sure."

"Have a seat. I'm just getting ready to do the eggs. How do you like yours?"

Apparently, whatever had been bothering him last night was forgotten. She took what had become her place at the table. "Scrambled."

He smiled. "Scrambled it is."

She liked this cheerful, relaxed version of Gabe. This was the man she'd gotten to know in Chicago. The charmer. She suspected his charisma was at full force.

Gabe placed a plate with fluffy eggs, two slices of crisp bacon and buttered toast in front of her. It looked as delicious as it smelled. She gave him a genuine smile of gratitude. "Thanks."

He soon joined her with a plate twice as full as hers in his hand. Over the next few minutes they ate in a companionable silence. Zoe was glad their camaraderie had returned. Slowly chewing bacon and studying him as he ate, she decided she'd like it to always be that way between them. She watched as his gaze met hers. He raised a brow.

"Thank you. This is wonderful."

Gabe looked pleased. "You're welcome."

His phone that was always nearby buzzed. He picked it up. "Dr. Marks."

As he talked she continued to eat, paying little attention to the conversation. "I'll be in this afternoon to review the charts." Gabe ended the call.

"Problem?"

"I implemented a new protocol. It's not popular, so I'm getting some pushback. Do you have a certain time that you have to be at your mother's?"

"It's Saturday, so I can go whenever I wish."

"Then do you think you can be ready to leave in half an hour? I have to go in to the hospital later." He picked up his toast.

She pushed at her eggs. "Then why don't you just go pick out furniture while I go see Mom? Cut down on your stress."

"No, I've got time. I just need to check the charts after shift change this afternoon."

She was amazed at his dedication to detail. "You really oversee all the details."

"It's important that my program be cutting-edge."

She pursed her lips and nodded. "Or you're just a bit of a control freak."

He grinned. "And maybe a little bit of that as well."

An hour and a half later they were walking into Shorecliffs House.

"This looks nice," Gabe said as he held the front door open for her.

"It is, but I still hate that Mom can't take care of herself anymore and, worse, that I can't do it either."

Gabe's arm came around her and pulled her into a quick hug before dropping away.

"You're doing the best you can for your mother. She knows you love her."

Zoe wished his hug had lasted longer as she held back tears. "I hope so."

They walked down the long hall and took the first right, stopping in front of a door on the left. Zoe knocked. Pushing it open with some trepidation about what she would find, she was pleasantly surprised. Her mother sat in a cushioned chair near the window. A book lay on her lap. Zoe's heart lifted. Her mother had always loved reading, but Zoe hadn't seen her pick up a book in months. Even if she wasn't reading, at least she'd thought to try. "Hi, Mom."

Her mother looked up. A smile came across her face. "Hey, sweetheart."

Relief washed over Zoe. Today her mother recognized her. The doctors had told Zoe there would be times when her mom would know her and then her memory would fade again.

"How're you?" Her mother was having a good day.

Zoe smiled and kissed her on the cheek. "I'm doing fine." She sank into a nearby straight chair.

Her mother looked to where Gabe stood. "You brought someone with you."

"Hello, Mrs. Avery. It's nice to see you again," Gabe said as he stepped forward.

Her mother gave him a blank look but soon the brightness of recognition filled her eyes. "I know you. You brought chicken."

"That's right." Gabe sat on the edge of the bed. "How do you like your new place? It's nice, and your daughter has done a lovely job of furnishing it."

"I want to go home," she said earnestly.

Zoe's chest tightened. She hated hearing those words. Gabe reached over and took her hand, giving it a gentle, reassuring squeeze. She appreciated the support. It was good of him to notice her distress. "I know, Mom, but right now this is the best place for you."

"Can I go home?"

"Mrs. Avery, do you dance?" Gabe asked.

That was an odd question. Zoe was thankful for his timely redirection of her mother's thoughts, but was perplexed by the new topic of conversation he'd chosen.

"Dance?" her mother asked in a tone Zoe hadn't heard in a long time.

"I noticed on the activity board on our way down the hall that there's a dance on Saturday night. I was wondering if you were going." Gabe leaned forward as if greatly interested in her answer.

Her mother actually blushed. Zoe couldn't help but smile.

"I don't know."

"I bet there are a number of men who would like to dance with you," Zoe said to further encourage her. "I also saw that they have game day, music and people coming in to sing."

Her mother gave her a bleak look. Zoe had lost her again. She forged forward. "We're on our way to buy some furniture."

"Furniture?" her mom said.

"Yes. For my patio," Gabe answered.

"He wants me to help him pick it out." Zoe watched closely, hoping her mom would come out of the place she'd disappeared to.

Her mother looked down at her book.

Together they struggled to converse with her mother for the next fifteen minutes. Her memory came and went all the while. When Zoe became frustrated, Gabe stepped in. She admired his patience. More than once her mom had asked what his name was and each time he'd clearly and calmly told her. Finally, her mother showed signs of frustration.

With a heavy heart, Zoe said, "Mom, it's time for us to go." She kissed her mother's soft cheek, straightened, hoping her mom would say goodbye. All she got was a vaguely puzzled smile. Gabe followed her out of the room, softly closing the door behind him.

As they walked down the hall on their way out, he took her hand. "I know how increasingly difficult visiting her is for you."

Zoe blinked back tears. "It is. I hate that she's losing her memory in general, but I know soon it will be to the point that she'll stop recognizing me altogether." She laid her hand over her middle. "She'll never really know her grandchild. The baby won't know her."

"Then you'll just have to make a special point to tell him or her about your mother." Gabe stepped ahead of her and held open the front door.

"You make it sound so easy." Zoe stepped past him.

"Never said that. My mom never talked about my father much. I wished she had. I don't feel like I know him."

She had a father who had decided he didn't want her. Zoe wasn't sure which was worse—never having a father to begin with, or having one who didn't want you. "My father left us when I was ten. He went to work one day and didn't return."

"I'm sorry. That must have been awful."

Her chest tightened. "It was bad but at least I had him for a little while. The worst is knowing it was that easy to walk away from us."

"Sounds like both of us might have father issues. Not a great thing to have in common, but something." There was sadness in his voice.

"I guess you're right." She looked at him. "Thanks for coming with me." Somehow Gabe's supportive presence had made it easier. She was starting to depend on him. That mistake she had to constantly guard against. He hadn't made any promises to her. He could be gone just as easily as her father, but Gabe was there for her right now.

"You're welcome," he was saying. "I'm glad to see your mom has a quality place to live. You're doing the right thing."

"Then why do I feel so rotten about it?"

Gabe stopped her. Waited until she looked at him before he said, "Because you can't do anything to make the situation better."

She nodded. "I guess."

They arrived at the car.

"So where should we go for this furniture? You're the person who knows the area." Gabe unlocked the doors.

After a minute Zoe answered, "I guess Abrams Furniture is the best place to start. It's the biggest furniture store in the area. Turn left out of the parking lot."

Thirty minutes later, Gabe parked in front of the entrance to the large building with windows showcasing furniture for many different rooms of a house. Gabe held the glass door open for Zoe to enter.

They were quickly greeted by a middle-aged woman. "Hello. What may I show you today?"

Gabe smiled. "We'd like to look at patio furniture."

The lady was quick to return his smile. "Come this way. I'm sure we have something you'll like."

They followed her along a path leading through groupings of sofas and chairs, then dining-room suites, toward the back of the store. The smell of new furniture and polished wood was nearly overpowering. Along the way they passed the nursery section. Before Zoe was the most perfect white crib. Beside it stood a matching chest of drawers, changing table and even a rocker.

She stopped, unable to resist running her fingers along the top of one side of the crib. The image of pastel ruffled drapes on the windows as the sun beamed in filled her mind. A white rocker sat nearby. When she had her own place this would be what she'd like to have for the baby. She was so mesmerized by the pictures in her head, she had to hurry to catch up with Gabe. He waited by a door leading to the outside.

"Did you find something you like?" he asked as she walked by him.

Zoe shook her head. He was already more involved in her life than she had intended to allow. She wasn't going to open her heart to another man who didn't share her dream of commitment and marriage. Heart still healing from her failed relationship with her ex, she certainly wouldn't repeat it when she already knew how Gabe felt.

The woman was waiting for them in the middle of the large covered area. There were all kinds of chairs and tables suitable for outdoor use. Some had metal frames while others were made of wicker. Many appeared nice enough for inside use. There were numerous cushions, in every color choice, both in floral prints and plain fabric. The space was almost overwhelming.

"What do you think would be best on the patio?" Gabe asked her.

"Oh, I don't know. There's so much here. Let me look around some." She shouldn't be making these types of decisions with him. She wouldn't be staying at his home long. Furniture implied longevity, and that she wouldn't have.

Gabe walked around from one grouping to another. She joined him, making her own path through the jumble.

She wasn't sure what was best for him, but she did know what she liked. "I prefer the wicker look."

"Then that's what we should look at," he said as if pleased.

His attention turned to the saleswoman, who was swift to direct them toward a space with nothing but that style of outdoor furniture. A particular suite caught Zoe's attention. It included a table with a large orange umbrella and four black chairs. Next to them were a matching two-person settee, a lounger, and two chairs with orange cushions and a low table situated between them. The entire set was perfect for Gabe's patio. Classical, yet functional. Zoe headed straight for it.

"Why don't you have a seat and see how it feels?" the saleslady suggested. "See how comfortable it is."

Zoe took a seat in one of the chairs at the table. Gabe

sank into an armchair with high sides. It accommodated his large body as if tailor made for him.

"So what do you think?" Gabe looked at her.

"I like this chair. It's sturdy enough, which you'll need if it's going to be outside all the time. But do you really need all of this?" Zoe waved her hand in a circle.

He shrugged. "I have plenty of room for it, so why not? Come try the lounger. You'd use it more than me."

She lowered her voice so the saleswoman couldn't easily hear. "I'm not going to use it that long."

"Please just try the lounger and tell me what you think." There was a pleading note in his voice.

The saleslady must have picked up on it as well because she said, "I'm going to let you two discuss this. If you need me I'll be right over there." She pointed toward the door through which they had exited.

With some annoyance Zoe sat on the lounger, pushed back until she was comfy and put up her legs. It would be the perfect place to read a book, feed their baby. *Their* baby. When had she started thinking of the baby as theirs instead of hers? She glanced at Gabe, shaken on a disturbing level. How did he think of the baby?

She had to stand. Those thoughts weren't ones she needed to have. Heartache, disappointment and disagreement were all they would bring between her and Gabe. Zoe shifted on the cushion, moving to get off it.

Gabe quickly rose and offered her a hand. "So what do you think?"

"It's very nice," she murmured.

He raised a brow in question. "Should I get it?"

Though reluctant to do so, Zoe nodded. "I think so."

"Now, that wasn't so hard, was it?"

She was grateful he didn't give her time to respond before he walked off toward the saleslady.

If Gabe furnished the rest of the house as nicely as the patio, their child would have an amazing place to visit. She wouldn't have to worry about the baby having what he or she needed. Gabe would see to it. In fact, he was quite willing to let her see to it, but she mustn't give in to that temptation. It would be too easy to think and act as if Gabe's house was hers as well and, worse, as if he was.

Gabe was kind, caring and generous. He'd be a good father based on that. Even if he didn't think so. A child deserved both a mother and father in their life. As long as she and Gabe could agree on how the baby should be raised, he or she should have a good life. Not the perfect one like Zoe dreamed of, but a good one nonetheless. What they had to do was remain civil. When their emotions became involved that was when heartache and anger would take over and create strife. She couldn't let that happen.

Zoe followed Gabe and the saleswoman into the building. As they walked past the nursery furniture, she made a point not to look at it, sighing. It would be nice to bring the baby home from the hospital to a finished nursery, but that wasn't the plan. When the time was right she'd set one up. Until then, she'd settle for a cradle in her bedroom.

She joined Gabe at the counter where he'd just finished paying for the furniture.

"All done." Gabe turned to her with a pleased smile. "Thanks for your help."

The saleslady said as they headed out the door, "It has been a pleasure to help such a nice couple."

Zoe's heart caught. A warm feeling raced through her. She looked at Gabe. Was there any chance that one day that could be true? He was an honorable and steadfast person. Just the type of man she'd been looking for...

She started to correct the woman, but Gabe placed a hand at her back and said without missing a beat, "Thanks for your help." To Zoe he said, "How about an early lunch before we head home?"

Gabe settled onto a metal chair on the patio of a local restaurant after seeing Zoe properly seated. The sky was bright and there was a slight breeze, making it comfortable outside. They had both ordered a sandwich, chips and a drink. He'd carried it to the table on a tray, thoroughly delighted with their morning together.

Visiting her mother had been difficult for Zoe and he was glad he could be there for her. Shopping, even for something as mundane as furniture, wasn't high on his list of fun things to do but he'd enjoyed the trip with Zoe. The only catch in the morning had been when she'd resisted sitting on the lounger. She was using the fact she wasn't going to live at his house long as an excuse to avoid taking any interest in it. He wanted her to feel comfortable while she was there. To his amazement he was in no hurry for her to do so. He would miss her.

Zoe captured his attention when she said, "This is one of those places I've always wanted to go but have never taken the time."

Her light brown hair glowed in the sunlight. There was a touch of color in her cheeks, giving her a healthy look. "Being pregnant seems to agree with you."

Her look quickly locked with his as her hand moved to her middle. He'd come to expect her to do that anytime the baby was mentioned. "It has been easier than I expected, despite the first few months of morning sickness."

Something close to guilt assaulted him. "I'm sorry."

"It's not your fault."

It had better be. His eyes narrowed. "Who else's would it be?"

"I...uh...only meant there's nothing you could have done about it."

"I was just teasing you." Reaching across the table, he brushed away a stray strand of hair from her cheek with the tip of his index finger. "I know what you meant. I still haven't gotten used to the idea that I'm going to be a father."

"You might need to. It won't be that much longer," she said softly.

"Have you picked out names?" Gabe watched her closely. Would he like them? Would she care? Or ask for his suggestions? She didn't have to.

"I've thought of a few." She picked up a chip.

He watched her closely. "Such as?"

"If it's a boy I'd like to name him either William or Michael."

"Those are both good strong names. My father's name was Gabriel Harold." He didn't miss the slight upturn of her lip at the last name.

Zoe said with a dip of her shoulder and an unsure look, "I like Gabriel."

He grinned. "Not a Harold fan?"

She shook her head. "Not really."

Gabe took a bite of his sandwich. He'd like his child to have a name from his side of the family. But it wasn't a demand he believed he could make. "What about girls' names?"

"I was thinking Laura, Mandy, Maggie. My mother's name is Sandra. I wasn't going to make any real decision until I knew the sex."

"And you'll find that out when?"

She glanced at him. "This week. I have a doctor's appointment on Wednesday. I could have known a few weeks ago but I had to push the ultrasound back because of Mother."

Gabe gave an understanding nod. "What time?"

"What time?" Zoe gave him a quizzical tilt of her head.

"What time are you going for the ultrasound? I'll need to make sure I don't have a surgery scheduled." At her flabbergasted look he added, "I told you I wanted to be there."

"Is that really necessary?"

Why would she care if he went? "Is there any reason I shouldn't be there?"

Zoe didn't look at him. "No, not really, but I can just call you when I'm finished."

"I'd like to be in on the surprise as well." Why did it matter to him that he be there for the actual event?

"Okay." She didn't sound convinced but at least he wasn't going to have to persuade her further.

"You know, I've never lived on this side of the country," Gabe said, picking up his sandwich.

Zoe's face brightened. "You'll love it here. There's so much to see and do. Of course, there's everything in Washington but there are historical homes, battlefields, museums and all the seasonal events."

"Do you go to see those things?"

"I used to stay pretty busy attending concerts and festivals until Mother got worse. I've not got to do much of that in a long time." Sadness filled Zoe's eyes.

"Then maybe we should do some of those things before the baby gets here."

An expectant, hopeful look came over her face. He had her full attention. "Would you have time?"

Would he? He had no idea. "I could try."

"I'm sorry. That wasn't a fair question. I know you're busy."

He'd disappointed her. Just as he had other women he'd been interested in. Except it really bothered him that it was happening again with Zoe. There just wasn't much time in his life for extracurricular activities. He wasn't being fair to Zoe to suggest there was. He wanted to make her happy. Maybe he could work something out in a few weeks. He checked his watch. "I'd better get you home. I'm due at the hospital."

"I'm ready." She stood and pushed the chair in.

She didn't say much on the trip home. He pulled up to the front door. "The deliverymen said they could be here today at three. Will you be around?"

"Yes."

"Great. Do you mind seeing that they get the furniture in place?"

"I can take care of it." Zoe climbed out of the car. "Thanks for lunch and going with me to see Mom."

"No problem. See you later."

The doorbell ringing brought Zoe out of sleep. It took her a few seconds to clear her head enough to get off the bed and head up the hall.

She hadn't been surprised when Gabe hadn't even gotten out of the car before he'd left for the hospital. For a moment at lunch she'd hoped that what he said might be different from what he felt. That he would take time for himself. Do something other than work. Then maybe they could do some touristy things together, but as quickly as the hope flickered it had been snuffed out.

Part of knowing Gabe was accepting those types of things weren't high on his priority list. She, on the other hand, believed they were important for a balanced and happy life. With that in mind, she wanted to make the most of the beautiful day, so she took a walk around the neighborhood before settling in for an afternoon nap. She'd forgotten all about the furniture being delivered until the bell rang. She opened the front door to find two uniformed men waiting.

"We're here to deliver your furniture. Would you show us where it goes?"

"Through here." Zoe opened the door wider and led the way through the living room to the patio.

The men followed quietly, nodding as they surveyed the area, then left her. Soon they returned with the armchairs.

"Where would you like these?"

Zoe pointed to the area that received the most sun. They returned to the truck. While they were gone Zoe moved the chairs into position. In just a few minutes all the furniture was sitting on the patio. Even the umbrella was in place and up. She turned around and smiled. The floral and striped cushions with the matching colors added interest. The patio looked perfect. Gabe should enjoy using it. If he took the time to appreciate it. Until she moved she planned to make the most of the lounger as often as possible, starting that afternoon.

One of the deliverymen asked, "Where would you like the rest of it to go?"

"What? I didn't know there was any more." She followed him into the house.

He pulled a paper out of his back pocket and studied it. "We have a whole room of nursery furniture that's supposed to come to this address."

Zoe's heart jumped. Gabe had bought nursery furniture? She'd not seen him even look at any. Maybe he'd done it online.

"Oh, okay."

"So where do we put it?" The man sounded as if he was losing patience.

"In here." Zoe showed him the empty front room.

He left again and returned with his partner. They had a chest of drawers in their arms. Zoe's breath caught. It was the chest in the group she'd liked so much.

"Where do you want it?" one man grunted.

Zoe looked around the room for a second, totally disoriented by what was happening. "Uh, over on that wall." She pointed to the space between the window and the door. Still in a daze at what Gabe had done, she watched as the men brought in the rocker and changing table.

Gabe had been paying attention when she'd admired the crib and had even noticed how much she liked the set. Had any man ever been that in tune with her? He may have little time to spare, but when he was with her he was totally present.

On the next trip, the men brought in the pieces of the baby bed. One returned to the truck and came back with a tool bag. In less than thirty minutes the bed was together and the mattress in place.

"Where would you like this?" one of the men asked.

"Catty-corner, between the windows." She pointed to the area.

They did as she requested. Soon Zoe was showing them out. She returned to the nursery, taking a seat in the rocker. Feeling overwhelmed, she looked around the room. It would make a perfect nursery. She imagined the walls decorated and envisioned the drapery for the windows…

A tear ran down her cheek. The room would be so beautiful. But it would never be hers.

Zoe didn't have a chance to talk to Gabe about what he'd done because he wasn't home when she went to bed. She couldn't question his commitment to his job. Gabe seemed more than willing to put in the hours required. He'd earned her respect for that alone, but then, there was much to admire about Gabe. Too much for her comfort.

Midmorning the next day she was sitting on the patio, reading a book, when the sound of footsteps on the bricks drew her notice.

A moment later Gabe joined her with a glass in his hand. After placing the drink on the low table, he dropped into one of the chairs facing her. "Mornin'. Mind if I join you?"

It was his home. Gabe didn't have to ask her. "Sure."

She stared at him. Every feminine cell in her body stood at attention and tingled. He acted rested and relaxed. His hair was still damp and tousled as if he'd dried it with a towel and done nothing more to it after his shower. A T-shirt fit close to his chest and his jeans were well-worn with holes in the knees. He was gorgeous.

As if unaware of her admiration, he placed his feet on the table, crossed his ankles and leaned back in the chair. "It looks great out here. I like the way you arranged everything."

Zoe was pleased by his praise. Too much so. "I'm glad you do. I didn't know how you would want it."

"I had no doubt I could trust you." He grinned.

"Why didn't you tell me that you were buying nursery furniture?"

He pursed his lips and shrugged. "Maybe because

I thought you might argue with me about it. I needed something for the baby anyway. You don't like it?"

"I like it very much."

A smug look covered his face. "I thought you might. I saw you looking at it."

He had noticed her interest. She confessed, "I was thinking about getting it for the nursery at my place."

"Why don't you fix up the room the way you like it? You can take it all with you when you go. I'll get more furniture."

"I couldn't do that."

"Sure you can. The baby'll be coming home to this house. He or she needs their own space. Wouldn't it be nice for it to have some continuity from here to your house?"

That really wasn't necessary but Zoe liked the idea of having a special place for the baby from the beginning. "I had planned to just use a cradle for the few weeks I'm still here. I'll think about finishing the nursery."

Gabe picked up his glass, took a long draw on the iced tea and set it down again. "Good. I promised I'd come up with a figure for your rent. But before I give you that I'd like you to consider a proposition."

Her heart leaped. Proposition? What kind of proposition?

"I've been thinking, and don't want to offend you, but you've been cooking meals, even doing some shopping, and I appreciate you have your own job to deal with, but I've not had time to find a housekeeper. If you'd be willing, and thought you had time, to just keep things straightened around here for a little while, then I would forgo the rent altogether. I don't want to imply that I think you should be my housekeeper or anything…"

Zoe hadn't expected this. The extra money she would

save would make a nice down payment on the house she wanted. She enjoyed cooking and was doing that for herself anyway. The housekeeping wouldn't be that much. Gabe wasn't home long enough to get anything dirty. Plus, he was neat. She was already taking care of her side of the house. "I think that would work."

"Excellent." He stood. "Then I'm going to catch up on some reading and watch the ball game."

"Okay. I'll make lunch in a little while."

"Sounds great." He strolled to the house.

They were acting like a married couple on Sunday afternoon now. It should have made her feel uneasy but instead there was a satisfaction there, contentment. She looked into the living area at Gabe. He was sitting in his chair with his legs stretched out and his attention on the TV. Wouldn't it be nice if it was always this way between them? It was a wonderful dream. But just a dream. Gabe had never mentioned his feelings regarding her. He was a decent man but that didn't mean he cared for her the way Zoe wanted him to.

CHAPTER SEVEN

GABE STUDIED ZOE. She'd been reading for the last couple of hours while he had supposedly watched TV. Even though he wasn't outside with her, he was very aware of her movements. From his chair he could see her better than she could him. Was she aware of how many times her hand went to the rounded area of her stomach? Just from that small action he had no doubt she loved and wanted their baby.

Her gaze met his through the glass. She gave him a small smile before she returned to her reading. Only by a force of will did he stop himself from getting up and going out to kiss her. Or more. But he'd promised not to touch her again unless she initiated it. He would keep his promise even if it killed him.

Sometime later Zoe came in and quietly went to the kitchen. Now he was listening to her moving around as she prepared a late lunch. Something about having her in his home, being around her, sharing meals and even picking out furniture seemed right. She brought a softness to his life that he hadn't known he had been missing. Did he want to let it go? Was he capable of hanging on to it?

Would Zoe consider staying if he asked? They got along well. But she wanted a husband. Could he offer her that? Be the husband she needed? What if he didn't measure up to her expectations? Could he even be the father to his child that he should be? How would he ever know? He'd had no firsthand experience, not seen a father in action close-up. Could he find enough balance in his life to make it work? Which would be worse: not taking the chance or failing?

Zoe brought him a plate with a sandwich and salad on it.

"Thank you."

She smiled. "You're welcome." She continued outside to the table.

He watched her. She hadn't invited him to join her. Would she mind if he did? One of the things he liked most about having Zoe in the house was sharing meals and conversation.

Taking his plate, he went to join her. Zoe didn't look up as he approached. He'd like to know her thoughts. "Do you mind?"

Her head jerked around. "Uh, sure. It's your patio."

Annoyance ran hot through him. "I wish you'd quit thinking like that. This is your home for as long as you stay. I want you to treat it that way."

"I'll try."

"Don't try. Accept it." He took a chair beside her.

She pushed a leaf of lettuce around on her plate. "It just seems strange to live with someone you know so little about."

"What do you want to know?" He bit into his sandwich. Was it so good because of the sliced ham and cheese or because Zoe had made it?

"I don't know," she said slowly, as if giving it thought. "What's your favorite color?"

"Green." *Like your eyes*, but he didn't say that. "What's yours?"

"Red. But I'm supposed to be asking you questions."

He grinned. "Ever think I might like to learn a few things about you?"

"Okay, then. Do you like a dog or a cat?"

"Dog. Big dog. And you?" He looked up from the fork he was filling with salad and raised a brow in question.

"I always wanted a Labrador retriever but didn't have a good place for one to live." A dreamy look came over her face.

"Nice dogs. Good with children, I've heard."

She focused on him again. "Favorite vacation spot?"

"I like the beach but the mountains are nice too. What I like is to be active and learn something wherever I go."

"Learn something?" She pulled her sandwich apart and took the cheese off it.

"Yeah, I like taking trips centered around a subject where there are lectures and visits to places where events happened. History, social service, medical missions."

Zoe nibbled at the cheese and then said, "I haven't done that. Maybe I've been missing out on something." She paused in a pensive manner before asking, "Where have you been on a medical mission?"

"I've made a couple of trips to South America, another to Arizona."

"Oh!" Zoe jumped.

Gabe leaned forward, concern making him study her. "What's wrong? You hurt somewhere?"

Her smile turned to a sweet, reflective one. "The baby kicked."

He looked to where her hand rested. Despite being a doctor, the action filled him with awe.

She hissed and looked at him. "There it was again."

"May I feel?" he asked softly. The need to know the small life growing in her would take him to his knees, begging, if that was what it took to get her to agree.

She nodded. He placed his hand where hers had been. There was nothing. Zoe flinched again but he didn't feel anything. Placing her hand over the top of his, she moved it slightly and pressed. A second later there was a thump against his palm. His gaze snapped to meet hers. At that moment she took his heart.

He leaned forward with the intention of kissing her. But he'd promised. "Zoe..."

She wanted and deserved assurances he wasn't prepared to give. He needed space. Gabe stood and picked up his plate. "Thanks for sharing that with me."

Zoe looked at him with big wide eyes before he stalked away.

Fifteen minutes later he was on his way to the hospital.

Wednesday morning Zoe sat in the obstetrician's office, waiting for the nurse to call her name. She'd not seen Gabe since Sunday afternoon. He'd been gone Monday by the time she'd gone to the kitchen. She'd heard him come in once but it had been late and she'd already been in bed.

His new job might be demanding but the thought had crossed her mind that maybe he was dodging her. She wasn't sure why he would be but something about the way he'd abruptly left on Sunday made her question his actions.

She'd texted him the time of the appointment and the address. Maybe he'd changed his mind about being there. She wasn't sure how she felt about that. His insistence had taken her by surprise. Although she knew she shouldn't, she wanted to share the moment of discovery with him.

A nurse standing at the door leading back to the examination rooms called Zoe's name. She searched the entrance to the outside of the building as disappointment filled her. Apparently Gabe wasn't coming. After all he'd said about being involved and the one time she'd agreed, he wasn't taking advantage of it. She'd let herself believe… What, she wasn't sure. That there might be a chance for them? That Gabe could really care about the baby beyond being honorable? Or that he could want to be there for her? All of it was just wishful thinking. Nothing based on reality.

She followed the nurse back to the examination room. Inside she sat on the table with shoulders slumped and waited. Her situation with Gabe reminded her of her relationship with Shawn and her father. She hadn't been able to depend on them. They were unreliable, would hurt her. She saw it one way when in reality it was all another. With Gabe she needed to keep what was truth separated from wishful thinking.

Zoe had been waiting a few minutes when there was a quick rap on the door. Fully expecting the doctor, she was shocked to see Gabe step in. She couldn't deny the joy surging into her chest. He had come.

"I'm sorry I'm late. I got tied up at the last minute," he said, puffing as if he'd been running. He came to stand beside her. "Have I missed anything?"

His breathless enthusiasm made her smile. He was acting like a kid looking for a piece of candy. "No. The doctor hasn't been in yet."

"Good." He sank into the only chair in the room.

Moments later the door opened and this time it was her doctor. He gave Gabe a questioning once-over.

Gabe stood and offered his hand. "Gabe Marks. I'm the baby's father."

Zoe didn't miss the proud tone of his voice. Another gentle wave of happiness washed over her.

"Nice to meet you," the doctor said, then turned to her. "This visit is the one where we do the anatomy ultrasound. The question is, do you want to know the sex?"

Before Zoe could speak Gabe said, "I'm more interested in knowing if Zoe and baby are all right."

Tears sprang to Zoe's eyes. She'd not expected that statement.

"That I can let you know as well, but I don't anticipate a problem with either one of them." The doctor smiled at her.

"That's good to hear," Gabe said, then looked at her. "We do want to know the sex, don't we?"

Zoe nodded.

"Okay," her doctor said. "The tech will be in in a few minutes to do the ultrasound. Then I'll be back to do the examination." That said, he left, closing the door behind him.

"Are you okay?" Gabe asked now that they were alone.

"Yeah. Why?"

"You just had a funny look on your face a few minutes ago." Either she'd revealed too much or he'd been watching her too closely.

"I'm just excited."

Gabe took her hand. "I know this wasn't what either of us planned, but I have to admit that bringing a new life into the world is pretty amazing." He kissed her forehead.

The tenderness of the moment dissolved when there was another knock at the door, but the lingering contentment would last a long time.

Gabe held the door open for the tech, who was pushing a large machine on wheels. "Hi, I'm Sarah. I'll be doing your ultrasound." She positioned the machine beside the exam table. "Are you Dad?" she asked Gabe.

"Yes."

"Then what I'd like you to do is sit in the chair until I get everything all set up. Then you can come and stand beside Mom." She started getting the cables organized.

A perplexed look came over Gabe's face. Zoe couldn't help but grin. Her guess was that Gabe did most of the ordering in his world and to have this woman in control of the situation had to go against the grain. Despite that, he did what the tech requested but watched her with narrowed eyes.

"Let's get you further up on the table." The woman helped Zoe scoot back. "Now, please pull up your shirt."

Zoe did, revealing the roundness of her belly, made more pronounced by lying down. She looked over at Gabe. His attention was fixed on her middle. There was something telling and intense about his focus. Seconds later his gaze rose to meet hers and his eyes softened. What was he thinking?

Soon the tech squirted a glob of gel on Zoe's belly and had the transducer moving over her skin. The swishing sound of the baby's heart beating filled the room. "Okay, Dad, you can come and stand beside Mom."

Gabe didn't have to be asked twice. When he was beside her, he placed his hand over hers where it rested on the exam table, curling his fingers into her palm. It was as if he had to be touching her. For a man who had asserted he didn't have time or room in his life for a family, he seemed very interested in her and this baby. Maybe he didn't know what he really wanted.

The tech continued to watch the screen as she moved

the transducer over Zoe. "All right, I understand you want to know what gender this baby is. Let's see if we can find out."

Zoe glanced at Gabe. He was watching the screen intently.

Before Zoe could look back the tech said, "I believe with that anatomy it's a boy."

Pure joy filled Gabe's face. He squeezed her hand and breathed softly, "A boy."

Zoe looked at the screen. There was their baby boy. Would he look like Gabe? She hoped so. Tall, dark-haired with magnetic blue eyes. What child could go wrong with that combination?

A ringing sound had Gabe letting go of her hand and digging into his pocket. He looked at the cell phone and stepped away from her. Just that quickly the special moment evaporated.

"Dr. Marks." He listened then said, "I'll be right there." He ended the connection and considered her, his face grave. "I have to go. I have to be there to supervise."

His mind was already somewhere else.

"I know." Zoe did understand. She was glad that at least he'd made it there for their special moment.

He moved around the machine and slipped out the door.

Zoe watched it close between them. It was just one more reminder nothing had changed and she shouldn't get her hopes up.

Gabe would have never thought he'd be this absorbed in a baby. Was it because the child was his or because Zoe was carrying it? Or both? There had always been an attraction between him and Zoe, but in the last few weeks it had grown into something more. A feeling he didn't want to put a name to or analyze, but that was taking control nonetheless.

He'd hated to leave her so abruptly, especially after his almost too late arrival. They had shared one of the most surreal moments of his life. He had been watching his son on the screen. More than that, he'd shared it with Zoe. For heaven's sake, he was a physician and he'd gone through the OB rotation in medical school, but this time it was his child.

Although it was late in the evening before he headed out of the hospital, he still had a stop to make. Less than an hour later he pulled into the garage beside Zoe's car. With a smile on his face, he picked up the brown bag in the passenger seat and climbed out of the car. Would Zoe think his purchase was silly or give him an understanding smile? It didn't matter which, because he'd been unable to help himself.

There was a light burning in the kitchen but no Zoe. With the bag in his hand, he went to her hallway. "Zoe." There was no answer. He took a few more steps toward her room. "Zoe?"

Seconds later the sound of music playing met his ears. She must not be able to hear him. He went to her bedroom door. "Zoe." Still nothing. Now he was getting worried. Had she passed out? Fallen in the shower?

He stepped to the bathroom door and jerked to a stop. His throat tightened and his heart pounded. Zoe stood in front of the large mirror over the sink. She had her nightgown pulled up to below her breasts and was looking down while her hands slowly roamed over her expanded middle. A serene smile of wonderment lit her lovely face.

Gabe shifted.

Her head whipped toward him, her eyes wide. She reached for her gown.

"Please, don't." His words were soft and beseeching. "You're so beautiful. Breathtaking."

Zoe's hands stilled but she watched him with unmistakable wariness.

Gabe placed the bag on the counter and slowly stepped behind her. Their gazes locked in the mirror. There was a question in her eyes. His arms circled her. She trembled when his palms touched her warm, smooth skin. Would she push him away?

His heart thundered in his ears when her hands covered his, her fingers interlacing with his. She moved them down and around until they cupped the tight globe encasing their baby. Zoe closed her eyes and leaned back against him. Gabe had never seen her look more angelic. Inhaling, he took in the soft, subtle scent of her freshness. He could do nothing more than stare. What he had in his arms was precious.

She once again moved his hands to rest at what had once been the curve of her hips. There was a small push against one of his palms. Gabe hissed. His heart swelled. Emotions too strong to comprehend grew in his chest and spread out to overtake him. This was territory he'd never been to before. "Zoe, thank you."

Zoe stood perfectly still. Gabe's voice was like a tender kiss upon her neck. She opened her eyes, meeting his intense, passionate gaze. He'd said he wouldn't touch her again unless she asked him to, so it was up to her to make the first move. Turning in his arms, she wrapped her arms around his neck and pushed up on her toes. Her lips lightly touched his. "No. Thank you."

Gabe's mouth pressed into hers, igniting that fire

that only he could. He pulled her closer. His lips slid over hers, leaving sweet waves of sensation radiating out through her body. She put her fingers to the hair at the nape of his neck, ran them through it. Moments later, Gabe's gentle touch traveled over her back, grasping and releasing as his arms circled her, lifting her against him. She went willingly.

Where their previous kisses had been frantic, this one was loving and exploring, wondering and appreciating. Zoe moaned and melted further into him. She was sure she wasn't taking the most rational action, but she could no longer fight her emotions.

Gabe's mouth left hers to skim along her cheek, leaving small caresses that held more reverence than passion. He kissed her temple then the shell of her ear. "I want you. Just to hold you."

"I want that too," she purred against his lips.

Releasing her, Gabe lowered the gown covering her. He took her hand, leading her out of the bathroom and across the house toward his room. Zoe had resisted going into his space. Had even put off cleaning there. Something about it was just too intimate. Now she was being invited in. Wanted.

Gabe let go of her hand at the door, moving into the dark room alone. Seconds later, a small lamp on a bureau lit the space. Gabe's furniture was massive. It suited him. The king-size bed was the centerpiece with its dark green spread. On either side were two end tables. At one end of the room was a fireplace with enough space for a sitting area, but there was nothing there.

He returned to her, offering his hand. Zoe took it. She wanted this. Needed the closeness. Gabe led her to the bedside. His blue eyes seemed to glow with emotion. She was unable to identify which one before his lips found hers. His mouth touched hers gently, giving instead of taking. It was as if he was trying to convey his feelings without voicing them.

For the first time Zoe dared to hope that there might be a future for them.

When Gabe pulled away, he gave her another searching look. Going down on one knee, he took the hem of her gown and rolled it up. She sucked in a breath. With her heart in her throat, Zoe watched him lean in and place a kiss where their baby grew. Gabe turned his head, placing his cheek against her. Her hand cradled his head and held him close. Moisture filled her eyes.

He rose, bringing the gown up with him. Seconds later he stripped it off over her head. She shivered, her arms instantly covering her breasts.

"Please don't hide from me. You're stunning." Gabe knelt and slowly slipped her panties to her feet.

Zoe stepped out of them as he pulled the bedspread back. Gabe turned and swept her up against his chest. One of her arms went around his shoulders as she buried her face in his neck, her mouth finding heated skin. He worshipfully placed her between the sheets then stood gazing down at her as if memorizing each curve and dip.

"You're so beautiful. I just don't have the words."

Zoe's heart danced. She lifted her arms, inviting him to join her. Gabe sat beside her instead. Their gazes held as he placed a hand over the baby. Hers came to rest on his before he slowly leaned down to kiss her. His sweet, tender ways were her undoing. This was the affection that love was made of. In her heart she'd known it when she'd invited him into her hotel room that fateful stormy night. Cupping his face in both hands, she held his mouth to hers.

His kisses were easy, caring, loving. She was being

cherished with each touch of his lips. He controlled their kiss, refusing when she wanted to take it deeper. Her soul played joyous notes as he lightly skimmed his mouth over hers.

Zoe sucked in a breath as his attention left her lips to travel over her cheek. His mouth found the sweet spot behind her ear, pressed and suckled. His fingertips trailed down along the length of her arm and up again. She shuddered. Every nerve in her body was alive where Gabe's next touch landed. He moved to her shoulder, leaving a kiss in the dip there before dropping more along a path to the rise of her breast.

Her breath hitched then caught when he cradled her in his hand. He shifted her breast, looked for a second before his mouth covered her nipple. Fireworks went off inside her, her breasts grew heavy, and her core tingled. Her fingers funneled into his hair as she relaxed on the pillow, closed her eyes and took in each precious nuance of his caresses.

"Gabe." She lifted her shoulders, tugging his head toward hers.

He resisted. "Shh. Just feel."

Could she take more? That was all she was doing—feeling. Her body was on fire with want. Her body throbbed, ached, begged for relief.

Gabe suckled then circled her nipple with his tongue. Her body clenched. As he continued to worship her with his mouth, his hand traveled tantalizingly slow over her hip then across her middle. A finger traced the circumference of her belly button before it glided downward. It brushed her curls and Zoe's hips flexed. Gabe kissed the baby once more before his mouth returned to cover hers.

He pulled away too soon and she groaned, reaching for him in protest. Gabe chuckled lightly as he shifted on the bed so that her calves lay across his lap. The firm bulge of his manhood was visible beneath his pants. A slight smile came to her lips. He hadn't remained unaffected by their kisses.

Zoe watched as he picked up her foot and began to massage it. When she pulled at a corner of the sheet in an effort to cover herself, he tugged it away.

"I want to admire you. Watch your body turn all rosy for me."

She'd never lain naked in front of a man, much less while he touched and kissed her all over. There was something titillating and erotic about it to be desired so.

Gabe paid special attention to each of her toes, pulling gently before moving to the next. When he was done, he brought her foot to his mouth and placed his lips to her arch. Zoe sighed. This was heaven. How it should be between a man and a woman. Their gazes met and held. She bit her bottom lip as Gabe slowly ran his hand from her ankle up to her thigh, slipped inside the crease of her legs and then moved down again.

How much longer could she take his ministrations?

His wicked smile was equally sexy as he picked up her other foot. Confidence covered his handsome face. He was aware of what he was making her feel, enjoying it. After giving that foot the same attention he had given the other, he grabbed a pillow, placed it beside her, then another and did the same before he said, "Turn over."

"Gabe, I don't think—"

"Trust me."

In spite of all her precautions, she'd found she could do just that. Gabe was so much more than she'd first given him credit for. Rolling not very gracefully onto her stomach, she allowed Gabe to help place the pillows so that any pressure was off the baby. She glanced back to see he had moved again so that he sat beside her hips. Over the next few minutes she concentrated on the provocative feel of his fingers as they teased their way up one leg, slipped between it and the other long enough for her center to burn with need, before moving away, leaving her wanting. Too soon his hand moved on to the other leg, teasing her to the point she quivered all over. When she believed Gabe could do nothing more to raise her arousal higher, his mouth found the curve of her back. His lips kissed their way up her back one vertebra at a time. At her neck, he pushed her hair away and gave her a sensual nip as his hand brushed the side of her breast. Zoe groaned.

"Roll to your back." Gabe's voice was gruff as if he were grasping for control. She couldn't have moved without his help. Gabe's magic hands had reduced her to nothing more than a lump of putty held together by bones. When she'd returned to her back, his attentions went directly to the V of her legs, touching, withdrawing and approaching to tease once again.

"I want to watch you find your pleasure." His voice was low, coaxing. His lips settled on hers as his finger slipped into her center. She jerked upward, eager for relief only Gabe could provide.

His mouth slowly released hers before his look captured hers, held. He moved his finger faster. Tension built in her, squeezed, pulsed, before the dam burst. Her eyes widened as she flew off into paradise. She saw the look of wonder on Gabe's face as she shuddered before her eyelids fluttered closed.

"Thank you," she murmured.

He kissed her forehead. "My pleasure, honey."

CHAPTER EIGHT

GABE'S FINGERS TRAILED across Zoe's shoulder as he pulled back and stood. He covered her. What he'd experienced with Zoe had never happened to him before. He had always thought of himself as a generous lover and seen to his partner's release, but he'd never given anyone the attention he had given her. He'd not worried about his own desires but hers instead, determined that Zoe understood all he felt.

She was special. Very. If she was willing, he wanted to work something out. Find a way they could stay together after the baby. When the time was right he would talk to her about it. See if she felt the same way. But still he worried he couldn't give her all she wanted. Could he be that present husband and father she dreamed of? Was he willing to find the balance in his life that would make it work?

He headed for the shower. It would be a cold one tonight. Sometime later he turned off the lamp and crawled under the bedcovers, pulling the warm, sleeping Zoe to him. With a sigh he drifted off to sleep. This was too right.

It was still dark when Zoe's warm bottom rubbed against him. In an instant his body responded.

"Mmm…" Zoe murmured, before she turned to face him, her hand resting on his chest.

Gabe wasn't sure she was awake but he certainly was.

Zoe slid her hand up his chest and behind his neck. When she kissed his chest he sucked in a breath.

"You awake?" Her sleep-laden voice sounded so sexy.

"Yes, honey. I'm awake." And in pain.

"Honey." She kissed his chest again. "I like it when you call me that."

Gabe brushed his hand over the lower part of her back. He'd never called a woman that before.

"I like it," Zoe mumbled. "And I like you."

"I like you too." His lips found hers.

She pulled closer, moving and shifting so the baby pressed more into his side than on his middle. Her mouth opened for him. Gabe took her invitation. His tongue found hers, performing an erotic dance that was theirs alone.

"If you continue that, I won't keep my promise to just hold you."

"I'd like being held but I like other things too." Her hand moved lower.

"Are you sure?" If she continued, he would do anything she asked.

Zoe pulled his face to hers, kissing his eyes, his cheek, his chin before her lips found his. She squirmed, brushing against his arousal. That was more than Gabe could take. He rolled Zoe to her back and braced himself over her on his hands.

Gently, he entered her. Zoe lifted her hips, helping him to settle deep in her. As he entered and withdrew in the age-old manner, Zoe hissed while her fingers gripped his shoulders as he moved. His lips found hers.

He increased the pace. She squirmed beneath him as if trying to work closer. With uncertain control, he built their pleasure until Zoe moaned and the tension in her relaxed. Gabe thrust a few more times, before he groaned his release. He fell to Zoe's side and pulled her close, kissing her shoulder. Would life ever be this good again…?

The buzzing of his phone woke him. He was needed at the hospital. Only hazy sunlight was coming through the windows when he slid out of bed. Minutes later he was ready to leave when he leaned over and kissed the still sleeping Zoe. He wanted to climb back in beside her but he was being pulled away. He took a moment to watch her. Would it always be this way for him? Leaving her behind? What was he allowing to happen? If he could stop it, would he?

But what would he have missed if Zoe hadn't come into his life?

With the tip of his finger, he pushed a stray lock of hair off her cheek and forced himself to walk out of the room.

Zoe woke to cool sheets beside her, but the hot memories of the night before had her whole body still tingling. The room was bright with light. She jerked to a sitting position. Apparently she had overslept. She didn't ever do that. Making her way to her room for her phone, she called in and told the office she would be in soon.

She stepped into the bath and saw the bag sitting on the counter. Unable to resist, she peeked inside. A smile spread across her face. How like a man. Not wanting to spoil Gabe's surprise, she took the bag to the kitchen and placed it on the table. On the counter, she found a note.

Honey, I'll bring dinner home.

Honey. The word was like golden sunshine on a cloudy morning.

Zoe went through the day with a smile on her face. More than one person at her office commented on how happy she looked. She just smiled and kept her reason to herself. Saying why might make it disappear, and even if she did, what could she say? That she was in love with a man she wasn't sure was in love with her. Their relationship wasn't any more secure than it had been before. With her past, she'd learned the bitter lesson that not everything was always the way it appeared.

Gabe invaded her thoughts in every spare moment. Had they turned a corner where things would be different between them? Could they, would they find a future? Did Gabe want to? The baby was a life-changing event in their lives and she couldn't help but hope last night had been as well.

He'd given so completely, been so tender and caring during their lovemaking. There had been none of the frenzy of their first time, but the experience had been just as satisfying. The night had included passion but it had been wrapped in caring, sharing, getting to know each other on a level like never before. Had Gabe been expressing his feelings through his actions?

She could only hope. Yet a nagging fear remained that it might go away in the reality of everyday life. Zoe pushed away the negativity, determined to enjoy what they had shared and what she hoped would be between them in the future. She planned to make the most of Gabe's attentions for as long as they lasted, even if it was only for a few months. Her mother's illness and her father's defection had taught her not to take any day for granted. She would grasp all the happiness she could.

It was late afternoon when she arrived home. As she suspected, Gabe wasn't yet there. It was such a nice day and she'd been inside too much of it, so she planned to take a walk around the neighborhood. Zoe had reached the bottom of the driveway when Gabe pulled in.

Her heart fluttered just at the sight of him.

He stopped and rolled down the window. "Hi."

Zoe couldn't help feeling nervous and a little shy. "Hey."

He watched her too closely for her comfort. "What're you up to?"

"I was going for a walk." She shifted from one foot to the other.

Gabe smiled. "Give me a sec and I'll go with you."

She wasn't sure but she was afraid she might have looked at him as if he was from another planet. That had been the last thing she'd expected out of his mouth. "Won't dinner get cold?"

"It'll need to be warmed up anyway."

"Okay." Wasn't this the man who'd said he didn't have time for family? Now he was home early, with dinner in his hand, and he wanted to go for a walk? It was too good to be true.

He continued on up the drive. She walked behind him and waited at the porch while Gabe parked. Zoe watched as he strolled toward her with a sense of pride. Gabe was a tall, handsome male with a swagger of confidence that made him even sexier. The collar of the light blue shirt that matched his eyes was open and the sleeves were rolled up on his forearms. His pants were classic and fit him to perfection. All of this magnificence was hers. Gabe could be any woman's dream, but he was hers to enjoy.

When he reached her, he smiled and took her hand. "So how was your day?"

She was still uncertain around him. After all the emotion of the night before, he seemed so calm when she was still walking as if on clouds. "Good. I stopped by to see Mom on the way home. She's doing about the same. How about yours?"

"The usual—but I do have some news I think you'll like."

She looked at him. "What?"

"The committee agreed to list Mr. Luther."

She grabbed his arm, stopping him. "That's wonderful. Thank you!" She wrapped her arms around his waist and hugged him.

He pulled her close. "None of it was really my doing. The committee all voted yes after the social worker and psychiatrist had spoken to him. He assured them that he'd do what he needed to do."

"Still, you were the one who agreed to see him in the first place." If she had believed him wonderful before, he was her hero now.

"You're welcome."

Gabe was so humble about what he did for other people. Just another reason she was crazy about him.

They continued down the sidewalk, their hands clasped between them.

"You know, I've never taken you for a person who might enjoy a walk around the neighborhood. But I like it that you came with me."

"I can be full of surprises." Gabe squeezed her hand.

He was. Just a few weeks ago she would have sworn this day would never happen.

They walked a couple of blocks and turned around. As they did so, Gabe said, "I called my mother today. Told her we were having a boy. She was excited. Said she was looking forward to meeting you."

What did his mother think about their situation? "I look forward to meeting her too."

That worrying thought was interrupted by someone calling, "Hi."

Zoe looked to see an older couple standing near a manicured flower bed.

She and Gabe stopped.

The balding man, followed by his wife, stepped closer to the walk. "You must be our newest neighbor. The one who moved into the brick house with the curved drive."

"Yes, sir, that's us," Gabe said, offering his hand to the man. The man took it and they shook. "I'm Gabriel Marks." He put his arm at her waist and said, "And this is Zoe."

The way he left the introduction implied that they were married. Zoe wasn't sure how she felt about that. Had Gabe just not wanted to go into the details of their relationship at a casual meeting?

"I'm Richard Mills, and this is my wife, Maggie."

"It's nice to meet you both," Gabe said.

Maggie stepped closer and smiled. "I see that you're expecting a little one."

Zoe placed her hand on her middle. "Yes. He's due in a couple of months."

"A little boy. How wonderful. We'll need to get the neighbors together and give y'all a baby shower."

"Oh, that's sweet but not necessary." Zoe didn't want to have to go into explaining her and Gabe's relationship. The bubble of happiness she'd had minutes before had popped.

"We could make it a block party and shower. It'd be a wonderful way for everyone to meet each other." Her enthusiasm made her voice higher. "It'd be a lot of fun."

Zoe just smiled.

Maggie continued, "A lot of us who live around here are grandparents but our grandkids are no longer small. To have small children around will be wonderful. Ooh, to get to buy one of those cute little outfits." She all but rubbed her hands together in glee.

Zoe felt like a fraud. This couple thought her and Gabe were a happy couple in the process of becoming a happy family. She wished it was true. But Gabe had said nothing about that happening.

Gabe's smile had turned tight. "We need to head home. We've supper waiting for us."

"Great to meet you," Richard said. "See you soon."

"You too," Gabe said, as they started down the sidewalk.

"They seemed like nice people," Zoe said quietly. "They think we're married."

"Yeah, I suspect they do." Gabe didn't look at her while matching his pace to hers.

What was he thinking? Some of the joy of the day had dimmed. They continued in silence until they were in front of his house. She wanted their earlier camaraderie back. "I enjoyed our walk."

"I did too."

Zoe gave him a suspicious look. "What's happening to you?"

"Uh?"

"I'd have never guessed the always-busy type A doctor would've ever said something like that."

He grinned. "Could be you're a good influence on me."

Did she really have that kind of effect on him?

As they entered the house through the carport door, Gabe said, "I brought us some of the best Italian in town. Or so I've been told. It's from a little restaurant close to the hospital. I'll get it warmed up."

"Then I'm on dish duty." Zoe headed for the kitchen. She'd forgotten about the bag waiting on the table. Picking it up, she held it out. "By the way, you left this in my bathroom last night."

He gave her a wolfish grin. "I had other things on my mind."

Heat warmed her cheeks. She'd had other things on her mind as well.

Gabe took it from her. "You didn't peek, did you?"

She shrugged and tried to look innocent. "Maybe a little."

"Why am I not surprised?" He dug into the bag. "What do you think?" Gabe proudly held up a ball and a tiny baseball glove.

She smiled. "I think it'll be a while before he can use them."

Gabe grinned. "Maybe so but he'll have them when he's ready."

"Yes, he will." But would Gabe be around to play with him? Go to the games?

They worked around each other for the next few minutes. During one of her passes by him, Gabe caught her hand and pulled her to him. "I haven't had one of these in too long." He gave her a tender yet searching kiss.

The insecurity of earlier disappeared, replaced by the bliss of being in his arms again.

His lips left hers. "I could do without a meal to have you again but you need to eat. You tempt me so much."

She tempted him? Had she ever received a more exciting compliment?

After dinner Zoe stood at the sink, washing up the few dishes they had used. Gabe came up behind her. The heat from his body warmed her from shoulders to hips. His arms circled her before he pushed her hair away from her neck and gave her a kiss.

She could get used to this attention. His change in attitude and all his actions were almost surreal but they were everything she had dreamed of having in a husband.

"Forget those and let's go outside and sit for a little while."

Her heart opened more. Even that simple statement made her melt. He wanted to spend time with her. The impression she'd had of him when they'd first met had been that he would never have slowed down long enough to enjoy anything as simple as sitting outside under the stars. Then his life had seemed to center on his career. "Almost done here. You go on and I'll be right there."

Minutes later she wiped her hands off on the dishrag and headed to the patio. Gabe was sitting on the settee with one foot propped on the table. He looked relaxed and content. With his stressful job, he needed downtime. She was glad he could find it.

She moved to take a chair but he grabbed her hand and tugged her toward him. "You'll be too far away if you sit there."

She sat next to him. His arm went around her shoulders, pulling her close.

"This is much better."

Zoe sighed softly. *Much.* The evening sounds of bugs and the occasional bark of a dog joined the sound of Gabe's soft breathing. Could life get better than this? Only if it could be like this forever.

"I've been thinking about a baby name now that we

know what it's going to be." She sat so near she could feel the tension of anticipation in Gabe's body. Did he hope the baby would be named after him?

The calm of his voice didn't give anything away. "Have you decided on something?"

"I have."

"Will you tell me?"

"William. Call him Will. What do you think?"

"I like it." The hint of disappointment in his voice didn't escape her.

She couldn't help but tease him, prolonging saying more.

In a huff he asked, "What about the middle name?"

"Well…" She turned so she could see his face. "…I was thinking about Gabriel, after his father and grandfather. What do you think?"

"William Gabriel Marks. That's a fine, strong name."

"Avery. William Gabriel Avery."

He gave her a searching look. Would he argue? He couldn't expect the baby to have his last name if they weren't married. He nodded. Was it acceptance or appeasement?

"Tell me what you know about your daddy. I'd like to know something about Will's heritage."

Gabe didn't like the sour taste in his mouth that came with knowing his boy wouldn't carry his last name. Yet he didn't believe he could demand the name be different. He was well acquainted with Zoe's strong will and determination. She wouldn't easily change her mind. Neither probably should she.

He wasn't sure he was qualified to answer the question about his dad. This wasn't how he would have imagined their romantic moments on the patio going. But then, he'd have never guessed he'd be enjoying an evening like this.

Zoe wouldn't let the question about his father go either. He could only name a few people he'd ever share the story with. "I don't know a lot about him. Like I said, Mother never told me much. I think it's too painful even to this day. He was from Arizona and a teacher. He liked the outdoors. I think my parents had a good marriage but a too short one."

He'd never thought about how deeply his mother must have cared for his father. Had his mother never remarried because she'd missed his father so badly she couldn't bear the hurt of losing another? What would it be like to love that deeply? Could *he*? Did he already?

"That's a shame. It can be hard to find the right person, and when you do, to lose them so…" Zoe's voice trailed off, as though she'd said more than she wanted to.

She must know from experience. Her father had run out on her and she'd lost him, and now for all intents and purposes her mother was gone as well. She had to understand loss far better than he. Possibly love as well.

"Zoe, if you don't want to answer this I'll understand, but would you tell me about *your* father?"

She was close enough he felt her body stiffen.

He squeezed her shoulder. "You don't have to talk about it if you don't want to."

"It doesn't make the hurt any less by not talking about it. I was crazy about him. He could do no wrong. If he was at home I was under his feet. I don't know if I just didn't want to see his unhappiness or I couldn't, but it had to have been there."

She was too hard on herself. "You were a kid. You weren't supposed to see."

"I know, but it would have been easier than him just not coming home one day."

He hugged her again. It would have.

"I asked Mom what happened and all she could say was that he just wasn't happy. That he had to leave."

"You never saw him again?"

"No. We found out a few years later he had died of an overdose." The last few words were but a whisper.

Her pain must be at a level he'd never experienced, yet she still believed in and wanted a marriage, husband and family. Misery filled him. That wasn't something he felt he had the ability to give her, even if he wanted to. What if he failed her? He cared too much to have her hurt like that again.

It was time for a change in subject. Talk about something more pleasant. "Have you given any thought to decorating the nursery? Especially since you know the sex now."

"Not really…" Her voice trailed off as if she wasn't really listening.

"I wish you would. Will needs a place to come home to."

"Mmm…" Her head rested heavily against his shoulder.

Gabe just held her as she slept. A while later, he gently shook her. "Come on, sleepyhead. We need to go to bed."

"I didn't mean to go to sleep on you," she mumbled.

"Not a problem." He walked her inside.

Zoe headed toward her side of the house.

"Hey, where're you going?"

"To bed."

"Wrong way. You're with me." He extended his hand. For a second he worried she might not take it. To his relief, her palm met his. She curled her fingers around his as they walked to his bedroom. There he led her into the bath and turned on the shower, adjusting the water temperature.

"Are you getting a shower?" Zoe asked, her voice drowsy.

"We're getting a shower." Gabe begin to remove her clothes. She put up no resistance.

"You and me?"

Gabe grinned. She really was out of it. "Yes, honey, you and me." He cupped her face with his hands and kissed her before he turned her and opened the door to the shower stall. "In you go." Gabe gave her a gentle nudge at her waist before she stepped under the water.

He quickly removed his clothes and joined her. Zoe was so tired she was just standing beneath the water, letting it fall on her shoulders. They'd had an intense night the night before with little sleep. He picked up the soap and started washing her. She purred as his hands slid over her. He was deeply aroused but Zoe needed rest more than he needed release.

When she shivered, Gabe increased the temperature of the hot water and put her further under it. He quickly soaped up and rinsed. Cutting off the shower, he opened the door and jerked a towel off the rack. He dried Zoe and wrapped her in a towel. A minute later he'd dried, dropped his towel on the floor and guided Zoe to the bed. He jerked the spread back then removed the towel from Zoe. "Climb in, honey, before you chill."

She did as he said. Seconds later he joined her, pulling her to him and the covers snugly over them. In no time Zoe relaxed against him and was softly sleeping.

Contentment settled over him and he joined her.

* * *

The next evening when Gabe arrived home Zoe wasn't there.

The security he'd found in having her waiting for him was suddenly gone. How had she, in such a short time, managed to become such an important part of his life? He looked forward to coming home to her. The house was empty—not just the space, but the life force that made it a home was gone. Could he survive if she moved out?

An hour went by and still Zoe hadn't come home. Then another. He should have stayed at work. Guilt crept in. He had plenty of policies and procedures to read before he could start making serious changes to improve the program. He'd been leaving the hospital early far too often as it was to come home to see her. Now he was here and she wasn't.

As time went by, guilt turned to anger then to worry, which grew like a virus in a lab tube to the point where Gabe kept checking his phone, thinking he'd missed her call. More than once he'd stopped himself from phoning her because he had promised not to question her movements or try to control her. This anxiety and the waste of his time was drama he didn't need.

He loved having Zoe in his bed, but the emotionally draining side of their relationship would soon eat at him. Might even affect his job. He couldn't have that. But letting Zoe go was unthinkable.

Relief flooded him at the sound of the garage door opening. She was home. He was waiting at the house door before she could get out of the car. Gabe said, more casually than he felt, "I've been worried about you."

"I went by to see Mom for a few minutes. Told her about William Gabriel, then did a little shopping for the nursery."

"You did?" Any residue of concern completely disappeared with the sound of happiness in her voice. At least the joy over the baby was overcoming her despair about her mother's health.

"Come and help me bring these packages in." Her head disappeared inside the car.

Gabe moved to stand beside her. She handed him a couple of huge plastic bags filled with fluffy items. "You did do some shopping."

"You said you'd like me to fix up the nursery. I got off a few minutes early today, so I thought I'd pick up some things."

"This is a little more than some." He chuckled as he headed toward the door of the house. His pleasure at seeing her and his relief over her being home safe made any discord he'd felt earlier disappear.

"Babies need a lot." Her tone held a defensive note.

"Hey, I was just kidding." He put the bags down in the hallway and wrapped his arms around her waist. "You can buy twice as much, for all I care."

Her hands were full of bags but her arms came around him anyway. "It was so much fun. I can hardly wait to show you what I got. I'm going to need your help."

"You've got it. Have you eaten yet?"

"No."

"Then why don't I fix us some breakfast for supper? You can sit at the table with your feet up for a while and tell me about your day and how your visit with your mother went." Who had he turned into? Nothing about those suggestions sounded like the person he thought he was. Zoe was changing him.

"That sounds great. Let me put these in the baby's room." She held up the bags in her hands. "I'm going to change into something more comfortable too."

"Sounds like a plan. I'll get started on dinner. Just leave these bags here and I'll get them later."

After eating, they spent the next two hours working in the nursery, and now Zoe sat on the floor, pulling open another package. She was dressed in baggy sweatpants and a shirt she had asked to borrow from him. Her skin was glowing, her eyes sparkled and she giggled as she showed him each new item. He couldn't think of a time she'd looked more amazing. But didn't he think that daily?

During the last hour he'd hung curtains under her direction and helped her place a bed skirt on the crib. He wasn't sure it was particularly useful but he didn't voice that out loud. All the time she had been chattering about her decision to get this or that and opening bags. Gabe didn't care one way or the other about any of it but he was enjoying listening to Zoe. Her excitement was infectious.

"This is the last thing." She opened the clear package and pulled out some material with a triumphant look.

"I have no idea what that is." It wasn't the first time he'd thought that about some of the objects she'd bought.

"It's a crib sheet."

"Oh." He nodded sagely. "Should have known that right away. Hand it here and I'll put it on and that way you don't have to get up."

"Are you saying I can't?" There was a teasing note in her voice.

"No. I was just trying to be helpful. That's all."

"You weren't implying I was fat."

He grinned. "I know better than to do that."

"You'd better not."

After a struggle with the mattress and sheet that had Zoe giggling, Gabe finally had it in place. Done, he sat behind Zoe, spread his legs wide and wrapped her around her middle to bring her back until she rested against his chest. She placed her hands over his. He rested his chin on the top of her head.

He scanned the room, looking at the yellow and gray plaid curtains whose panels hung straight on either side of the windows, to the gray pillow with the yellow polka-dot cover, to the crib with a yellow sheet and the same plaid as the curtains on the bed skirt. He would have never thought to put those combinations together. He liked Zoe's taste. "So, are you pleased?"

"Hmm… I am. I still need to get a mobile and I want to do his name above the crib."

Gabe smiled. Her mind was still racing with ideas. "For someone who I had to talk into fixing up a nursery, you sure have run with it."

"It's fun, and you were right. Will needs a nice place to come home to."

But not live. There was that sick feeling in his gut again.

Zoe yawned.

"I think I need to get you to bed. You've had a long day." Gabe stood and then helped her up.

"I need to clean up this mess." She started to pick up a bag.

He took her hand. "Leave it until tomorrow." Gabe ushered her out of the room and turned off the light. He wanted her attention now.

Zoe was so tickled with the way the nursery had turned out. Gabe was a great help and even seemed to enjoy it. She hadn't even hesitated when he'd led her to his bedroom. In a few short nights she had started to think of it as hers. Sleeping without being in Gabe's arms would be impossible.

They were climbing into bed when he said, "I called my mother today. Told her what name we had decided on. I think she cried."

Zoe wasn't sure what to say to that. "She liked it, then?"

"She loved it. She said my father would be so proud." He gave Zoe a nudge to move further into the bed.

"What have you told your mother about me?"

"Nothing much really."

"She didn't ask any questions?" Zoe rolled to her side so she could see his face.

"I didn't say that."

Was he ashamed of her? Had he told his mother how easy Zoe had been to get into bed? She moved away from him. "Like what?"

"I told her your name. What you do for a living. That your mother is sick and you're wonderful with her. That sort of thing. Enough about her." He pulled Zoe toward him. "Let's think about us."

Zoe stopped his advance with a hand on his chest. Her look met his. She hated that she might ruin the happiness they had found together but she had to ask. "Gabe, what are we doing?"

"I don't know" was his soft reply. "Let's just see what happens."

For tonight she could accept that but for how long? She was afraid that what happened would end up with her heart getting broken. Gabe drew her to him, giving her a deep kiss that had her thinking of nothing but what he made her body feel.

Their lovemaking had a desperate edge to it. As if what they had found they feared would soon disappear.

CHAPTER NINE

A WEEK LATER Zoe was on her way out of her office to make her weekly rounds to area hospitals. Her cell phone rang. Gabe's name showed on the screen.

She and Gabe had spent a blissful week together. They had taken walks, visited her mom, enjoyed the patio and spent precious moments in bed, many times just in each other's arms, talking. Yet there had been no more discussion of where their relationship was headed or what would happen after the baby was born. It was as if they were living in a bubble of happiness and they were the only ones who existed. They were pretending nothing would ever change, therefore no decisions needed to be made. Gabe's silence told her that he hadn't changed his mind about what his life would be. She couldn't accept less than what she wanted. They were living on borrowed time. Despite all that, her heart did a flip at the mere thought of him.

She touched the button.

"Hi, honey."

Would she ever get over the thrill of Gabe's voice calling her that? "Hey."

"I just received word there's a match for Mr. Luther."

"Really? That's wonderful." She couldn't believe it.

So soon. The wait was usually much longer. The match must have been perfect.

"I've already made the call for him to come in. Hold on a sec." Gabe spoke to someone else then said, "He should be on his way now. I expect to be in surgery late this evening."

"I'm on my way."

He hurriedly said, "I don't know if I'll have a chance to see you or not."

"I understand. I'll be busy with Mr. Luther anyway."

Gabe had been keeping exceptionally normal hours for the past week but she was sure that wouldn't always be the case. As often as possible, liver transplants were done during business hours, but there were always emergency situations. She worked in the medical field, understood that better than most. Tonight was an example.

Forty-five minutes later she arrived at the hospital and took the elevator up to the third floor, where the liver transplant unit was located. She went to the nurses' station and showed her credentials to the unit tech before requesting to look at Mr. Luther's chart. Zoe had just finished her review and was headed to his room when Gabe walked up.

He smiled. "Hey, I thought I'd miss you."

"Glad you didn't."

She glanced at the desk to find the unit clerk and a couple of nurses watching them.

"Come on. We'll go and see Mr. Luther." He put his hand on her back and directed her toward the other end of the hall.

At Mr. Luther's door she knocked. When there was no answer, she pushed the door open slightly. "Mr. Luther?"

The room was dark and the TV wasn't playing. Had

the OR tech already come to get him? She moved further into the room with Gabe close behind. "Mr. Luther?"

A movement caught her attention. The man sat in a chair, looking out the window.

"Mr. Luther, it's Zoe. May I come in?"

"If you want."

It was as if all the blustery wind had gone out of the man. What was going on? "I needed to finalize some things before they come to take you to the OR. Dr. Marks is here too. May I turn the light on?"

"Please don't. I'm enjoying the sunset."

She knew that tone. It was the same one her father had used just before he'd left. The hopeless one. The one that said he had nothing to live for. Zoe wasn't going to let the same thing happen to Mr. Luther that had happened to her father.

She glanced back at Gabe then went to stand beside Mr. Luther. "Mind if I watch with you?"

"If you want to."

Gabe came to stand behind her. His hand came to rest on her waist. Would he have taken the time to do the same a few weeks ago?

The sky, already orange, slowly darkened to black. With the sun below the horizon, Gabe stepped back and she did too.

"I need to listen to you, Mr. Luther, before I have to go to the OR," Gabe said.

The man nodded and moved back to the bed. After he settled in, he focused on Gabe.

He pulled his stethoscope from around his neck. "You know, Mr. Luther, I'm good at what I do. I've done many liver transplants. I don't anticipate you having any problems."

"If you say so."

"I do. I want you to try not to worry." Gabe listened to Mr. Luther's heart.

"I thought if you didn't mind I'd stay right here with you," Zoe said as she stepped closer to the bed. "Maybe walk down to surgery with you. Would you mind?"

Mr. Luther, who had hardly had time for her when she'd visited, looked at her and smiled. "I'd like that."

"Zoe," Gabe said in a sharp voice and with a direct look. "It might run late."

She met his glare. "I know."

"You need to take care of yourself," Gabe insisted.

Mr. Luther nodded toward Gabe but looked at her and asked, "So what's the deal with you and the doctor here? That baby?"

Was their relationship that obvious? Apparently so. Under normal circumstances their conversation wouldn't have taken place in front of a patient. At least it had Mr. Luther thinking of something besides his impending surgery.

Zoe stared at Gabe. What should they say? How like Mr. Luther to ask such a direct personal question.

Gabe straightened. "Zoe is carrying my baby. We're having a boy."

She liked the pride she heard in his voice.

As if Gabe's statement had confirmed what he thought, Mr. Luther said, "Congratulations. Now, Doc, do you think you can put in that new liver?"

Zoe blinked at his change of attitude and subject.

"I can and I will. I'll see you in the OR." He looked at Zoe. "Can I speak to you in the hall?"

Zoe placed her hand on Mr. Luther's arm. "I'll be right back." She followed Gabe out the door.

"You shouldn't be spending long hours here," Gabe

hissed before she could completely close the door. "I don't want to have to worry about you."

"I'll be fine. If I start feeling bad I'll get one of the security guards to walk me out if necessary. I'll just be in the waiting room." She glanced toward Mr. Luther's room. "He needs to know someone is here for him. I promise to only stay as long as I feel up to it."

"I guess there's no point in arguing with you." Gabe sounded resigned to the fact he couldn't fight her.

She smiled sweetly. "No, I don't think there is."

"Okay, but if you do leave, will you please text me and let me know you made it home?"

"I will. Thanks for caring."

Gabe's look captured hers. "I do, you know."

Joy flowed through her as hot as a beach in the summer. That was the closest Gabe had come to expressing his feelings. She smiled. "It's always nice to hear. I care about you too."

"Maybe we should talk about how much when I get home." He checked his watch. "I have to go. My team is waiting."

There was something about Gabe that hummed like electricity when he talked about doing surgery. His thoughts were already on the job ahead. He was in his element. Gabe knew how to save lives and did it well. She was proud of him. "I understand. I still have to do vitals on Mr. Luther."

He briefly touched her hand before walking away. Hope burned bright. Were her dreams coming true?

Gabe couldn't believe he had almost admitted to Zoe that he loved her in the middle of the hospital hallway. He had truly lost his mind where she was concerned. In his wildest dreams he would never have imagined opening his home to her would have also opened his heart. The last couple of weeks had been the most wonderful of his life. He'd never felt more content or cared for. Even going home had become more appealing than working late at the hospital. That had never entered his mind as a possibility or a desire before Zoe.

"Hello, ladies and gentlemen." He spoke to his transplant team less than an hour later. He was pleased with how they were slowly coming together to create an impressive group. "I appreciate all of you making it a late evening." With only their eyes visible over the masks they wore, they nodded. "This is our patient, Mr. Luther. He'll be getting a new liver today. Let's make sure he receives it in short order and with top care."

A couple of his staff gave him a questioning look. Gabe moved to stand beside the table. He said to the anesthesiologist, "Are we ready?"

"He's out and vitals stable," the woman answered.

"Scalpel," Gabe ordered.

His surgical nurse placed it in the palm of his hand. Seconds later Gabe went to work.

They were in the process of closing when the fellow, Dr. Webber, released a clamp.

"That needs to stay in place while we look for bleeders," Gabe said sharply.

"But this has been the process before," Dr. Webber replied.

"Not this time. I am trying a new procedure."

"Yes, sir." Dr. Webber replaced the clamp. "It's your patient and your call."

When Mr. Luther's incision had been closed, Gabe said, "Well done, everyone." He looked at the fellow.

"Thank you. It's been nice working with you. I believe we have a world-class team here."

Despite the masks, he could see their smiles in their eyes. He left the OR and stepped into the next room to remove his surgical gown. A couple of the other staff followed.

"Nice job, Gabe," one of the team said.

"Thanks. I thought it went exceptionally smoothly." Gabe threw his gown in a basket.

"You were a little hard on the fellow in there, weren't you?" another said.

Gabe shrugged. "My OR, my call."

"Yeah, it was."

Gabe headed straight for the surgery waiting room to see if Zoe was still there. Hopefully she'd gone home, but if not, he could at least walk her to the car. He wasn't surprised to find she was still there.

Zoe stood and met him at the door. "Well, based on that smile on your face, everything went well."

"It did. There were no complications. Barring any infection, Mr. Luther should recover quickly and I anticipate him doing well with a much-improved quality of life."

She wrapped her arms around his waist and hugged him. "Thank you."

He pulled her close, not caring who might see them.

When Zoe eased away, he said, "Now it's time for you to go home. It's late. I have to stay a while longer, but I'm going to walk you to the car."

As they stood beside Zoe's car, Gabe pulled her into his arms and kissed her. Zoe gladly returned it. His kisses made her forget the noise of an ambulance approaching, cars on the nearby freeway whizzing along and the clang of a large truck going over a bump. There was nothing but Gabe.

There was a promise in his kiss. Something that hadn't been there before.

Gabe released her. "I'll be home as soon as I can. Now, in the car with you."

A little later, with a large yawn Zoe pulled into the carport and parked. It had been a long day. A few minutes later she climbed into what had become her and Gabe's bed. Tonight she missed his welcoming body next to hers.

Sometime later she was aware of the moment Gabe slipped underneath the covers. The bed had gone from cool and lonely to warm and heavenly. He snuggled her in, just as he always did.

"What time is it?" she asked.

"Late."

"Mr. Luther?"

"In ICU and doing great. Now shush, go back to sleep." He kissed her forehead.

The next time Zoe woke, the morning sun was high and beaming into the bedroom windows. Gabe still snored softly next to her. She slowly slid out of his arms and from the bed. Picking up one of his shirts, she covered herself.

Knowing she would be out late, seeing about Mr. Luther, she had called the office and told them she wouldn't be in that day. She would go by the hospital and check on Mr. Luther later in the day. Zoe smiled. Since she lived with the transplant surgeon, she could get a personal update.

She'd just started the coffeepot so it would be ready when Gabe walked into the kitchen.

"Mornin'."

His voice was extra-low and gruff from sleep. Oh, so sexy.

She smiled. "Hey."

He took her in his arms. "Before you even ask, I just called the unit. Mr. Luther is doing great. They have already started weaning him off the respirator."

"I can't say thanks enough."

"Why don't you kiss me and we'll call it even." Gabe's head was already moving toward hers.

Her arms circled his neck and she eagerly went to him. She put all the love she felt into showing him how much.

As she pulled back, Gabe said, "You keep that up and I'll have to take you back to bed."

"I don't have a problem with that." She smiled at him.

He chuckled. "That's nice to hear but we should talk."

"Why don't we make breakfast first? Then we can talk while we eat." Zoe was already pulling a pan out of the cabinet.

"Sounds like a plan."

Half an hour later she and Gabe sat down at the table to what had turned into their favorite meal of eggs, bacon and toast.

Zoe had just picked up her fork when her phone rang. She looked at it. Shorecliffs. For them to be calling, something must be wrong with her mother. She answered.

"Ms. Avery, this is Ms. Marshall."

"Yes?"

"I'm sorry to have to tell you this but your mother is missing."

"What!" Panic shot through Zoe, mixed with disbelief

and shock. She looked at Gabe, who had stopped eating and wore a concerned look.

"One of the new employees left a door propped open and she walked out. We have it on video. We're searching for her now. I have called the police. I wanted to let you know in case she comes to you."

No one would be at the apartment. Her mother wouldn't remember that Zoe now lived with Gabe.

Zoe stood. "I'll help look. Please keep me informed."

"We will. Again, I'm sorry about this."

Zoe ended the call. To Gabe she said, "Mom's missing. I have to go."

Before he could respond his phone buzzed. Zoe rushed to her bedroom, already stripping off Gabe's shirt as she went. Where could her mother be? What if she was hurt? Guilt assaulted Zoe. Her mother should be living with her. Instead, Zoe was busy playing "happy home" with Gabe.

He came to the door. "Tell me what happened."

As she pulled on clothes, she told him what the woman had said. "I'm going to the old apartment to see if she's there, even though I can't imagine how she would get there."

Gabe came closer. "That call was from the hospital. There's an emergency and I'm needed. I'm sorry but I can't go with you. I have to see about this."

Zoe glared at him. "What? My mother is missing. You aren't going to help me look for her?"

He gave her an imploring look. "I've got to go. It's my responsibility."

"Couldn't someone else fill in for you just for a little while?"

"I'm the head of the department. It's my job."

"Go. Do what you need to do. If you're needed, you're needed." She pulled on her pants. But she needed him too. Still, his job was important. It hurt that he couldn't be there for her. When had she last been this scared? When her father had left.

"You take care of yourself. Don't do anything crazy. She has to be near the home."

"You don't know that. She could be anywhere!" Zoe lashed back. She jerked her shoes on.

"Call me the second you find her."

Zoe pushed past him and hurried down the hall toward the garage. "Okay. I've got to go and find my mother."

Gabe shook his head. As nice as the day had started, with Zoe sharing his bed and the plans he'd had for them coming to an understanding about the future, it had all turn upside down and ugly with two quick calls. He had left the house with the thought he would clear up the problem at the hospital and join Zoe in the search, but it didn't work out that way.

When he arrived at the hospital, he soon learned the patient would need surgery and he was the most qualified to perform it. Any hope he held of being at Zoe's side slipped away.

Going into the OR, he told the unit tech, "Please let me know if I get any messages."

She gave him a curious look but nodded. "Yes, Doctor."

Most of the time he left a "Do Not Disturb" request. This time he was worried about not only Zoe but her mother.

It was a couple of hours later while Gabe was busy suturing the vein that had been bleeding that the OR phone rang. A nurse answered and relayed a message. "Dr. Marks, the mother has been found. She is well."

Gabe didn't let himself falter as he continued to work,

but relief washed over him, along with sadness. He wasn't there to support Zoe. She must be so relieved. Her desperation and fear had been written all over her face but he had still left her in her time of need. It gnawed at him. She'd needed him then and now, and he wasn't there for her. Would be, if he truly cared. Zoe should be the number one thing in his life, always come first.

The very thing he'd feared the most and had tried to avoid had happened. He'd proved he was right about himself. He had chosen his career over her. For him, his profession and a family didn't mix. He didn't know how to make them mesh. Others could do it, he'd seen it, but he just wasn't capable of doing it. He'd not even grown up watching a marriage. And to think he had started to believe he could have one. Zoe had made him care enough to want to try. But now...

On his way home he made a decision. He had to let her go. For her sake, she needed to find a man who could give her what she needed. Today had just been an example of how he wasn't that person. Zoe deserved better than him. He would be there for Will, but Zoe wanted more from their relationship than he could give. It might kill him but he would have to let her go.

It was turning dark before he pulled into the drive. The lights shone brightly in the house. Zoe was waiting for him. He had no doubt of that. There would be a hot meal there as well. His chest ached for what had been and what he was about to do. Her day must have been emotionally exhausting yet she'd thought about him. Zoe had such a capacity to love. Her mother, he himself and Mr. Luther were all evidence of that, and soon Will would be.

Gabe pulled into the garage, cut off the engine but didn't get out immediately. He needed to gather his thoughts, think through what he was going to do. He couldn't continue to live in the house with Zoe. Having her so close and not being able to touch her would slowly drive him mad. He would have to move out. Go stay in a hotel. No way would he ask her to go. The baby was only weeks away. She wouldn't like the idea but he would make her accept it.

He slammed his hand down on the steering wheel. This was just the drama he wanted no part of. The kind that would steer him away from his goals. Made him think of other things besides his career.

The door to the house opened. Zoe was silhouetted there. Oh, heaven help him, he was going to miss her. He climbed out of the car.

"Hey, are you all right?" she called.

"Fine. Just on my way in." Gabe stepped closer to her. "Tell me about what happened with your mom."

She smiled and headed toward the kitchen as he closed the garage door. "Thank goodness it sounded worse than it was. She did leave the home but didn't get far. The door she went out of was the one to the garden area. They found her in the potting shed, filling pots with soil. You were right. She was close by. I'm sorry I acted so irrationally. I shouldn't have demanded you stay with me."

"They didn't look there before calling you or the police?" Anger filled Gabe at the distress they had caused Zoe.

"Someone had, but apparently my mother had stepped around to the back of the shed to look for something to dig with and they missed her. On the second pass, there she was."

"I'm sorry they scared you."

They continued into the kitchen.

"I have to admit all kinds of things were running through my head at what could go wrong." She stopped near the sink and turned to face him. "I fixed supper. Thought we could eat out on the patio tonight. You hungry?"

He was. For her more than anything. "Yeah."

"Then you go wash up while I get it on the table."

Gabe went to his room. Zoe had no idea what was coming. Her mother's successful return hadn't changed his mind. If something like that happened again, where would he be? Beside Zoe or off seeing to a stranger? No, he couldn't do that to her again.

When he returned to the kitchen, Zoe wasn't there. She waved to him from outside where she sat at the patio table, waiting for him.

"I just filled our plates. Simpler that way. I hope you don't mind."

"No." There was little he minded about Zoe. As far as he was concerned, she was near perfect.

The weight of what he was about to say made each of his steps feel as if he were wearing lead shoes. Nothing in his life had been more difficult. He would wait until they had eaten before he explained how it must be. At least they could share this last meal.

As he settled in his chair, Zoe asked, "So how's your patient doing?"

How like Zoe after the day she'd had to show concern for someone else. "She's stable and should recover without any issues."

"I'm sure that's due to your superior skills." She nibbled at a roll.

It didn't make what he had to do any easier, hearing her vote of confidence. "I have a good team." He took a bite of the chicken she had prepared. "This is good. Thanks for going to the trouble after the day you've had."

"Not a problem. After things were settled with Mother and I calmed down, it turned into a perfectly nice day."

Which he was getting ready to ruin. Suddenly his food had no taste. "What kind of arrangements did Shorecliffs make for what happened this morning not to occur again?"

Zoe took a sip of the hot tea she was having. "They were going to fire the guy that propped the door open but I told them that wasn't necessary. It had scared him enough that he won't do it again."

"You're a better person than I am." He had no doubt she was.

"I don't know about that."

When they finished their meal, Zoe stood and picked up their plates. "I made a pie as well. Want some?"

He'd put off what needed doing long enough. "Maybe later. Leave those. I'd like to talk to you for a minute."

Zoe put the plates down, sank into her chair and clasped her hands over her middle. He held her attention. "I know we promised to talk but—"

"Zoe, please…"

Confusion filled her eyes and she pursed her lips. "What's going on, Gabe?"

"This—" he waved a hand between them "—isn't working for me."

"What're you talking about?" Her voice was flat as fear replaced confusion in her eyes.

"I've been leading you to believe that our relationship is moving toward something more permanent. It can't."

"You said you care about me." She watched him closely, as if searching for the truth.

"I do."

"So what does that mean?" Zoe's eyes narrowed.

He shrugged both shoulders. "That I care about what happens to you. To the baby."

"I don't get it."

Gabe wasn't surprised. He wasn't making any sense. "I'm not who you need."

"Isn't that my choice?"

He wasn't sure how to answer that. "Yes," Gabe said with hesitation. "But I'm not going to let you."

Zoe straightened her shoulders, glared at him. The stubborn look he knew so well came over her face. She was no longer on the defensive; she was taking the offensive position. "For a man of your intelligence you aren't making any sense. Just what's the problem? Tell me."

"I can't be there for you like I should be. I've been pretending for the last couple of weeks. I had thought we could make a real go of it, but this morning just proved I'd been right all along."

"And just how's that?" Her tone had turned patronizing.

"My career, my choices would always go to my patients. Your mother was missing and I get a call from the hospital and choose them over being with you. A real relationship is about caring for the other person. I let you down."

"So you think I'm weak?"

His eyes narrowed. What was her point? "I didn't say that."

"I believe that's what you meant. You think I can't handle something like what happened today with Mother on my own. I've been doing that for years. Just because you came into my life, it doesn't mean I still can't. You had a patient who needed you today. I understand that."

She pointed to her chest. "Remember, I work in the medical field too. I get it better than most women do."

"But I should have been there to support you."

"Next time you will be. Today you were needed elsewhere. You had a good reason."

"But you're the one who told me you wanted a husband and a family. Isn't that what someone does when they're a husband, be there for the other person?"

"Sure they do. When they can. As for what I want, mostly it's for someone to love me."

"I'm not that guy." The devastation that filled her eyes almost had him on his knees, begging her to forgive him. But he'd never be the man for her. "You expect a marriage to be perfect. I don't even know how to do marriage. Today proves it. I'd make a horrible husband."

"Sure seems like the last couple of weeks you've been doing a fine job of playing the part. Everything about our day-to-day lives looked like a marriage. The neighbors even thought so. Were you just playacting?"

Gabe didn't want to answer that question. He hadn't been, but if he told her that then he'd offer her hope. "Zoe, it's just not going to work."

"You didn't answer the question, Gabe."

He pushed back from the table. "No, I wasn't pretending." Why couldn't she just accept what he was telling her and let them move on? Zoe reached out but he pulled back. If he allowed her to touch him, she would melt his resolve.

"Gabe, forget all the shouldn'ts and let loose. We can make this work together. Let yourself feel. Trust me enough to love you. I do. I have for a long time."

He could hardly breathe. Was a truck running over his chest? One slight woman had a hold on his heart and was squeezing. "I've let things get out of hand. I knew this would happen. I shouldn't be putting you through this. My patients will always come first. You don't deserve that."

"Don't I get to decide that too? I understand you're a doctor."

"You shouldn't have to. I want better for you."

"Do you really? Or is that the excuse you're using?" She paused then looked at him as if she'd realized something. "Oh, I get it. I've just been one in the long list of people you feel you need to help. Your patients, strangers in airports, your child. You took me in because you're a good guy. That's it. It has had nothing to do with loving me. It must be hard to carry all those needs of the world on your shoulders and still not let yourself feel. Such a burden." Her tone dripped sarcasm. "How noble, and unnecessary. The problem is you do care. You know, Gabe, I would've never have thought you, of all people, would be running scared."

Gabe jerked to his feet. He'd taken all he could. Right now he didn't like her and liked himself even less. It must be this way. He loved her too much to fail her like her father had, and he would if they continued down the road they were traveling. The sudden need to get away clawed at him.

He'd had enough. Of Zoe. Of what could have been.

"We're done here. I'm going to move to a hotel. I want you to stay here as planned until after the baby is born. Hell, keep the place, for all I care." He stalked off.

Zoe called to his back as tears spilled, "I don't need noble. I need your love."

She had told Gabe the truth when she'd said she understood about that morning. It wasn't as if he had chosen to watch a ball game over going with her. His surgical skills had been required. In her heart she'd known he would be there beside her if he could have been. Frustration rolled through her. Why couldn't he see that?

What was she going to do now? Chase after him and beg him to reconsider? She couldn't do that but she was living in his home. That couldn't continue. She would have to find a place sooner than she'd planned. What about her mother? She wouldn't survive a second move. Zoe would have to figure something out. To put Gabe out of his house would be wrong. Staying here without him would be just as impossible. The memories would be more than she could stand.

She picked up the dishes and carried them to the sink. The sound of the door to the carport opening and closing screamed that Gabe had left. Zoe's hands covered her face and she let the tears of misery flow.

CHAPTER TEN

IT HAD BEEN two weeks since Gabe had driven out of the driveway, his intention to only return for clothes later. His contact with Zoe would only have to do with the baby after it was born. He couldn't continue seeing her and keep his promise to stay away. He wasn't even sure it wouldn't be a good idea for him to sell the house when she moved out. Facing the memories might be more than he could manage. It would never be home again unless Zoe was there.

Just seeing her would make his resolve disappear like mist on a sunny day.

Gabe couldn't imagine being more miserable than he had been over the last couple of weeks. He'd missed everything about what his life had once been and it all hinged on Zoe. The way she looked when he called her honey. Or her laughter as he told her something that had happened at work, the joy in her eyes when she'd heard Mr. Luther was doing well. The unconscious way she'd put a protective hand over their baby when they'd talked about it.

Shoving the take-out paper bag away, he groaned. He missed her delicious meals and their simple conversations. She'd been what had been absent in his life, and now that he'd had her, he wanted her back. His personal life was in a shambles.

It was starting to affect his work. The lack of sleep because he was living in a hotel and didn't have Zoe was starting to take its toll. A couple of his coworkers had given him questioning looks when he said something too sharply. He tried to remember to think before he spoke but it didn't always work.

It was Tuesday and his clinic day. He wasn't looking forward to seeing the next patient. He lightly knocked on the door. A gruff voice called for him to come in. As he entered the small room, Gabe said, "Hello, Mr. Luther. How're you doing?"

"Better. The scar doesn't hurt as much as it used to."

Gabe nodded. "Good. That sounds like you're making progress."

The man had only stayed a few days in ICU and had been out of the hospital in less than a week. Gabe had seen Zoe's name beside notes on Mr. Luther's chart a few times but Gabe hadn't run into her. He couldn't keep dodging her but he needed a little more time to adjust to what his life was now.

"I feel better than I have in years. My neighbors are taking good care of me."

"I'm glad to hear that. I'm going to give you a good listen then look at the incision site." A few minutes later Gabe said, "Every day you should be improving and you're doing that. I'll see you back here in a couple of weeks. Is there anything you have questions about?"

"Yeah. I'd like to know what you did to Zoe. She looks sad all the time."

Gabe's chest ached. Of course, Mr. Luther would notice. "How is she?"

"Why don't you ask her yourself?"

"It's complicated." Gabe stepped toward the door.

"That's what she said. One thing I've learned through all this is that life can slip away before you know it. Think about it, Doc."

Gabe did regularly over the next few days. Still, he couldn't see how things could be any different. For Zoe to find that man who could give her what she wanted, she couldn't have Gabe hanging around. Even the idea of Zoe being with another man made him feel physically sick. Surely with time it would get easier, but so far that didn't seem to be the case.

While in his office that evening, his phone rang. He looked at the ID. "Hi, Mom."

"Hey, Gabe. I've not heard from you in a few weeks."

"I'm sorry, Mom. I've been busy." He sounded so much like his mother used to when he was a child, never having enough time when he wanted to talk.

"So how's Zoe and the baby doing?"

"Fine."

There was a pause. "What's going on, Gabe?"

"Nothing I can't handle." He wished he felt as confident as he sounded.

"I'm here if you need me."

She might have worked a lot when he had been a kid, but he'd always known she was there to support him. With or without a father, his mother had been there when she could be. "Mom, why did you never remarry?"

Again there was a pause. This one was longer than the last. "I guess I never found the right man. Your father was a hard act to follow. Then I just got too busy. I worry that you're doing the same. I learned too late that you can't make more time. Don't let it slip by. Especially with the little guy coming."

"I heard you say once that you were worried I had no father figure to model myself on."

"I did?" Amazement was evident in her voice. "Single mothers worry about all kinds of things. Big and small. Gabe, you're one of the most intelligent, caring, giving men I know. I have no doubt that my grandson will have the best father ever."

A sense of relief came over Gabe. His mother believed in him. Hadn't Zoe said close to the same thing? So why couldn't he believe in himself?

"By the way, I'm planning to come for the birth," his mother added. "Help out. Is that okay?"

"I'll have to check with Zoe." He wasn't prepared to go into all the details about his and Zoe's relationship with his mother at that moment. He would have to sometime soon but he wasn't up to explaining it right now. Even if his mother came, she'd have to stay in a hotel and see the baby through a window.

How was he going to explain what had happened between him and Zoe? His mother had been so excited when he'd told her he'd found someone special. When he told her he and Zoe were no longer together, his mother would be so disappointed. "It's great to talk to you, Mom. I'll see you soon."

Zoe wasn't sure her heart would ever completely recover. The pain she'd feared would come with the loss of Gabe was nowhere near as strong as that she was carrying now. Her days had become a foggy existence. Every night was a struggle without Gabe next to her and every morning an act of survival to meet the day. She had become reliant on him so quickly and now he wasn't there.

Going home daily to Gabe's house compounded the pain but she had no choice. She couldn't move her mother, and the only way Zoe could afford a new place was to move her mother. So she was stuck living at Gabe's. It seemed wrong that she was and he wasn't. Her life had become so twisted. At least she'd just have to endure for a few more months. The only bright spot in the mess her life had become was that Will would arrive soon. That she could get excited about.

Had Gabe changed his mind about his involvement with Will? Had he broken it off not only with her but their child as well? He'd been so adamant about being involved, but with the change in their relationship, had he decided staying away was better? That decision was his. Gabe would have to approach her about it, not the other way around.

Because of Will, she and Gabe would always be connected. She would have to figure out some way to control her emotions when they had to meet. Even though she was certain a little bit of her would die each time they did, knowing the happiness she'd once shared with Gabe was gone.

At her obstetrician visit, the doctor was concerned about her weight loss. She promised to take better care of herself. Only with great effort did she make herself eat and do what was necessary for the baby's health.

She'd not heard or seen Gabe since he'd left. The day he'd come to pick up his clothes, she'd noticed his car in the drive and had driven around the neighborhood until it had gone. Now she'd do almost anything for a glimpse of him. Even when she visited Mr. Luther she'd not seen Gabe.

It didn't take Mr. Luther long to zoom in on her unhappiness. As she would have guessed, he commented on it.

"What's wrong with you?" he asked as she wrapped the blood-pressure cuff around his arm.

"Nothing."

"Yeah, there is. You've got that pitiful look. Usually you come in here with a smile on your face. I bet your face would break if you smiled right now."

"I think we should concentrate on how you're doing." She pumped the bulb attached to the cuff.

For once Zoe wished Mr. Luther would go back to being the sad, self-centered man she'd known before the transplant. At least he wouldn't be focused on her.

"You know, the doc doesn't look much happier when he comes in."

He didn't? Why did the idea make Zoe's heart beat a little fast? Maybe Gabe was as miserable as she was. Zoe continued to do vitals. "I'm sorry to hear that."

"You two have a fight or something?"

"Mr. Luther, I appreciate your concern, but Dr. Marks and I are fine."

He grunted. "Don't look fine to me. That baby deserves happy parents."

That statement Zoe couldn't argue with.

On the way home that afternoon, she stopped by to visit her mother. Now that Gabe wasn't at the house, Zoe had made a habit of going each afternoon. Going home to Gabe's house wasn't comforting for her. It was just a place to lay her head, no longer the place of dreams it had once been.

With the exception of the one escape episode, her mother seemed to have stabilized and was thriving since moving to Shorecliffs. She seemed more aware, and despite most of what she talked about being in the past, it at least made sense. With her confusion remaining at bay for the time being, Zoe's guilt had eased. Her mother was as happy as she could be.

Today her mom was well dressed and sitting in a

cushioned chair in the lobby. There were a number of other residents there as well. Zoe took an empty chair beside her. "Hey, Mom, how're you today?"

Her mother smiled.

The tightness in Zoe's shoulders eased. Her mother was having a good day. There was a sparkle in her eyes, not the dull look of reality slipping away. "I'm fine. How're you?"

Zoe ran her hand over her extended middle. "Me too."

"Baby?" her mother asked.

"Yes, I'm having a baby." Zoe had to remind her almost every visit. Anything that had happened recently her mother couldn't remember, but she could recall almost anything in detail from her childhood. "He's growing."

"Your daddy and I had a big fight about you."

Was she making that up? Zoe had never heard this story. To her knowledge, they had never fought.

"He was mad when I told him I was going to have a baby. He didn't want a family." Her mother's face took on a faraway look.

"Mom, I've never heard you say anything like that before."

"That's not something you tell a child. A baby should be wanted. Loved."

A deep sadness filled her. "He didn't want me?"

"After you came he loved you dearly, but he never adjusted to family life. He was always looking for a way out."

Was she expecting Gabe to embrace an ideal he wanted nothing to do with? Was she asking the impossible from him? Was that why he had left? They had been happy together for two weeks without more commitment. Could she settle for that if it meant having Gabe in her life? Her child having a full-time father?

Was there some way she could convince Gabe she would take him any way she could get him? Make him feel like what he could give was plenty.

Gabe searched the patient's open abdomen. Something was wrong. He could feel it.

"Suction." He looked again. Nothing. The surgery was going by the textbook. So why the nagging feeling?

The phone on the OR wall rang. One of the nurses answered. "Dr. Marks." The nurse held out the receiver. "Do you know a Zoe Avery?"

"Yes. Why?" Was the baby coming? It was too early. It was at least another six weeks away.

"This is the ER calling."

Gabe's heart went into his throat.

The nurse continued, sounding perplexed. "They said they found your card in her purse. She'd had a bad car accident."

Zoe hurt! The baby?

Gabe looked at Dr. Webber standing on the other side of the surgery table. He was more than qualified to handle the rest of the operation. Gabe had to get out of there. See about Zoe. He spoke to the fellow. "You've got this. I gotta go." Gabe didn't wait for a response before he hurried out the doors, leaving them swinging. Zoe needed him and he would be there for her and Will this time.

He flipped his surgical headlamp up on his head and didn't bother to remove his gown as he raced toward the staff stairs that would get him the two flights down faster than the elevator. Less than a minute later he burst through the ER doors, one of them hitting the wall.

"Whoa," one of the techs said as he put his hand out to stop Gabe. "Can I help you, Doctor?"

Gabe pushed the man's arm away. "Where's Zoe Avery?"

"Let me check the board." The tech turned to the large whiteboard on the wall. "Trauma Six."

Gabe looked around wildly. "Where's that?"

"This way. You must be new here. Were you called in to consult?"

"No. She's my...uh..." What did he call Zoe? His friend, girlfriend, lover, the mother of his baby? Thankfully he didn't have to explain more before they reached the room. Gabe rushed inside.

His heart sank and his belly roiled. The stretcher was surrounded by people working on Zoe. Two different monitors beeped, one giving Zoe's heart rate and the other the baby's. Oxygen hissed as the doctor gave orders.

With his gut churning with fear at what he might see, Gabe stepped closer. "Zoe." Her name was barely a whisper over his lips.

The doctors and nurses were so busy they didn't even respond to him. Gabe looked over one of their shoulders. Zoe's eyes were closed and she wore an oxygen mask. Around it and beneath he could see her pale, bruised skin. Her right arm lay to her side with an air cast on it. The real focus was on Zoe's leg. There was a large gash on her thigh.

"We need to get her to surgery, stat. She's lost a lot of blood. Do we have a next of kin?"

"I'm it," Gabe said. "She's my girlfriend."

The ER doctor turned and looked up and down at Gabe. "Aren't you Dr. Marks?"

"I am."

"Okay. Let's get her up to the OR," the doctor ordered. To Gabe he said, "You take care of the paperwork and the surgeon will be out to speak to you in the waiting room."

"I'll see him in Recovery," Gabe shot back. He watched helplessly as Zoe was pushed away. The first chance he had to tell her how he felt about her he was going to. If she would have him, he'd promise to do whatever he could to make her happy.

Zoe worked at opening her eyes. Why were they so heavy? Someone held her hand. She shifted. That hurt.

"Don't move, honey."

That voice. She knew that voice. *Gabe.*

Dreaming, that was what she was doing. Her eyes fluttered closed.

Zoe woke again and blinked as the lights were so bright. Where was she?

"Honey, stay still."

There was Gabe again. He sounded worried. Why? "Gabe?"

"Right here." His hand squeezed hers as his face came into view.

"You're here." *He was here.*

"I am, and I'm never leaving you again." He kissed her forehead.

All the pain of the last few weeks washed away. Gabe was next to her. Touching her. Calling her honey. What had happened? Why did he look so scared?

A nurse moved around her bed, checking the IV lines and doing vitals. "Ms. Avery, we're getting ready to move you to your room."

When the nurse left, Zoe searched Gabe's face. "What happened?"

"You were in a car accident."

The haze started to clear. She'd been driving home and had been hit from behind. The next thing she'd known, she was being slammed into the car in front of her. Tears filled her eyes. Zoe reached for her middle with her un-injured hand. "Will?"

"Shh, honey. Our baby is just fine." Gabe's hand came to rest over hers.

Zoe drifted off again.

When she woke next, it was dark outside and she was in a hospital room. She looked around. Her eyes focused on Gabe, who was sitting in a chair facing her. His hand held hers as if it was a lifeline. "Gabe."

He straightened quickly. "Right here. Is something wrong? How are you feeling?"

"I ache all over."

Gabe stood, but didn't let go of her hand. "I'm not surprised. You're lucky it wasn't worse. I saw pictures of the accident." His voice hitched with emotion. "I could have lost you both."

She squeezed his fingers. "We're right here. My leg hurts."

Gabe's doctor persona returned. "You have a broken arm and had a deep laceration on your thigh. Both were taken care of in surgery."

Zoe looked at her arm, which was in a cast. Tears threatened to spill over. "I won't be able to take care of Will when he comes."

"With any luck, it'll be off before then. Either way, I'll be there to help."

"You will?" She watched him closely. Did he really mean it? But he'd never lied to her, only to himself.

"I can't wait any longer to say this. I'm sorry for how I treated you. You were right. I was just afraid. Still am. I know nothing more about being a husband or a father than I did before, but what I do know is that I can't live without you. I promise to put you and our family above anything else in my life. If you'll just have me. I love you, Zoe."

Gabe's plea squeezed her heart. "Of course I will have you. I love you."

His lips found hers. The kiss was tender but held a promise of many to come.

They were interrupted by a nurse entering the room. While she was seeing about Zoe, Gabe stepped out into the hallway. As soon as the nurse was finished, Gabe reentered the room.

"Why're you wearing a surgical gown?" Zoe asked.

Gabe gave her a sheepish grin. "When they called me about you, I was in surgery. I left in the middle of the procedure and didn't stop to change."

He had? "You shouldn't have done that."

"Yes, I should. I'll always be there whenever you need me somehow or some way. I won't leave you again."

"Gabe, your work is important. It saves lives. I understand that." Zoe could only imagine the drama he'd caused.

"I left the patient in good hands. He's doing fine. I just checked in."

"I love you," Zoe mumbled.

"I love you more," she heard as she slipped off into sleep once more.

She had no idea how much time had passed when she woke again, but Gabe was still there beside her. He was leaning back in the chair with his eyes closed. His long legs were stretched out in front of him and his ankles crossed. Zoe couldn't take her eyes off him. He was such an amazing man with such a large capacity to love. And he'd chosen her. She was blessed.

"You're staring at me." Gabe opened his eyes and smiled at her. "How're you feeling?"

"Pain meds are a good thing."

"Yes, they can be." He stood.

Zoe didn't miss his professional habit of checking all the monitors and lines before his attention returned to her. "Gabe, you know you don't have to stay here with me. You need to go home and get some rest."

"My home is right here. You are it."

Her heart melted. If he hadn't already owned her heart, he would have after that statement.

"What made you change your mind about us?" She had to know. Believe that it wasn't just because of the accident.

"Honey, I've been miserable without you. Nothing has been right. It was even starting to be noticed at work. No hospital needs a lovesick surgeon heading a transplant program. And I spoke to my mother. When I was a kid I overheard her say something about me not having a role model for fatherhood. She didn't even remember saying it. That seed grew in my mind to the point I believed it."

"You have so many qualities that'll make you a great father."

"I think with you at my side I can be." He kissed her. "Zoe, I know this isn't the best time to ask this but I need to know—will you marry me?"

Gabe was everything she'd ever wanted in a husband but she didn't need marriage to prove they loved each other. "You don't want to get married. I understand that. Accept it."

"Yes, I do. I want people to know you belong to me. I want my son and any more children we have to carry my name. I love you."

"My mother had a lucid moment and we had a conversation about Daddy. It seems he never wanted a family, felt strangled by one. I don't want you to ever feel that way. If not being married is what works for you, then I'll be satisfied just to be in your life."

Gabe leaned over until his face was near hers. "I love you and *want* to marry you. Now, will you please answer my question? I'll beg if I have to."

With effort and some discomfort, Zoe circled his neck with her good arm. "Yes, I will marry you. I love you." Her lips found his.

EPILOGUE

GABE LEFT HIS mother in his kitchen, fussing with dinner, and went to find Zoe. He stopped in the nursery doorway and looked at the picture Zoe and their baby made as they slowly rocked in the sunshine. A glow that could only be love radiated from Zoe as she looked down at the perfect baby boy in her arms. His family.

She must have heard him because she looked up with an angelic smile and met his gaze. The love he'd just seen for Will was now transferred to Gabe. It didn't waver. What he'd done to earn it, he had no idea. The thing he did know was he would spend the rest of his life honoring it.

"Hey, honey." Zoe's smile grew, just as it always did at his endearment.

"Come in and join us. Your son would like to say hi."

Gabe walked to them and gently kissed Zoe on the forehead. "You did well, Mrs. Marks."

"Thank you, Dr. Marks. I think we both did well." Gabe carefully took Will from her, cradling him against his chest. Zoe's cast had only been removed a few days earlier.

Gabe looked at the peachy chubby face and he worried his heart might burst from the amount of love filling it. "Hello, William Gabriel Marks."

Zoe rose to stand beside him.

He looked at her, at the tears filling her eyes. His lips found hers. "I love you."

"And I love you."

"Just think, in my stupidity I almost missed out on this."

She leaned her head against his shoulder. "But you didn't and that's what matters."

* * * * *

COMING SOON!

We really hope you enjoyed reading this book. If you're looking for more romance, be sure to head to the shops when new books are available on

Thursday
26th July

To see which titles are coming soon, please visit
millsandboon.co.uk

MILLS & BOON

MILLS & BOON

Coming next month

THE SHY NURSE'S REBEL DOC
Alison Roberts

She had to catch his gaze again and she knew that her curiosity would be evident. What surprised her was seeing a reflection of that curiosity in *his* gaze.

'It was a one-off for more than the fact that neither of us do relationships,' she said. 'We work together. It would be unprofessional.'

Blake snorted softly. 'It's pretty unprofessional to be thinking about it all the time.'

Again, Sam seemed to see her own thoughts reflected in those dark eyes. He had been finding this as difficult as she had? Wow…

Could Blake hear how hard her heart was thumping right now? 'Um… maybe we just need to get it out of our system, then.'

His voice was a low, sexy rumble. 'Are you suggesting what I think you're suggesting? Another… one-off?'

'Or a two-off. A three-off, if that's what it takes.' She took a deep breath and then held his gaze steadily as she gathered her words. Yes, she did want a real relationship that was going somewhere but it had to be with the right person and that person wasn't going to be Blake Cooper because she could sense that his demons were even bigger than hers.

But, oh… that didn't stop the *wanting*, did it? The lure of the bad boy…

'We both walk alone, Blake,' she said quietly, 'for whatever reason – and at some point we'll know it's enough.

Maybe we just need to agree that when one of us reaches that point, the other walks away too. No regrets. No looking back.'

Somehow, she had moved closer to Blake as she'd been speaking, without realising it. Her head was tilted up so that she could hold his gaze and he was looking down.

Leaning down… as if he couldn't resist the urge to kiss her.

Then he straightened suddenly and Sam could feel the distance increasing between them with a wave of disappointment. Despair, almost…?

But he was smiling. That crooked, irresistibly charming smile of a man who knew exactly what he wanted and was quite confident he was going to get it.

'What are you doing tonight, Sam?'

Her mouth felt dry. 'Nothing important.'

'Give me your address and I'll come and get you. You up for a bike ride?'

Sam could almost hear her mother shrieking in horror at the thought but her rebellious streak wasn't about to be quashed. She might only get one more night with this man so why not add an extra thrill to it?

She could feel her smile stretching into a grin. 'Bring it on.'

Continue reading
THE SHY NURSE'S REBEL DOC
Alison Roberts

Available next month
www.millsandboon.co.uk

Copyright ©2018 Alison Roberts

LET'S TALK
Romance

For exclusive extracts, competitions
and special offers, find us online:

 facebook.com/millsandboon

@millsandboonuk

@millsandboon

Or get in touch on 0844 844 1351*

For all the latest titles coming soon, visit
millsandboon.co.uk/nextmonth

*Calls cost 7p per minute plus your phone company's price per minute access ch

Want even more
ROMANCE?

Join our bookclub today!

'Mills & Boon books, the perfect way to escape for an hour or so.'

Miss W. Dyer

'Excellent service, promptly delivered and very good subscription choices.'

Miss A. Pearson

'You get fantastic special offers and the chance to get books before they hit the shops'

Mrs V. Hall

**Visit millsandbook.co.uk/Bookclub
and save on brand new books.**

MILLS & BOON